FINDING
JACKSON

FINDING
JACKSON

A Novel by:
Anne Holster

For Mom . . . miss you

CHAPTER 1 - LEAH

It was an unseasonably hot night in mid-June. The kind of hot night that sneaks up on you after an unusually cool spring. The sudden change catches you by surprise even though it shouldn't. That's the way I remembered it, anyway.

My best friend Molly and I were headed to a graduation party that her cousin Heather had invited us to and we were psyched about it. Heather said it was going to be wild. Reed, the guy throwing the party, lived just a few blocks from her in Saddle River and apparently came from a very wealthy family. You know the kind – they let their kids run amok just to keep them out of their hair. They'll let them invite however many people they want so long as they promised to keep it under control – which of course never happened.

"Just get a ride here," she told Molly, "and the three of us will walk over together."

That night, I stared out the window of Molly's dad's car, watching the blur of huge homes and endless perfect lawns and wondering which one of these fat cats was having the party. Finally, he pulled into Heather's large, circular driveway and for the tenth time made us promise to be careful. Molly rolled her eyes at him, but she was smiling as she leaned over to give him a peck on the cheek.

Heather opened the door almost before we knocked, and immediately started jabbering about how glad she was that we came and about how much fun we were going to have.

Molly's cousin was pretty and popular and confident – one of those perfect blondes with a perfect body, perfect teeth, and clothes right out of

Vogue. Basically, she was everything I wished I could be. Even Molly was somewhat in awe of her, though she would never admit it.

As we walked the two or so blocks to the party, Heather told us about Reed, basically how hot and filthy rich he was. As we got closer, I could slowly hear the music getting louder and louder. It was live, too; apparently, his parents had hired a local rock band to perform. Obviously, an attempt to help him outdo his fellow classmates, but judging from what I saw when we arrived I couldn't imagine *anyone* outdoing this shindig.

There were people everywhere, but I could still see that the wood floor in the entrance hall was as shiny as a mirror; the paintings on the walls resembled works of art I'd seen on a field trip last year to the Metropolitan Museum of Art. Straight ahead was a red-carpeted staircase that was right out of *Gone with the Wind*.

We were no sooner in the door when I saw a tall, built, impeccably dressed guy striding confidently toward us. I knew even before Heather introduced us that this was Reed. She'd insisted they were just good friends, but from the way Reed was looking at her it seemed like there was a lot more to it than that.

I tried to keep my jaw from dropping as Reed led us in through the kitchen and several other enormous rooms until finally we reached the doors leading out to the backyard, which was the size of a small park. On the far side was the band I'd heard from down the street; a few feet away were several buffet tables piled high with food. This was where the real party was happening.

"Ladies, help yourselves," Reed said, as he swung a well-defined arm toward the tables, "I have to go mingle." He flashed a perfect smile at us, then squeezed Heather's arm before heading back into the house.

"Is he hot or what?" Heather asked, obviously smitten.

"He's hot, alright," Molly agreed and I nodded my approval even though Reed wasn't really my type.

Then again, I didn't know what my type was. I'd never even had a boyfriend.

The three of us maneuvered through the throngs of people, coming to a stop at the edge of the gorgeous inground pool. I can't speak for Molly, but I'd certainly never felt so cool in all my life. Heather pulled us aside and whispered that there were coolers full of beer behind the pool house but we should keep the drinking on the downlow so we didn't get Reed in trouble.

Though neither one of us were drinkers, it wasn't long before Molly and I were sidling over to the pool house. Once the coolers were in view we stood there awkwardly, not knowing what to do. We really were geeks.

"Come on, let's go," Molly said as she grabbed my elbow.

We each took a can and emptied it into our cups like everyone else was doing, then deposited the empties in a big black trash bag next to the coolers.

Feeling suddenly awkward standing amongst the sea of obvious in-crowders, we decided to grab a table, listen to the band play and people-watch for a while. We laughed, we drank, we laughed some more and before we knew it, we were making another trip to the pool house, and then another.

"I think I need to use the bathroom," Molly announced as she pushed her chair back and stood up.

"Okay," I nodded then watched as she disappeared through the crowd of people.

For a while I just sat there, alternating between stolen glances at the crowd and stolen sips of beer. It was my third, and I was feeling a slight buzz and an accompanying urge to get closer to the music. When a few more minutes passed and Molly still hadn't returned, I got up and wandered over toward the stage at the edge of the yard. I weaved through the crowd, trying not to spill my beer, then lifted my gaze toward the band and Oh. My. God. I did a double take then froze, my heart thudding in my chest.

You hear people talk about this feeling, that once-in-a-lifetime, struck-by-a-thunderbolt feeling; you know, like when two cartoon characters are staring at each other and their eyes look like two big hearts bugging out of their heads. You hear about it but never really believe it could happen in real life. That is until it happens to you and then it completely consumes you, leaving you exhausted and worn out from falling for someone so hard so fast. It's a high that you never, ever want to come down from. I think they call it *love at first sight* and, well, that's exactly how I felt when I saw him. I can't even explain why I was so taken with him – he definitely wasn't what you'd call "classically handsome" - I just knew I couldn't take my eyes off him.

Almost without realizing it, I inched closer and closer until I was just a few feet from the stage. Just then they finished the song they were playing and announced that they'd be taking a short break. I watched as he placed his guitar down and joined his bandmates on the side of the stage.

I had to meet him. If it was the last thing I did, I just had to. With my last bit of common sense, I waited for a few minutes to make sure that he wasn't with anyone, because how could he *not* be?

While I waited, I studied him closer. He had this crazy, dark brown hair that sprouted in all different directions. I couldn't decide if it was supposed to look like that or if it was just the humidity and quickly decided it didn't matter. His eyes were a bright blue - or green, maybe? - that stood out starkly against his olive skin. He looked a few years older than me, but that might have been the light scruff that covered his angular jaw.

My eyes travelled down to the jeans, worn and faded, that he had paired with army-style boots. He had a slim frame but his arms were subtly defined, and though his chest appeared sculpted beneath his gray t-shirt I got the feeling it was natural, that he didn't put in any extra effort to look the way he did. Just then he shifted his body, giving me a view of his back and shoulders. He couldn't have been more perfect.

I waited a few minutes, watching and considering my next move. When no lovestruck females rushed the stage, I took a deep breath and started slowly moving toward him. I was about to do something I'd never done before, had never even thought about doing. Although one might argue that it was the alcohol spurring me on, I was sure it was something more – it had to be.

One of his bandmates must have said something funny, because he suddenly let out a laugh and slapped the guy on the back. I paused for a beat, wondering if I was about to make a huge jackass of myself, then decided that wasn't as bad as leaving the party without talking to him. Positioning myself right behind him, I then slowly reached out and tapped him lightly on the back without any idea what I was going to say when we came face to face.

He turned and looked down at me, his full lips turning up in a slightly crooked, totally sexy grin. His eyes, which were definitely green and even more piercing up close, paralyzed me for what felt like the longest moment in history. Finally, I quietly croaked out a simple *hi* and felt my own mouth stretching into a smile.

CHAPTER 2 - JACKSON

I was talking to Clutch about the last set when I felt the lightest tap on my back. It was so light I might have ignored it, if Clutch hadn't jerked his head to indicate that someone was standing behind me.

I turned around, surprised but pleased by what I found. She sure was a tiny thing – couldn't have been more than fifteen, either. Probably someone's little sister who tagged along for the night. *Jailbait.*

"What's up?" I asked, but she just stared up at me with this silly grin on her face. I glanced behind me to see if Clutch was watching this, but he'd disappeared, probably to find the others. I turned back to the girl and asked what her name was.

"Leah," she answered quietly, her amber eyes still glued to mine.

"Well *Leah...*" I began as I stuck out my hand for her to shake, "it's nice to meet you. I'm Jackson."

She tentatively reached out and shook my hand.

Amused at the fact that she still hadn't really said anything, I asked her who she was here with.

"Um, my friend, uh, Molly," she stumbled nervously, "Her, uh, cousin invited us."

I nodded, smile in place, as I tried to think of what to say next. It wasn't often that a girl just came up to me out of the blue, and this one seemed really friggin' nervous.

This could be fun.

"What did you think of Blow Torch?" I asked; then, seeing her blank stare I jerked my head toward the makeshift stage set up at the rear of the yard. "The band...?"

"Oh! It was great!" She answered over-enthusiastically.

"We weren't even supposed to play this party," I explained as I grabbed a beer out of Clutch's cooler, which he brought, fully stocked, to every gig. "We got a call last minute from this hip-hop group the family had originally booked, asking us to fill in. Something about a scheduling mix-up. I don't even think these people know the difference." I laughed, then leaned over conspiratorially. "But, shhh, don't tell anyone." I tossed her a wink as I leaned back and was shocked when her face lit up like it was Christmas morning. *Yes, this was definitely going to be fun.*

Blow Torch had been together for about a year, although we still seemed to be trying to find our groove. I'd been working with Clutch – our drummer – at a small local ski joint the past couple winters and he brought me into BT.

When I asked Leah if she wanted to meet the rest of the band her eyes got all wide and she said "Sure!" like I was going to introduce her to the Stones or someone equally as big.

"Come on," I said, jerking my head for her to follow me.

We walked across the yard to where Clutch was now standing with Jerard and Deal. I high-fived them, telling them what an awesome job I thought we did, then I turned to Leah. She had that wide-eyed look again.

"Hey guys, meet Leah." Then, unable to help myself, I slipped my arm around her shoulder. I felt her tense nervously and, I gotta admit, I ate it up.

Clutch and Deal just nodded at her, but Jerard said, "Hi, Leah, nice to meet you," in his best laid-back musician voice. He was so full of shit. He loved it when anyone wanted to *meet the band*. Probably 'cause it didn't happen very often.

"Did you graduate with Reed?" Jerard asked.

Leah giggled nervously but shook her head which made me wonder again how old she was.

"Well, we're going to get some food," he said, "Nice meeting you, Leah." Then he pulled out a stack of "business cards" and handed one to her, adding, "Our website's on there. You can check out all our upcoming shows."

She looked at the card and quietly thanked him, then quickly slipped it into the pocket of her denim shorts.

I found myself checking her out more closely. She was very small and slight – like she weighed a hundred pounds soaking wet. Her long wispy brown hair had natural-looking golden highlights, and she wasn't wearing flashy clothes like most of the girls at the party. Actually, I kinda liked the way she was dressed – denim shorts with a yellow t-shirt that rode up slightly when she turned, revealing a stretch of deeply tanned, toned abdomen.

"Do you want to meet my friend Molly?" she asked.

"Sure," I said, then began following her back across the yard as she craned her neck from side to side looking for her friend.

She stopped short and I bumped into her, nearly knocking her over. I looked up and there in front of us was some girl who I assumed was her friend sitting on some wannabe rapper dude's lap. I could tell Leah didn't know what to say so I cleared my throat and said loudly, "Hey Leah, did you find your friend yet?"

Upon hearing that, the girl quickly pulled away from Snoop-Dog and looked around, quickly spotting Leah. She jumped up.

"Leah, where've you been? I've been looking all over for you."

Really?

She glanced in my direction, and I smiled and said, "Hey," then stuck out my hand for her to shake. "Jackson."

"Oh, hi," she said as she shook my hand, then glanced sideways toward Leah.

"Yeah, um, we met earlier...when you were in the bathroom. Jackson's with the band."

While the two of them briefly discussed their whereabouts, I looked over the guy her friend was with. Like I said, a typical wannabe-rapper. You know the type...blonde buzz cut with designs shaved into the sides and a thick silver chain around the neck. Long basketball shorts with an almost equally long white t-shirt and a baseball cap with the nose flipped up and of course, the standard issue red and black Air Jordans. He even jiggled from foot to foot when he spoke. *How did this guy get in here anyway?*

When he introduced himself as "Double Jay" I almost laughed in his face.

"Hey J.J., what's up," I said, knowing it would piss him off.

"Name's Double Jay, dude," he corrected me.

"*Riiiight*," I drawled, keeping my eyes on his.

Leah and her friend were giving each other the eye the way girls do when they're trying to convey some sort of secret message to one another. I pretended not to notice as I continued to scope out the scene in front of me. Her friend was just slightly taller than Leah, but her frame was bigger and while I wouldn't call her heavy, she could've stood to lose a few. She had shoulder-length curly-ish brown hair that was almost the exact same color as her eyes.

I glanced over at the guy and could tell by the look on his face that he was hoping Leah and I would make a quick exit so he could get back to business. I tossed him a bone.

"I'm gonna grab some food," I said, turning to Leah, "You wanna come?"

"Okay," she agreed, then I saw her make eyes at her friend again before I led her over to the table of sandwiches.

We grabbed some sandwiches and hung out until it was time for Blow Torch to play the last set. When we took to the stage Leah's eyes didn't stray for even a minute. It was as if she were watching an actual *Bon Jovi* concert. Actually, in Leah's case, it was as if she were watching an actual *One Direction* concert. I wasn't sure which way she swung when it came to music but she certainly seemed to be enjoying herself.

She was still there and staring at me expectantly when we finished for the night. The yard cleared out pretty quickly after that, with just pockets of kids here and there. I didn't see her friend, but Leah didn't seem too concerned about it; she just hung out while me and the guys packed away our equipment.

"Maybe I'll see you around," I said when it was time to go. A flash of disappointment crossed her face before she tried to act cool about it. I'd had a decent time hanging out with her but I wasn't going to take it any further. Leah was a girl I'd categorize as the "girlfriend type" but she wasn't going to be mine. She was nice and even kind of hot in an understated sort of way but definitely not someone I'd pursue. First, she lived in Franklin Lakes, which meant for me backroads with a ton of traffic lights. I didn't do geographically undesirable, at least not for girls who didn't put out, and I would have bet my guitar that this one didn't.

"Hey," I said to Clutch as I headed toward the pool house, "Gotta make a pitstop."

He nodded then walked with the others to the house.

A few minutes later I walked out and noticed that Leah and her friend had been joined by a friend of Snoops. He actually could've been his twin, their outfits were so much alike. I stopped and watched momentarily as the friend tried to cozy up to Leah. I squinted, my head cocked to the side, then made a split-second decision. I didn't know it at the time but that decision would end up changing my life in ways I never could've imagined.

I slow-jogged over. "Hey Leah."

She turned, looking surprised but happy to hear my voice.

"Almost forgot to get your number," as if I planned to all along but it had just slipped my mind.

I glanced sideways at J.J.'s friend and smirked as she eagerly got out her phone and we exchanged numbers.

"I'll give you a call," I said as I took a few steps backward, slipping my phone into my back pocket. By the time I left the party I had forgotten all about her.

▲   ▲   ▲

The following Friday I woke up to pouring rain. *Fuck*. That meant no work and a smaller paycheck. It was my second summer working with my neighbor, Mr. Slater, who owned Silver Maple Tree Service. When the season ended at the ski joint, I got a few weeks off and then started my summer job with Slater. He'd been happy with my work last summer and was even talking about putting me in charge of my own crew. I looked out at the grey day and swore again. But not today.

I stumbled downstairs to find the house in its usual state of disarray, with a sink full of dirty dishes and the fridge empty except for some leftover Chinese. I don't know why I was surprised; this had been the norm for years and even more so since Beth moved out.

My sister and her boyfriend Brody had rented a small house together on the other side of town. That left just me and my dad, which basically meant I was living on my own. We barely spoke to each other, which was actually fine with me since at this point in my life I had little use for him. I was surprised Beth stayed as long as she did, especially after our brother Tim enlisted. He left right after graduation a few years back and we hadn't seen him since. The last time we spoke he was somewhere in or around Afghanistan but said he wouldn't be stationed there much longer.

I nuked the Chinese and ate standing by the counter. I hated days like this, when the weather was shitty and there was nothing to do but think. That's when I remembered Leah, the jailbait I'd met at the rich kid's party. I wandered into the living room then pulled out my phone and placed the call.

"Hello?" she tentatively said when she answered on the second ring.

"Hey, it's Jackson. . ." I said casually as I hopped onto an uncluttered space on the couch, "...from the party last weekend. What's up?"

"Oh, hi Jackson!" she said in that I'm-going-to-meet-Springsteen voice she'd used at the party.

We talked for a while and then I asked her if she wanted to hang out.

"Sure!" she said as if I'd just offered to take her to Hawaii or something.

"Cool, how 'bout I pick you up around three?" I asked and then almost as an afterthought added, "What part of Franklin Lakes you from?"

She hesitated for a second and then asked, "Would it be easier if I just met you somewhere? The mall, maybe?"

"Sure." It would be a hell of a lot easier than hauling my ass all the way over to Franklin Lakes.

"Great, I'll see you there. Is three o'clock okay? The bench outside of Macy's?"

"How about inside the mall," I suggested, "You know, because of the rain...?"

"Oh, right, of course," she said quickly, as if she was afraid I'd change my mind, "What about by the food court?"

"See you there." I smirked to myself, but as I hung up the phone I found myself looking forward to seeing Leah again.

After taking a shower, I grabbed the keys to Tim's Nissan and headed for the door.

I had my hand on the doorknob when I did an about-face and went back up to my room to grab some weed out of my top drawer. She looked like a straight arrow but who knows – maybe Leah would want to get high with me. Smoking weed was a harmless habit I'd picked up a few years back. It's not something I did every day; just something I used once in a while to take the edge off after a particularly shitty day or after a run-in with my dad. Although sometimes I just used it for fun or to forget about things – old shit that would invade my thoughts sometimes – shit I didn't like to think about.

Leah was waiting in front of the food court when I got there. She didn't see me right away so I got a chance to check her out. She had on shorts again, black ones with a gray cotton tank top and tan sandals. Her long hair was pulled up into a high ponytail with the tip brushing just between her shoulder blades. She looked so . . . *neat?* I know that's a weird word to describe a pretty girl but it was true. Her clothes looked perfectly pressed, and there wasn't a hair on her head that was out of place.

She certainly wasn't my type. I'll admit I liked to party and seemed to attract girls who did too. Girls who'd cut school with me and hang out in my room all day getting stoned and then having sex and then getting stoned again. This girl was different; I'd known that the minute I laid eyes on her at the party.

I came up behind her and tugged her ponytail, startling her.

She jumped, then smiled when she saw it was me. "Hi!"

"Hey there," I said to her, feeling like a giant. I wasn't that tall but next to her I might as well have been Paul Bunyan. "Waiting long?"

"No, no I just got here."

"Mind if I grab something to eat?" I asked, because the Chinese hadn't cut it. "Do you want something?"

"No, thanks; I'm good."

I glanced around the food court, weighing my options before finally settling on pizza.

"Sure you don't want anything?" I asked again as I placed my order for two slices and a Coke.

She shook her head.

I got my pizza and we got a table way in the back away from the crowds. I kept waiting for her to talk, but she seemed content to stare at me while I ate. It was a little annoying.

"So, did it take you long to get here?" I finally asked.

"Um, about twenty minutes, maybe a little less. There wasn't much traffic this afternoon."

"Which lot did you park in? I lucked out, got a space right out front," I told her as I took a sip of Coke.

"Oh, um, actually my mom dropped me off. My car's in the shop and she needed hers to run some errands.

After I finished both slices we sat there for a while. She was very soft-spoken and seemed to be getting a kick out of the numerous silly observations I had about the various people at the neighboring tables.

"See those two," I said as I discretely pointed out a heavy-set twenty-something couple sitting a few tables to the right of us.

She nonchalantly turned her head and then turned back, nodding slightly.

"I betcha he took her here to break up with her."

"Why would you say that?" she asked, and no sooner were the words out of her mouth when the woman burst into tears, noisily pushed back her chair and ran off. The guy stared after her for a beat, then shrugged and went back to his burger.

Leah's eyes bugged out. "Oh my gosh! How'd you know that?"

"Fucking body language," I said as I slid back in my chair. "Theirs was screaming 'breakup'."

She giggled and shook her head.

I folded my arms across my chest and studied her for a moment and I knew by her fidgeting that it was making her uncomfortable. She cleared her throat nervously before she spoke and once again, I found myself feeling almost flattered by it. I never thought of myself as intimidating but apparently to Leah I was.

"So, um, how long have you been with Blow Torch?"

If Leah was trying to distract me from what she clearly perceived as scrutiny, it worked. I loved to talk about anything to do with my music.

"Oh, maybe about a year or so, but I've been playing guitar on my own since I was a kid." I opened the lid of my empty soda cup and fished out a piece of ice, popping it into my mouth.

As I sucked on the ice cube I thought about mentioning the fact that I also wrote some of my own music, but for some reason I stopped myself. She might ask to hear it and I'd never even played my stuff for Clutch and guys. I'd hate to play it for her and find out it sucked. It might ruin the whole *cool intimidating guitar guy* thing I had going on.

"What kind of music do you like?" she asked, sounding genuinely interested and a tad less nervous.

"Classic Rock, mostly - Stones, Zeppelin, Clapton, that kind of thing. The Eagles are pretty cool and I like some of the Beatles' older shit too. How 'bout you?"

"I'm not too familiar with most of those bands except the Beatles, but I'm not into anything in particular anyway." She shrugged. "I'll listen to whatever's playing on the car radio."

Then she asked me what high school I went to.

"I went to Lakeland, but I graduated in June."

"Oh, so college in the fall?" she asked.

"Na, taking some time off and then I'll decide what I'm gonna do."

I don't know why I lied to her. I'd always struggled in school and I had no intention of ever stepping foot in a classroom again. Besides, any spare time I had was spent working on my music because that's the only thing I gave a shit about. My gigs with Slater and at the ski joint were just temporary until I could break into the music industry. Maybe wishful thinking on my part, but a guy can dream, right?

"How 'bout you? Where do you go to school?"

"I'll be a senior at Indian Hills in the fall."

"Ah, Indian Hills, home of the Braves – do you play?" I asked because everyone in our area knew about the Indian Hills girls' soccer team.

"Yes, I play; varsity the last two years."

"Oh, cool," I said, genuinely impressed.

"Did you play any sports at your school?"

"Nope," I shook my head. "I'm not much for organized sports." And then for some reason I added, "I used to play travel baseball when I was a kid, but not since." As soon as the words were out of my mouth, I regretted it. That was a different life, one that I didn't like to talk about.

"Oh really? My younger brother plays travel baseball in the spring and summer. He even plays fall-ball on a club team. He loves it." She went on a bit about the brother but I have to admit I wasn't really paying attention. Then she asked, "Why'd you stop playing?"

"Just lost interest," I lied again, then changed the subject. Too late, though, because in a flash I was back in that time, the spring just after my mom died.

Things had been sort of getting back to normal - as normal as could be expected anyway – and I wanted to play again. I was good. I mean I wasn't going to be the next A-Rod but I was just as good as any of the other players my age. Better, even, because I was seven years old but played "up" with the eight-year-olds. It may not sound like a big deal but when you're seven it's a *huge* deal. I was even hoping to play on the nine-year-old team that year. Beth filled out all the paperwork for the tryouts and I made sure to turn it in on time.

I reminded my dad the night before tryouts and the following afternoon I got all my equipment ready and was dressed and waiting for him to get home and take me. He never showed. He rolled in around nine o'clock that night, reeking of beer and cigarettes, and promptly passed out on the living room couch. And that was the end of my baseball career. *Asshole*.

It was still raining, so Leah and I just walked around the mall a few times. She seemed to relax a little as she told me about her family and her friend Molly, who sounded like a bit of a nutjob. She also didn't seem to notice that I kept steering the conversation away from myself.

I think we were on our third lap when she pulled out her phone to check the time. "I should probably get going..."

"I could drive you home," I suggested but she shook her head.

"Really, I don't mind," I told her.

She squirmed a bit. "It's probably not a good idea."

I looked at her quizzically.

"It's just that I didn't mention to my mom that I was meeting you here and . . ."

"And what?"

"And . . . I really wanted to see you again," she said and then gave me a half smile.

"Ah, so you're sneaking around," I chuckled as I nodded, my head cocked to the side.

She giggled nervously again, which she'd done a lot that day.

"Hey, maybe next time we could hang out at my place. I could teach you how to play a few simple cords on the guitar," I suggested but immediately regretted when I noticed her eyes widened slightly. I could only imagine what she was probably thinking - *His place?!*

"Uh, yeah, maybe," she agreed anxiously and I chuckled to myself but didn't say anything else since my intention certainly wasn't to scare her off.

Leah called her mom and in true gentleman style I waited around until she spotted the car coming through. Then, with a quick see ya later, I headed out.

I thought about her the whole drive home. Yep, Leah was definitely different from the girls I usually hung out with. I had her pegged from the start as a real straight arrow and I had been right. I wasn't sure how I felt about that, but straight arrow or not she was definitely hot and also kinda cool in a subtle sort of way. Plus, she didn't know anything about me or my past, and I planned to keep it that way. It was obvious from our conversation today that she was tight with her family, and I envied her for it. I used to have that too, once upon a time, before everything turned to shit.

CHAPTER 3 – JACKSON

I was about seven years old when things really went south. Life was mostly good before then and I say *mostly* because I chose to block out what wasn't.

My mom was the best. We were real tight and I always knew I was her favorite. No, really, I was. All kids like to think they're their parents' favorite and all parents say they don't *have* a favorite, but I knew different. My older brother and sister didn't have fun with Mom like I did. They didn't laugh and joke together like we did. She'd play with me for hours on end, especially in the summertime. There was a lake in town not far from where we lived and she'd take me there almost every day as long as the weather was good. When it rained we played inside with my buckets of army men. We'd set up forts and then have battles that went on all afternoon.

My father was a different story. When I was a real little kid, Dad, or "Ace" as my mom called him, was a hero in my eyes, but as I got older that changed. To tell the truth I can barely even remember when he was *Superman*. It's vague in my mind but I know there was a time that he was.

It didn't happen overnight. The change was slow, subtle, until one day, things were just *different*. Suddenly it seemed Dad wasn't happy with anything Mom did. No matter how hard she tried, it was never enough. Then he started going out drinking at night. He'd call her from the bar to pick him up because he was too trashed to drive home. If no one else was around to watch me I'd go with her and see his antics firsthand. She'd make up excuses for him, like he was working or helping out a friend. But then he started drinking at home too and when he did we all knew to stay out of his way. He never did anything to me or my siblings; it was Mom who took the brunt. That's when I learned words can hurt as much as a fist. He never raised a hand to her, but he said terrible things, and the more she tried to please him the nastier he got. One night I overheard her crying on the phone to my grandmother. That was the beginning. That's when I started to hate him.

After that I was glad when he went to the bar because him being at the bar meant I had Mom all to myself.

I'd lay in her bed and we'd watch TV together or she'd tell me stories from when she was young. When I was little, my favorite story was how she'd met my dad and why she called him "Ace." I loved that one because it made my dad sound really cool. After he changed I thought the story made him sound like a dick, but for some reason I would still ask to hear it.

"Tell it again, Mom, the one where Dad knocked you down and stole your candy."

"Jacky, you know that's not the way it happened. He didn't knock Mommy down on purpose," she'd say.

"I know," I sighed, "but it sounds way cooler that way."

Mom would always laugh when I said that, then she'd give in and tell me the story. I can still hear her voice, so clear and animated, like it was only yesterday . . .

Anna - 1977

It was Halloween the first time I laid eyes on him. I'll never forget it because Halloween had always been my favorite holiday, maybe because for some reason I was allowed to run wild. Things I'd never get away with were suddenly okay to do on Halloween. For instance, staying out after dark or eating candy before dinner, dressing inappropriately, and by inappropriately, I mean going out without a coat when the weather dipped below fifty degrees. Things you think are cool when you're ten years old, which was how old I was that year. Most people may not clearly remember their tenth Halloween, but I do and with very good reason, because it was the day I fell in love. You might think it crazy for a fifth grader to arrive home after a night of trick-or-treating and announce that she's in love and you probably wouldn't be the only one, but that's exactly what I did — and I was totally serious.

It was dusk, and the air was electric with excitement. It had been a lucrative afternoon and my three friends and I had split up just long enough to empty our bags of candy, grab something to eat, then regroup in an hour to hit the other side of town. Not wanting to waste any time I decided to cut through the woods by my house, something I didn't usually do with darkness approaching. It was a fateful decision that would end up altering the course of my life.

I hesitated, but only briefly, before scurrying down the path and into the woods for the ten-minute walk. When I was about halfway through the woods, I heard a rustling in the distance. I quickly snapped my head toward the sound which was closely followed by the echo of several sets of feet sprinting through the overgrown brush and dead leaves. I picked up the pace but within seconds it seemed the footsteps were upon me. I glanced over my shoulder only to see a band of four Indians barreling swiftly towards me. Panic-stricken, I tried to move quicker but the long white flimsy material of my Princess Leia costume got tangled around my legs. I froze as three of them flew past me, seemingly oblivious to my presence. It was just some boys, taking a shortcut, like me. The sigh of relief had barely left me when suddenly I was knocked off my feet, my pillowcase full of candy going airborne. I landed on the ground with a thud, surrounded by an array of assorted Hershey Bars and Turkish taffy and my carefully pinned Princess Leia buns now unraveled on one side.

"What the heck?!" I heard someone yell as I lifted my head and turned around.

There at my feet lay the fourth "Indian," but on closer inspection he wasn't dressed as an Indian at all, but a member of the rock band, Kiss, complete with teased hair and white face paint. I didn't know many of their songs, but I had certainly seen enough posters, not to mention all the boys I'd seen dressed like them that day. Whole groups of them were roaming the streets in high-heeled black boots, calling themselves members of the "Kiss Army."

"What the heck's your problem? You're the one who ran into me."

"Well what are you doing out here," he yelled, "taking up the whole path? This is our turf."

"Your turf?" I squealed as I got to my feet, brushing the dirt off my white dress. "You don't own the -"

I was suddenly struck speechless at the sight of the beautiful blue eyes peering out from behind his painted face. He had a mop of shoulder-length dark brown hair that was a wild-looking mess. He wore a black hooded sweatshirt with Kiss emblazoned across the front in big shiny silver letters, along with a pair of navy-blue corduroys that were worn and faded at the knees. Wrapped around his waist was a scuffed black leather belt with a huge silver Kiss belt buckle.

"Hey cool, you got grape Pop Rocks," he said excitedly, not noticing my stare as he reached down and picked them up. "How 'bout they're mine if I help you pick up the rest of your stuff? Deal?"

"Uh, deal," I was able to muster, unable to take my eyes off him.

I watched as he got down on all fours and quickly started gathering the spilled candy that now littered the worn dirt path. Once he got everything - including a few stray leaves - back in the bag, he handed it to me with one hand and held up the packet of Pop Rocks with the other.

"Deal, right?" he said with his head cocked to the side and wearing a wry grin.

"Deal," I agreed as I grabbed my bag of candy from him.

"Thanks," he said as he began to walk off.

"Hey," I yelled to him when he was a few yards away, "Who are you anyway?"

He turned and smiled. "Name's Ace," he said, pointing his two index fingers to his painted face. Then he turned back around and broke into a slow jog to catch up with his friends.

Ace?

He must not live in my neighborhood, I thought to myself, because I'd never heard of anyone by that name.

When I got home I had my mom fix my bun, sidestepping her questions about how it had gotten disheveled. If she knew I'd gone through the woods she'd never let me go back out. After a slice of pizza and a Pepsi I was back on the street, this time with a new purpose. In addition to once again filling my bag to the brim with candy, I was determined to find out more about "Ace." Who was he? Where did he live? Which school did he go to?

None of my friends seemed to know anyone by that name so I thought perhaps that he was a relative of someone in the neighborhood.

Weeks went by and the identity of "Ace" remained a mystery.

"When did you find out who he really was?" I'd always ask, even though I knew what she was going to say.

"How many times have you heard this story, Jacks?" she'd ask, rustling my shaggy hair as she laughed. "About a thousand?"

I'd look at her sheepishly. "Can we make it a thousand and one? Please?"

It would be almost six months before Ace's identity was revealed. By that time I'd all but given up any hope of finding him. No one I knew was familiar with the name and I had resigned myself to the fact that he was someone's distant cousin who had been in town for a rare visit.

One Saturday at the end of March my friend Amy and I went to a basketball game at the middle school we'd be attending the following year. Her brother Ben was playing and it was already nearing halftime when we arrived. We scooted into an empty row about halfway up the bleachers and settled in to cheer him on. Just after the cheerleaders finished their halftime show a group of boys arrived and squeezed by us to get to the other end of the row.

I glanced at the boy sitting closest to me and instantly did a double-take when my eyes caught a glimpse of his shiny silver belt buckle. Could it be –? Yes, it was the exact same one Ace had been wearing on Halloween. I inched closer to him. I'd know for sure it was him if I could just get a glimpse of those powder blue eyes that were etched so clearly in my mind.

I cleared my throat. "Uh, excuse me, do you know what time it is?"

He looked down at his watch, then cut his eyes to me and mumbled, "Four thirty" before returning his attention to the game. The exchange took all of a second, but it was enough.

It was him. All these months of sleuthing and here he was, sitting right next to me at a basketball game!

"Ace," I said tentatively, "Is that you?" When he didn't turn around I thought he may not have heard me so I said it again.

Abruptly he turned his head. "Huh? You talkin' to me?"

"You're Ace, right? From Halloween?" I asked, but he looked at me blankly. "You ran into me? Knocked me down? Princess Leia? The grape Pop Rocks?"

Finally recognition flashed across his face, "Oh yeah! The grape Pop Rocks! I remember now." Then a look of bewilderment appeared, "What'd you call me?"

"Ace. You told me your name was Ace that day, right?"

He paused for a beat then chuckled and said, "Uh, yeah, Ace, that's right," before turning back to the game. And that was it. I waited a few more minutes, praying he would say something else, then finally slid back over to Amy.

I pointed him out to Amy, who in turned asked her brother, who didn't know him but said he went to a lot of games. It was true; over the next few weeks I "accidentally" bumped into him at a few, only to have him completely ignore me.

Doesn't matter what his name is, I told myself, he doesn't know you're alive.

▲　　▲　　▲

I nearly died of shock when I walked into the cafeteria and saw Ace standing there in a cap and school jersey. As if I wasn't nervous enough my first week of high school!

We hadn't spoken since the basketball game nearly four years earlier, but I had seen him a few times. My face would flush and I'd feel all jittery and I'd have to remind myself that he had absolutely no interest in me. I dreaded having to see him every day at lunch and – God forbid – have him see me eating. The one comfort I had was that he probably wouldn't notice.

"Princess Leia," he stated one day when he got behind me in line as I waited to pay for my turkey sandwich and fries.

Remembering all his years of ignoring me, I decided I would play it cool.

"Oh, hi Ace," I said, trying to sound nonchalant, but I could feel my face flushing and my heart beating wildly. Ace had actually spoken to me! Though I prayed he would say more, I didn't dare turn back around. I didn't dare let him see the effect he had on me.

The conversation ended there, but it didn't matter; lunch period officially became my favorite part of the day. Ace would always make his way over to my table at some point to say hello. Then, one day out of the blue, he asked if I'd be interested in coming to see his band practice. He said they were practicing in his friend's garage which happened to be only a few blocks from my house.

"Maybe," I shrugged noncommittally, although inside I was doing backflips.

He gave me the address and said he'd be there around three-thirty.

"Maybe I'll see you later then," he said as he walked back over to his group of friends.

Later that afternoon I showed up at the address he gave me and rang the doorbell. The door was answered by a middle-aged, auburn-haired woman who smiled when she saw me.

"Oh, hi, I'm uh looking for Ace. He told me he'd be at this address this afternoon . . . practicing with a band...?"

"Ace?" she questioned. "Hmm, I'm not sure who Ace is but my son and some of his friends are playing in the garage out back. Come, I'll show you."

I followed her through the house and out the back door where she led me to a garage situated at the end of a long driveway.

"Justin," she called out as she banged on the door. "There's a girl out here looking for someone named 'Ace'. Is that a friend of yours?"

Just then the door swung open and Ace appeared, smiling sheepishly. "Yeah Mrs. Russo, that's me; she's here to see the band practice."

"Oh, okay Keith, um, I mean 'Ace,'" she said as she curled her fingers into air quotes. "Didn't realize you boys were going by aliases these days."

I eyed them both quizzically as the woman laughed lightly and held the door open for me. That's when I got my first glimpse of "the band" - four guys, two acoustic guitars, and one keyboard balancing across a pile of cardboard boxes and a single drum and cymbal.

"Hey guys, this is . . . um..." He paused awkwardly, then shrugged, "a friend from school."

We both started to laugh, realizing that neither of us knew the other's real name.

"Annalise, my name's Annalise – Anna for short," I told him. "Nice to meet you, 'Keith.'"

He introduced the rest of the guys – Justin, Henry and Dixon – and then they began to play a song they claimed was New York Groove. I couldn't really tell what it was, all I knew is that they sounded awful. I didn't care. I was with Ace and that was all that mattered.

Our eyes didn't stray from one another's, not for even a second, the whole time I was there. And it wasn't just me. I knew he felt something too.

An hour later they were packing up their gear and Ace asked if he could walk me home. Of course I said he could.

On the way to my house I asked, "So, how come everyone calls you Ace?"

"Uh, actually you're the only one who calls me that," he admitted.

"But back on that Halloween that's what you said your name was, right?"

He shrugged. "I just said it 'cause my face was painted like Ace Frehley, you know, from Kiss. It just popped into my head so I went with it."

"Yeah?" I smiled smartly as I poked him in the chest, "Well, you know what? Just for that I'm gonna keep calling you Ace, like it or not."

"Like it," he said with a wink. And then he took my hand and led me home...

"That's like the best story ever, Mom," I'd tell her sleepily as she tucked me in. "Dad was like the coolest, right?"

"That's right, Jacks, he was the coolest."

CHAPTER 4 - JACKSON

My world shattered into a million tiny pieces just before my eighth birthday.

By that time, my father's tirades had become the norm. Almost every evening he'd get pissed off over some imagined affront my mother had committed, like cook something he didn't like or not being home when he called. Sometimes I think he made stuff up just so he could storm out.

After he left that night me and Mom cuddled up on her bed to watch Sponge Bob before I went to sleep. As soon as I heard the phone ring I knew it was him. The usual short, tense conversation followed, then she hung up the phone and turned to me.

"I need to go pick up your dad, sweetie; do you want to take a ride with me?" She smiled, but I could tell she was sad. "Timmy's home, so if you want to stay and watch the rest of your show it's fine."

"I'll stay," I answered, my eyes turning back to the television screen as Sponge Bob and Patrick bickered back and forth.

"Alright…" She got me another pillow and tucked it behind me, propping me up even further.

"I'll be quick," she said as she kissed the top of my head and then made her way to the door. "Love you."

"Yeah, me too," I said, again my eyes glued to the television.

It wasn't until the second episode of Sponge Bob ended that I realized Mom still hadn't returned. She had gone out to get my father plenty of times and it had never taken this long.

I padded down the hall towards Tim's room, pushed open the door and poked my head inside. He was lying on his bed and resting on his elbow as he spoke to someone on the phone. I could tell by his voice that it was a girl.

"Scram, twerp," he barked when he noticed me standing there, then he hurled a Nerf football at my head. I ducked quickly as it whizzed past me.

"Mom never came back," I stated. "She went to pick up Dad while I was watching Sponge Bob and she never came back."

"She's probably downstairs," he snapped, "Now beat it." He turned and went back to his phone call.

I went down to the immaculately kept kitchen and looked around. As I feared, it was empty and silent – so silent that the ringing phone totally scared the crap out of me.

"Hello?"

"Where the fuck is your mother?" my father yelled, so loud I jerked the phone from my ear. "I called her over an hour ago and she still hasn't showed. Put her on the phone, will ya?"

"Sh-she's not here," I said tentatively, afraid to get her into trouble. I explained how she'd left to pick him up while I was watching Sponge Bob.

"Jesus Christ, can't she do anything right? Idiot probably went to the wrong fucking bar. I'll find my own way home I guess." He slammed the phone down without saying goodbye.

I walked into the living room and peered out the front window, hoping to see her pull in the driveway, but there was only darkness. I climbed onto the couch and waited, thinking she'd be home any minute. About twenty minutes later, I heard a car, then the room was flooded with light from the high beams. My relief was short-lived, though, because when I looked out again, I saw my father climb out of a cab. He stumbled a few times as he walked up the path to the front door, then I heard his key in the lock.

Just then the phone began to ring again. Thinking it was my mother letting me know she'd be right home, I dashed into the kitchen to pick it up. An unfamiliar male voice was on the other end, asking for my father.

"Who's that?" Dad barked as he motioned to the phone.

I shrugged and told the person to hold on, then held out the phone to him.

"Yeah?" he said brusquely as he tossed his keys and wallet onto the kitchen table. As he listened to the man on the other end, I watched his expression go from confusion to fright and saw his hand white-knuckling the back of the kitchen chair. Something was wrong. Very wrong.

Whatever the man said, it seemed to sober Dad up. As soon as he hung up he started yelling for Beth and Tim, then there was a flurry of activity as he hustled us all into the car. The whole time Beth and Tim kept asking him questions and Dad kept telling them that he didn't have any details. All he said was that there'd been an accident, and Mom was hurt.

I kept quiet. I had a weird feeling in the pit of my stomach that was telling me that this was bad – really bad. When we got to the hospital me, Tim and Beth were told to sit in the waiting room while Dad went with the doctor. Grandma and Grandpa arrived a little while later and I noticed that Grandma's face was all puffy, like she'd been crying. Grandpa kept wiping his eyes.

"Don't worry, Jacky," he said gently as he pulled me onto his lap, "your mom'll be alright. I heard the doctors here are the best in the state. They'll fix her up good as new."

But even as he said it he kept glancing at Grandma and wiping his eyes with the wrinkled hankie that he always carried in his pocket.

Finally a nurse came to the entrance of the waiting room and told Grandma and Grandpa to come in. I stood up and looked pleadingly at her, hoping she'd tell me I could come too.

"You wait here, honey," she said sweetly, then turned to my sister and brother. "Your father will be out in a minute, okay?"

I sat close to Beth and she put her arm around me, but neither she nor Tim said anything. I remember feeling embarrassed that I looked like such a baby, with my fuzzy slippers and my rodeo pajama pants sticking out from beneath my winter coat. I wished I had put on jeans or sweatpants before I left.

Just then Dad appeared. The three of us looked up at him silently.

"Mom's busted up pretty bad. It don't look good. You need to come in and see her."

We silently followed him through the long sterile hallway until we got to her room. *Busted up pretty bad?* Dad's words were woefully inadequate. Then again, nothing could have prepared us for what we saw. Mom was virtually unrecognizable. Her features were completely distorted. She had a tube down her throat and she was hooked up to several different machines that all seemed to be beeping at different intervals.

"You need to tell them, Keith," I heard Grandma whisper to Dad in between her quiet sobs. "They need to hear it from you."

She turned to Grandpa and nearly collapsed into his arms. The nurse helped the two of them to a small couch in the hallway right outside Mom's room.

I turned to my father feeling suddenly very small amidst the sterile surroundings of the hospital room. I knew right away what he was going to say. My fists were clenched so hard that my nails drew pricks of blood on the palms of my hands, but I didn't even feel it. Dad didn't say anything; he just stood there with his head down, pinching the bridge of his nose, then he walked out of the room. Tim went after him, leaving just Beth and me.

"Is she gonna be alright?" I asked hopefully, but Beth just burst into tears and ran from the room. I glanced after her and saw Dad talking to Grandma and Grandpa. Grandpa looked mad and I could see that they were starting to argue. One of the doctors came over to calm them down.

I turned back toward my mother's bed and slowly moved toward it. When I was close enough I reached out and tentatively touched her hand, surprised by how cold it felt. I looked around for a blanket to cover her but there were none.

I leaned closer to her and whispered, "Mom?" Then I slipped my hand into hers and quietly called out to her again. I felt her faintly squeeze my hand, but a few seconds later alarms were going off and the machines she was hooked up to started beeping wildly. Two doctors rushed in and pushed me to the side.

"Get him out of here!" one of the doctors yelled and I was quickly whisked out into the hallway by one of the nurses.

A week later she was gone – buried in the cemetery at the edge of town.

Anna – Spring 1985

Spring semester of senior year had finally arrived and everyone was excited about it, but none more than me and Ace. We had big plans for our future, huge in fact. As soon as I graduated we were headed to California so he could break into the music business. Since his own graduation the year before he had been working nonstop – two jobs! – to save for the move. We'd get an apartment somewhere in L.A. and find jobs, just something to hold us over until he became the next Eddie Van Halen. Then we'd be living the high life, with a mansion in Bellaire and a limo with our very own driver. That's what Ace said anyway. He had a way of making anything sound not only possible, but probable; it was just a matter of time.

In the meantime, he used whatever spare time he had to work on his music – writing songs and practicing his guitar. He wrote the music and I attempted to write the lyrics. Both needed to be fine-tuned, but for two amateurs the songs weren't half bad.

As the schoolyear came to a close, Ace decided that we should stay here on the East Coast and work through the summer to save up a bit more money. He wanted to make sure that we were flush with cash when we got to L.A. in case things started happening right away. Interviews, auditions, those kind of things. As much as I couldn't wait to get started on our new life, I had to admit what he said made sense. Ace always seemed to know everything.

We had been inseparable ever since that day I saw him play in Jason's garage. My parents, on the other hand, weren't all that crazy about him, especially when I told them about our plans to move to L.A.

"Annalise, you can't be serious," I remember my dad saying. "Have you listened to him play, I mean really listened? The boy is practically tone deaf!"

My dad felt that Ace had "delusions of grandeur" where his music was concerned, but I didn't care what he or anyone else thought. If Ace said he was good enough to make it big then that's the way it was going to be – end of story. Even after our high school's Battle of the Bands last year, when Ace's band didn't place in the top three, he wasn't discouraged. He blamed it on the changing tide in music, away from the hard rock he played and more towards pop. It was just a fad, he assured me, the pop scene had just about run its course in the big cities. The big-time producers would recognize his raw talent when they heard him play. I agreed.

"Honey, your father's right," my mom said, as usual agreeing with him. "We both want better for you. He's not going to make anything of himself with that music he plays. And now you're going to give up college to follow him clear across the country to chase his pipedream?"

"Let him go to California on his own," Dad urged. "Stay here and start college in the fall; there's still time to enroll at State."

They didn't get it. They didn't understand that this wasn't just Ace's dream, it was our dream. We'd been planning this for close to two years and now it was about to become a reality.

I told them in no uncertain terms that I'd made my decision. Come September we'd be heading to California whether they liked it or not.

In the meantime, I had other things to think about, like senior prom. I couldn't wait! I'd be arriving on the arm of the hottest guy in town, maybe in all of Jersey.

Ace looked so handsome that night in his silver-gray tuxedo and lavender bowtie that perfectly matched my lavender dress. He had grown out his hair that year and it hung way past his shoulders and was really full and wild-looking. He looked every inch the rock star that he aspired to be.

I had to admit, I was looking pretty spectacular myself. The shade of eye makeup I wore made my green eyes pop and my light brown hair was teased to the max and looked just like a lion's mane. My friends and I were always competing for who would have the biggest hair. That night mine was a close second to my friend Amy's but it wasn't really fair since she had hers done by her cousin, who was a beautician in Cliffside Park.

My dress was a strapless number that fit me like a glove and made me look much curvier than I actually was, and my three-inch satin heels had been dyed to perfection. My jewelry – all large, fourteen-carat gold pieces, completed the ensemble. Ace's jaw dropped when he saw me, confirming I'd definitely made the right choice where my dress was concerned.

It was perfect. A few of Ace's friends were dating girls in my class, so basically the whole crew was together again. After dancing all night, we headed down the Jersey Shore for a long weekend - a time-honored tradition in the area. Ace got us a room at the Aztec Hotel, right on the boardwalk, that we would share with Amy and Dixon.

On our last night there we were partying in one of the other rooms with a bunch of our friends. After days of beer we had switched to vodka and O.J. and everyone was *really trashed. That's when Ace got the idea to go to the beach and watch the sunrise. No one else was up for it, so after stopping at our room to grab a blanket, Ace and I staggered down toward the sand. It was a cloudless night on the deserted beach and for sure the sunrise was going to be beautiful.*

It wasn't long before Ace leaned over and kissed me and of course one thing led to another and the next thing I knew we'd forgotten all about the sunrise.

"Ace, wait, let's go back to the room," I told him, fearful that someone might see us.

He turned his head from side to side. "Look around, we're the only ones here."

I smiled, because he was about to convince me that sex on a public beach was perfectly okay so long as no one was around to see it.

"Did you bring anything with you?"

"Anna," he groaned as he continued to kiss me, "you're ruining the mood."

"But Ace . . ." I protested feebly.

"It's only one time, it's not a big deal. Dixon says him and Amy do it like this all the time and nothing happens. Can't you just be spontaneous for once?"

When I didn't say anything, he proceeded to slowly slip my shorts down on one side. And, before I knew it, I found myself helping him out of his.

"Do you really want me to stop?" he whispered as he pulled the edge of the blanket up to cover us.

"If, if you're sure it'll be alright..." I trailed off breathlessly.

"Yeah," he gasped, "definitely, I'm sure . . ."

CHAPTER 5 - JACKSON

I'd thought Dad was a mess before Mom died; turns out he was a prince compared to what he was like after.

Those early days were the worst. He could barely get out of bed and that was only for fear of losing his job. And as for us kids, I don't know what would've happened if it weren't for Grandma and Grandpa.

They practically moved in with us – they were there when we got up in the morning and stayed until we were in bed at night. Grandma cooked and cleaned and helped us with our homework while Grandpa took us to all of our appointments and afterschool activities. Looking back, I don't know how they did it. We were all so wrapped up in our own grief that everyone seemed to have forgotten the fact that they'd lost their only daughter. Sometimes I'd catch Grandma staring at Mom's picture and getting teary, but I'd always look away. It scared me when I saw her like that.

About four months after Mom died, everything came to a head.

We waited forever for Dad to come home from work and when he finally did show up, he was drunk off his ass.

"What the fuck are you two still doing here?" I heard him ask my grandmother. I couldn't see him from my perch at the top of the stairs, but I could hear the annoyance in his voice.

"Excuse me?" Grandma said, and then all hell broke loose.

I inched my way toward the bottom of the stairs and peered into the kitchen, just in time to see Grandma burst into tears.

"This whole thing is your fault!" she screamed, "You're nothing but a no-good drunk!" Grandpa went to her and put a hand on her shoulder, but she shook it off. "If you were home where you should've been that night and not out drinking yourself half blind this never would've happened! She'd still be here!" Her hands had been clenched into fists at her sides, but now she shook one at him. "You're the one who should've been hit by that drunk driver! YOU! Not her, not my Anna!"

I stared from her to my father, waiting for his reaction, but he just stood there with his mouth open. My grandmother lowered her fist and for a moment I thought she was finished; I was wrong.

"She wouldn't listen," she said, her voice dropping almost to a mutter, "I told her to stay with us, go to college and we'd help her out! But no, she had to marry you. Dad was still staring at Grandma but now his face was twisted with a mix of rage and shock. "She should have moved out as soon as she decided to leave you instead of waiting and hoping things would get better. If she had, she'd still be alive."

My father stood there another minute, then he snarled, "Get the *fuck* outta my house! I don't want you back here and you better stay the hell away from my kids – you hear me?"

Grandma was crying even harder and Grandpa was trying to calm her and my dad down.

"Listen Keith," he began evenly, "It's late; we're all upset. We're saying things we don't mean." He looked pointedly at Grandma, giving her arm a gentle squeeze. "Let's just take a day or two to cool off, okay?"

Before my dad could say anything else, Grandpa was leading Grandma to the front door. I waited until I heard it close quietly behind them, then I quickly scampered back to bed before Dad could notice me.

Grandma and Grandpa weren't there the next morning, or the morning after that. I forced myself to wait a week then finally asked Beth what was going on. She told me that she'd heard Dad and Grandpa on the phone - Dad told him that they weren't allowed back at the house. Said he didn't want them talking bad about him to us. He said that if he caught them around here again he'd pack us up and move us clear across the country to Arizona, where our Uncle Ronnie lived.

Every time I thought things couldn't get any worse, they did. Without my grandparents around things quickly spiraled out of control. It was like living in a frat house day in and day out. There were no rules whatsoever. Dad didn't care what we did as long as we left him alone to wallow in his grief. For a guy who had treated Mom like shit all the time he sure took her death hard. It wasn't until I was much older that I would come to fully understand what had gone wrong between them and the guilt that ate away at him day after day once she was gone.

Anna – June 1985

Ace's unbridled enthusiasm for our "great escape" - as he referred to it - was contagious. Each night we'd talk on the phone until all hours, meticulously planning every detail out.

"What about all the groupies, Mr. Soon-To-Be Rock Star?" I asked him playfully over the phone one night.

He chuckled when I said that. "You and me, Anna," he began, "We're the real deal. We're gonna make it. No way I'd let some crazed fan ever come between us. I love you, Anna, more than anything; you know I do."

"I love you too, Ace," I said with a sigh. I hated the moment those calls ended and couldn't wait until we could spend all night, every night, together.

The morning of graduation I felt queasy but I chalked it up to nerves. I couldn't believe that high school was actually over. It had flown by like lightening. Three more months and Ace and I would be on our own. It all seemed just too good to be true.

After graduation came the endless string of pool parties and late-night celebrations, and while I was having fun, there was a strange feeling that persisted.

"You're not going to Dixon's?" Ace asked incredulously when I called to tell him I wasn't feeling up to another night of partying.

"I'm sorry. I know how much you were looking forward to it, but I just feel so rundown. I think I need a night off to recharge. You go, Ace, I don't mind."

He hesitated for a beat. "Okay, but you'll come to Jason's on Saturday, right? 'Cause he's setting up a stage in the yard and we're gonna be playing."

"Wouldn't miss it," I assured him, then after the usual I love yous, we hung up.

A week later, I still wasn't feeling like myself. I was also late, really late. It wasn't that odd, I thought, trying to push the fear to the back of my mind, probably just nerves about graduation and all the late nights. Still, one thing was gnawing at me - that night down the Shore, on the beach. We weren't careful, but it was only that one time and Ace said it would be alright. I pushed the thought once again to the back of my mind. I'll give it another week. Surely I'd get my period by then.

But another week went by, then two. I could no longer ignore the fact that something was wrong, but when I told Ace he didn't seem too concerned.

"Anna, no way. It was only that one time," he assured me, "There's just no way."

"Well, maybe I should go to the clinic and let them do a test, you know, just to make sure."

"Fine, take a test if it'll ease your mind, but I'm sure you're fine." He wrapped an arm around my shoulders. "You're just tired from all the partying, that's all."

Much as I wanted to believe him, something inside knew otherwise. Still I waited another week, hoping against hope, then I phoned the clinic and made an appointment for that afternoon. As I drove there I kept telling myself to relax and it worked so well that by the time I'd gotten there I'd actually convinced myself that everything was going to turn out fine. I wasn't even feeling queasy anymore.

Half-hour later I was walking back to my car with their card in my hand. They told me to phone them the following morning for the results. Until then I was going to put it out of my mind. No sense in getting myself all worked up over nothing. I definitely wasn't going to mention it to Ace until after I'd gotten the good news. He had a lot on his plate with all the preparations he was making for L.A. and I didn't want to add to his stress.

The next morning I awoke feeling great. In fact, I was feeling so good that I was nearly out the door on my way to work – I had gotten a job as a lifeguard at the local lake - when I remembered to call the clinic. I gave the woman on the other end of the line my name, then impatiently listened to several minutes of hold music while she went to get the results. I was debating whether to hang up and call back when she came back on the line and matter-of-factly announced that my results had come back positive.

A wave of lightheadedness forced me down onto my bed. The phone slipped from my shaking hand to the floor, where I heard a disembodied voice asking if I was still there. Even if I had been holding the receiver, I would not have been able to speak. Positive. The results were positive. This couldn't be happening.

Beneath the daze, the thoughts were beginning to race. But I was not thinking, "Holy crap, my parents are going to kill me when they find out," but, "Holy shit, this will destroy our plans for the Great Escape." Ace and I had messed up, big time, and I didn't even want to think about his reaction when I told him.

Somehow I managed to get it together enough to go to work, but I spent the day there in a complete and utter fog. I couldn't have told you about one thing that went on during the day; all I could think about was how I was going to tell Ace when I saw him that night. I kept rehearsing the words in my mind, both at work and on the ride home, but I couldn't picture myself saying them aloud.

Ace came to my house straight from work. We decided to go for a quick slice of pizza in town, then maybe head back to his house to hang out. We took a booth in the back and ordered our pizza and sodas. While we waited, Ace went on and on about things we were going to need when we got out to California. He didn't want to clutter the apartment with a lot of junk in case he was picked up right away and was needed in San Francisco or San Diego. He wanted to be able to just pick up and go. It took every ounce of strength for me to focus on his words.

"So?" I heard him say just as the waitress arrived with our order.

"Oh, sorry. What'd you say? Must've zoned out."

"I said," he replied, annoyance creeping into his voice as he slid a slice onto his plate, "that I think we could get away with just a studio apartment since we'll probably only need it to sleep." He gave me a pointed looked. "What's with you tonight, Anna? You've been in another world since I picked you up."

I watched as he picked up the pitcher of Coke and filled our glasses.

"Listen, I need to tell you something," I began as I shifted nervously in my seat.

"Yeah? Shoot," he said as he took a large bite of pizza.

"Ace . . ."

"Anna...?" he imitated with eyebrows raised.

"Um, I'm . . . I'm pregnant."

The words just hung in the air for a few seconds and then Ace shook his head.

"Anna, no, you're not. It was only that one time. It's, it's impossible," he said, sounding exasperated.

"No, Ace, it's definitely possible. I went to the clinic and they did a test and it came back positive. I am definitely pregnant."

He stared at me in disbelief for a moment, then tossed the slice back onto his plate.

"Fuck," he quietly said as he leaned his head on the back of the booth and closed his eyes.

After another moment he opened his eyes and said, "I think I lost my appetite; let's just get outta here."

I just nodded and he signaled for the waitress to bring the check. He left the cash on the table and then the two of us walked out to his car.

Neither of us said anything as he drove the short distance toward his house. When he got to his street he drove past it a couple blocks and pulled into a deserted lot across from a neighboring baseball field.

He put the car in park and turned the ignition off. He didn't say anything at first, he just fiddled with the radio dial, not looking at me.

Finally, I broke the silence. "Ace, say something. I've been freaking out about this all day."

"You've had all day to think about it," he said, still not looking at me as he continued to fiddle with the radio dial. "You just dumped it on me ten minutes ago so give me a fucking break."

I flinched at his tone. He'd never spoken to me that way before.

He turned sideways in the seat and looked at me. "So . . . what do we do?"

"I . . . I don't know," I said, my eyes filling with tears.

His face seemed to soften a bit. "C'mere," he said as he pulled me over and wrapped me in his arms.

I cried quietly against him until I felt the sleeve of his Def Leppard t-shirt begin to dampen; then I pulled away and began to wipe my eyes.

"It'll be okay, Anna," he said gently as his hands cupped my face, "We'll figure it out."

CHAPTER 6 - JACKSON

By the end of that first year, Beth, Tim and I had missed so much school that we were all in danger of being held back. That seemed to light a fire (well, a spark anyway) under my dad, who went up to the school and calmly explained how rough things had been for us since Mom died. The principal listened with a sympathetic ear and agreed that due to the tragic circumstances we deserved special consideration. That didn't mean a free pass, though. Our teachers would test us and if they felt that we were prepared to move on without struggling, then he would allow it. If not, well, he couldn't in good conscience promote us to the next grade knowing we weren't prepared.

Finally at the end of June a letter from the school arrived. "Two outta three ain't bad," Dad growled as he ran his fingers through his overgrown hair. "Sorry, Jacks, looks like you'll be repeatin' second grade."

I watched him toss the letter onto the kitchen table, then amble over to the fridge and grab himself a beer as if it were no big deal.

For me, it felt like another piece of my world was crumbling.

"Please, Dad," I cried, "I'll do anything, just please, please don't let them leave me back. Everyone will make fun of me. They'll call me stupid!"

"Well, if the shoe fits," he huffed under his breath as he sat down on the living room couch and turned on the TV with me still crying after him.

"Beat it, Jackson," he said, somehow managing to sound stern and dismissive at the same time, "Shoulda tried harder."

Try harder? I was seven, for fuck's sake! A seven-year-old living with no mother and a drunken ass for a father. What did he expect?

That September, I entered Ms. McShane's second grade classroom, the humiliation clinging to me like a wet blanket. I slid into a desk way in the back, but when she took attendance she made me move to the front seat in the first row.

"Principal Goodwin wants me to keep a close eye on you, Jackson," she said, "and make sure you have a successful year."

She smiled, trying to be nice, but it didn't help, not when I felt the eyes of every kid in the class upon me. I stared at the floor as I slunk into my new seat.

Nothing much changed after that, not at school or at home either. My dad wasn't any more attentive than he was before, and I soon found myself struggling. Ms. McShane tried to engage me, but I was distracted by absolutely everything – from the fly buzzing around the front of the room to the sound of the garbage truck driving past the school. Ms. McShane's mismatched shoes were a particular favorite. Anything was more interesting to me than being in that classroom. I barely eked my way through the second grade, but it was good enough for me.

There was only one good thing about that year – I discovered the guitar. One day, I was holed up in the basement after a particularly shitty day at school. There was a lot of junk down there, and I began going through it, more out of boredom than curiosity. There, buried under a pile of old clothes, was the little acoustic my dad had given Tim for his fifth birthday. Tim had always been more interested in sports and hanging out with his friends than music, and after a few unsuccessful attempts to engage him, Dad gave up and tossed the instrument down into the basement.

I'd lugged it upstairs to my room and fooled around with it for a while before finally asking Dad for help.

"Dad," I said quietly as I approached him, guitar in hand, "Can you show me how to play?"

I should have known better. He stared at me for a long moment, breathing steadily, all bleary-eyed from another night of drinking. "Get lost, Jackson," he said finally, "It's too complicated for a kid like you to understand." Then he turned and slowly went up the stairs to bed.

I felt like I had been punched in the stomach. *A kid like me?* What was that supposed to mean? I stared at his retreating figure as he climbed the stairs, feeling wounded by yet another one of his jabs. I vowed right then and there that I'd teach myself to play the guitar if it was the last thing I ever did.

It wasn't just our schoolwork that Dad didn't keep on top of. If we didn't want to clean up after ourselves, we didn't. If we wanted to eat potato chips for dinner, then bon appetite. If we didn't want to take a bath at night, we stayed dirty. There was a time when the three of us were pretty filthy. And our house – it was a fucking mess. Everyone remembers at least one family in town that they referred to as dirty or strange, and in our town that was us. Parents didn't let their kids come to our house and we rarely got invited over to anyone else's.

Beth and Tim were older, and it wasn't long before they cleaned up their act. Me, well that's another story. Let's just say it was still a few more years before I introduced myself to a bar of soap on a regular basis. Even then, it was only because I'd developed a crush on Tara Bradford. She was kinda dirty, too, but in a good way.

Flash forward a few years, and our oddness had become cool; our house, the go-to spot to party. My dad was usually out at night and when he wasn't, he was usually passed out up in his room. I was exposed to a lot of wild shit at a very young age – drinking, drugs and what I thought was "sex" but was actually just people making out on the couch.

Beth really began to straighten out senior year of high school, when she met Brody through a friend. Brody was a burley-looking bearded guy a few years older than her; he was also a straight-shooter who'd had a steady job working construction since the day he graduated. I called him the lumberjack dude, which she didn't always appreciate, but even I could see he was a good influence on her. Beth attempted to rein me and Tim in – setting a curfew and assigning us chores, all the things our father should have done - but by then we had been on our own too long to start playing by her new set of rules. Eventually, she gave up and started spending most of her time at Brody's house.

When I wasn't partying with Tim and his friends I was usually up in my room, practicing the guitar. I had outgrown the little acoustic pretty quickly and had been able to pick up a better one at a garage sale in town. It was cheap, too, and I used the few dollars I'd saved up from shoveling snow from my neighbors' driveways. The guy who sold it to me even threw in a packet of old sheet music.

Although he never actually said it, my dad made it pretty clear that he thought I sucked, rolling his eyes or turning up the TV whenever I played. It only reminded me of my vow to get better. I practiced even more, and even cleared out a spot in the garage so I could go there when he was home – which thankfully wasn't very often.

I was still in middle school when Dad started bringing women around. Women that he picked up in the dive bars where he hung out. Real winners, these women; some of them actually made *him* look classy. Holed up in my room, I'd listen to their drunken giggling and want to scream. There was only one good thing about them - they kept Dad occupied which meant he wasn't around to dump on us.

Anna – July 1985

I felt better after we spoke about our "issue," as Ace referred to it. He would figure out what was best for all of us. Maybe I'd meet him out in California after the baby was born, or maybe we'd postpone the trip until next summer. Maybe he'd want to just go ahead with our plans and then I'd have the baby out there. Mom wasn't going to like that third option. I hadn't told either of my parents yet. I figured I'd wait until me and Ace had decided on a plan before I broke the news.

I didn't see Ace for the next few days. He was working extra hours and then the band was practicing at Jason's. He wanted me to come but I wasn't feeling up to it, so we made plans for that Wednesday. I was looking forward to it. Nauseas or not, I missed him.

On Wednesday Ace came over as soon as he was done with work. We went to watch TV in the basement, out of earshot from my parents. For a few minutes we were silent as he flipped through the channels.

"Ace, we need to talk about what we're going to do," I finally said.

He sighed in response and reluctantly turned his attention away from the TV. "Anna, I don't really think we have any options."

"What do you mean?" I asked, confused.

"Anna," he said, giving me a pointed look, "You know exactly what I mean."

"No, Ace, I really don't," I responded, still confused. He didn't say anything, just kept staring. When I realized what he was getting at, I squirmed away from him and stood up from the couch.

"Ace, you don't mean -"

"Yeah, I do," he said unblinkingly. "Oh, come on, Anna. Don't act like it's so outrageous. It happens way more than you think. I could name three people we know right off the top of my head who've done it. Don't act like it's such a big deal."

"Not such a big deal?" I repeated, unable to believe what I was hearing; unable to believe his callous attitude. "You can't be serious."

"Yeah, Anna," he snapped, "I'm fucking serious. We have plans, remember? California? Does it ring a bell?"

"Ace -" I began, but again he cut me off.

"There is no way, no fucking way I'm arriving in L.A. with a baby in tow. No one's gonna take me seriously if we show up to auditions with a kid. That's not the image I want."

"Oh, well excuse me!" I said, folding my arms across my chest, "I wouldn't want to ruin your 'image' with our child. Better I just get rid of it than risk that."

"Anna, this isn't what either of us wanted."

"Yeah, Ace, I know, but it's what we got."

He glared at me angrily as he searched for a retort. "This is bullshit!" he shouted as he too stood up from the couch. I glanced toward the door at the top of the stairs, praying my parents couldn't hear. "I don't need this right now; I'm outta here."

Then, without another word, he turned and stormed out of my basement and up the stairs. A few seconds later I heard the front door slam followed by the faint sound of his car pulling out of my driveway.

Stunned, I collapsed back onto the couch. In all the time I'd known him, Ace and I had never had such a heated argument before. In all my life I had never felt so alone.

"Everything okay?" my mom asked me when I went upstairs, "I thought I heard yelling."

"Oh, no, he was just playing the TV too loud." I ignored her suspicious stare and started moving toward the staircase. "Well, I'm tired. 'Night, Mom."

Once up in my room I stood staring at myself in front of the full-length mirror on the back of the door. I turned sideways, smoothing my t-shirt over my still flat belly and trying to imagine what I was going to look like five or six months down the road. I'd have to tell my parents long before that, and just the thought of it made me sick to my stomach.

I didn't sleep a wink that night.

A week went by and I still hadn't heard from Ace. As hurt as I was, I refused to call him. He was the one who'd stormed off so he should be the one to make the first move. My parents were certainly in chipper moods in his absence; I knew they were hoping that he was out of the picture for good. My dad even brought up enrolling at State again, but I brushed him off.

On Sunday evening I was lying on my bed with a magazine when there was a knock at the front door. I heard my father's footsteps, then the disappointed tone in his voice as he made small talk with Ace. I waited in my room a moment or two before I went downstairs.

"Oh, there you are, Annalise," Dad said as he turned to me, "Keith's here for you." My dad refused to refer to him as Ace.

I nodded, then waited for him to join my mother in the kitchen for coffee before I turned to Ace.

"You got a minute?" he asked, barely able to meet my eye. His hands were stuffed in his front pockets as he kicked at some imaginary dirt on the carpet.

"Yeah," I nodded.

He cocked his head in the direction of the front door, and I grabbed my sweatshirt and followed him outside.

"Take a ride?" he asked.

"Okay."

I climbed into the passenger seat of his black Camaro and the two of us drove in silence to a park not far from where I lived.

He pulled to a stop, then reached into the backseat. When his hand reappeared, it was clutching a single red rose. "Truce?"

"Truce," I repeated as he handed me the rose.

"Anna, I'm so sorry. I acted like a total jerk."

I didn't argue with him because he definitely had acted like a total jerk.

"But Anna . . . I haven't changed my mind." He held up his hand when he saw my face. "Wait, I mean I haven't changed my mind about wanting a kid. I'm not gonna lie to you, Anna - I don't. At least not right now. But... I've been thinking things over, trying to come up with a plan that works for both of us."

"Go ahead, I'm listening," I said, motioning for him to continue.

"You know as well as I do that we're not ready to be parents. So I was thinking, what if we gave it away? You know, let someone adopt it or something...?"

I didn't say anything at first. It's not like the thought hadn't crossed my mind.

"I don't know, Ace. My parents would never go for that if they found out. They'd want me to keep it."

He thought for a minute. "Well, what if we didn't tell them – or anyone? What if we just went to L.A. like we planned and did it out there? I mean, you could pop out a kid just as easily in California as you could in Jersey, right? No one would ever have to know."

Ace had a point. Neither of us were ready for the responsibility of having a family and his idea did make sense. We'd be sidestepping our parents and by the time we came back to visit the whole ordeal would be long over with.

"Do you think we could really pull it off?" I asked.

"Why not?" he shrugged. "I haven't told anyone. Have you?"

I shook my head.

"So nobody knows. There's no chance of it leaking to our parents." He waited a beat, "So . . . what do you say?"

I mulled it over but finally came to the conclusion that he was right – it was the only option that worked for the both of us – so I agreed.

CHAPTER 7 - JACKSON

After Beth graduated we saw less and less of her. She was working full time at a local bank and practically living at Brody's. Dad spent most of his free time holed up with one of his whores, leaving me and Tim alone in the house. It was just fine by me. I had little interest in schoolwork and with Dad not around I was free to hang out in the garage or up in my room with my guitar. For obvious reasons, lessons had always been out of the question so I tried to play along with the songs on the radio. It was slow at first but eventually I was able to play most of them by ear. I actually wasn't half bad and I knew that if I had a tuned-up new guitar instead of the garage sale special, I'd be able to play a lot better.

I think that was the year I stumbled across a box of my dad's old record albums in the basement. Most of them were warped thanks to several floods over the years, but I was able to salvage a few. I was even able to play some of them on an old stereo, also in the basement but stored high enough off the ground to avoid damage. There was only one working speaker but it was enough for me to tell that I definitely liked what I heard. I eventually replaced my favorite albums with CDs so I could play along with them out in the garage. I'd pick up that guitar and just disappear into the music. Nothing else existed.

Tim, a junior in high school, ran with a pretty rough crowd. Then, halfway through his senior year he began to get his shit together. Maybe it was his looming graduation, or maybe it was just the thought of living the rest of his life under Dad's decrepit roof that lit a fire under his ass. Well, that and the novelty of our bohemian-like lifestyle was probably beginning to wear thin on him. He started subtly distancing himself from his friends, then in the spring he dropped the bomb that he'd gone and enlisted. He'd leave for bootcamp a week after graduation and then he'd be shipping out to wherever they needed him. Dad grunted a "keep in touch," then went back to watching TV. I was too shocked to say much of anything. I was just a freshman – thanks to being left back in the second grade - and counting the days until I too could escape the house.

With Tim gone I was alone even more than before. Since I was also always short on cash, I decided it was time I found myself a job. A job hunt meant that I'd need some form of identification, and since I couldn't yet drive I'd have to dig up my birth certificate. One particularly dull afternoon I went up to the attic and began rummaging around. Eventually I found what I was looking for - in the far corner of the dusty attic was a box with "Important Docs" scribbled across the front in black sharpie. *Must be in here,* I thought as I carefully carried it down to my room.

I began with a manila envelope stuffed with papers, and there at the bottom was my birth certificate. I was about to bring the box back up to the attic when I decided to go through the rest of it. I sifted through some old books and other crap, then another smaller manila envelope – this one containing a few old pictures – caught my eye.

I emptied the pictures onto my bed and began scanning through them. Most were of my mom and dad, but real old. There were a few of my dad as a kid and some of his friends dressed up like Kiss – *fucking loser.* A prom photo that made me laugh because in it they both had those really big eighties hairdos. A black and white of my mom and dad sitting on the hood of an old Camaro. It had something scrawled across the back of it but the words were faded and I couldn't make out what it said. That one had a crease in the center; probably from being folded over in a wallet or something. The last two in the envelope were grainy Polaroids my mom must've taken of my dad playing with his band. I wondered briefly if the band had been any good but doubted it. If they'd been even halfway decent, he wouldn't have given up playing to go work at the post office.

I was putting everything back in the box when I saw the words "marriage license" at the top of a faded document. I knew it belonged to my parents so I picked it up.

June 7, 1986? That couldn't be right, I thought as I looked at the date. I quickly pulled out Beth's birth certificate and read it carefully to confirm my suspicions which ended up being correct - Beth was born a good six months *before* they were married.

Anna – August 1985

Ace and I went about our business that summer as if nothing was out of the ordinary. We didn't even discuss it between ourselves. It was just swept under the rug. We planned for our big move across the country as if our "issue" no longer existed.

My parents had finally come around and accepted the fact that Ace and I would be leaving. Well, not so much "accepted" as realizing there was no changing my mind. My mom went on about how she was going to miss me and that I'd better make sure I was home for Christmas.

"I don't know, Mom..." I began, knowing full well it wasn't possible, not in the condition I would be in by then. "Ace has got a lot of stuff lined up and if things start happening for him we're not going to be able to just pick up and leave."

"Well, try at least. Christmas won't be the same without you here."

I told her that we'd try, but that next summer would probably be more doable for us.

By mid-August there was no hiding the fact that I was pregnant, at least not in my regular clothes. Ace and I were scheduled to leave on September 4, meaning I had almost three more weeks of hiding my pregnancy from Mom and Dad. I took to wearing baggy sweatshirts, using the excuse that I was cold. I don't know how they bought that, what with the temperatures hovering around ninety degrees nearly every day.

Despite their new, relatively cool attitude about the move, I was genuinely surprised when about two weeks before our departure date my mom announced she was taking me to the mall to get some new clothes.

"I want you to have some nice things, honey, and it'll be fun to spend the day together. I'm really going to miss you." She sounded so sad.

"I'm really going to miss you too, Mom," I replied, trying to keep my voice neutral. I hated lying to her.

The next day we got an early start, arriving at the mall as soon as it opened. After a quick stop for drinks at the food court, we went from store to store, picking up a bunch of cute little tank tops and shorts along the way.

Our last stop was Macy's, where I found a ton of stuff on sale being that it was the end of the season. I tried all the clothes on in the dressing room and although most of them were tight around my expanding middle I figured they would be perfect for afterward.

I was just pulling one of the tops off over my head when I heard my mom call out as she opened the dressing room door, "Annalise, I found these really cute -"

She froze mid-sentence, her eyes growing wide as she looked at my abdomen.

"Oh my God, Anna . . . you're pregnant!"

CHAPTER 8 – JACKSON

No doubt about it, finding the pictures and my parents' marriage license had me intrigued. There was obviously a lot about them I never knew, and now I wanted more. Problem was, I didn't know who to ask.

Asking Dad was out of the question; we were rarely home together and when we were we avoided each other like the plague. Tim was gone. That left Beth, and I wasn't sure I wanted to go there. What if she didn't know?

A couple days later she happened to stop by the house.

"Hey Jacks," she said as she poked her head into the kitchen.

"Oh, hey Beth; what brings you here? Checking up on me?" I joked.

"Na, just looking for my winter boots. It's supposed to snow later in the week."

"Oh." I nodded absently, wondering how I could broach the topic. *Hi Beth, I'll help you look for your boots, oh, and by the way, did you know you were illegitimate?* Not exactly a smooth transition.

In the end I bit the bullet and went with the direct approach, showing her the hard evidence I'd found. She just rolled her eyes at me as if to say, *Well, duh.*

"So, you knew about this?"

"Of course I did, Jackson. I'm not stupid; I mean, really, do the math."

"Does Tim know?" I asked, wondering if I was the only one who was out of the loop.

"I don't know, I guess so. I thought everyone knew."

I sat silently for a moment, then switched topics. "Do you know anything about the band Dad was in?"

"Not really. Just that he played guitar. Why?"

I shrugged. "I found some old pictures and was just wondering about it, that's all."

"Well whatever you do, don't ask him," she bristled as she shook her head, "I mentioned it once and he nearly bit my head off. You'd have to ask Grandma or Grandpa, they'd probably know."

I looked at her incredulously. "Uh, Beth, they're dead. Did you forget?"

"Duh, Jackson. I mean *Mom's* parents. Grandma and Grandpa Keller."

My sister was full of surprises today. "You've been in touch with them? Do you know where they are?"

"No, I haven't been in touch with them since they left, but I'm sure you could find them. Try googling them."

Dad had forbidden my grandparents from any contact with us after Mom died, even threatened to move us out of state if they ever came near us. Turns out it wasn't an issue, because they moved out west shortly after. Grandma had some health problems and the stress from my mother's death, and the arguments with my father – not to mention losing us kids – made them a hell of a lot worse. The doctors told my grandfather he'd better get her to a warmer climate because her weakened lungs would never have been able to withstand another Northeast winter.

We were allowed to say goodbye to them but thanks to our father it was a strained conversation. They promised to write but never did. I checked that damn mailbox every day for nearly a year but no letters ever arrived – never even got so much as a birthday card. Eventually I gave up. By then I was all too familiar with disappointment.

Anna – September 1985

Well, the cat was definitely out of the bag. My mother berated me all the way home for being so irresponsible. I didn't say anything, choosing instead to just stare down at my hands folded in my lap

"Take a seat in the kitchen, Annalise, and do not move," she said sternly, then called out to my father, who was upstairs.

"What's all the yelling about?" I heard him say, then she climbed the stairs. A second later I heard them whispering in the hallway.

"Jesus Christ, Joanna," Dad said, "I said you were giving her way too much freedom. This is what happens when you don't keep an eye on her!"

"Oh, so it's my fault?" my mom hissed. "You're the one's who's been spoiling her rotten since she was a little girl. She's grown up thinking there's no consequences for her actions. You're the one to blame."

I flinched at every word. It wasn't either of their faults; both had been model parents. I turned as I heard them enter our small kitchen.

"So, what are your plans? Let's hear it," my mom demanded as she roughly pulled out a chair and sat down.

Before I could answer, Dad said, "Calm down, Joanna, she's obviously upset and what's done is done. Let's just hear her out." He turned to me. "Annalise?"

I calmly explained what Ace and I had decided. "I didn't tell you because we had it all figured out."

"Figured out!" my mother shouted as she threw her hands up in disbelief. "You think you can just give away a child like it's a stray kitten? This is our grandchild you're talking about and there is no way you're going to hand him or her over to complete strangers. And in California, no less? And how did you expect to pay for all the related expenses? Hospital bills, doctors? Have you thought about that?"

"Uh..." I began because I hadn't thought about it much at all.

"It sounds like maybe you don't have it all figured out."

"Mom, I -" I started, but she quickly cut me off.

"Don't 'Mom' me, Annalise!" she warned. "Do Keith's parents know about this?"

I shook my head.

She stood from the table. "Get in the car – now!"

"Where are we going?" I asked.

"We're going over to the Foxxes'; I think they'd like to hear what you two have 'planned.'"

I stood, knowing that there was no arguing with her.

"Dad?"

"Get in the car, Annalise," he said, struggling to stay calm, "I think the three of us need to sit down with Keith and his parents."

On the drive over all I could think about was how freaked out Ace was going to be when the three of us showed up at his door.

When we arrived Dad banged loudly on the front door. I was mortified, especially when Ace's mom opened it wearing her bathrobe and a surprised expression on her face.

"Oh, Mr. and Mrs. Keller, Anna, what a nice surprise," she said, trying unsuccessfully to mask her bewilderment, "Come in."

"We need to speak with you and your husband," Mom said matter-of-factly.

Ace's mother had us wait in the living room while she went to get her husband.

"What's this about?" Mr. Foxx asked after greeting the three of us.

My mom then proceeded to relay the whole story to them as they looked on in complete shock. Ace's dad then went to find Ace, who was out back mowing the lawn and obviously hadn't heard the commotion.

To say Ace was shocked when he found us all sitting in his living room was an understatement but I could tell he knew the reason why.

Ace's mom relayed to Ace an abridged version of what my mom had told her. "Is this true, son?"

"Yeah, it's true. So now you know," he said as he sat down on the arm of the chair I was sitting on and put his hand on my shoulder. "And you should also know that Anna and I've got it all figured out. Everything's settled." He looked at me. "Right, Anna?"

Before I could answer my dad blurted out, "Settled? Oh, I don't think so." He turned to Ace, "If you think for one minute I'm going to let you take my pregnant seventeen-year-old daughter trekking across the country with you, you're crazy, boy."

"Wait a minute-" Ace began, but my dad put his hand up.

"No, you wait a minute. You just try to take her with you and I'll have the cops on your ass so fast your head'll spin." He turned to Ace's dad. "You better have a good lawyer ready, Foxx, 'cause you're gonna need it when your boy here tries to transport a minor across state lines."

"Dad!" I yelled.

"Calm down, everyone," Mrs. Foxx said. "We need to settle this like civilized adults. This is our grandchild too."

I was exhausted when we finally left Ace's and I was dying to talk to him alone and explain how this whole thing blew up in the first place. In the end nothing was actually settled but at least no one was yelling anymore.

Things calmed down the next day and my parents and I talked rationally about the whole thing. They were right about the hospital and doctor's bills. The fact that these things never entered the equation just proved that me and Ace were definitely not ready for this kind of responsibility.

Ace and I finally got to speak alone two nights later when he came over after work. My parents were a bit frosty to him when he arrived but if it bothered him it didn't show.

"That was seriously fucked up the other day," he said, shaking his head.

"Totally," I agreed as I took a seat next to him on the basement couch.

"So, I guess L.A.'s out of the question," he sighed.

"Ace," I said quietly, "You should still go to California. You don't need me. All I'd do in this condition is slow you down. And besides, my parents are right. I should stay here and have the baby. It'll be safer and I'm still under their insurance so it won't be a financial strain on us. Besides, it'll be easier handling all the legal stuff with the adoption with their help."

He looked at me in shock. "But . . . but what about us?" He sounded almost choked up. "I . . . I can't do it without you, Anna."

"Yes, you can, Ace. And it's only six months, eight at the most, before I can meet you out there."

"I can wait," he suggested, but I knew that he had already started setting up auditions.

"There's no sense waiting; it took you months to set up those auditions and who knows if you'll get another chance. It's fine. I'll be fine. We'll both be fine."

A week later we had a tearful goodbye at the airport, and just like that, he was gone.

CHAPTER 9 - JACKSON

Back in the day tracking down my grandparents would have taken a private investigator and a whole lot of cash. These days, it was a lot cheaper and a lot less dramatic. A couple of Google searches later and I was staring at their current address on my computer screen. Guess they didn't like the West too much because at some point they'd returned to Jersey. The address was for a retirement community in Rockaway, about an hour or so from where we lived.

Finding them was the easy part; the hard part was deciding whether I wanted to reach out. I couldn't forget how they'd totally bailed on us after Mom died. Sure, my Dad was an asshole and my grandmother's health wasn't great, but why hadn't they ever bothered to call or write? It was as if they'd just disappeared off the face of the earth.

I sat on the information for a couple of days but eventually curiosity got the better of me.

"You want to go *where*?" Beth asked incredulously when I called to tell her of my plan.

"You heard me, I wanna go see Grandma and Grandpa," I repeated, "So, will you take me?"

"But that's crazy, Jackson," Beth exclaimed. "So what if they're back in Jersey? They haven't called. And like you said yourself, they bailed on us." She paused a moment, then I heard her mutter, "Can't believe you actually found them."

"I know what I said, but after finding all that stuff in the attic I have a lot of questions." I waited for her to say something, but she was quiet.

"Can you just take me there? You don't even have to come in; wait out in the car if you want."

There was more silence as she mulled over my request. "Fine, I'll take you," she said finally, "but you're on your own once we get there."

▲   ▲   ▲

The following Saturday Beth and I pulled into an empty parking space across from our grandparents' condo.

Beth turned to me and sighed. "Are you sure you want to do this, Jackson?"

"Yeah. Sure you don't wanna come with?" I asked, hoping she'd changed her mind, but she shook her head.

"Okay, whatever." I shrugged and got out of the car.

A couple minutes later I found myself standing outside number 9212 but just as I raised my hand to knock a breathless Beth appeared at my side.

"Knew you'd come," I lied.

She rolled her eyes. "Just knock, Jackson."

I rapped on the door a few times, then took a small step back. I glanced at Beth's profile and could tell that she was nervous too.

A moment later the door pulled open slowly and suddenly there we were standing face to face with our grandfather.

At first he just gave us a questioning look, then his jaw slowly dropped open in shock. "Beth? Jackson?" he said, his eyes filling with tears, then his arms went around us.

I didn't know about Beth, but I was stunned. It had only been about eight years since we'd seen him but from the way he looked you'd think it was more like twenty.

"Who's at the door, John?" I heard a familiar voice call out.

"Joanna, come, it . . . it's the *kids*!" He slowly pushed the door open wider so she could see.

My eyes shifted to his left and locked onto those of a frail-looking woman sitting in a wheelchair. There was a blanket draped across her lap

"Good Lord!" she said, squinting as she reached for her glasses. She looked between the two of us and then wheeled closer to the door. "My prayers have finally been answered."

He stepped aside and motioned for us to come in. Beth and I had yet to utter a word. Obviously she was just as shocked at their appearance as I was.

"I was beginning to think this day would never come," Grandma said, her voice cracking as she struggled to get up from her wheelchair. Once on her feet she steadied herself and then reached out to embrace us. That's when my stoic sister suddenly burst into tears.

For a few minutes we just stood there clinging to each other, and I may have even wiped a tear or two away myself.

"Well, let's not just stand here in the foyer," my grandmother said finally. I helped her back into the wheelchair and we all headed to the living room. Grandma gestured toward a couch and Beth and I took a seat.

"John, get the kids some lemonade out of the fridge," Grandma said, then smiled at me and Beth. "Is it still your favorite?"

"Sure," Beth said, while I just nodded like an idiot. Grandpa returned with the drinks and the four of us talked for a long while. Actually Beth did most of the talking, which was surprising since she hadn't been too keen on coming in the first place. It was fine by me, though, because I suddenly seemed to have lost my voice. I felt like a little kid again. It was mostly casual talk anyway. Beth filled them in on her boyfriend and her job and about where she lived. I just sat there, waiting for the right time to address the six- hundred-pound gorilla in the room, namely, *Why the fuck did you not keep in touch after you left?*

After a while Grandma took Beth into the bedroom to show her some things that had belonged to Mom. My grandfather asked me about Tim and how long he'd been gone and about how I was doing in school. I answered him with short answers until finally I couldn't take it anymore.

"Why the hell did you just leave us like that?" I blurted out.

He stared at me, confused, but before he could reply I added, "You just left. I know Gram was sick and you had to move but I don't get why you just dropped us like that. Never a call or a letter. Not even a friggin' birthday card." He started to interrupt, but I put up my hand to stop him.

"You guys were the only normalcy we had after Mom died. Do you have any idea how bad it was with Dad?"

He let out a sigh as he stood up. "Come with me for a minute, Jackson; I want to show you something."

I stood and followed him down the narrow hallway and into a small spare bedroom.

"Have a seat," he said as he motioned to the bed and then went over to the closet. He slid the closet door to the side and gestured with his hand to the many boxes stacked on the floor of the closet.

"See those boxes, Jackson?" he said as he began to pull one of them out. I quickly jumped up to help him and we carried the box to the bed.

"Open it," he told me.

The tape came off easily enough. I pulled open the folds and peered inside. *What the -?* When I looked up at my grandfather, his eyes were once again filled with tears.

"That box," he began, "along with all the others, is filled with every letter, birthday card, Valentine, Christmas card and postcard that your grandmother and I sent to you kids over the past eight years. Every single one of them was sent back unopened and marked *return to sender*."

I stared at the contents, slowly thumbing through them, each postmarked with different dates over the years.

"But how. . .?" I let my voice trail off because I already knew the answer.

"Your father worked for the post office, Jackson. He made sure not a single one got through. We kept sending them anyway, hoping that one day he might relent, but as you can see..." He motioned again to all the boxes. "...he never did."

"He changed the phone number too and made sure it was unlisted. I'm sorry, Jackson, with the distance between us – not to mention all Grandma's health issues - there was nothing more we could've done." He placed his hand on my shoulder and hesitated before adding, "It nearly killed her, though."

▲   ▲   ▲

"Can you believe how old they look?" I asked Beth as we drove back from Rockaway.

"Give them a break, Jackson, they've been through a lot." She glanced at me. "And they weren't that young when they had Mom - I think Gram was in her mid-forties and Grandpa was nearly fifty. She told me that Mom was like a gift because she didn't think she was able to have children."

I told Beth that I'd asked Grandpa why they never kept in touch.

She nodded. "I asked Gram the same thing."

"Can you believe Dad kept all those letters and cards from us?"

Beth took her eyes off the road long enough to give me an incredulous look. "Why? You can't?"

"Yeah, you're right – stupid question."

We drove for a while in silence, then I said, "I want to go back again; I don't want to lose touch with them, Beth."

"Yeah, me either."

"I have a lot more questions." I looked over at her. "I wanna know about Dad's band and if they were any good."

She huffed. "Yeah, well, you wanna know what I want to ask them?" She didn't wait for me to answer. "I want to ask them if they know why Dad started treating Mom like shit all the time. I'm not sure if you remember, but it wasn't always like that."

"Yeah, they looked real happy in those old pictures I found. What do you think happened, Beth? What could've changed?"

She shrugged. "Beats me."

I agreed and then reclined the seat and closed my eyes against the setting sun.

Anna – Fall 1985

When Ace left for L.A. we missed each other like crazy. We burned up the phone lines every night, talking for hours. Mostly it was him, telling me how great it was out there and how bad he wished I was with him. But after a few weeks the phone calls started to get shorter, then we started skipping nights here and there. When I did talk to him he seemed moody and not himself. When I asked him how things were going he always gave me vague answers, like, "It's going great" or "Things are really beginning to take shape" or "Stuff's happening," but he never really told me what the "stuff" was.

I chalked it up to nerves and his being overly exhausted from all the running around he was doing between working and auditions. He'd gotten a job waiting tables, which he hated but helped him pay the bills.

Then it started getting harder and harder to get in touch with him and when I left messages on his machine they would often go unanswered.

I called his older brother Ronnie, but he told me that neither he nor his parents had heard much from Ace either.

The next time I spoke to Ace, I asked him if something was wrong, but he just snapped at me and told me to stop nagging him.

"Nagging you? What are you talking about? I'm not nagging you. I just wanted to know how things are going, that's all."

"Yeah, well it feels like nagging so just lay the fuck off."

"Lay the fuck off?" I challenged. "I don't need this crap, Ace. I'm dealing with a lot of shit here and I don't need shit from you too."

"Well, if you don't like it then don't bother calling anymore."

"You can go to hell, Ace," I told him, then I slammed the phone down.

Soon my anger turned to hurt. Every time the phone rang I would jump, thinking it was him, but it was always a friend from school or someone calling for my parents.

I found myself alone in my bedroom one night, staring blankly across the room and wondering how things could've gone so horribly wrong. When I looked up my eyes caught sight of the black and white photo of us that was sticking in the corner of my dresser mirror.

I crossed the room, then slowly pulled the photograph down and flipped it over, reading what Ace had written on the back of it, "Anna – Livin' out our dream! Luv ya, Ace." My eyes misted over as I thought back to the night it was taken. Ace had just gotten his first call-back from one of the producers he'd contacted about an audition and we were all out celebrating. All our friends were thrilled for us and Ace and I were both so excited. I remember he kept saying, "This is it Anna! It's really happening! This time next year we'll be livin' out our dream!" I slowly folded the picture in half and then placed it in my drawer so it was out of sight. I didn't need a daily reminder of my shattered dreams.

Thanksgiving came and went without a word from Ace and it was the same thing at Christmas. His family hadn't heard from him either. It was like he had dropped off the face of the earth. I finally had to accept the fact that he was done with me. He'd probably met some skinny non-pregnant groupie with bleached blonde hair and big fake boobs. Mom did her best to console me though neither she nor my dad had ever been very fond of Ace.

She asked me again after Christmas if I'd consider keeping the baby and continue living with them. Maybe enroll at community college for a year and see how I liked it.

I snapped at her to leave me alone and she wisely retreated. I was cranky and bored sitting around the house all day and I couldn't wait for this pregnancy to be over and done with.

A week later, I got my wish.

I woke in the middle of the night with severe cramps. The pain was excruciating but I knew it was way too early for the baby to be coming. I got out of bed to try to walk it off but when I turned on the light the lower half of my nightgown was covered in thick dark red blood. I made my way to the bathroom but as I did I could feel the blood running down my inner thighs.

Mom heard my screams and came running. I thought she'd pass out when she saw all the blood - her face went white - but she just yelled to my father to call an ambulance.

I leaned onto the edge of the sink and then everything started to blur. The last thing that flashed through my mind before passing out was that despite everything that'd happened, I wished to God that Ace was here with me.

CHAPTER 10 - JACKSON

A few weeks later Beth and I went back to our grandparents' condo. I brought some of the old photos I'd found and after lunch we sifted through them, along with a bunch of others Grandpa had pulled from the closet. When we got to the pictures of my dad, I asked what they knew about the band and whether they were any good.

"I don't know, Jackson," my grandfather sighed, "that was a long time ago."

He hesitated, as if debating whether he should say anything else. "I know he moved out to California for a while... something to do with his music... but I don't know what ever happened with it."

I raised an eyebrow at him, trying to reconcile the lazy drunk I knew with a kid moving across the country to follow his passion.

"California, really? When was that?"

He and my grandmother glanced at each other as if not sure how much they wanted to reveal.

"It was a long time ago, Jackson," she repeated my grandfather's words, "before you kids were born."

"Well, how long was he there?" I asked, not ready to let the subject drop.

My grandfather shrugged. "I don't know, six months maybe?"

He was in California for six months? For his music? Could he have actually been good? I sat back for a moment to let this new information sink in, but by the time I opened my mouth to ask another question Beth had started talking - something to do with her job. I wasn't really paying attention.

"Why did he come back?" I interrupted.

"Let it go, Jackson," Beth said pointedly.

"No, Beth, I wanna know and we both know I'm not gonna get any answers from Dad." I looked away from her and back towards my grandparents. "Tell me, did he come back because he was no good and couldn't make it?"

I could tell I was making them uncomfortable but I wasn't going to back down.

"Jackson, I'm sorry," my grandfather said gently, "but I don't know anything about your father's music or how good he was or what happened while he was away. As far as I know he came back to be with your mother after Beth was born. If you want to know more, you'll have to ask him."

I couldn't tell whether he was putting me off or if he didn't really know anything, but either way I decided to let it drop. For now it was enough to know that there was way more to my father's story than I had ever imagined.

Anna – January 1986

I came awake slowly, with no knowledge of where I was or how I had gotten there. My eyelids felt swollen and weighted down with sand. Sudden flashes went through my mind. The pain. The blood. The baby. Try as I might I wasn't able to open my eyes. Someone was sitting beside me; I could feel the weight of their head leaning on my arm and the pressure of their hand holding mine. I could hear their quiet sobs. If I could just move my fingers and let them know that I was okay, that I knew they were there... It took all my strength but I was finally able to move my index and middle fingers of the hand being held.

"Anna?!" I heard Ace whisper hoarsely, then he squeezed my hand tighter.

"Anna!" he said again, louder this time. Then I heard him call for the nurse and a moment later I heard footsteps rushing into the room.

"She moved!" he exclaimed, "She moved her fingers! She'll be okay now, right?" I felt myself drift off again.

I don't know how long I was out, but when I awoke again my eyes felt less swollen. When I cracked them open, I saw Ace's tall frame slumped in the chair in the corner, his head in his hands.

"Ace...?" I croaked out so quietly I don't know how he heard it.

He shot out of the chair and was at my side in seconds.

"Anna, Anna, it's okay; I'm here." He buried his head at my shoulder. "I'm sorry Anna, I'm so, so sorry. I never should have left you. Never."

"Ace . . ." I whispered, ". . . the baby, what about the baby?"

He didn't answer right away.

"Please, Ace . . . tell me."

"Oh, Anna," he sobbed, "she's, she's so small. They thought she wasn't gonna make it."

"She? It's a girl? I need to see her," I gasped as I struggled to sit up.

Ace shook his head. "You can't, she's in Intensive Care. No one's allowed in."

"I'm her mother," I said, my voice growing louder, "She needs me, Ace, and I want to see her."

Ace yelled for the nurse again and a second later a stout woman rushed in, along with a doctor. They tried to calm me.

"You've been through a lot, Annalise," the doctor said, "I need to examine you again and make sure everything checks out."

"Yes," the nurse added reassuringly, "We just want to make sure you're okay before we take you up to Intensive Care."

I reluctantly laid back down and allowed the doctor to examine me. After what seemed like an eternity, he and the nurse gently maneuvered me into a wheelchair, then Ace wheeled me toward the Neonatal Intensive Care Unit to see our daughter.

We weren't allowed in but there was an enormous window than ran the length of the room. She was the only baby in there, and although she was alarmingly small and hooked up to several monitors, I could see she was beautiful. Her eyes were closed and I could see her little chest rising and falling with every breath.

"Ms. Keller?" I heard someone say and I turned toward the voice.

"I'm Dr. Corliss," the man said as he stuck out his hand to shake mine, "I'm in charge of the team that's been taking care of your daughter."

"Nice to meet you, Doctor," I replied.

"It's good to see that you're up and around. You gave everyone quite a scare. Great to see you're out of the woods and it looks like your daughter is too."

"Thank God," I whispered, and heard Ace's sigh of relief. The doctor proceeded to explain everything that the team had been doing regarding the baby's condition, then *reiterated that she was doing much better. I could tell from his expression that it had been touch and go and was almost grateful I had been unconscious.*

The doctor patted my shoulder. "We think she'll be able to go home as early as next week."

"Thank you so much, Doctor," Ace said. It was a tone I'd never heard him use before.

After telling us he would touch base with us again the next morning, the doctor excused himself to go do rounds. Ace and I turned back towards the glass and gazed at the baby until the nurses took her to another area for more tests.

Ace wheeled me back down to my room where I found my parents waiting for me.

They wrapped their arms around me, saying what a scare I'd given them. Apparently the two of them had sat vigil at my bedside since they brought me in.

"Figures you wake up the minute we leave for a shower and a change of clothes," Dad laughed.

I was exhausted and at ten o'clock the nurse came into my room and kicked Ace and my parents out. "Visiting hours are over and our new mom needs her rest. You can come back tomorrow morning."

"Okay," I said, swallowing my disappointment. I really wanted to speak to Ace but not in front of my parents.

After they left, I lay in bed thinking about the baby and wondering when someone would arrive with the adoption papers for me to sign. I hadn't even held her yet and already I was having second thoughts.

I tossed and turned all night, wrestling with the biggest decision I'd ever have to make.

When I woke the next morning, Ace was sitting in the chair beside my bed, looking down at the pink bundle nestled snugly in his arms.

When he saw that I was awake he smiled, then stood and placed her in my arms. "What about Beth?" he asked.

"Hmmm," I said, not really listening to him as I looked down at her; so light she felt, like a feather resting against my chest. She was absolutely perfect and I knew in that moment that I never wanted to let her go.

"I said, what about Beth?" he repeated, then added, "She needs a name, right?"

"Beth?" I asked blankly. I hadn't given much thought to names since I hadn't planned on keeping her.

"Yeah, Beth, like the song by Kiss from when we were kids . . . Princess Leia. Kinda reminds me of us. What do you think?"

"Ace," I whispered as realization dawned, "are you saying you want us to keep her?"

"Anna, I can't imagine not keeping her," he said laughing.

I laughed too, thinking if I lived to be a hundred I would never feel happier than I did in that moment.

"Beth," I said again as I let it sink in. "Yeah, I think it's perfect."

CHAPTER 11 - JACKSON

With all the excitement of tracking down and reconnecting with our grandparents, I had almost lost sight of what had started the search in the first place. If I ever wanted to get myself a new electric guitar, I needed to earn some serious cash. Bright and early the following Saturday morning, I began looking for a job. Unfortunately, without a driver's license my search was very limited.

In a little over an hour I'd hit every business within walking distance, with no luck. Hot and pissed off, I almost passed right by the bagel shop on the corner of Grant and Franklin, but then I figured, what the hell? As soon I walked inside, I knew I'd hit pay-dirt. There was a line of customers at the counter and two guys behind it, running around like chickens without heads. The owner, Mr. Hoffman, hired me on the spot, and the following Saturday at six a.m. I found myself slicing bagels and pouring coffees. The hours sucked but the money was good, and before I knew it I had saved up enough to buy a decent electric guitar.

The difference between it and the instrument I had at home was like night and day, and in no time at all I had mastered it. Not bad for someone who'd never even taken a lesson! I loved playing the guitar, probably more than anything, but I soon discovered that there was something else I loved doing: writing my own music.

It started as a goof one day. I'd string a couple of cords together, then write a few stupid rhyming lines. Soon I was singing the tunes on a pretend stage in my garage on rainy afternoons and having a laugh at my own expense. I never played my stuff for anyone else - it was just something I did for fun. I'd often wonder though where songwriters got their inspiration, since all the ditties I came up with were just a few steps above a dirty limerick.

Anna – Winter 1986

The next few days went by in a whirlwind. I found out that my parents had never even contacted a lawyer about the adoption.

"I knew as soon as you laid eyes on that baby you weren't going to give it up," Mom said, "And besides, there was no way in HELL I was letting you hand my grandchild off to strangers."

When I heard the word hell I drew my head back in mock surprise. My mother never swore unless she was deadly serious.

I was, however, genuinely surprised when Ace announced he was staying put. There'd be plenty of time to pursue his dream of rock stardom in the future, he said, and there was no way he was leaving me and little Beth behind. At first I found it hard to believe – after that big fight on the phone I'd thought it was over between us - but he promised he was serious.

He even hinted that he wanted us to get a place of our own. Although I wanted to, I wasn't about to just forget the way he'd treated me while he was in California. For now, I told him, Beth and I were staying with my parents.

He seemed to accept my answer, until about a month later, when he showed up at the house with a ring and on bended knee asked me to marry him.

"Anna, you and Beth are all I want. Being away from you for those months made me realize that this is where I belong. I'm not saying I'm giving up on the dream, but for now it's going on the backburner. Whaddaya say, Anna? Marry me?"

I laughed. "Of course I will!" He slipped the little diamond ring on my finger, then scooped me and Beth into his arms.

Needless to say, my parents were not happy about the arrangement.

"Honey, I just don't think it's a good idea for you two to get married right now. He's not very umm…" My mother searched for the right word. "…stable. Who knows when he'll get the bug to up and leave again? Stay here with us and go to college, get something of your own."

"Your mother's right, Anna. He wants to live that wild life and he's eventually going to get bored here playing house. At least if you get some college behind you, you'll have something to fall back on. We'll help you take care of Beth."

Though I shrugged them off I couldn't totally dismiss what they were saying. What if Ace did leave again, or stay with us and regret it? I finally decided I'd feel him out — give him every opportunity to take back the proposal.

"Ace," I began the next time we were together, "I wanted to talk to you about something."

"Yeah?" he said but he sounded distracted; he was staring down into Beth's bassinette, just watching her sleep.

"I was thinking that maybe we don't have to get married right away."

He blinked over at me in surprise. "What do you mean?"

"Well, I'm just saying if you maybe wanted to go back out to L.A. and, you know, finish what you started, that would be okay with me. I mean, the three of us could go, or you could go ahead and send for us after you're settled."

He opened his mouth but before he could say anything I added, "I'm not having second thoughts about getting married, Ace, I'm just saying that I want you to be sure."

Ace walked over and sat next to me on the couch. "Anna, I told you, this is where I want to be, with you and Beth. Everything else can wait as far as I'm concerned. Maybe I'll go back out to California one day and maybe I won't, but one thing's for sure - if I do, my two girls are coming with me."

"Ace, this has been your dream since you were a little kid. You have to be sure about this because otherwise it's not fair to any of us."

"I've never been more sure about anything, Anna." He took my hand in his and gave it a little squeeze. "So how about we put this to rest for now."

While I was happy to hear Ace wanted to put California "to rest," I found it odd that he never wanted to talk about what had happened when he was out there.

"Ace, what went on when you were in L.A.?" I finally asked. "Did you . . . did you meet someone? Is that why you suddenly stopped taking my calls?"

"No, of course I didn't meet someone!" he said, sounding slightly offended, "It was nothing like that." He thought for a minute. "I was just under a lot of pressure, that's all."

He moved in closer and put his arm around me. "Anna, there's never been anyone for me but you; you know that. And we're gonna have a great life here — the three of us."

"Okay," I smiled as I snuggled into him, "then I guess we have a wedding to plan!"

CHAPTER 12 – JACKSON

It had been weeks since I saw my grandparents, but I still wasn't able to get the conversation about Dad's stint in California out of my mind. One afternoon I decided to try baiting him into telling me more about his past, specifically his music. It was going to be tough since he rarely spoke a kind word to me, but I was determined. I made sure he was home and in his bedroom watching TV when I brought my guitar upstairs and plugged it into the amp. I started to play a few simple cords but kept purposely messing up.

"Damn," I said out loud, as if I was really having trouble getting it right.

A second later there was a loud bang on my wall. "Sounds like shit, Jackson," my dad yelled, "Go back down to the garage if you can't do it right."

I ignored his comment and kept purposely playing it wrong, figuring that he'd eventually storm over to my room.

I didn't have to wait long. A few minutes later the door to my room swung open. "Christ, Jackson, you can't play that thing for shit," he said as he grabbed the guitar from me.

"Watch," he said, and underneath the annoyance I thought I detected something else in his voice. Pleasure? Satisfaction? I wasn't sure. He then proceeded to play the simple cords with ease. "See, it ain't so hard. Any idiot can do it."

I wondered whether he was insulting me or himself. Probably both of us.

He handed the guitar back to me and turned to leave but before he could get out the door I repeated exactly what he'd done *and then some*. He stopped short but didn't turn around.

"Like that?" I asked dryly after I'd finished.

"Yeah," he said quietly, "Something like that."

Before he could slip away I asked, "Hey, was this your band?" When he turned around I held up the picture of him and a group of other guys playing on a makeshift stage in someone's backyard.

He walked toward me, his eyes narrowing at the picture. "Where'd you get this?" he asked as he took it from me.

"Found it in the attic with a bunch of other ones," I said as I motioned to the array of pictures on my bed.

He moved closer until he was standing at the foot of my bed, his eyes flicking over the pictures.

"So, was that your band?" I repeated.

He seemed distracted, almost like he hadn't even heard me, as he reached down and retrieved one of the snapshots. I glanced over his shoulder and caught a glimpse of the one he'd picked up. It was the black and white of him and my mom sitting on the hood of an old Camaro, each holding a bottle of Budweiser. They were laughing at something and my dad had one arm around her and the other raised up in salute. He stared at the picture for a moment longer, running his finger over the crease in its center before tossing it back on the pile.

"Yeah, that was my band," he confirmed without much emotion.

Just then I heard my cell go off with a text from Beth. I turned to grab the phone from my nightstand, and when I turned back around my dad was already on his way out. After answering Beth's text, I began to put the photos back in the envelope but noticed right away that the one of him and my mom that he'd been staring so intently at was now gone.

Anna – June 1986

Six months later, before a small group of close family and friends, Ace and I were married. It was the smart move; my parents gave us the rest of the money they had put aside for my wedding, which turned out to be just enough for a down payment on a

70

small fixer-upper in the next town over. We closed on it the Friday before Labor Day. A couple months before we got married Ace had taken the civil service test and a couple weeks after we moved into the house he got a job at the post office. It was as if everything had magically fallen into place.

"Hey, so it's not the music industry," Ace happily conceded, "But there's plenty of time for that, right babe?"

"Right," I agreed.

Ace worked hard while I took care of the house and Beth. She was a good baby, never gave us an ounce of trouble. She even slept through the night from the time she was six weeks old.

Ace still worked on his music whenever he could, but as time went on it got more difficult, what with lawn work, repairs, and all the other chores that go along with home ownership. When the roof needed repairing, Ace took a second job at night at an auto parts store to earn some extra money. Money — there just never seemed to be enough. Every time we turned around something else needed fixing or to be replaced. Eventually Ace had to sell his car because driving a baby around in a Camaro wasn't very practical. I knew it broke his heart to see it go but he just smiled at me and shrugged it off.

When Beth turned one I took a job a couple days a week at the local grocery store while my mom babysat. The extra money really helped; it also meant that Ace could take less shifts at the auto parts store, which freed him up to work on his music.

Despite our money troubles we were happy — almost deliriously so! We had lots of friends in town who'd come over for weekend cookouts and they all doted on little Beth. Ace and I would look down at our daughter and there was no question that although we'd had a lot of responsibility hoisted upon us at a young age, we wouldn't change it for the world.

I took on a few more shifts at the grocery store, and with Ace's regular raises at the post office things finally began to ease up financially. That's when we got hit with another curveball. I was pregnant again.

When our son was born Ace was ecstatic. He talked about all the stuff they would do together and how he was going to teach him to play the guitar before he could even walk. Unlike Beth's birth, Timothy's arrival was an easy one, but Tim was not the easy baby that Beth had been. He cried constantly and hardly ever slept. Beth was a toddler by then and getting into everything, so, needless to say, between taking care of her and an infant, Ace and I were exhausted. Two children were definitely the limit for us.

Fate had other plans, though.

"You're pregnant again?!" Ace shouted, "Christ, Anna, we can barely afford the two we have and now another one's coming?"

"It's not all my fault Ace."

"Well, either you do something about it or I will because this is definitely the last one."

Of course when Jackson arrived it was love at first sight for the both of us. Ace was thrilled to have another son and unlike Tim, Jackson was a very good baby. It had seemed unthinkable, but somehow we managed to adjust to life with three small children, and we were all very happy.

We didn't have much in the way of extras but Ace's job was stable and our parents helped out where they could. I picked up hours here and there at the grocery store but with three kids at home it was nearly impossible so eventually I quit altogether.

One night I was feeding one-year-old Jackson when I heard Ace's keys in the front door. I picked up the baby and went to greet him, only to gasp at the unfamiliar figure standing there. It was my husband, alright, but his beautiful long rock-n-roll hair was gone, trimmed down to a sensible easy-to-care-for men's haircut.

"What?" he asked when he saw me staring, then he shrugged. "I'm sick of the upkeep. This'll be a lot easier."

I didn't say anything, but I remember feeling slightly uneasy about it. It was as if cutting his hair meant he'd officially given up on the dream.

You're just being silly, Anna, I told myself. It doesn't mean anything.

CHAPTER 13 - JACKSON

I got my first taste of freedom on my seventeenth birthday when Beth drove me down to the DMV to take my road test. After passing with flying colors I dropped Beth off but instead of returning to school like I was supposed to, I filled the tank of Tim's Nissan and spent the rest of the afternoon cruising around town. Just before returning home, I stopped in at the bagel shop and promptly told Mr. Hoffman I was quitting. Hell, a guy with a set of wheels certainly doesn't have to haul his ass to a bagel shop every weekend at dawn, now does he? Having a car opened up endless possibilities, right?

Not exactly.

I spent the next few months dipping into my small savings to pay for gas while I looked for something better.

Eventually I lined up a gig working after school and weekends at Powder Peak Mountain, a very small family-friendly ski slope about five miles from home. It was only open for about four months out of the year but they paid well and it was a blast. At first I helped out the maintenance crew but when an opening came up for a ski lift operator I jumped at the chance. I loved working outside and on my days off I was able to use the facilities for free. I'd always wanted to learn to snowboard so I took a few lessons and in no time at all I was sailing down the mountain with ease.

I made a lot of friends working at Powder Peak, but my favorite was Clutch, the guy who managed the operation of all the lifts. Turned out he was also a musician. I told him about my guitar playing and he introduced me to the rest of the guys from his band, Blow Torch.

Even before my gig at the ski slope ended, I had my next one lined up. Mr. Slater, our neighbor and owner of Silver Maple Tree Service, offered me a job on one of his maintenance crews. He said that if things worked out, when I graduated he'd put me in charge of my own crew which meant a nice raise. It was the perfect deal – for the time being. For although I made good money and was happy enough, I held out hope that one day I'd be able to make a living doing what I really loved – music.

Anna – October 1992

As time went on, I got used to the haircut and forgot about the odd feeling it had evoked. When he wasn't working, Ace was home every night, playing with the children or helping them with their homework. I couldn't have asked for a better husband or father.

At first the change was so subtle I barely noticed it. If I had to pinpoint an exact time that things began to shift, I guess I'd say it was around the time Jackson turned three. Ace became quiet, even sullen. I'd often find him watching me with kind of a blank expression on his face as I fussed with the children or made dinner or was cleaning up after it.

He started to nit-pick at little things, like the kids' toys weren't put away or the rugs needed vacuuming. At first, I didn't think too much of it; he'd worked all day and should come home to a tidy house. I tried my best to stay on top of things and for the most part I thought I did a pretty good job. Ace's mood, though, just seemed to get worse.

Then there were subtle digs he made about me not working. About how much easier things would be if I got a job. So when Jackson began preschool I took a part-time job as a classroom aid in one of the local schools. Then the jabs began about my cooking.

"Chicken again, Anna?" he'd complain.

When I tried my hand at some new recipes, he'd complain that they were either too spicy or too plain or too greasy or too something else.

Again, I let it go, making excuses that maybe he was having a rough time at work or something else was bothering him. Whenever I tried to talk to him about it, he'd just brush me off.

One afternoon we had some friends over. It'd been a while since we were all able to get together, what with everyone's busy schedules, so I was really looking forward to it and I know Ace was too.

Ace threw burgers and chicken on the grill and I made some salads, then we all hung out on our deck like old times.

Amy showed up with an amazing new outfit and – after years of busting her butt in the fashion industry – news of an amazing new job in Manhattan. Jason came with another new girlfriend – Mandy I think her name was – and he was doing well working at his father's architecture firm. Dixon was a sound designer and had worked on several big name Off–Broadway shows. Henry was a software developer and still played in a band on the side. I don't know how good they were or what kind of music they played but he seemed happy about it. He was still dating the same girl, Megan, and he brought her along.

After we ate I put the kids to bed and rejoined everyone on the deck for a few beers. It was the most I'd laughed since I couldn't remember when, but even better, Ace seemed like his old self. It was close to midnight when, amidst I-love-yous and let's-get-together-again-soons, our friends stood to leave. We walked them to their cars then Ace went back to the deck to finish his beer and I headed to the kitchen to clean up. That was all he needed, I told myself, a day to kick back and hang with his friends. I was just putting the last dish into the dishwasher when I heard him come back inside.

"I'm gonna turn in," he said as he placed his empty can of Bud on the counter. He had an odd look on his face but I chalked it up to a beer buzz.

"Okay, I'll be up in a little bit."

When I went upstairs fifteen minutes later, I found Ace lying on the bed staring up at the ceiling. I made small talk as I rummaged through the dresser drawer for a pair of pajamas.

"What did you say, hon?" I asked after he mumbled something that I didn't hear.

"I said you really got everything you wanted," he repeated.

I looked at him, confused. "What do you mean?"

He paused for a beat. "Well, let's see, you got your house, you got your three kids, you got me. You got it all, right?"

"Uh…yeah," I said, uneasy with the sarcastic tone he had used.

"Yup, everything went according to plan." He turned on to his side and raised himself up on one elbow to glare at me. "You never really wanted to go to California, did you, Anna?"

"Ace, you're drunk. You don't know what you're saying," I said, trying to control the quiver in my voice.

"Daddy's girl wanted to stay right at Mom and Dad's side, didn't she?"

"Ace, you know that's not true so cut it out, now. I wanted to go to L.A. just as much as you did and you know it." I felt tears coming but I fought like hell to keep them at bay.

"Like hell it is, Anna. You trapped me into staying here with you. Probably planned it all along. Couldn't stand the fact that I might've made something of myself. So afraid that I'd have left you if I did . . ."

"Stop it," I yelled loudly, and from down the hallway I could hear Jackson let out a cry.

Ignoring the baby, Ace flipped onto his back again. "One of your chicks is calling for you, Ma. Better run and see what he wants." Then he closed his eyes and pinched the bridge of his nose as if staving off a headache.

I rushed out of the room, as much to get away from Ace as to go to our son. It took several minutes to get Jackson back to sleep, and by the time I returned to our room Ace was passed out and snoring lightly.

When I woke the next morning he was gone, but I didn't have time to think about him because I had to feed the kids breakfast and then run a few errands. It wasn't until I returned home with the kids and saw Ace in the driveway tinkering with the car that his words came flooding back.

After putting Jackson down for his nap and getting Beth and Tim settled in the kitchen with a snack, I went back outside. Did he even remember what had happened? Before I could say anything, he put down his wrench and shot me a guilty look.

"Anna, I'm sorry about last night. I was drunk and I didn't know what I was saying. I've just had a lot of crap on my mind lately with work and all the stuff I've got to get done around here and with the guys over yesterday it just got me thinking a lot of shit. I'm sorry, I shouldn't have said those things. I didn't mean any of it."

I was still deciding how to respond when he reached over and hugged me, burying his face in my hair.

I ended up accepting Ace's apology, opting to keep the peace and chalking it up to too much alcohol mixed with the nostalgia of visiting with old, arguably more successful friends. Everything would be fine, I told myself, and it was...for a while.

Later I would realize it had been a mistake to let it drop. I should have made him sit down and talk about it and maybe I could have prevented the calamity to come. Then again, maybe it was inevitable.

CHAPTER 14 - JACKSON

I wasn't a guy who usually "dated"; it was more like I hung out with girls here and there. It had always been that way for me, probably because from the time Tim started high school our house had been party central and there were always girls around.

Though I was two years younger than Tim, I was never shielded from the goings on at Casa de Foxx on the nights Dad wasn't home. And it wasn't long before I was sucked in – albeit willingly - to the endless stream of sex and partying. At first it was just silly shit, like girls flashing "Tim's cute little brother" their bras and then giggling when my jaw dropped to the floor. That is, all except for Brittany Turner. Britt started out as one of the bra-flashers, but one night, much to my shock and delight, she flashed me her bare tits when she thought no one was looking.

That happened a few times and then late one afternoon she arrived with a few of her friends to party with Tim and his crew. She ended up staying pretty late and by the end of that night she'd shown me a whole hell of lot more than her tits. After that our encounters became a regular occurrence. She was really hot, and I had no idea what she could've seen in me - that is, other than my endless enthusiasm.

About six months after we first hooked up, she and her family moved down to South Carolina – *lucky southern bastards* - leaving me with a seemingly chronic case of blue balls.

I tried to concentrate on my music but found it increasingly difficult due to constant thoughts of the hot sex I was no longer having. I knew an actual girlfriend would have been far too demanding of my free time, so I decided to focus on looking for a certain *type* of girl. I steered clear of the bookworms, the varsity athletes and of course the virgins – all of whom probably had little interest in hanging out with me anyway. The academic types tended to talk way too much. The varsity athletes couldn't sit still for any length of time and always wanted you to join in whatever their sport-de-jour was. And I'd witnessed enough of Tim's romantic agonies to know that if you screwed a virgin that they were bound to get all clingy.

The girls who liked to party were definitely best, mostly because they didn't need much convincing. I'd invite them over with the promise of a fun night with some decent weed and a few beers, and usually found at least one or two who were willing to have sex with me. Best of all, they usually left right after or were gone when I woke up the next morning.

No doubt, I had a hell of a sweet gig going, and I had little intention of messing with it. So it was weird that after meeting up with Leah at the mall that day I couldn't get her out of my head. She obviously wasn't the type of girl I went for and I was surprised at how much I enjoyed hanging out with her.

After wrestling with it a few days, I decided to give her a call and ask if she wanted to get together for the Fourth of July. Maybe we could go see fireworks somewhere. Girls like Leah liked that kind of stuff, right?

"Sure!" she said excitedly. "There's a great display in Glen Rock every year and it's not too far. We can even take the train so we won't have to worry about parking."

We ironed out the details and then made plans to meet at the train station.

I arrived there a little before seven on Friday, and on a whim bought two tickets to Hoboken instead of Glen Rock. It sounded like a lot more fun and I had a feeling Leah would be up for it.

"Hoboken!" she exclaimed when she got to the station, "Are you sure you know your way around there? Because I've never been."

I shrugged. "It'll be an adventure."

The next thing I knew the train pulled up and the two of us were headed for Hoboken, which turned out to be *a lot* more fun than Glen Rock. Glen Rock was pretty similar to where we were from, but Hoboken, man, Hoboken was a whole different world. It was right on the Hudson

River and jampacked with all kinds of people hoping to get a glimpse at the awesome fireworks display they put on every year.

That night turned out to be the first of many "adventures" that summer, though to be honest Leah seemed to think of everything as an adventure. I was beginning to think she didn't get out much. Damn, the girl had never even been to a Mets game!

When we got to Queens that day, she was astonished to find out that I didn't actually have tickets – *yet*.

I explained to her that if we waited until after the game started any scalper left with tickets would get rid of them for a fraction of what they were worth.

When you grow up with a dad who barely speaks to you, let alone takes you to a ball game, you figure out ways to do things on your own. Dad would've never given me or Tim the money either so we became experts at scamming the system when we wanted to do something. Nothing we did was actually illegal, but we were at times on the fringe.

Any concern I had about Leah's reaction quickly evaporated.

"Wow, Jackson! That's so cool!" she exclaimed when I flashed her two tickets for the second row right on the third baseline. *Yep, this girl made me feel like I was king of the hill.*

Halfway through the game I left to use the bathroom. After braving a line as long as a city block, I returned to find Leah reading over a discarded program, a pair of trendy, dark brown horn-rimmed glasses perched on her nose. I'd never really dug glasses on girls, but this was different. Leah looked sort of like a sexy librarian and I began to imagine what she'd look like with nothing on but the glasses.

"Hey, Jackson, look what I found!" she said excitedly as she nonchalantly removed the sexy specs and returned them to her bag. "Now we can figure out which players are which."

"Oh, yeah...cool," I replied, still a little distracted. The rest of the night I couldn't get the image of "Sexy Librarian Leah" out of my head and began to wonder if perhaps she would turn out to be more *fun* than I had originally thought. Wishful thinking, no doubt.

Like a lot of other guys, I was usually able to tell right off the bat whether a girl put out or not. Leah had been especially easy to read; in fact, when I met her, she was pretty much holding up a neon sign to the contrary. It was why I hadn't asked her for her number at first. It was only after I saw her talking to that wannabe rapper dude's friend that I changed my mind, and even then, I only reached out because I was bored on that rainy afternoon. Now, as I cast a sideways glance at her, I decided I was definitely glad I had.

Anna – May 1994

It started a few months later, when I got a call from Ace saying that he wouldn't be home for dinner. He and Henry were meeting up for a few beers after work.

I told him no problem and to have a good time and then went about making dinner for me and the kids. I was already in bed when at eleven o'clock, I heard a knock at the door. When I answered it, there was Ace, leaning drunkenly against Henry.

"Sorry," our friend said sheepishly, "he couldn't find his keys."

Annoyed as I was, I didn't say anything, not that night or the next day when Ace awoke with a nasty hangover. There was nothing to say, I reasoned; he needed to go out with his friends once in a while. I actually thought it was good for him.

It turned out to be more than once in a while. Before long, after-work drinks became a Friday night ritual, though it wasn't Henry he usually went out with, but a group of older guys from the post office, guys I didn't know. He'd stumble in late and drunk, then he'd climb into bed and have some very unromantic, almost angry sex with me. It was so unlike him that the first few times he actually apologized afterwards. Before long though he didn't bother to muster up a sorry, not even when he heard me crying.

One night a week soon turned into two and then three. Eventually he was out four nights a week drinking.

I knew I was kidding myself when I said it was just a phase he was going through. One night, when he came home and started pawing at me, I decided I'd had enough.

"Cut it out, Ace," I said as I pushed him off me. "What's with you lately?"

I could hear him breathing heavily in the dark and I could smell the liquor on his breath.

"What? Don't like it, Anna?" He fell back on the pillows and snickered in the dark. "What are you gonna do? Leave me?" He laughed again. "Where're you gonna go?"

Before I could say anything, he added, "You gonna run back to Mommy and Daddy?"

"Ace . . . you're drunk and . . ."

"Yeah, I'm drunk, Anna. I'm drunk because I can't fucking take it anymore. The goddamn house, the kids, the fucking post office, for Christ's sake." He laughed almost maniacally. "I'm twenty-seven years old and I got a wife, three kids and I'm working at the goddamn post office! Man, never woulda guessed it."

I was on the verge of tears and thanked God for the darkened room. "Ace, if you want to get back into music then you should do it."

"Gimme a fucking break, Anna. It's too late. I lost too much time taking care of this fucking mess."

I was definitely angry with him for all the rotten hurtful things he'd just said, but mostly I felt terrible for him. I so vividly remembered how much we were both looking forward to a new life in California, with all the promises it held. I reached out to gently rub his shoulder but he flinched at my touch.

"Just leave me alone, Anna," he sighed, "Leave me the fuck alone."

CHAPTER 15 - JACKSON

Early on I had figured out one thing for sure, and that was that per my dating "rule" book Leah had three strikes against her – she was an athlete, a bookworm *and* a virgin. I had hit the trifecta with this girl and not in a good way. So why was it that I couldn't seem to stay away from her? I'd asked myself that question on numerous occasions but still hadn't been able to come up with an answer.

I decided to keep seeing her but keep things casual and see what happened. Unfortunately, between the sexy horn-rimmed glasses I spied her wearing at the Mets game and the barely-there hot pink bikini she donned at the beach one hot August day it was only a matter of time before I caved. Now, if she showed up at my house wearing both the horn-rimmed glasses and the hot pink bikini I knew I couldn't be held responsible for my actions.

Although I didn't want to admit it at first, I knew my partying days were over the first time I turned down one of my "regulars." Samantha had turned up at my door wanting to hang out, something I used to enjoy but now sounded completely unappealing. I knew how lame I sounded when I told her I was getting over being sick and not up for a late night, but Sam didn't seem to question it. Just gave me a peck on the cheek, then I heard the click-click of her very high heels on the driveway as she headed back to her car.

The nail in the proverbial coffin came around midway through Leah's soccer season. Leah really wanted me to come to one of her games but so far I had resisted. It just seemed like too much of a "boyfriend" thing to do, something Leah would think was the mark of a real relationship, which I wanted to avoid. Lucky for me, between work and jam sessions with Blow Torch I always had a ready-made excuse as to why I couldn't go. Then one Friday night, after Clutch and Deal both bailed at the last minute, my curiosity got the better of me. I headed over to the field, figuring I'd sit in the back of the bleachers. She would never even know I was there.

By the end of the first half I was floored by her talent on the field. For a girl her size she had unbelievable strength and stamina. I left to get a Coke and when I returned there were two douchebags in football jerseys where I'd been sitting so I took the seat in front of them. When the game started back up I focused all my attention on Leah but was distracted when I heard one of them mention her name.

"Leah Miller's definitely looking good this year."

"Yeah, I hear ya," said his buddy, "she's in my economics class this semester." He laughed and nudged his friend, "Her ass is looking pretty hot in those black jeans she wears."

I had this uncontrollable urge to punch the dude right in the face for discussing Leah's ass like that.

"She seeing anyone?" Douchebag Number One asked.

"Don't think so." The other guy elbowed him and laughed. "I definitely wouldn't mind hittin' that some time."

I turned around to face them and the words shot out of me like a cannon. "Watch your fucking mouth, asshole. That's my girlfriend you're talkin' about."

A look of surprise crossed both of their faces as they gave me the once-over.

"Who the fuck are you?" they said almost in unison.

"I'm Leah Miller's fuckin' boyfriend, that's who the fuck I am, so let me say it again: Watch. Your. Fucking. Mouth."

I wasn't huge by any means and didn't really consider myself to be all that intimidating but I had no intention of stepping down from a fight with either of these assholes if it came to that.

"Yeah, right," one of them snickered and then turned back toward the game.

I let it go, deciding two against one was definitely not a good idea. Still, the exchange with the douches had certainly been a wakeup call. I had this beautiful sweet girl who was like totally into me and I'd been holding her at arms-length for months now. What the hell was I thinking? Surely it was only a matter of time before some other guy . . . *or guys . . .* took notice of her. Christ, how much longer did I expect her to wait around? *Fuck.*

I stood from where I was sitting and maneuvered my way to the bottom of the bleachers, where I found an open area at the fence surrounding the field. The game ended a few minutes later and as soon as I caught Leah's eye her face lit up.

"Jackson! You came!" she said excitedly as she ran over and wrapped her arms around my waist. She immediately pulled back and giggled, "Oh, sorry, I'm all sweaty."

"I like sweaty," I said as I dragged her back into a hug.

And just like that, I had myself a girlfriend.

Anna – June 1994

I kept hoping things would get better. There were still some good days, but they grew fewer and farther between. After a while I learned to just stay out of Ace's way and give him as little to complain about as possible. That meant that I kept the house spotless, cooked a nice dinner every night whether he ate it or not and, above all, did my best to keep the kids quiet when he was around. That part was the easiest because the kids sensed when he was in a mood and steered clear of him.

It would have been so easy to just pack up the kids and leave. The four of us could've moved in with my parents, but I was too embarrassed. I didn't want them to know what was going on between us. I guess I wasn't ready to admit that maybe they had been right about Ace all along. And besides, I wasn't ready to give up on him just yet. I just kept telling myself that he'd snap out of it and that brighter days were just around the corner.

The kids became my world, especially little Jackson, who was a lot clingier than his older siblings. Whereas Beth and Tim thrived in preschool and enjoyed interacting with the other children, Jackson tended to be shy and a bit withdrawn. When I took him to the playground, he'd stand quietly beside me rather than running around with the other kids.

Yes, Jackson and I were quite literally joined at the hip. Not that I'd say he was my favorite; he just needed me more than the other two and with everything that was going on with Ace, I needed to be needed.

I doted on him and he ate it up, always sidling up to me for a cuddle when no one was looking. When Beth and Tim were in school fulltime Jackson and I spent every afternoon together, either going to the park or coloring at the kitchen table on a rainy day. When he got a little older he traded in his crayons for Tim's bucket of army men. He would play for hours with them, always wanting me to join in on the battle, which of course I did.

Jackson and the other kids were a welcome distraction from my deteriorating marriage. Although he never mistreated the children, Ace wasn't overly warm to them either, especially Jackson. Ace seemed to hate the way our youngest clung to me. The kids got used to Ace's moods and it became normal to them, but the palpable tension took its toll on me. Then came the day when after holding it together for so long, I just cracked.

It was the beginning of summer and the kids were out of school and I had promised to take them swimming at the lake in town. The three of them had a great day splashing in the water and playing on the sandy shore with their friends. Even Jackson joined in with the other kids, which was great to see. When I told them it was time to go they begged me to stay just a little longer. I figured why not? There was no school the next day and I was just grilling up burgers for dinner which wouldn't take me very long at all. We ended up losing track of time and didn't get home until nearly seven o'clock.

I knew as soon as I walked in that Ace was ready to blow his stack, so I hustled the kids upstairs so as not to get them in the middle of it.

"Nice life you got, Anna. I work all day and I can't even get dinner when I get home 'cause you're out having fun."

"It'll only take a minute, Ace," I said as I hurried around getting the burgers out of the freezer, "Just go relax and I'll call you when it's ready."

"Fuck it, I don't need this shit," he said as he grabbed his keys, "I'll get something at the bar." He stormed off and tossed a "Don't wait up" over his shoulder before slamming the door behind him.

It was something he'd done dozens of times but for some reason it put me over the edge. I collapsed onto a kitchen chair, put my head in my hands and let the tears come. The phone began to ring and I almost didn't answer it, but I figured the kids would think it was weird and come downstairs. When I heard my mother's voice on the other end I tried to sound normal, but she knew right away that something was wrong. Then, in a moment of weakness, I blurted the whole thing out.

"Oh Annalise, I'm so sorry. I can't say I'm too surprised, though. Your father and I felt that something's been off between you two for a while now."

"It'll be fine, Mom," I told her, now fearing I'd said too much, "Ace is just going through a rough patch, but things'll get better."

"Anna, you know you and the children are always welcome here."

"No, Mom. I shouldn't have said anything. I'm just having a bad day, that's all. Just forget it, alright?"

"Anna..."

"No, really, Mom. Everything'll be fine. I... I have to go make dinner for the kids, okay? Call you tomorrow," I told her, then I hung up.

I grabbed a tissue from the box on the counter and blew my nose. As I was dabbing my eyes with another tissue I turned around and saw Jackson standing there. How much had he heard, I wondered.

"Hey Jacky, you all ready for dinner?" I asked, trying unsuccessfully to mask the rush of sadness the conversation with my mom had evoked.

He didn't look scared by the exchange... he looked angry.

He shot towards me like a cannon and wrapped his little arms around my legs and squeezed tight.

"Jacky," I said softly as I loosened his hold on me and bent down to his level. I put my hands on his shoulders then and said, "Don't be upset, everything's alright."

He reached out and put his arms around my neck, then pulled me into a tight hug before softly whispering, "I hate him."

CHAPTER 16 – LEAH
(The following summer)

"**I**'m really going to miss you, Jackson," I said, looking up at him, my eyes squinting against the bright late-August sun.

He smiled as he reached down and tucked a stray hair behind my ear. "Hey, not nearly as much as I'm gonna miss you." He paused for a moment. "But this is what you've been working so hard for, right?"

"Yes, I guess you're right." Even as I said the words I felt the doubts creeping into my mind. If someone had told me last year that I'd be having second thoughts about going away to college, I'd have said they were crazy. Jackson was right, of course. I had worked hard for this and it's what I'd always planned to do. Or should I say, what my parents had always planned for me to do. I knew I wasn't being fair to my mom and dad – I had been on board all the way...until Jackson. Meeting and falling in love with him had never been part of the plan, but now that it had happened I didn't know what I wanted. I just knew I didn't want to be separated from him.

When I casually tossed out the idea of maybe attending a local college my parents nearly flipped. I had never been good about standing up to them so after seeing their reaction I didn't bring it up again.

There was another reason I didn't fight harder to stay at home: I was never quite able to gage Jackson's feelings about me. I'd been crazy about him from the get-go, but it seemed like he saw me as more of a friend than a romantic interest. We'd talk on the phone a lot and do couply-type things like going to baseball games and day trips to the beach. He'd put his arm around me or hold my hand sometimes, but I couldn't help but feel that it was more in a "buddy" sort of way. Back then I tried everything short of throwing myself at him but nothing seemed to work. I even went so far as to buy myself the skimpiest, sexiest hot pink bikini I could find, and wore it when he took me down the Shore, but I swear he didn't even notice.

After a whole summer of trying everything under the sun to inch our relationship to the next level, I finally had to admit it was time to throw in the towel. Then, out of the blue, everything changed. Whereas before we used to talk on the phone every few days, now it seemed a day didn't go by without us speaking at some point. He also became a lot more physical. Now when he had his arm around me or was holding my hand it was in a more possessive sort of way, like he wanted people to know we were together. It was as if someone had flipped a switch. I didn't know what caused the change in him and, honestly, I didn't really care. All I knew was that I couldn't remember a time when I'd been happier.

Unfortunately, I couldn't say the same for my best friend, Molly, who wasn't at all thrilled about our blossoming relationship.

"Jackson was just supposed to be a summer fling," she pointed out. "We both agreed we didn't want to be tied down our senior year, remember?"

At the start of last summer Molly and I had made a pact to make our last high school summer the most memorable one ever. And for Molly there were three key ingredients to a memorable summer: sun, sand and a summer fling, which she defined as a *passionate relationship that came to a natural, amicable conclusion when the parties went their separate ways.* In laymen's terms, *a sexual adventure free of hassles, commitments or drama, sandwiched neatly between Memorial Day and Labor Day.*

I agreed to the pact, though at first I thought of it as a pipe dream. You see, I'd been skating through high school in what was known as the "invisible crowd." Actually, I'd never had much in the way of a social life but that wasn't all my doing. My parents had always been of the mindset that "idle hands are the devil's workshop." This meant that my days were scheduled from the time I could walk - soccer, ballet, piano lessons, art classes, karate. I was so busy running from one activity to another that I barely had a moment to socialize with anyone.

When high school rolled around I had to cut down on the glut of activities in order to make more time for studying. The goal now was to maintain a 4.0 GPA – something else my parents insisted on. I did continue the soccer, and whenever I wasn't studying I had a soccer ball at my feet. By sophomore year all my practice had paid off – I had earned my first varsity letter, not an easy feat considering the Braves were the number one high school team in the county. I never complained about how busy my parents kept me, and why would I? I'd never known any different.

Molly was in a similar boat, at least when it came to guys. Not that there was anything wrong with either of us, it was just that guys didn't seem to notice us, ever. Like I said, *invisible*. It was fine, though. We'd gotten used to it; it was just the way it was.

Then Molly planted the "summer fling" idea in my head, and once she did I couldn't shake it. I'd often fantasize about who it would be with. I imagined meeting some tall, dark and handsome lifeguard at the beach. Or maybe a stocky, fair-haired soccer player at one of the many tournaments I played in. Or maybe he'd just be some nondescript guy of average height who worked at the mall. Truth be told, most of our "summer fling" talk was just that – *talk*. I never said it to Molly, but although it was fun to daydream, I never thought it would actually come to fruition – *that is until I met Jackson.*

What Jackson and I had last summer obviously didn't fit Molly's definition of a summer fling. First, there was no passionate sex involved - he hadn't even tried to kiss me. Second, it had lasted well beyond the summer; in fact, I made the argument that he was my "fall fling" since there was definitely a lot of kissing going on by then. I'd hoped Molly would appreciate that, but she didn't.

"I don't know what you see in him anyway, Leah; on scale of one to ten I'd say he's *barely* a five."

I let the comment slide. As rude as she was, Molly did have a point. Jackson was not what you'd call classically handsome, with big green eyes peering out mischievously from a dark, disheveled mane. He may have appeared merely thin to the casual eye but I knew that hidden beneath the faded jeans and loose concert tees was a lean but athletic build that rivaled any model. Anyone who'd seen him playing his guitar shirtless in his garage on a hot summer day – which he did often - would agree.

It was more than just his edgy look that attracted me to him, though. Jackson was *cool*, and whenever I was with him, *I* felt cool too. He was everything I wasn't. He dressed the way he wanted. He never cared about what anyone thought of him. He took everything in stride, never worrying about tomorrow. I, on the other hand, liked to blend in with the crowd and remain unnoticed. I was also easily frazzled, even by minor things. Things like being late for practice or not getting a perfect score on an exam or even a simple disagreement with someone caused me undue anxiety. Some days it felt as if my stress levels were on overdrive but it was never that way for Jackson, not by a longshot. He just went about his business each day as if nothing fazed him.

"Lee, relax, it'll all work out," I remember him saying one night when I was once again fretting over some college issue.

"I can't relax," I said nervously, throwing my hands up, "What happens if I don't get into any of my top schools? What'll I do then?"

"C'mere," he'd said, pulling me onto his lap. "You'll get in. You have nothing to worry about. Your grades are great. Your SAT scores are through the roof and I hear ya play a pretty mean game of soccer. What school *wouldn't* want you?"

I'd melted into his embrace and immediately felt myself relax. It was like Jackson was my very own personal stimulant and tranquilizer, rolled into one.

⋏　　⋏　　⋏

My parents had never hid the fact that they didn't want me dating anyone seriously while I was still in school; in fact, they'd always drilled it into my head that my studies were most important. I went along with their ideas, partly because there weren't many other options. Soccer and homework kept me busy during the year and, like I said, it's not like guys were lined up around the block waiting to ask me out. My parents had nothing to worry about...that is until Jackson came along.

Maybe that's why it took me so long to introduce them. When I did, my parents didn't say much, leaving me to believe that they didn't have a problem with it. Of course, this might have been because I played it off as more casual than it was. I didn't want them getting the idea that Jackson might distract me from my studies because that definitely was not the case.

I'd have Jackson over on occasion, but most times we hung out at his place, which was just fine with me since there were no rules at Jackson's house. It was pretty much anything goes. Whereas at my house we had to hang out in the family room with my parents always close by, no one cared what we did at Jackson's house – *so needless to say we did a lot*. Not right away, of course. I wasn't about to make the same mistake Molly made with Double Jay. Molly had met Double Jay at the same party where I'd met Jackson but things with those two ended up moving *much* quicker, on their *second date*, if memory serves me correctly. After that it seemed they never got together for anything but sex, and although she said she didn't care, that she was just using him anyway, I had my doubts.

Whatever the case, Molly's "relationship" with Double Jay was a real eye-opener for me which is why I decided to proceed with caution where Jackson was concerned. Turned out I had nothing to worry about, because Jackson was nothing like Double Jay. He never pressured me, not even after things became more serious between us. In the end, I was the one who decided we'd waited long enough... that *I* had waited long enough. I knew it was only a matter of time anyway, especially since whenever we were alone we couldn't seem to keep our hands off each other. Besides, after listening to Molly's stories about sex with Double Jay, I wanted to know what all the fuss was about. So one night I just bit the bullet and it had been hotter than heck ever since! I didn't go into detail with Molly like she had with me, and sometimes I thought that was part of the reason she was so testy where Jackson was concerned.

▲   ▲   ▲

"You better get going," Jackson chuckled as he opened the driver's side door of my grey Honda, "Molly's probably about to blow a gasket wondering what's taking you so long."

I sighed, then reached up to give him one last kiss before sliding behind the wheel. Even as I drove away from Jackson's house I kept stealing glances at him in the rearview mirror until he disappeared from sight. My eyes now glued to the road ahead, I inhaled deeply for what seemed like the first time in weeks.

That morning had been chaotic at my house. My mother, with her endless list of instructions and my father with his constant lecturing about highway safety, had my head spinning. The good news was that they'd already helped me move all my stuff into my dorm the week before, so there was no need for them to make another trip. I didn't think I could take being subjected to another round of goodbyes.

I took another deep breath, then allowed myself a smile. It had certainly been a crazy year, crazy and wonderful. I had aced my finals, my soccer season had culminated with our team going to States and winning in double overtime, and Molly and I had both gotten into the same prestigious university. But Jackson was definitely the icing on the cake. It was as if the Universe had decided to hand me my heart's desires, one by one.

When I got to Molly's house she was waiting on her front porch with two small bags and an annoyed expression on her face. She seemed to have that expression more often than not these days, and it usually had something to do with Jackson. I rolled my eyes and tried for the thousandth time to put myself in her shoes. How would I feel if I suddenly had to "share" her with a boyfriend? Probably not so good.

Before I could even get out of the car she was already down her front steps with bags in hand and her parents following close behind. I quickly jumped out and opened the truck, then after another round of hugs, we were finally on our way.

Not long into our trip Molly turned to me and quipped, "This thing with you and Jackson'll never last; you know that, right? Once you meet all those hot upper classmen at all the frat parties we'll be going to you'll forget Jackson ever existed."

"Maybe," I replied, with a casual shrug to hide my annoyance. Going off to college was supposed to be an exciting, carefree time, and I was not about to let her goad me into an argument or convince me that being a few miles apart would ruin what Jackson and I had.

Deep down, though, her comment bothered me more than I cared to admit. Especially since I'd learned over the summer that Molly wasn't the only one who had a problem with Jackson and me. One morning over breakfast my mom casually asked how Jackson felt about my leaving for college. I'd been taken aback by her question; it was only the beginning of July and Jackson and I hadn't spoken all that much about our impending separation, though it had certainly been on my mind.

"He's okay with it, I guess. I mean it's not like we're breaking up over it or anything like that."

My mom looked surprised, but only said, "Just don't let it affect your studying. Your father and I expect your grades to be top notch and we won't settle for anything less." When I went to get up from the table, she added, "Has Jackson decided what he's doing about college yet? You mentioned he was taking some time off - is that still the case?"

I squirmed a bit because I knew Jackson's aspirations – or lack thereof – concerning higher education would be a sticky subject with my mother. I'd somehow managed to avoid the subject, until now.

"What do you mean?" I asked.

She shot me an annoyed look to let me know she knew I was stalling. "I mean, what are his plans? How much longer will he be taking off? It's not a difficult question, Leah."

"He's just not sure what he wants to do yet or where he wants to apply, that's all," I huffed, knowing full well that I was going from stalling to outright lying. Jackson's passion was his music and he eventually hoped to earn a living at it; he wasn't about to waste time in a classroom. Besides, it wasn't like Jackson was some sort of loser who just loafed around. He worked hard all day at the mountain, and for the tree company, then worked late into the night on his music. I certainly didn't have a problem with him not going to college, so why should my mother?

I turned to leave before she could say anything else, making it clear that the conversation was over.

I managed to get through the remainder of the summer without Mom bringing it up again, but I knew that she wasn't likely to let it drop.

"Leah, pull off the next exit; I want to hit the bathroom," Molly asked, pulling me back from my thoughts.

"Molly, we left less than an hour ago. How can you have to go already?" I knew it was a stupid question because it was something she did without fail whenever we were on the road for any length of time.

"Look, there's an exit coming up; just pull off," she said, ignoring my comment.

I pulled off the exit and into the nearest gas station. Molly quickly scurried into the store and emerged a minute later, happily waving the key to the ladies' room in my direction as she scooted toward the undoubtedly filthy bathroom.

I leaned against the car, thoughts once again flooding my mind as I waited for her to return. Molly was ecstatic about starting this new chapter in our lives, and while I wanted to share in her enthusiasm, I was decidedly torn. Not about starting college – I was super-excited about that – but not being able to see Jackson as much. I knew I was being silly; Eastern Pennsylvania, where our college was located, wasn't all that far from northern New Jersey. It was a good thing, because once I was settled I intended to come home most weekends to see him – or so I thought.

Anna – Late September 1997

The years ticked by but despite my best efforts, nothing changed where Ace's behavior was concerned. If anything, it got worse. One rainy night in late fall I got the phone call that I'd been dreading. It was a school night and the kids were all in bed, though Jackson was the only one who was actually asleep. He had been turning in especially early since starting first grade that September. He wasn't used to being in school for the full day and he was usually wiped out by bedtime.

"Get to sleep, you two," I yelled over my shoulder to Beth and Tim as I hurried to the ringing phone.

"Hello?" I answered and was surprised to hear our neighbor Jeff's voice on the other end. Jeff was a police officer in town who had lived three doors down from us ever since we'd moved in. He and his wife Rosemary had two college-age kids who were attending school out of state. They were a nice couple and had even helped me out in a pinch when I needed someone to watch the kids.

"Hi, Anna, it's Jeff," he said, and I knew right away by his tone that this wasn't a social call.

"Oh, hi Jeff, what's up?"

"It's Keith. I was called down to Dune's about a disturbance that broke out and he was one of the guys involved."

Dune's was a local dive bar in town that I knew Ace hung out in sometimes. I asked him if Ace was okay.

"Yeah, he's fine. The situation was straightened out and they're not pressing charges against anyone involved, but Anna, Keith was trashed. Didn't even recognize me at first."

"Oh," I stammered, embarrassed.

"Listen, I'm all for letting loose once in a while but after it was over he was actually going to get into his car and drive to another bar. Drive, Anna. And he would have if I hadn't stopped him." He hesitated. "I took his keys and told him to call a cab. My shift ends at eleven so I'll drop the keys off then. He's lucky I caught him when I did because if one of the other officers had seen him take off in his car there's nothing I could've done. They would've hauled him down to the station and booked him."

"I'm so sorry, Jeff. I'll talk to him, it won't happen again."

"Anna . . . It's none of my business, but is everything alright?"

I cringed with embarrassment. "Sure Jeff, everything's fine."

"Well, you know if you ever need anything Roe and I are just a stone's throw away. Don't hesitate to ask."

"Thanks Jeff, but everything's fine," I lied again. "He's just been under a lot of pressure at work."

"Okay, well, take care then. I'll pop the keys into your mailbox so I don't wake the kids."

"Thanks again, Jeff," I said as I hung up the phone.

The last thing we needed was Ace charged with a DWI, so the next morning I approached him about the conversation I'd had with Jeff the night before.

He knew Jeff saved his ass and the last thing he wanted to deal with was losing his license for six months, but he wasn't about to "let me win" by giving up the partying.

"If you got a problem with me driving, Anna, then it looks like you're just gonna have to pick me up 'cause otherwise I'm taking the car."

He thought I'd try to argue and I think he was actually disappointed when I didn't. He always seemed to be looking for a fight.

I shrugged. "Whatever, Keith." I think I surprised us both when I used his real name. I saw a brief flash of sadness reflected in his eyes, but in an instant it was gone again. Without another word I rose from the kitchen table and went upstairs.

CHAPTER 17 – JACKSON

I played it cool about Leah leaving for college, but the truth was I hated the idea. It's not like it was a surprise – she'd been talking about it since the day we met. Sure, she went on about how she wasn't going that far away and that she'd come home on weekends, but I knew better. She'd get sucked into college life and then who knows when I'd see her?

My pessimism was put to the test two Fridays later when I answered the doorbell and found Leah standing on my porch with a shit-eating grin on her face.

"Surprise!" she exclaimed, her eyes drinking me in.

"What are you doing back already?" I asked excitedly as I scooped her into a big hug.

"I just missed you too much, Jackson," she said as she returned the hug and stepped inside. "Besides, it's not that far."

"Well, I bet Molly wasn't too happy," I chuckled as I closed the door behind her.

She shrugged, confirming my statement. "Well, she'll just have to deal with it." Then she grabbed my hand and led me up to my room.

After a round of *I really missed you* sex I casually asked her what her parents thought of her decision to come home so soon.

"They don't care. I have my car at school so it's not like I'm inconveniencing them or anything."

"True," I agreed, but I couldn't help but think that they weren't any happier than Molly.

After that, Leah came home every weekend. I'd work all week during the day and concentrate on my music at night. I had begun recording demos of the music I wrote to have on hand, *just in case*. It wasn't like any big-time producers were clamoring to hear my work, but hey, a guy can dream, right? Before I knew it, it would be Friday, and Leah would beat rush hour traffic to get to my place in time for dinner. We saw each other nearly as much as we did when she lived at home. It was great.

One Friday at the end of October Leah showed up looking like something was on her mind. When I asked what was up, she told me that her parents were insisting she start spending the weekends at school so she could get what they called the "full college experience."

She seemed surprised, but I knew it was bound to happen. The only thing that surprised me was that it took them as long as it did to say something.

"Lee, it's not a big deal," I said, trying again to play it off, "Thanksgiving break is just around the corner and then before you know it winter break will be here."

Leah nodded but she still looked upset.

"And besides," I added as an afterthought, "I could come up and see you on the weekends instead. I don't mind making the drive, it'd be fun." And I meant it.

Anna – October 1997

Our new normal started the following weekend when Ace headed out for the bar with the guys. I'm sure one of them would've had no problem taking him home but come hell or high water he called me to pick him up. It was almost like he was "fixing my wagon."

It was a real pain in the neck having to pack the kids into the car at all hours of the night, but it was better than him getting behind the wheel. Besides, who was to say his friends were in any better condition?

Sometimes I'd leave Beth and Tim home, but Jackson always wanted to come with me, which meant I still had to make excuses as to why I was picking his father up and why his father was in a stone-cold stupor every time I did.

I held out hope for a while after the incident at Dune's but finally had to admit to myself that things were never going to get better. I could no longer live with Ace's constant hostility towards me and even though it wasn't directed towards them, I knew it wasn't good for the kids either.

I swallowed my pride and one afternoon after I got out of work I went to see my mom. I told her about everything that'd been going on between us, though I glossed over Ace's drinking and the fact that he'd almost gotten a DWI. It just made him sound so trashy, like he was some sort of bum. I hated to admit it, even to myself, but another reason I didn't tell her was because I was secretly still holding out a tiny glimmer of hope that things would get better. What if I told her everything and Ace and I ended up working things out? She'd worry every time she saw a beer in his hand that he was headed back down that path.

She listened calmly to everything I had to say. "Anna, I'm so sorry," she said when I was finished, "I knew things hadn't been right between you two for a while but I had no idea it was to such an extent."

"Mom, I've tried everything to make him happy but no matter what I do it's not enough. He's so bitter and angry all the time. He just seems to hate me." I threw my hands up in defeat. "What am I supposed to do?"

She shrugged. "There's nothing you can do. You can't force him to stop being angry all the time. His anger is something he has to deal with."

"But do I pack up the kids and leave him? Because I can't live like this anymore, Mom. I'm just so . . . so lonely. If it weren't for the kids keeping me busy all the time I think I'd go out of my mind!"

She took my hand. "Annalise, I can't tell you what to do. You have to decide for yourself. But know that there's always a place for you and the children here with us."

"Mom, I can't," I said as I shook my head, "It would be too much for you and Dad."

"Nonsense, Anna; there's plenty of room," she said, motioning around the kitchen. "And your father wouldn't mind. You know how much he loves the kids."

We sat in silence for a moment before she said, "At least think about it. Okay?"

"Okay, I will."

CHAPTER 18 - LEAH

I was glad when Jackson suggested coming up to see me. I'd hoped that's what he'd say because I hadn't been completely honest with him about the reason my parents wanted me to spend more time at school. The truth was, it was less about me getting *the full college experience* and more about me staying away from him.

Mom and I had a heated argument about it one weekend in October, but I'd felt the storm brewing long before that. She had made some subtle (and some not so subtle) innuendos whenever Jackson dropped me off or his name came up in conversation, but I still hadn't realized the extent of my parents' dislike for him. To be fair, it wasn't actually *him* they didn't like. It was more his lifestyle choices - his job, his lack of education, his preoccupation with his music. I think it was his general laidback attitude that bugged them the most. Both of my parents were uptight go-getters and to them his *don't worry, everything'll work out* attitude sounded a lot like laziness.

But this was what I loved most about him. He had a calming effect on me that balanced out the pressure I'd always felt from my parents and, more recently, my college classes.

They waited for a night when my brother was spending the night at a friend's house. "Leah," my mom began calmly over dinner, "your father and I want to talk to you about Jackson."

"Oh, okay, what's up?" I asked as I slid a piece of roasted chicken onto my dish and then returned the platter to the center of the table.

"The thing is," she continued slowly, delicately at first, "We think that perhaps you and he have been spending a bit too much time together and it has us a little concerned."

"Concerned? Concerned how?" I asked as I took a sip of my raspberry iced tea.

"Well, we feel that he may be distracting you from more important things, like your studies, and we don't think it's good for you right now."

"Good for me? What's that supposed to mean and what's not *good* about it?" I was starting to get annoyed now. "My grades are fine; Jackson isn't a distraction."

A tense look passed between my parents.

"We'll cut to the chase, Leah," my father said gruffly, "Your mother and I aren't happy about this. In the beginning we let it go, thinking it would run its course, but it's been over a year now and we've had just about enough. You're not to come home from school on weekends anymore, and to make sure you don't, you won't be taking your car back. We'll drive you and you're to stay put until Thanksgiving break."

"Whoa, wait a minute -" I started to argue but he quickly put up his hand to stop me.

"It's not up for discussion, Leah. I'm not paying almost sixty thousand dollars a year for that school so you could end up with the likes of *that* kid."

From his tone you would have thought he was talking about some bum that laid around doing nothing all day.

"*That kid*?!" I said as I stood from the table, "How dare you refer to Jackson like that!"

"Sit down," he said sternly.

I glared at him for a moment and then slid back down onto my chair.

He slowly placed his elbows on the table, then laced his fingers together and rested his chin on them. He'd done this since I was a kid, as a sign that he meant business.

"Listen to me, young lady, and listen good," be began in a calm tone that made him sound all the more serious, "If I find out you came home to see him before break I will rip you out of that fancy school so fast your head'll spin. You hear me?"

Again, I went to speak and again he cut me off. "Maybe seeing how the other half lives - and by other half I mean those attending community college - would knock some sense into you."

Then, without waiting for a reply, he stood, pushed his chair back and marched into the living room. As soon as he was gone from sight I snapped my head toward my mom but before I could say anything she started to speak.

"Leah, this is not Romeo and Juliet," she said in an attempt to soften my father's words. "We're not forbidding you from ever seeing him again. Your father and I would just like you to branch out, maybe broaden your horizons a bit. You know, maybe date some other boys. Perhaps someone from school; someone more on par with you, with us."

On par with us? I'd never heard my mother sound like such a snob before.

"Look around you, Leah," she said motioning around the room, "you grew up in a comfortable house, surrounded by nice things. He's never going to be able afford the kind of life you're used to."

"Mom, hold up, this is crazy. I'm barely nineteen and you've already got me married off."

"It's not so crazy," she argued, "it happens all the time. One thing leads to another and the next thing you know you end up pregnant and -"

"*Pregnant!* Who's pregnant?" my father bellowed from the doorway behind me.

"Calm down, William, no one's pregnant." My mother rolled her eyes. "We're just talking."

"What a minute, is she *sleeping* with that kid?" he said with disgust, at first directing the question to my mother then turning to me. "For the love of Pete, Leah, *are you* sleeping with him?!"

Oh my gosh! Is this conversation actually happening?

"Christ, it just gets better and better," he roared, shaking his head as he threw his hands in the air.

"First of all, I am *not* sleeping with him," I lied, mortified that we were even discussing this. "Second of all, I don't think you're being very fair. You're judging him without even knowing him."

"I know all I need to know, Leah," my father declared angrily. "That rat trap of a car he drives around in. That house he lives in. His father's a drunk, Leah. Are you aware of that? Are you?"

"Says who?" I snapped, "You've never been to his house or met his family."

"I did a little research over the summer." He took in my expression. "That's right. Do you think I'm not going to check out a boy my daughter is spending so much time with?"

"How dare you! How dare you spy on him!" I gasped as I jumped up from the table. I felt the inevitable tears begin to spring free when suddenly something inside of me just snapped. All the years of them controlling me, trying to run my life, making all of my decisions for me – it all came bubbling to the surface and exploded like fireworks on the Fourth of July. "You might be able to keep me away at school but you can't keep us apart. Jackson loves me and I love him and we are *not* breaking up - not by a long shot - so you better just get used to it."

Before he could get another word in edgewise I took a chance and called his bluff. "I'm over eighteen, I can do what I want. Maybe I'll forget about college altogether. I can move in with Jackson and get a job at the ski slope where he works. What do you think of that?"

I held in a breath, praying he wouldn't take me up on it. We glared at each other before my mom finally intervened.

"Calm down, both of you," she said evenly, "Let's sit down and discuss this rationally. No shouting, I mean it."

My stomach was in knots as we all returned to the table. I had never had such a heated argument with my parents and though I was shaken it felt good to stand my ground. In the end we agreed that I would only come home for major breaks and holidays. In return they would not interfere with me and Jackson. I knew they felt they'd claimed a small victory, but that was okay because so had I.

When I finally was able to escape up to my room I quietly shut the door and then let out the breath I'd been subconsciously holding. I loved Jackson, no doubt about it, but I also loved school. I had goals, ambitions, and I certainly wasn't going to reach them by dropping out of school and working at the mountain with Jackson. After a lifetime of playing it safe, I'd taken a gamble and won.

I smiled smugly as I leaned my back against my closed bedroom door. It'd felt so unbelievably good to lash out at my parents like that. Suddenly it dawned on me that my father's threats were empty ones. He'd never pull me out of school, never. They both loved bragging about me to their friends. My grades, my soccer career, my acceptance into a prestigious university - I was the one who held all the cards, not them. I recalled the look in my father's eyes when I threatened to drop out and go to work at the mountain – pure fear.

I'd stick to our deal about not coming home on the weekends to see Jackson, but they'd never said anything about him not coming up to see me.

▲   ▲   ▲

Of course I downplayed the incident with my parents to Jackson; all it would do was upset him. When he offered to come up to see me at school, I knew I had made the right decision – he might not have done so if he knew how strongly they felt about him. It was much better this way, with him thinking everything was status quo and me looking forward to his visit each week.

Before I knew it, Thanksgiving had arrived. It was the first time I'd seen my parents since the big blowout, and at first things were a bit strained, mostly on their part. After returning to school I hadn't given much thought to how much my threat affected them, but it was obvious when I saw them that they had taken it very seriously. Clearly, I had the upper hand now and I intended to play it to the hilt.

The first order of business was informing them that Jackson would be joining us for Thanksgiving dinner.

"Oh sure, honey, I guess that would be fine," my mom said as Dad stood by with gritted teeth. He looked like he was going to blow a gasket but kept himself in check, just nodding curtly.

I didn't stop there. On Wednesday I called Jackson and told him he should come over early on Thanksgiving so we could watch the football game with my dad and brother.

I felt a little bad about putting Jackson in the middle of all this but the idea of rubbing my father's face in it was too good to resist. I took every opportunity, too, grabbing his hand all the time and snuggling up to him on the couch while we were watching the game. I told myself that it was okay since Jackson had no idea how my parents felt about him; they were always very sweet to his face and that day was no different.

When it came time for dinner we all moved into the dining room to take a seat at the impeccably set table. Conversation flowed and Jackson seemed to be very comfortable and oblivious to the tension that surrounded him.

"So, Leah," my dad began, "have you thought any more about what we talked about, you know about maybe getting some work experience while you're home for winter break? It'll look good on your resume, especially if you could get something in your field. I could talk to Uncle Kevin, see if his firm has anything available. What do you think?"

"I don't know," I shrugged, "Maybe."

Before my dad could add anything further Jackson spoke up excitedly, "Hey Leah, if you're looking to work when you're home I could pull a few strings and get you something at Powder Peak." He looked toward my dad. "I'm pretty tight with upper management and I could put in a good word."

My dad nearly gagged on what he was chewing and I grabbed another golden opportunity to piss him off.

"Really, Jackson? That'd be great!" I said excitedly, then slid my eyes to my dad to catch his expression. "It'd be so much fun working together! We'd be together like all day! Thanks so much!"

"No problem, babe," he said as he slipped his arm around my shoulders and gave a gentle squeeze.

After we ate dinner we hung around for a bit, then I announced to my parents that Jackson and I should probably get going. We were having dessert at Jackson's grandparents' house. This time I was rewarded with a subtle frown from my mother, who was clearly not happy about the fact that I was leaving with him, and before she had served the pie.

We grabbed our coats and then said our goodbyes.

"Thanks so much for having me over, Mr. and Mrs. Miller," Jackson said as he reached out to shake my father's hand.

I saw Dad's tight smile and almost laughed out loud. This was the most fun I'd had in months.

▲   ▲   ▲

We arrived at the neat little condominium complex about forty-five minutes later. I didn't really know what to expect since I'd never met his grandparents before. I had never met his brother either, because he was stationed overseas, but of course I knew his sister, Beth. I'd only met Jackson's father a handful of times, not that it mattered though because Jackson had told me he wouldn't be there anyway. Jackson's family dynamic was odd, to say the least. In the year and a half that we'd been together I could probably count on one hand the number of times I'd even seen his father; he was usually either not home or holed up is his room, that is, when he wasn't passed out on the living room couch.

Jackson rarely if ever talked about his family, and when I asked he'd mumble some sort of non-answer. I knew his mom had died in a car accident when he was young, but he'd never elaborated on the circumstances. When I tried to question him about it, he shrugged me off so I never brought it up again. I never mentioned his father's drinking either, because I knew Jackson was embarrassed by it.

I was pleasantly surprised by what I found when we arrived at his grandparents'. The condo was as neat as a pin and very tastefully decorated, unlike Jackson's home which always looked like a tornado had just swept through it. His elderly grandparents seemed totally normal, a sharp contrast to the disarray in which Jackson seemed to have grown up.

His grandparents were extremely friendly to me, and they positively doted over Jackson and his sister.

After we ate our fill of homemade pie and ice cream, we gathered in the cozy living room where Jackson's grandmother got out some old photos.

Some of them were really funny, especially those of Beth and Jackson when they were little. It was cute when his grandfather said that Jackson was a "pistol" when he was a kid but "cute as a bug's ear." When I remarked that this was still the case, we all had a good laugh.

On the way home I told Jackson what a good time I'd had with his grandparents.

"I would've loved to see more pictures," I chuckled. "And not just the cute little Jackson pictures I saw tonight. Next time I want a glimpse of middle-school-awkward-Jackson."

"Oh, I'm pretty sure that's all they have. They moved out west when I was seven or eight – I guess my grandma was sick and the climate there was good for her. Anyway, we didn't have any contact with them for years."

When I looked at him questioningly, he added, "Yeah, after my mom died they had some big blowout with my dad. He didn't want us to have anything to do with them. It sucked for me and my brother and sister, but what are you gonna do? At least they moved back and we found them again."

"Gee, that's too bad..." I said, my voice trailing off lamely. I had no idea what else to say.

"Hey," he began, switching topics as he usually did when the subject of his family came up, "you really interested in coming to work at the mountain? 'Cause I could definitely get you in."

I thought again about how pissed off my father seemed when Jackson first brought it up. Working at my Uncle Kevin's firm would definitely be a lot cushier than working at Powder Peak, but toying with my dad – that was priceless.

"Of course I'm interested," I said as I slipped my hand into his.

▲ ▲ ▲

Jackson continued to come up to college each weekend, much to Molly's annoyance.

"But Leah, he's here every single weekend!" she whined. "You haven't been to one single frat party since we got here. Aren't you sick of him yet?"

The truth was, I wasn't sick of him – not by a longshot. He was just so different than anyone I'd ever known. He was cool, and kinda quirky, and as far as I was concerned, hot as all hell. And, as an added bonus, his presence really pissed off my parents which was something I had begun enjoying a lot more than I should have.

I didn't even care what Molly thought about him, a first for me. What was she complaining about, anyway? She'd made some new friends and always seemed to be headed to one party or another; she certainly didn't need me to hold her hand.

Besides, me and Jackson were too busy having *I missed you all week* sex to be bothered with the drunken goings-on around campus. I did promise her that if Jackson couldn't make it up one weekend I'd go wherever she wanted.

There were only a few weeks of school after Thanksgiving and then I was home for the long winter break – and starting my job at Powder Peak Mountain with Jackson. He'd hooked me up with a job at the front counter checking in skiers. There wasn't much time for fraternizing – I dealt with the constant stream of patrons and he spent most of his time with the other snowboard instructors - but we managed to squeeze in a few minutes alone here and there.

Molly, who'd gotten a job as a cashier at a convenience store in town, came up to visit me on her days off. She never missed an opportunity to point out that most of the instructors Jackson worked with were female and even repeatedly hinted that he was fooling around with at least one of them. It was the same conversation every time.

"Molly," I'd say, exasperated, "I told you, management likes to have one guy and one girl when they give lessons to the kids. They say it makes the kids feel more comfortable."

Molly would once again conveniently overlook this detail.

"Leah," she'd say, choosing to focus on a different girl each time she came, "Just look at the way she's looking at him; I'm telling you, she's got the hots for him."

"Molly, you're being ridiculous. Jackson's not doing anything with her or with any of the other ones, for that matter."

I tried not to get angry with her, but it wasn't easy. This wasn't about concern for me, or any real suspicion about Jackson's loyalty. Molly wanted Jackson out of the picture and she made no bones about her feelings.

"Leah," she'd huff, "You're missing out on your college years, your *partying* years. You'll regret it, I know you will."

I'd just smile at her and shake my head. How could I make Molly understand what true love was when she'd never even experienced it herself?

All too soon winter break was over and it was time to head back to school.

It turned out that the workload for my second semester was a lot more rigorous than my first. Jackson's schedule was a lot fuller, too; Jersey had gotten a lot of snow and he was working most weekends. We talked on the phone a lot but it wasn't nearly the same as seeing each other. I really missed him.

Molly finally got her wish one Saturday night when I announced I'd finished my paper due on Monday. I'd been working on it all week and now I needed to let off some steam.

"I'll go to the party with you," I told her, "but I'm not staying late. Jackson said he might come up for the day tomorrow."

She was ecstatic. "Sure, just be ready by ten o'clock sharp."

I rolled my eyes at her, but as I started getting dressed I found myself looking forward to a night out. Maybe Molly was on to something.

Anna – November 1997

I planned to leave him, really, I did, but the timing just never seemed to be right. First I decided it would be too traumatic for the kids while school was still in session. Then when school let out I couldn't bring myself to ruin their summer. Then when September rolled around I found myself using the school's-back-in-session excuse. Finally I told myself that when the time was right, I'd know it.

That time came one chilly Friday night a couple of weeks before Thanksgiving. It was around eleven o'clock when I heard Ace come in. I was surprised, not because of the late hour, but because he hadn't called me to pick him up from the bar.

He stumbled, bleary-eyed, into the kitchen and without a word to me pulled open the refrigerator door. After a few minutes of rummaging around he finally pulled out some bacon.

"Really, Ace? You're not going to start frying up bacon at this hour, are you?"

"Maybe," he snapped as he grabbed a frying pan out of the cabinet below.

For some reason that really pissed me off. It wasn't that he wanted bacon, and he had certainly been much nastier to me, but that night I was tired and fed up and just wanted to go to bed. I knew he'd leave a mess as usual and I'd be scrubbing bacon grease at midnight. Plus, I was afraid that in his drunken stupor he might burn down the house.

"No way, Ace. If you want something to eat I'll make you a sandwich, but I'm not cleaning this up," I said firmly.

He looked at me through squinted eyes like he couldn't believe that I'd just denied him bacon. Then he just turned his back to me and proceeded to put the pan on the stove.

It was the final straw. I grabbed the pan from the stove and then snatched up the bacon and tossed it back into the fridge. Still clutching the pan, I stormed up the stairs toward the bedroom. Halfway up the stairs I turned and yelled over my shoulder, "Sure gonna have a hard time fryin' it up now."

I went into the bedroom and quickly slid the fry pan under the bed as I heard him bounding up the stairs after me. Seconds later, he burst into the room.

I knew it. I knew it before it even started that this was it. This was going to be the argument that finally did us in. Bacon.

"Gimme the fucking pan, Anna," he said through clenched teeth.

I faced him, arms crossed. "No."

He came towards me and roughly grabbed my upper arm, squeezing it tightly as he pushed me back towards the wall. "Gimme the fucking pan, Anna. Now."

I tried to jerk my arm away but he held it tighter. "Ace, you're hurting me. Let go."

He pushed me back roughly, causing my head to slam against the wall. The sharp pain I felt caused me to cry out.

"Dammit, Anna, look what you made me do! Just gimme the fucking pan!"

Clutching the side of my head, I stepped away from the wall and slid the pan out from under the bed toward him with my foot.

"Get out of here, Ace," I said as I slowly sat down on the edge of the bed, refusing to even look up at him.

He paused breathing heavily before he bent down and picked up the pan. Then he turned and went back down the stairs.

He never came up to bed that night and I didn't go downstairs the next day until I knew he was out of the house. I knew when I woke up that morning that I was done. I'd had it. I was leaving.

CHAPTER 19 - JACKSON

It sucked not getting to see Leah every weekend, especially after spending so much time together over winter break, but I tried to make the most of it. My paycheck had nearly doubled, I was working so much, and I also had more time to spend working on my music and jamming with Blow Torch.

When by myself I mostly worked on the lyrics to my own music. I hadn't made a lot of progress with it but was hoping to try and play one or two of the songs the next time I had a gig with BT.

As much as I loved working on my own stuff, I found myself looking forward to spring so I could have weekends off again and be able to go up and visit Leah.

Leah was the real deal. She didn't care that I didn't have a lot of money or lived in a crappy house or drove my brother's hand-me-down car. She just loved me for who I was. I didn't believe in God, not after everything that'd happened in my life, but I had to believe that this was no fluke, that someone up there must've been looking out for me. It was the only explanation I could come up with. All I knew was that she was hands down the best thing that had ever happened to me.

And it wasn't just Leah, it was her family too. They had money, education; they could have taken one look at me and decided I wasn't good enough for her, but instead they had given me a fair shake. In fact, they really seemed to have taken a shine to me. Like on Thanksgiving at her house, when we watched the game together with her dad and brother. It was like being part of a real family. I couldn't even remember the last time I'd felt like that.

It was the same thing at Christmas but at Christmas her *whole* family was there – grandparents, aunts, uncles, cousins – and Leah made sure to introduce me to everyone. The guys in the family had an annual football game that they called the "Snow Bowl" and Leah told her dad to make sure and pick me for his team so she could root for the both of us. Then again, he probably would have picked me anyway, seeing as I hooked Leah up with the job at the mountain.

It felt as though in such a short time my life had taken such a dramatic turnaround. It wasn't so long ago that if I had a free weekend I'd spend it either drunk off my ass with my friends or up in my room, stoned outta my mind with some slut from town. Now I can't even remember the last time I'd gotten high and the funny thing was, I didn't even miss it.

One day I was gonna make it big with my music. I just had to make the right connections, get the right people to hear it because I knew it was *that* good. And when I did make it big I was gonna take care of everyone who stood by me, who believed in me. Then I'd stomp all over the one person who treated me like dirt, who always told me I sucked and couldn't do anything right. My darkened thoughts turned to my father. I'd crush him the way he'd crushed my mom, the way he tried to crush me.

Anna – October 1998

After the bacon incident I'd started squirreling a few dollars away here and there so when I did leave Ace I wouldn't be arriving at my parents' house penniless. I didn't know how Ace would react when I told him I was leaving and I needed to be prepared. Maybe I was fooling myself, maybe he'd actually be glad I was leaving. I felt like I didn't even know him anymore. He definitely wasn't the same person I fell in love with as a teenager. Not by a longshot.

There was no question about how my parents felt about my ending my marriage. In their minds I would just be undoing a mistake I should have avoided long ago. I would be starting over. My mother had even actually convinced me to sign up for a few classes at the community college.

"It's never too late to get an education, Annalise," she said. "A few classes here and there and before you know it, you'll have your degree."

I wasn't so sure, but I was willing to give it a shot. Every time I got scared to move forward, I thought about all the effort I had put into my marriage, all of it fruitless.

I set a deadline for the end of the month. That's when I'd tell him.

With Ace still not home from yet another happy hour with his coworkers, I was microwaving some popcorn for me and Jackson to eat while we watched Sponge Bob. Jackson loved Sponge Bob and although I wasn't a big fan of cartoons it was fun watching with him. Beth and Tim were both holed up in their rooms and weren't interested in joining the festivities.

"It's nice and hot, Jacky, just the way you like it," I said, smiling at the way his eyes lit up at the sight of the bowl. I placed it on the nightstand and slid onto the bed next to him. Jackson liked to watch TV together in my room because there was plenty of room to cuddle up together, not to mention the TV was much bigger than the one in his room.

"Is it extra salty?" he asked as he leaned up from the pile of pillows and rubbed his palms together.

"No extra salt, Jacks, you know it's not good for you."

"But I like extra salt," he whined as he grabbed a handful and shoved it into his mouth.

"What episode's on tonight?" I asked as I stuck my hand into the bowl.

"The one where Sponge Bob and Patrick get the baby clam," he said excitedly, "my favorite!"

"Mine too," I agreed and then tossed my arm around his shoulders and pulled him closer.

About ten minutes into the episode the phone rang and I knew before I answered it that it was Ace, wanting me to pick him up. This will all be over soon, I thought as I reached over and grabbed it. I could barely make out what he was saying over all the noise but I knew he indeed wanted me to get him.

As I hung up the phone I turned to Jackson. "I need to go pick up your dad, sweetie; do you want to take a ride with me? Timmy and Beth are home so if you want to stay and watch the rest of your show it's fine."

I was surprised when he said he'd stay since he almost always came with me.

"Alright," I said as I grabbed a few more pillows and then proceeded to tuck them behind him so he was propped up even higher.

"I'll be quick," I said as I kissed the top of his head and then made my way to the door. "Love you."

"Yeah, me too," he said with his eyes glued to the television.

I smiled as I sighed to myself. He was such a good kid, they all were. I just hoped I was doing the right thing by leaving their father.

I yelled to Beth and Tim that I'd be right back but as usual got no answer. Then I grabbed my keys and purse and slipped into my jacket as I left through the front door.

I hadn't realized it was raining and cursed the fact that my jacket didn't have a hood and I hadn't grabbed an umbrella. I thought about going back for it, then decided not to bother. I just wanted to get this over with.

I pulled out of the driveway and started on my way downtown towards Dune's where Ace would probably be waiting near the front door.

As I was waiting for the traffic light to change to green I found myself thinking once again about the upcoming changes in my life. It was pretty much all I thought about these days, but to my surprise I found myself feeling cautiously optimistic about it. Hey, community college might actually turn out to be fun and who knows where it might lead. I smiled to myself - That's right, Anna, turn your lemons into lemonade.

The light turned green and I pulled forward into the intersection with the silly smile still on my face. Suddenly, out of nowhere I heard the loudest noise I'd ever heard in my entire life. It sounded like thunder, an earthquake, a grenade all rolled into one. Then came the pain. The most excruciating pain I'd ever felt and it blanketed my entire body. And then, silence . . .

CHAPTER 20 – LEAH

I felt my head pounding the following morning when I woke up. Even my eyelids ached in protest when I tried to open them. My very first hangover, and it was a doozy. I felt around the little nightstand next to my bed until my hand curled around the small bottle of Advil. After popping two I reached for the can of warm Sprite resting on the floor beside my bed and downed some before sinking back into a deep sleep.

I awoke several hours later feeling somewhat better. I rolled onto my side to see if Molly was awake and had to squint to make sure I was seeing correctly. Molly's bed was still made as if she'd never come home last night. I slowly pulled myself up into a sitting position, careful not to make any sudden movements that might make me hurl what was left in my stomach from the night before.

A shower, I thought to myself, I need a shower to make me feel human again. I gathered my things and shuffled down the long hallway toward the bathroom I shared with the rest of the floor.

I stood beneath the soothing needles of warm water until I started to come alive. While I did, I tried to piece together the fragments of the night before. It was definitely fun, that much I remembered.

When I got back to my dorm room Molly had returned, still clad in the clothes she'd had on the night before.

"Where were you all night?" I asked as I bent over and began towel drying my hair.

"I stayed at Chase's place," she said nonchalantly as she sat down on her bed and began to remove her shoes.

"Chase?" I questioned as I stood upright and flipped my damp hair back.

"Yeah, Chase from the party last night. You remember – the tall blonde; body like Ryan Reynolds." When I didn't answer, she looked up at me even as she continued rubbing her sore feet. "Leah, how can you not remember? You were talking to him like half the night."

I vaguely remembered talking with a tallish guy for a while but I didn't remember what his name was, or anything else about him for that matter.

"That is until you wandered off with Gabby, never to return," she added annoyed.

"I think we went to get something to eat," I told her, now remembering that my friend Gabby and I stopped off for some fish tacos at the all-night burrito bar. This would certainly explain my sour stomach this morning.

"I think he has the hots for you," she informed me as she collapsed back onto her bed.

I laughed. "And so *you* left with him?"

She tossed one of her pillows at me but I ducked and it hit the wall behind me. "I didn't leave with *him*. I left with Brent, but I ended up crashing on the couch at their place."

She looked over at me mischievously. "Admit it, you had a good time, didn't you?"

Before I could answer she added, "Don't deny it, Leah, you know you did."

"I wasn't going to deny it," I shrugged, "It was fun. Not something I'd want to do every weekend, but now and then would be okay."

"Well, Chase wanted to know where I'd been hiding my 'hot' roommate all this time."

"Hot? He said I was hot?" I asked as I sat down at the edge of my bed, my interest now piqued. 'Hot' wasn't generally a word that was used to describe me by anyone. Well, anyone other than Jackson, who did tend to say it quite a bit. The thought was flattering, no doubt. Not that I had any interest in pursuing Chase or any of the other guys here, but it was definitely nice to know.

"So, what should I tell him? You know, in case he asks about you again?"

I hesitated a moment for some reason before saying, "Nothing; don't say anything. I'm with Jackson and I'm not interested anyway."

I saw a slight smile tug at the side of her lips before she shrugged and said, "Suit yourself."

▲   ▲   ▲

The Saturday night frat parties soon became routine, at least on the weekends Jackson couldn't make it up, which lately had been more often than not. I still missed him but had to admit I was having a lot of fun.

One night in February Molly and I were getting ready to go out when there was a knock at the door. I was shocked when I opened it to find Jackson standing there.

"Surprise, babe," he said excitedly as he wrapped me in a hug.

I was thrilled. "Jackson! What are you doing here? I thought you were working!"

He loosened his hold and looked down at me. "I told management no way I was working another weekend. Hadta get up to see my girl." He winked to let me know that he *didn't* actually tell management that, which made me laugh.

As I led him into our room I saw Molly give a slight eye roll before tossing a friendly "Hey there, Jackson" over her shoulder.

"Hey, Moll," he replied as he sat down on my bed, "What're you up to tonight? Another party?"

"As a matter of fact, yes," she said not turning away from the mirror where she was carefully applying another coat of cherry-red lip stain. "Leah and I were going to head over to a frat party in about a half hour, but I guess I'm going solo now. Unless..." She sighed as she turned from the mirror. "Unless the both of you want to join me."

"Jackson doesn't want to go to one of those parties, Molly..." I said. The thought of Jackson hanging out with a bunch of frat guys was almost comical, or at least downright weird. But Jackson was full of surprises that night.

"I don't mind going, Lee," he said, "It might even be fun. Never been to a college party before. Besides," he continued as he stood and moved over next to Molly, casually tossing an arm around her, "we can't let this sexy lady wander over there on her own. Right, Moll?"

"Right, Jackson," she said with a huge smile on her face that I knew was meant for me.

Molly had purposely backed me into a corner. She knew I couldn't get out of going without it looking to Jackson like I was hiding something.

"Okay, cool," I said with more enthusiasm than I felt. It's not that I minded him going to the party with us, exactly, it was just that sometimes the guys at the parties got a little flirty. None of it meant anything, it was just innocent fun, but I wasn't so sure that Jackson would agree.

When we got to the frat house the party was already in full swing. I squeezed myself past the crowd around the keg and grabbed three beers. I had a feeling we were going to need them.

Jackson seemed to be comfortable enough, though to me he stuck out like a sore thumb. He was dressed in his usual attire of jeans, work boots and a t-shirt, which normally I had no problem with. I actually liked the way his lanky frame looked in the clothes he wore. I had always thought it was cool. But when I looked around at everyone else, he just looked... odd. Ninety percent of the guys there also had on jeans and t-shirts, but Jackson's jeans were kind of faded and frayed. And whereas most of the other guys had on t-shirts with either a college or a professional sports team logo, Jackson's t-shirt had the name of – well, I presumed it was some rock band no one had ever heard of – on the front. And the work boots – all scuffed with the laces untied! He just had them loosely laced, so he could just step out of them at a moment's notice without having to put in any effort. But the biggest thing - literally - was his hair which I had gotten so used but looked completely nuts compared to all the other guys' neatly cropped styles. And it wasn't just the length, it was the style – or lack thereof. If it wasn't hanging in his eyes then he was finger-combing it back, causing it to stick up in all different directions.

"Hey there, Leah, Molly," I heard Chase say as he approached. I snapped my attention back from Jackson's hair just in time to see him and Brent join our little circle.

Molly greeted each of them with an overly friendly hug and then turned back to face me. "Hey guys, I don't think you've ever met Leah's boyfriend. This is Jackson."

"Hey," Jackson said with a slight nod as he reached over to shake Brent's hand. I saw Chase's curious expression as he quickly gave him the once over just before Jackson turned to extend his hand to him.

For the next few minutes they made some guy-type small talk before Chase said he'd catch us later and he and Brent walked off.

The three of us actually ended up having a pretty good time drinking and talking amongst ourselves — that is, when Molly wasn't off talking to this one or that one and in general being a social butterfly.

On one of her return trips Jackson laughed, "Shit, Molly, you're like the mayor; is there anyone here that you *don't* know?"

"Um, actually no," she chuckled and then she was off again in another direction.

"What do you say we cut out," he said as he slipped both arms around my waist. He leaned in slyly and whispered, "Cuz I'm dyin' to get my hands on that hot little body of yours."

That made me laugh; he was always so blunt. When I looked up at him, suddenly I felt bad about being embarrassed by his appearance. I always thought he looked great — *hot as hell* is how I always described him.

I leaned up close to his ear and whispered back a crude phrase I'd never used before and he bent his head back, letting out a very audible laugh. Then he grabbed my hand and said *you're on* as he led me through the crowded house and out the front door.

▲   ▲   ▲

I was hoping Molly would stay over at Brent's again so me and Jackson could have the room to ourselves but there was no such luck. She texted me about ten minutes after we arrived back at the dorm that she was on her way home.

"Better make it quick," I teased, "Molly's already on her way back."

"Don't think that'll be a problem, babe," he said as he slid next to me on my tiny twin bed, but before he even had a chance to turn off the bedside lamp we heard Molly's key in the door.

"Damn," he whispered and I covered my mouth to keep the laugh from escaping.

"I'm home," she said loudly, her eyes mockingly averted. Then she laughed and hopped onto her bed.

"What're you doing home so soon?" I asked, "When we left you were still with Brent, what happened?"

"He said he had to get going because he had to get up early for lacrosse practice," she explained as she grabbed her pajamas and headed for the door. "So I told him I'd just catch him tomorrow."

The door slammed behind her and Jackson turned to me as he slipped his hands up the sides of my t-shirt, "Now how 'bout we get back to business."

I laughed as I pushed him off of me. "No way, she'll be back in like thirty seconds." No sooner were the words out of my mouth when I heard the door open again and saw Molly waltz back through.

CHAPTER 23 - JACKSON

With an early spring thaw, work at the mountain began to slow down, which meant I'd have my weekends free again. I'd miss the extra money but it was a small price to pay for being able to see more of Leah. I'd gone up there on Saturday nights whenever I could wrangle the Sunday off, but it was a bitch driving all that way for only one night.

Even worse were the weekends that I couldn't get there at all. Although I never mentioned it to Leah for fear of sounding like a jealous prick, I didn't like the thought of her at all those parties with just Molly looking out for her. Molly seemed to have her own agenda, that being flirting with any guy who happened to look her way. It wasn't that I didn't trust Leah - because I totally did - but I wasn't so sure about Molly or the guys from her school for that matter.

It was my first full weekend off and I was psyched. That Friday, I rushed home from work, showered, then quickly threw some things in a duffle bag and grabbed my guitar. I was passing through the kitchen on my way out when I suddenly realized how hungry I was. I set my stuff down and opened the fridge, hoping to find my leftover Italian from the other night. I never knew what Dad would polish off after one of his late-night benders. Luckily it had escaped his notice, and three minutes later I was sitting down to a plate of nuked spaghetti. Halfway through I came up for air and took out my phone. For at least the tenth time I reread the email I'd gotten the other day, because this email wasn't just any email, it was *the* email.

I'd been putting feelers out to musicians I'd connected with online, even sent demos out to a few, but this was the first time one of them had gotten back to me. The email was short - saying they were a four-person band based in Brooklyn with an "Indy-classic rock fusion" feel and were looking to replace their lead guitarist who'd decided to pursue a solo career. Then came the most important part: *they liked my sound and would be interested in hearing the stuff I'd written to see if we were on the same page.* My hands were shaking a little when I replied to the guy - Matt was his name - saying I was definitely interested. He said he'd get back to me next week with some days and times to meet.

Hard as it was – okay, *impossible* - I tried not to get too excited in case it turned out to be a total bust. I hadn't even told Leah yet, partly because I was sure Matt would write to tell me it had been a misunderstanding (he hadn't), and partly because I wanted to see her expression. I knew she'd be just as excited as I was.

When I was done eating I washed off my plate, then headed out the front door, duffle bag and guitar in hand. That's when I saw that my father had parked behind me, blocking me in. Must've come in when I was in the shower. I grunted in annoyance and went back inside to look for his keys. They weren't in the kitchen so I went out to the family room, where I found him snoring lightly on the couch, no keys in sight. Thanks, Dad, I thought, swallowing my frustration. It wouldn't be the first time I was late somewhere because of his bullshit. I jogged up the stairs, then hurried down the hall and into his room. The keys were on his dresser next to a small pile of coins and a pack of gum. I grabbed the keys, then slid a piece of gum out of the pack, unwrapped it and popped it into my mouth. I went to toss the wrapper in the trash can beside his bed when I noticed a half-opened shoebox lying on his unmade bed. It was a large box – one that a pair of work-boots might come in. For some reason, I don't know why, I stepped closer, removed the cover the rest of the way and peered inside.

What got my attention first was the picture that was lying on top of a bunch of papers. I'd seen it before but I picked it up anyway to take a closer look. It was the black-and-white of my mom and dad sitting on the hood of a Camaro, drinking a couple of Buds and laughing. I turned it over and held it up to the light, hoping this time I'd be able to decipher the faded writing on the back. No such luck, so I tossed it back onto the pile of papers, and that's when something else caught my eye. It wasn't just random paperwork that lined the box. Nope, what I found was more like a hidden treasure, worthless to most but priceless to me. Written on several sheets of loose-leaf paper was what could've easily been mistaken for poems, were it not for the note written on a small piece of stationery paperclipped to the pile. Even without the heading, "From the Desk of Annalise Keller," I would have known it was my mother's. After years of rereading her birthday and Christmas cards to me, I'd memorized her handwriting. The note said simply: *Ace, here are the lyrics I told you about. Let me know if you think they're good enough to put with the ones we're bringing to L.A. Luv you! Anna.* She had even drawn a big heart around her name and marked the bottom of the page with a bunch of Xs and Os.

I sat down on the edge of the bed, feeling a rush of emotion that I hadn't felt - hadn't *let* myself feel - in ages. I tried to make sense of what the note said. The gist of it was that they were *both* going to California, but in the end, I knew only Dad had made it out there. According to my grandparents, he had come back to be with Mom after Beth was born. Was that why she didn't go? Had he ditched her when he found out she was pregnant? I wouldn't put it past him. Then again, he had come back, and he had stayed. Was it really like my grandparents said, that he came back to be with Mom and Beth? Or was there another reason?

My mind spinning, I rifled through the pages, drinking in every word she'd written. Most were poetic and flowery, clearly written by the hand of a teenage girl. Some of the other ones, though, were dark, almost gritty ballads and I found it hard to believe that they were written by the same person.

I heard the door creak and instantly my head snapped up as my eyes locked with the furious eyes of my father.

"What the fuck are you doin' in here?" he hissed.

"What the fuck *is all this*?" I hissed back, refusing to let him intimidate me. "Mom wrote all these songs and you never thought to mention it?" I tossed the evidence onto his bed. "I'm a musician too, in case you haven't noticed. Even write a lot of my own shit. Woulda been nice to know I had something in common with someone who actually gave a damn."

"Stay the fuck outta my stuff, Jackson," he threatened.

"You piece of shit," I said, my voice getting louder, "You left her when you found out she was pregnant. You took off for California without her."

"You don't know *shit*, Jackson," he snarled. "It was *nothin'* like that."

"Oh yeah?" I moved closer to him until we were practically toe to toe. "Well, you know what I think? I think it was *exactly* like that."

I stepped back before he could respond, then I grabbed his keys and raced out of the room and down the stairs. My heart was pounding.

I set my bag and guitar down in the driveway, then jumped in his car and quickly moved it out of the way. By the time I got into my own car and tore down the street, angry tears threatened to fall.

I knew I'd hated him before but now I absolutely *despised* him. What kind of guy walks out on his pregnant girlfriend? I couldn't even wrap my head around that. How could I even be related to someone like that? I wondered what Beth would think about this latest revelation. She'd probably just shrug it off; when it came to our father nothing surprised her anymore.

I cringed at the thought of Leah ever finding any of this out. I'd always been tightlipped where my family was concerned, for the simple fact that I was embarrassed. She came from such a nice normal family where everyone got along and genuinely cared about each other, a stark contrast to the way I'd grown up. Of course, she'd been at my house enough to know that *something* wasn't right, but still, the less she knew the better.

By the time I pulled onto the highway I'd begun to calm down, and my mind drifted back to the packet of songs I discovered. Who would've guessed that me and Mom had a lot more in common than just our light green eyes and laid-back demeanor?

About a half-hour into my trip, traffic came to a dead stop. I couldn't see anything up ahead other than an array of brake lights. Eventually I heard on the radio that there was a jackknifed tractor trailer blocking all the westbound lanes. Sighing, I pulled out my phone and sent Leah a text. I wouldn't be there for another few hours, at least.

Anna – October 27, 1998 8:24 P.M.

Noise – an indistinguishable screeching – filled my ears. It was people screaming, I realized, and the angry whoop, whoop of an ambulance. Flashing lights slipped in and out of focus as I tried unsuccessfully to comprehend what had happened, then sunk into the beckoning darkness. The pain pulled me back, agonizing pain that spread like fire through every inch of my body. I heard the screeching again, had the sensation of bouncing on top of waves. A shadowy figure sat over me but I could not make out their features. There was another jolt as the ambulance went over a pothole. The figure applied pressure to my arm, then the pain faded and I returned blissfully to the darkness.

The next time I came to, the motion had stopped and I heard a rhythmic beeping sound. I knew I was in a hospital room. The pain was gone and I felt lightheaded but comfortable, although I was unable to find the strength to open my eyes. Although I couldn't see anything I felt a familiar presence in the room and could hear heavy, choked breathing approaching my side.

Two strong hands grasped onto my limp hand as if it were a lifeline, then I heard Ace choking back sobs as he clutched onto me, burying his head at my side.

"Anna . . ." he whispered but then sobs overtook him again.

I wanted to tell him I was okay and that I heard him, but I felt myself slipping away again, deeper into the peaceful abyss.

I felt Ace being pulled away from me, then heard another voice crying. Beth! I knew the other kids were there too, but though I wanted so badly to see them I could not open my eyes. There was silence again but then I felt a light touch and a moment later a small hand slipped into mine. I knew instantly that it was Jackson's. My sweet baby boy.

"Mom?" I heard him whisper.

Calling on every bit of my strength, I was able to muster a faint squeeze of his hand. I heard his breathing quicken and, smiling to myself, I drifted off for the last time.

CHAPTER 24 - LEAH

I glanced at the digital clock on the nightstand for the tenth time, wondering where the heck Jackson could be, when finally my cell dinged with a text. I grabbed it right away and my earlier annoyance melted when I saw it was from him. But my relief quickly turned to disappointment when I read that he was going to be late. *Could've been worse, though, he might not have been able to make it up at all.*

I texted back, telling him to stay safe and that I'd see him later, then I told Molly.

"Oh that's too bad," Molly said, trying unsuccessfully to hide her pleasure, "but there's no sense hanging around the dorm all night, right?" She didn't even wait for me to answer before adding, "Maybe we should hit one of the parties."

I was about to tell her I wasn't in the mood when there was a knock at the door. Molly crossed the room to open it, her face splitting into a grin when she saw Chase and Brent on the other side.

"Hey! What're you guys doing here?"

Brent said hi to Molly, then threw me a wave. "Me and Chase are heading over to a party one of the guys told us about, thought you girls might want to join us."

"Sure," Molly answered before I could object, then she looked over and gave me a slight shrug.

I hesitated; a party didn't really appeal to me, but neither did sitting in the dorm room waiting for Jackson.

"C'mon, Leah," Chase coaxed, "We're not staying long; both of us have to get up early tomorrow anyway." He gave me a look of mock pleading.

I laughed. "Sure, why not?"

▲ ▲ ▲

The party was even more crowded than usual. Chase and Brent went to grab some beers while Molly and I waded through the stiflingly hot room, finally carving out a corner of the living room for the four of us to hang out.

We were just shaking off our jackets when Molly spotted the guys and waved them over.

"Cheers, girls," I heard Brent say as he handed each of us a red solo cup filled to the brim.

One beer turned into two, then three, and before I knew it I was having a really good time. I could tell Molly was too. She and Brent were whispering and giggling to each other about something I couldn't hear over the loud music.

Chase was standing next to me, talking to one of his lacrosse teammates. I glanced over at him, and thought, not for the first time, how good-looking he was. He was tall, definitely over six feet, with sandy-blond hair that always seemed to look as if it had just been cut. He must have felt me staring because he glanced over and smiled before turning back to his conversation. When his friend walked off he turned back to me, his steel-gray eyes boring into mine, and for a moment I froze. I had never noticed until that moment how beautiful they were.

"Another beer?" he asked as he motioned to my nearly empty cup.

I didn't think it was a good idea but found myself nodding anyway, "Sure, thanks."

He nodded, then chugged the rest of his before taking my cup from me and heading off to the kitchen. The line at the keg must have thinned by then because he was back a few minutes later, two beers in hand.

He placed the two cups on the end table behind him and turned back to me, folded his arms across his chest, and smiled. I slowly drank in the broad shoulders, the sculpted chest beneath his fitted maroon lacrosse t-shirt, the clearly defined biceps, the slim waist. I came to my senses and stopped myself before going any lower but it was too late. He knew I was ogling him.

"So, uh, you play lacrosse?" I asked, suddenly nervous.

"Yeah, you should come to a game some time," he suggested.

"Uh, yeah maybe," I answered, growing even more nervous as he inched closer to me. But I didn't back up; in fact, I found myself wanting him to get closer. Our forearms were practically touching. I could smell the musky scent of his aftershave or shampoo or whatever it was that was making him smell so good and I knew that I probably shouldn't have been enjoying it as much as I was.

"So, your boyfriend . . . uh, Jackson, right?" he said as he cocked his head to the side, "He not coming up this weekend?"

"There was, um, a big tie-up on the highway. He'll be here later," I told him.

As soon as he heard that, Chase moved back. It was almost imperceptible, but I noticed and, even worse, found I was a little disappointed.

"Chase," I heard Brent yell from behind me, "We should head out, early practice tomorrow."

"Yeah, in a minute," he said to Brent but his eyes were still fixed on mine, "I should probably get going."

"Okay, we should probably head out too." I turned toward Molly. "Are you ready?"

Molly nodded, already grabbing our jackets.

The walk back to our building was almost more fun than the party itself. The night air felt good after the hot house; it also made my beer buzz stronger. I giggled as Chase helped me into my jacket, then laughed along with Molly as he and Brent told us a funny story about some guy from their team. I figured they'd leave us out front and continue on their way, but they didn't even break stride, just followed us up to our floor. I tried to catch Molly's eye to let her know I didn't want them there, but either she didn't notice or she was ignoring me. *This is not good,* I thought as I nervously looked over my shoulder for Jackson. As we approached the door to our room, I fully expected to see him there waiting for us, an annoyed expression on his face, but it seemed the coast was clear.

As Molly fumbled with her key, I tried to come up with an excuse to keep them from coming in. Suddenly, we heard sounds of a commotion at the other end of the hall. We all turned towards the noise, then Molly and Brent hurried down to see what it was.

I leaned back against the wall next to our door. "Molly's like the queen bee of the floor – she's always got to know what's going on." I laughed softly, trying to hide the nervousness that was springing up in my gut again.

"How about you?" Chase asked as he moved in closer to me. He reached over and tucked a stray hair behind my ear, letting his fingers linger there longer than they should have. "Would you like to know . . . what's going on . . .?"

"Uh, you mean down the hallway?" I asked, thrown by his tone as much as his touch.

He moved in even closer. Then he let his hand slip from behind my ear to my shoulder, where he started slowly running his fingers back and forth. I felt my breath quicken and knew I should step away but I didn't. He reached up with his other hand and slowly ran it up and down my other arm. *This was so not right and I knew it, so why wasn't I stopping him?*

"Yeah," he whispered, ". . . down ... the...hallway . . ."

I lifted my head as he spoke. My intention was to tell him he should stop but before I could get the words out his lips were pressed to mine. I froze, then tensed, but I didn't pull away and a second later found myself kissing him back. I felt him grip my arm and pull me closer as his other hand started moving through my hair.

"Leah," I heard Molly call out, then I heard footsteps bounding down the hall toward us. It was like someone had thrown cold water in my face.

I immediately brought my hands up to Chase's chest and pushed him away. For a few seconds, we just stared at each other, then he quickly stepped to the side before Molly got close enough to see us.

"You guys missed it!" she gasped as she came skidding to a halt in front of us. "The guys down the hall were building a human pyramid and it didn't end well!" She looked back at Brent and gave a breathless laugh. "Holy crap!"

Brent shook his head, but he was laughing too. Neither of them seemed to notice the awkward vibe hanging in the air.

I smiled and pretended to listen as they told the story, but I desperately wanted to get inside our room and away from Chase. That's when I heard the unmistakable sound of Jackson's voice calling out to us in the distance.

Chase heard it too because he suddenly said, "I'm gonna cut out; I'll catch you guys tomorrow." He turned to Brent, "Ready?" But he didn't bother waiting for Brent to answer, he just walked the opposite way down the hall and rounded the corner.

"Hey, wait up," Brent yelled, then turned to Molly and me. "Guess I'll see you guys during the week." A second later he too had disappeared around the same corner as Chase.

Suddenly I was overcome with the fear that Jackson would be able to tell what'd just happened between me and Chase. Like somehow he'd know as soon as he laid eyes on me that I was guilty of something. But as he got closer I realized how silly I was being; he was his usual smiling self. The fact that he was so happy to see me, even after sitting in hours of traffic, made me feel even shittier.

"Hey babe." Jackson placed his bag down and leaned his guitar against the wall.

"Jackson!" I said overenthusiastically as I jumped into his arms, causing him to stumble back.

"Whoa!" he laughed and then kissed me, "Missed you too, babe."

Molly gave a playful eyeroll as she scooted by us and threw a *hey Jackson* over her shoulder.

"What's up, Molly?" Jackson said good-naturedly as he loosened his hold on me and retrieved his bag and guitar. We both followed Molly into our room where he took a seat on my bed.

"Same old," she replied as she fished around for her pajamas and towel. "I'm gonna hit the bathroom now," she announced when she had gathered everything, "so you guys got like *ten* minutes, tops; better make the most of it." She giggled as she walked off.

Normally I would've laughed off her suggestion to *make the most of it* but something came over me. I don't know if it was the alcohol I'd consumed, the guilt I felt or the lingering effects of Chase's kiss – maybe a combination of all three. But as soon as Molly was out the door I turned the deadbolt, then moved closer to my bed where Jackson was removing his work boots.

"Molly's a trip," he chuckled as he shook his head.

I didn't reply, just pushed him onto his back and straddled him. I didn't even bother pulling off his shirt, instead choosing to get right down to business. When I attempted to undo his belt buckle, a look of mild surprise crossed his face.

"Uh, Molly'll be back in ten minutes, right?" he asked, a bit startled by my actions.

"Well, she exaggerated a bit; she's never *that* quick. But you might want to help me out here or she'll end up getting back before we even get started."

"You don't havta ask twice," he laughed as he easily undid his belt and maneuvered out of his jeans. Then he pulled my purple comforter over us as I slid my black leggings down.

"I think I like this side of you," he said as he playfully flipped me onto my back. Then he reached down and grabbed a condom out of his bag which was on the floor beside the bed.

"Here, let me," I said as I took it from him, tearing open the wrapper and quickly rolling it on. Then, not wanting to waste even a second, I did something I'd never done before - I squirmed out from under him and climbed on top. This is strange, I thought, as I reached down and guided him inside me. Strange that in all our time together I'd never taken the lead until I was fueled by guilt. All I knew was that I liked it, though I didn't know if it was the way Jackson moved his hips or the way he was looking at me with a slightly dazed expression. Afterward, I lay next to him, my heavy breathing matching his own, and stared up at the ceiling.

"Holy shit, Leah," Jackson said, breaking the silence, "that was seriously *hot*." He turned to me and joked, "How much did you drink tonight?"

"I'm completely sober," I said, forcing a smile. It was the truth, too. Nearly getting caught has a way of killing a buzz. "I guess I just really missed you."

There was a knock and then we heard Molly's unmistakable voice.

"Sorry, guys," she said from the other side of the double-locked door, "Time's up; gotta get some sleep!"

Jackson and I quickly scrambled into our clothes, then I jumped up to let her in.

She strolled in wearing her trademark fluffy melon-colored robe and matching slippers.

"Hey there, sexy mama," Jackson teased when her saw her attire.

"You know it, Jackson," she shot back, laughing as she pulled down the blankets and climbed into her bed. "You guys going to sleep soon? 'Cause I'm beat."

"*You're* beat? Hell, try sittin' in bumper-to-bumper traffic for nearly three hours!"

"Oh yeah, that must've sucked," Molly agreed, then without another word, she yawned and turned over.

I climbed back into bed with Jackson, then reached over and turned out the light. Within minutes Molly was snoring lightly and Jackson had me tucked snugly next to him.

"Man, I missed you so friggin' much," he whispered as he pulled me closer. "Can't wait 'til this semester's over."

I didn't answer, just nodded in the dark as I stared up at the ceiling and wondered who it was that I'd *really* just had sex with.

▲   ▲   ▲

The next morning, I was careful not to wake Jackson as I slipped out of bed and grabbed a towel and some sweats. It was still early for a Saturday, and as I headed down the hall I prayed I wouldn't run into anyone I knew because the last thing I felt like doing was making small talk. Thankfully, the bathroom was empty, and I was able to undress in peace. Once inside the stall I pulled the curtain closed and turned the faucet on full blast, then let out a long sigh. I felt as though I had been holding my breath all night. I stood there for a moment, just letting the steady stream of warm water caress my body, hoping it would wash away the guilt and tension. It didn't work, and with another sigh I picked up the shampoo bottle.

As I worked my hair into a lather, I tried to make sense of what'd happened. I had a boyfriend who I was crazy about, right? I had no excuse for what happened with Chase, other than a temporary lapse in judgment fueled by way too much beer. I was sorry it happened but I certainly couldn't undo it. Telling Jackson didn't make sense; I'd be hurting him over something that meant nothing, just to ease my own guilt. Sheesh, it was only one kiss anyway; it's not like I'd gone and slept with him or anything.

By the time I'd rinsed my hair I had convinced myself that the incident would end up being nothing more than a blip on my radar and was best forgotten.

When I got back to the room Jackson was sitting at the edge of my unmade bed, guitar in hand. He had on the same jeans he'd worn the night before and a navy-blue hoodie that was zipped only halfway. He didn't even have a shirt on underneath and on closer inspection I noticed that one foot was bare. For some reason the fact that he only had one sock on bothered me. *Who walks around with one sock?* Jackson, that's who.

"Hey, Lee," he said, not looking up, "listen to this new tune I'm working on. Molly thinks it's pretty cool."

"Yeah, Leah, you gotta hear it. It's really awesome," Molly agreed.

I pulled my gaze from Jackson's feet just as he looked up.

"Listen," he said again as he finger-combed his hair out of his eyes. Then he began to play. Listening to him quietly strum the intricate chords reminded me of just how good he really was. I listened intently until he brought the new piece to a close and decided that it was easily his best yet.

When he looked up at me, I moved closer to him and lightly touched his face, suddenly feeling bad for scrutinizing him so closely.

"That was great, Jackson," I said, nodding, "really great."

He gave me a satisfied smile as he put his guitar aside and stood. "I'm gonna hit the shower and then how 'bout I take you two ladies out to breakfast? The diner in town? You guys must be sick of the cafeteria by now, right?"

"Sounds like a good deal to me," Molly announced, always eager for a trip into town.

"Sure, Jackson. That'd be great," I said.

"Okay, ready in ten," Jackson said as he grabbed his bag and headed for the shower, one foot still bare.

▲ ▲ ▲

I knew I'd eventually have to face Chase but I was hoping it would be after Jackson had left. That Saturday, I grew eyes on the back of my head, looking every which way as Jackson and I searched the campus bookstore for a textbook I needed and went to a local pizza place for a couple of slices. When we got back to my dorm that night without any sightings, I had begun to think I was home free. Unfortunately, fate had other plans.

When we woke up on Sunday, Jackson and I decided to take an early morning hike, which turned out to be a late morning hike by the time the two of us got ready. There were a lot of cool trails on the outskirts of the campus and I'd been wanting to check them out for a while. Plus, I figured it would get me out of Chase territory for a few hours. We followed the winding paths, holding hands and enjoying the time alone, something that, given my living situation, was all too rare.

On our way back, we took a different route, one I had suggested because it appeared to be easier terrain. It wasn't until we were approaching the outdoor track and field area that I realized my mistake. The lacrosse team had apparently just finished practice and was walking off the field. Even if I hadn't seen the equipment they were carrying or their uniforms, I would have known Chase's tall, handsome figure and confident stride anywhere. *Shit.* Jackson and I went on holding hands, and I nonchalantly slowed my pace, hoping they would be gone by the time we approached. Ironically, it resulted in our crossing paths with the tail end of the team. By that time, I didn't see Chase anywhere and figured he was already gone.

"So, when do you think you'll be up again?" I asked Jackson.

He was about to answer when I heard a familiar voice call out my name.

When I turned I saw Brent waving. I gave a half-hearted wave back, hoping that would be the end of it, but then he began to slow-jog towards us.

"Missed you guys at Dylan's last night - what gives?" He laughed, leading me to believe that Chase hadn't mentioned anything to him about Friday. Dylan Stuart was a senior with an off-campus house he shared with a few other guys and everyone knew they threw the best parties around. I'd known about the party but not wanting to tempt fate I hadn't mentioned it to Jackson.

"Next time," Jackson laughed, "I had a bitch of a time getting up here Friday night and we just wanted to hang, right, Lee?" He slipped his arm around my shoulder and pulled me closer.

"Yeah, just wanted to hang," I agreed, hoping to make a quick exit. Unfortunately, Jackson had other ideas, because he started asking Brent about the lacrosse team. *Since when is he interested in lacrosse?*

"Well," I said as soon as there was a lull in the conversation, "we were about to -"

"Hey," Brent called out over my shoulder, "look who I ran into?"

I knew even before I turned around who it was. Sure enough, it was Chase, and though he was a good thirty feet away I could still tell from his posture that the last thing he wanted to do was come over. Then again, to not come over would make things look even stranger, especially if Brent really didn't know what was going on. I felt my stomach clench as I saw him reluctantly head toward us.

"Hey," he said in a normal tone. He even managed a smile, and I wondered if he was as uncomfortable as I was.

"Just telling these guys how they missed Dylan's house at its finest," Brent said.

Chase nodded and smiled again, completely at ease. We all chatted for a few minutes and just when I decided he hadn't given the kiss another thought, he abruptly said he had to head out. Just as he had done the other night in the hall, he turned and walked away, leaving a slightly confused-looking Brent trailing after him.

"Those guys seem pretty cool," Jackson commented as we continued toward the main campus.

"I guess," I shrugged noncommittally.

"Hey, I have some pretty big news," he announced as he grabbed my hand.

"Oh, what's that?" I asked, glad the subject had changed.

"I sent a few demos out," he told me proudly, "and I connected with some guys online who were interested in maybe working together."

"Oh my gosh, Jackson, that's great news!" I exclaimed, then swatted him playfully on the arm, "I can't believe you're just telling me this now."

"Waitin' for the right time, I guess."

"So, where're they from?"

"Brooklyn," he answered. "You know I wouldn't bother reaching out unless they were local."

I squeezed his hand and nodded. Jackson had told me more than once that he wouldn't get involved with musicians who were too far away. Our relationship was his first priority and he wasn't going to start flying across the country – or out of the country for that matter – until I was out of school and could go with him.

"Jackson, you shouldn't limit yourself like that. You might miss out on a fantastic opportunity. And who knows, this could end up being your big shot at Rock Stardom or -"

He spun me around and smothered the rest of my sentence with a kiss. "Stop," he said when he had pulled back. "You know how important you are to me; I can wait. And besides, you know how I feel about 'Rock Stardom,' as you put it."

I laughed when he emphasized *Rock Stardom* with air quotes. It had become something of a running joke between us.

"You know it's not about the fame, it's about the music," he explained even though I'd heard it many times before. "It's the music that I love and to be able to play *my* music for people who love it as much as I do, *that's* the dream. Hell, I don't care if I'm playing in front of three people or three thousand people - if they love it, I'm happy.

"Okay, but I still think it'd be much cooler to be able to introduce you as *my boyfriend the rock star* than *my boyfriend the guy who plays music to crowds in the single digits.*"

"C'mere," he said as he swung me around and kissed me again. "You know I'd be happy just playing for you, right?"

When I looked up into those beautiful green eyes another wave of guilt washed over me. I loved Jackson so much; how could I have let Chase kiss me?

"What about Blow Torch?" I asked because I had to switch the direction my thoughts had suddenly taken. "Are you still playing with them?"

"Yeah, but that's just for fun," he explained. "Those guys are a blast but it's just a side gig for them, not a career. I think I'm outgrowing them anyway. They're happy being a cover band which is cool but I want to do my own shit too."

"Well, your stuff is great. I love it, and I'm sure those Brooklyn hipsters will love it too."

▲　▲　▲

When we got back to my room Molly was hunched over her laptop, frantically working on an assignment due Monday. She was *under the wire*, she said. Considering how she was always scrambling to get her work done, the phrase had become something of a mantra.

"I should probably head out," Jackson said reluctantly as he pulled me into his arms and kissed me.

Molly tossed a good natured "*Get a room*" over her shoulder.

"Uh, we'd have one if you weren't always playing super student, Moll," Jackson quipped.

"Roommates suck, right Leah?" Molly said without moving her eyes from her computer screen.

I ignored her and sat on my bed while Jackson packed up his stuff.

"Think I'm ready," he said a few minutes later. "Walk me out?"

"Yep." I reached for his guitar and handed it to him.

"Don't get up, Molly," Jackson teased but Molly just waived over her shoulder, too engrossed in what she was working on.

Once we got out to Jackson's car he tossed his bag and guitar in the backseat. Then after another passionate embrace with several *I love yous* peppered in between, he was on his way back home.

▲   ▲   ▲

The following week was busier than usual; it was like all my professors had gotten together and decided to assign twice the work. As I ran from my dorm to class, from class to the library, and back again, I remained on high alert, knowing that any minute I might run into Chase. I hadn't seen hide nor hair of him since the brief encounter by the lacrosse field on Sunday. The fact that he hadn't sought me out led me to believe that he felt as I did - that what'd happened in the hallway was just one of those stupid things that happens in college when you've had too much to drink. Something you probably end up laughing about one day.

When Friday night rolled around Molly of course was ready to cut loose and made plans for us to go to a party she'd heard the wrestling team was throwing. Jackson would be a no-show this weekend, as he was driving to Brooklyn to meet up with that musician he'd connected with. If things went well he'd jam with the rest of the band on Saturday. It was all he could talk about on the phone and I had my fingers crossed that things would work out for him.

"Sure, sounds like fun," I told Molly when she brought up the party.

We arrived later than usual, and the party was already in full swing. Molly got us drinks and since it wasn't too cold we hung out for a while in the backyard where they had a firepit going.

An hour later, Molly and I were hanging with a group she knew from last semester when I spied Chase and Brent on the porch. They didn't see us right away and without even realizing it, I found myself discretely watching them. A group of girls had just approached them when Molly's hand suddenly shot up and vigorously waved them over. I had to give it to Molly – she had the uncanny ability to sense female competition and immediately squash it. Brent and Chase must not have been interested in the girls because they came right over and joined our group. At first I felt funny, like I didn't know how to act around Chase. It didn't help any that he wasn't saying much, preferring to let Brent do most of the talking.

The more we drank, the more the ice between us melted, and by the time the party was over things seemed to be back to normal. I was glad he never mentioned "the incident," as I had come to think of it. At this point I didn't know why I was even referring to it that way. Naked ping pong, three-ways, sex in public places – now, those things were incidents. A ten-second kiss in a dorm hallway hardly qualified.

On our way out Brent suggested we go back to their place and hang out for a while since it wasn't too late. Molly quickly agreed, then rolled her eyes when she saw I was on the fence.

"C'mon, Leah," she coaxed as she took hold of my arm.

Realizing how ridiculous I was being, I silently vowed to forget about the *non-incident* once and for all, since I was sure that was exactly what Chase had done. I nodded at Molly, and we made the short walk back to the house the guys shared with a bunch of other lacrosse players.

I had never been to their house before, and I was impressed by what I found. It was big, for one, and well-maintained on the outside, and surprisingly clean and tidy on the inside. Nothing like the typical sports team party house I was used to seeing.

While the three of them were rummaging through the kitchen for more booze and something to eat, I went into the huge living-slash-dining-room and began thumbing through a pile of DVDs.

"Hey, Leah," Molly called out, "you've got to see the rest of the house – it's huge!" She paused, then I heard her say something to Chase about a "grand tour."

I inwardly groaned; although things seemed cool between us, I wasn't anxious to be alone with him again. "Oh, that's okay -" I began, but Chase was already standing in front of me.

"C'mon, I'll show you around."

I nodded, knowing that if I said no I would either look rude, or worse, nervous around him.

He showed me the rest of the first floor, including two large bedrooms and bathrooms.

"Wow, this is really nice," I commented.

"Yeah, not bad, right?"

He started up the stairway and when we reached the top he pointed out the four other bedrooms, along with the master bath.

"My room actually has a balcony, wanna see it?"

"Um, okay," I said, then followed behind him.

He opened the bedroom door and led me into the darkened room. A second later I heard a click as he turned on one of the lamps. The room was huge – easily twice the size of my room back home – and much neater. Then he pulled back the blinds, revealing a small deck that looked out into the backyard.

"Wow, this is unbelievable," I exclaimed. "I don't know how I'm going to go back to living in my two-by-four dorm room after seeing how the other half lives."

He laughed and opened the sliders to the deck.

We stepped outside to admire the view of the backyard, but I kept finding myself glancing to my right and admiring the view beside me. I knew I shouldn't have been, but he was just so damn good-looking.

A cold wind was starting to blow and I involuntarily shivered and rubbed my palms together.

"Cold?" he asked.

"Little bit," I said as I nodded. He stepped behind me and began rubbing his hands up and down my arms in an exaggerated motion.

I laughed, and he wrapped both his arms around my neck and pulled me back against him.

"Warmed up yet?" he teased.

"Yes, I think I'm good," I giggled nervously. I was enjoying having his hands on me way too much. "We should get going."

"Okay," he said, and to my disappointment immediately dropped his hands. "Let's get back to the party."

I reluctantly followed him back through the bedroom, my eyes darting this way and that, and I realized I was curious about him. We were almost to the door when I noticed several pictures on his dresser. Most were of his family – Chase and his parents at high school graduation; he and his two brothers – each one hotter than the next - at a lake; and one of him and girl, probably his sister, sitting in front of a campfire. Then I noticed the picture of the whole lacrosse team. They had their uniform jerseys on and were carrying their sticks, but oddly, they were all wearing colorful Bermuda shorts.

"Hey, what's up with this?" I giggled again as I picked up the picture. "Was it taken at a tournament in the Caribbean or something?"

He walked back to me and took the photo from my hand. "Na, we were just goofing around when we were down in Orlando for training." He laughed at the memory. "Fun day."

"Yeah, looks like it!"

When he went to put the picture back on the dresser, his hand brushed mine and I felt an instant shiver bolt up my arm. I felt his gaze on me and knew he'd felt it too.

He moved a bit closer. "You ever been to Orlando?"

"Oh yeah, Disney, of course; a few summers ago with my family," I replied in what I hoped was a nonchalant tone. "The heat was a killer, though."

"Yeah, it gets hot down there in the summer," he agreed and added, "but it gets hot here too... right?"

I just nodded and swallowed the nervous lump forming in my throat.

He reached over and pushed my hair back over my ears on both sides, then ran his hands around the back of my neck. "I bet you pull your hair back when it's really hot, right? Like this?" he asked as he gathered my long hair into one hand and held it as it hung down the front of my sweatshirt.

"Uh huh," I whispered nervously.

He moved in closer and lowered his head and I knew he was going to kiss me. I also knew that I wasn't going to stop him.

He hesitated, giving me every opportunity to put on the brakes, but in that moment, every bit of common sense seemed to fly right out the window. Suddenly, all I could think about was the brief kiss we'd shared the week before and how I wanted nothing more than to experience it again.

He let go of my hair and brought his hands up so they were on either side of my face, then he leaned in and kissed me. It was gentle at first, then, when he was sure I wasn't going to push him away he began to kiss me more urgently. Before I knew it, we were feverishly making out, and not ten feet away from his bed.

He reached around and pulled me closer so that I was nearly pressed up against him. I knew this was wrong on so many levels but I still didn't stop him. Moments later he began to slowly slip his hands under my sweatshirt and slide them up my back. As soon as I felt his warm hands make contact with my bare skin bright red flags immediately shot up – *and I immediately shot them right back down.* Instead I ran my hands up under the front of his t-shirt, reveling in the delicious feel of his smooth hard chest beneath my palms. I couldn't stop my hands from roaming, it was like they had a mind of their own. It wasn't long before he moved in even closer so that there was no room between us at all and I could easily feel him right through his jeans. That's when I knew I had to stop before I did something I knew I would regret.

"Chase," I whispered breathlessly as he continued to kiss me.

"Leah, don't. Please don't tell me to stop," he whispered back as he pressed harder against me.

"No . . . Chase we . . . we have to. We . . . have to stop. I can't. I . . . I, I can't do this." I finally pulled away. "I'm sorry," I gasped, "I, I have to go."

He stepped back, equally breathless, and I hurried past him and back down the stairs.

Molly and Brent were eating in the kitchen when I got downstairs and I poked my head in and as casually as I could said, "Ready to head out, Molly?"

"Where've you been?" she asked with a mouthful of Doritos.

"Waiting for you," I lied, and fortunately she seemed to buy it.

I waited a few minutes for her but Chase never came back downstairs. I didn't blame him, either; it was the second time I'd pushed him away. Molly finally emerged from the kitchen and then the two of us headed for home.

"What's with you?" she asked after I'd been quiet for two blocks.

"What – me? Nothing?"

"That's bull, Leah. You've been acting weird all night." She gave me a knowing look. "I know you miss Jackson, but you have to learn to enjoy yourself even when he's not around."

I nodded. "I know..."

Oh, Molly, if you only knew the half of it.

▲   ▲   ▲

When I woke the next morning, I could tell it was late – probably after ten, judging from the way the light was streaming in through the blinds. Damn, I haven't slept this late in months, I thought as I reached my hands above my head. Halfway through my stretch, the events of the night before flashed through my mind. What was I thinking making out with Chase like that? And in his *bedroom* of all places! I could *not* let that happen again – *ever*!

I heard the door open and propped myself up on my elbows.

"Hey, you're up," Molly said as she moved across to her side of the room then added with a giggle, "You were like comatose when I left."

"Just really tired, that's all." I didn't bother to mention that before falling into my "coma" I had tossed and turned for nearly an hour.

She sat down on her bed and began running a brush through her tangled curls. "So, what happened last night? That tour Chase gave you took an awful long time. What gives?"

I shrugged, "Nothing, he was just showing me around, that's all."

". . . around his *bedroom*?" she teased.

"Jeez, Molly," I said as I pulled myself into a sitting position, "he just showed me the second floor and yeah, there were bedrooms up there but that doesn't mean anything happened. Chase and I are just friends, and besides, I *do* have a boyfriend, remember? So why don't you lay the fuck off with you little innuendos because they're really starting to piss me off." I glared at her with my arms crossed, almost daring her to say something else. Instead, she just gaped at me in shock.

Neither of us said anything for a moment . . . and then I caved. I felt my eyes begin to mist over and immediately brought my hands up to cover them, but not before a small sob escaped.

In two second, Molly had jumped up and crossed the room to my bed. "Leah, what's wrong?" she asked as she pulled me into a hug.

When I didn't answer, she asked again, this time more urgently. "What's wrong? *Did* something happen last night? Did Chase do something?" She pulled back from the hug and looked at me. "Oh my gosh, Leah, did he hurt you? That bastard! I'll kick his ass myself if he did!"

I just shook my head, my palms now pressed against my eyes.

When I finally felt composed enough to uncover my eyes, I found Molly staring at me with that dog-with-a-bone expression she got whenever she refused to let something go. "Listen, Leah, we can sit here all day if you want, but I'm not moving until you tell me what the heck is wrong. Is it *Jackson*? Did Jackson do something?"

At the mere mention of Jackson's name my sobs came quicker, but I managed to shake my head again. Eventually I calmed, but I knew I had no choice other than to open up the bag and let the cat leap out.

I started slowly, telling her only about the first kiss the week before.

"Is *that* what's got you so upset?" she interrupted. Clearly, she didn't think it was a big deal because *clearly* I hadn't told her the whole story. "One kiss isn't a big deal, Leah. You both had a lot to drink and it just happened, no biggie."

She stood and continued detangling her hair. "See, problem solved. Just forget it even happened. I'm sure Chase has."

When I didn't respond, she turned to me and repeated, "So, problem solved, right?"

"Well . . . not really."

"Leah, are you telling me the whole story?" she questioned, and I knew she could tell by my expression that there was more to it. "Spill it, Leah. We've known each other since we were kids and I *know* when you're holding back so go ahead, spit it out."

I proceeded to tell her about the second time he kissed me.

"I *knew* it. I knew that tour took way too long," she said, shaking her head. "Man, he actually had the nerve to try and manhandle you again after you pushed him away the week before. He's got some nerve!"

She plopped down into her desk chair, looking annoyed as she began rummaging through the desk drawer for her stash of candy. She pulled out a bag of Twizzlers but suddenly froze. She looked over at me and squinted slightly and I could almost see the lightbulb forming over her head. She tossed the Twizzlers back in the drawer.

"Unless . . ." she trailed off and then shot me a suspicious look. "Leah, did you *let* him kiss you? Oh my gosh, did you actually kiss him *back*? You *did*, didn't you?" She threw her hands up. "Holy *shit* Leah, this is *huge*!"

"Yeah, a huge *mistake*," I conceded. "I feel so guilty about it. Jackson can never find out – no way – he'd flip if he did."

"Okay, so this sheds a whole new light on the situation." She thought a minute. "Do you think this thing with Chase is something you might want to . . . to," she searched for the right word, "*explore*?"

Molly lived for this kind of drama.

"It wouldn't be fair to Jackson to go *exploring* behind his back and I don't even think I want to anyway. I just got carried away, that's all. It was a mistake."

Molly gave me a pointed look. "One time and it's a mistake; twice is . . . well, I don't know but I'd say twice means it isn't so black and white anymore."

"I need to talk to him, to Chase, I mean. Tell him this can't go on. I can't risk ruining what I have with Jackson, I just can't."

"Okay, if that's what you want to do then do it. And don't worry about Jackson, Leah; I totally got your back. He won't find out."

I nodded in agreement and decided that the next time I saw Chase I would tell him we could never be anything more than friends.

Ʌ　　Ʌ　　Ʌ

Telling Molly about what'd happened with Chase had put it into perspective. *I had really messed up.* I had to nip it in the bud, and I wasn't going to wait until I ran into him the following weekend to do it. I knew he had lacrosse practice every afternoon so the next day I went to the field and waited in the bleachers until I saw the players leaving the field. To say he was surprised to see me would be an understatement.

"You got a minute?" I asked, and although he said *sure* and that he'd meet me out front as soon as he changed, I couldn't tell whether he was happy about it or not.

I waited nervously, going over and over in my mind what I was going to say to him. My worst fear was that he would say I was making something out of nothing, like guys sometimes do when they don't want to deal with that "girl drama."

"Hey," he said when he emerged from the locker room, "What's up?"

"Listen," I began right away, sounding almost rushed, "I wanted to talk to you about the other night, what happened . . . you know, in your room."

"Leah," he cut me off, putting his hand up. "I'm really sorry about that. I totally misread you, I thought you were into it. My mistake, I swear it won't happen again." Then he smiled that mega-wide thousand-watt smile and said, "Friends though, right?"

I was so relieved that he'd made it easy for me. "Yeah, friends, definitely, Chase."

"Cool. Well, I gotta head out. There's a captains' meeting starting at four-thirty. I'll see you around, maybe this weekend."

"Yeah, this weekend."

I watched him walk away, then headed to the cafeteria where I was meeting Molly.

"So, how'd it go with Chase?" she asked eagerly as she bit into her grilled chicken sandwich. I hadn't even put my tray of food down and the questions had already begun.

I purposely took my time sitting down. "Do I start with the salad or the turkey-cheddar wrap?"

"Come on, what happened?" she practically begged.

"Nothing really," I began as I speared a tomato wedge. "He apologized, said he misread me and that it wouldn't happen again. That's all."

"That's it?" She sounded disappointed. "Oh jeez, what a letdown. I was hoping maybe he'd pledge his undying love for you or something equally as exciting."

"Sorry to disappoint," I said as I grabbed another forkful of salad.

I thought for a minute. "Molly, you do realize that Jackson can never find out about this, right? I know how you feel about me and him so you better not go 'accidentally' blurting it out when he's here."

"What do you take me for, Leah?" she said, sounding genuinely wounded. "I would never do that to you." She paused for another bite. "I may have been a little annoyed, okay maybe a lot annoyed, with how things went down when we first got here, but honestly Jackson's kind of grown on me."

For the second time in an hour, I smiled with relief. Although I didn't think she would've actually said anything to Jackson, well, let's just say some things needed to be said to Molly outright.

"Actually, when I look back it really worked out for me. You spending so much time with Jackson at the beginning of our first semester forced me to get out there and meet new people - it was either that or sit around the dorm every Saturday night." Molly sat back in her chair. "Hey, I just thought of something. If it wasn't for you spending so much time with Jackson, I never would've met Brent and that means *you* would've never met Chase. So, if you think about it, this whole thing is actually Jackson's fault anyway."

I rolled my eyes at her. Molly's logic was obviously warped, but it was logic nonetheless. Better still, it was logic that suited me.

CHAPTER 25 - JACKSON

If this wasn't the best weekend of my entire life, well, I don't know what would top it. On Friday night I drove over to Brooklyn and met Matt at some hipster place in Bushwick. At first I didn't know what to make of him - tall and wiry with shoulder-length blonde hair and blue eyes that peered out from behind a pair of wire-rimmed John Lennon glasses. Not at all what I was expecting, but we hit it off immediately. He told me that he did most of the vocals and played bass guitar and had originally formed the band with some guy named Damian, who played lead. Damian was the one who'd decided to part ways with the band and go solo, but he'd left on good terms and they still kept in touch.

After a couple of beers Matt and I walked around the corner to the garage where the band practiced. He played me some of their music and it was right in line with the stuff I wrote which, by the way, he really dug. He invited me back to meet the rest of the band on Saturday and we jammed all night – it was a blast.

Their talent was immediately obvious. Skid was an awesome drummer, probably one of the best I'd ever met. He was a tall skinny guy with dark hair pulled back into a ponytail that hung down his back and a sleeve of colorful tattoos down his left arm. He didn't say much, but his playing spoke for itself.

Then there was *Jayne*. I was thrown a bit when I met her because I had just assumed that the band was made up of all dudes. No big deal, it was just odd at first because I'd only ever jammed with guys before. Jayne was about five-five or so, with jet-black hair that was twisted into a knot on top of her head. Several piercings lined each ear and her deep-set pale blue eyes were heavily rimmed with dark makeup. She played keyboard but was pretty decent on the guitar too. Like Skid, Jayne didn't have much to say; in fact, she scrutinized me with an almost pissed off expression on her face and I wasn't sure if she had a problem with me personally or there was something else at play. Whatever the case, she did begin to warm up after we began to jam and by the time I left I felt I'd made a pretty good connection with all three of them.

This crew was certainly an odd-looking mix and at first glance you'd never guess they would jive as well as they did. Then again, who was I to judge? As long as they synced up musically, it didn't really matter what they looked like. Matt seemed to be the primary songwriter, but said he often collaborated with Jayne when he needed a fresh perspective. At first I assumed they were a couple, but then Matt took a call from some girl he was seeing, so clearly that wasn't the case.

I thought for sure we were on the same page until I was leaving late Saturday night. "Hey man," Matt said as he reached for my hand, "this was great."

"Yeah," I agreed, "Haven't had this much fun jammin' in a long time."

"Okay, so I have a few more guys I'm meeting with and then I'll be in touch when we decide which direction we're gonna go in."

It was as if all the air had gone out of me. I was so sure it was a done deal!

"Yeah," I replied in what I hoped was a nonchalant way, "sounds good; talk to you soon."

As I slid my car onto the expressway, I thought about calling Leah but decided it was too late. *Who was I kidding?* If I'd gotten a definite offer from Matt I would have called her no matter what time it was. Waking her up to say they would *be in touch* was ridiculous.

I got back to Beth and Brody's place around two a.m. and quietly crept in through the back door. I'd been crashing on their couch since the run-in with my dad the week before but I'd probably about worn out my welcome by now and knew I'd have to return home sooner rather than later.

As predicted, when I told Beth about the stuff I'd found in his room and how pissed I was that he'd kept it from me, she just shrugged it off.

"Jackson, does anything he's done surprise you anymore? You need to put this all behind you because at this point it doesn't make a bit of difference. Mom's gone and as much as I miss her, I can't dwell on the past. And you shouldn't either."

I knew she was right, she always was, but *putting it behind me* wasn't nearly as easy as it seemed to be for her.

CHAPTER 26 - LEAH

I looked up from my Western Civ book at Molly's pleading face. She'd been driving me crazy to go with her to the lacrosse game that afternoon and wouldn't take no for an answer. I slowly shook my head. Who was she kidding? Molly was about as interested in lacrosse as she was in watching paint dry.

"Molly, you've been in the friend zone for months now," I said, "What makes you think anything'll change at this point?"

"I felt a vibe last time we were together," she replied in a low voice, even though we were alone. "I think he's close to making a move."

Poor Molly. Unfortunately, the latest object of her affection – Brent – seemed completely indifferent to her.

"I don't know..." I said, half-heartedly gesturing to my book. The truth was I didn't have that much schoolwork to do; I just wasn't anxious to be in close proximity to Chase so soon after our little talk. I was finally getting to the point where I could talk on the phone to Jackson without feeling guilty. Though he'd tried to sound upbeat, I knew he was disappointed with how things had gone down in Brooklyn and I was determined to make this weekend fun for him.

An hour later, Molly and I were sitting on the sidelines of the lacrosse field. The game turned out to be more exciting than I expected, not that I was paying all that much attention. My eyes kept flicking over to Chase, how quickly he ran, the occasional glimpse of a bulging quad muscle. There was no denying he was a phenomenal athlete. *Among other things*, I thought as I felt the heat rush to my face.

After the game, I waited while Molly went down to the field to talk to Brent. I noticed that there were several girls hanging around waiting to see the players – lacrosse groupies? On closer inspection, though, it was apparent that they weren't *lacrosse* groupies, they were *Chase* groupies. Well, at least two of them, anyway, because I saw them rush over to him as soon as he came off the field.

Dodged a bullet there, I told myself. No way was I going to be competing with some hoard of girls.

I stood there a few more minutes, but when it looked like Molly wasn't returning I decided to go down and move her along. That's when I heard a familiar voice call my name.

I turned my head and sure enough, there was Chase, waving over at me. He said something to his admirers, then started walking towards me, leaving the girls staring after him with identical annoyed expressions.

I waved back but kept my expression neutral so he wouldn't notice my nervousness.

"Hey, you finally made it to a game," he said excitedly when he reached me. "What'd you think?"

"Oh, you guys were great!"

A proud grin split his face, making him look even more handsome. "Yeah, we're looking to take the conference title this year."

"Oh, cool."

"Hey, I gotta change and shower, but why don't you guys come over? We'll order a couple pies or something." As soon as he saw my expression he put his hands up in mock surrender and chuckled. "Just as friends, I swear."

I laughed. "Sure, that'd be fun."

Molly and I stopped at the dorm so she could primp, then headed over to their place. The way Chase made it sound, it was just going to be the four of us, so I was surprised to find their dining room overflowing with people. More were gathered in the kitchen, around the two large kegs or grabbing pizza from several boxes on the table. I looked over at Molly to see whether she had known it was going to be a full-fledged party and judging from the annoyed look on her face she definitely did not.

Several lacrosse players, including Chase, were sitting on the various couches and chairs in the living room. He waved me over and told me to have a seat on the arm of the recliner he was sitting on. Molly slid into the kitchen and since she didn't return, I assumed that's where she found Brent.

Someone popped in a DVD – some movie I'd never seen before because I'd always thought it looked stupid. Everyone else seemed to know it – they were reciting all the lines – and I found myself laughing right along with them. About halfway through Chase got up to grab another beer, and I slid off the arm and onto the chair. When he came back I went to stand but before I could, he squeezed in next to me. We stayed that way for a few minutes until he sort of wedged himself under me, and before I knew it I was comfortably nestled on his lap.

We stayed that way the rest of the night and I convinced myself that I wasn't doing anything wrong since we *were* just friends. He even introduced me to several of his teammates as his "buddy" Leah, which I conveniently took as confirmation.

Molly did a double-take when she finally came out of the kitchen and saw where I was perched. The movie had just ended and everyone was starting to leave.

"Ready?" Molly asked as she approached, eyeing me suspiciously.

"You guys cutting out?" Chase asked. He sounded disappointed.

"Yeah, we should get going, early class tomorrow," I said as I stood.

"Alright, see ya around . . . *buddy*," Chase said as he wrapped his arm around my shoulders and gave an exaggerated squeeze.

When we got outside Molly turned to me. "What was that all about?"

"What was what all about?"

"Leah, you were sitting on his *lap*. I thought you guys were just friends."

"We *are* just friends Molly," I huffed, "It's not that big a deal."

"You're kidding, right?" she challenged. "It was - what - only two days ago that you were bawling your eyes out because he kissed you. Remember, you were in a panic that Jackson would find out? That *is* what happened, right? Or am I crazy?"

"Molly, you're making way too much of this. Yes, I was upset about the kiss but this is totally different. I told you, we talked it out and both agreed to just be friends – notice how he used the word *buddy* when he introduced me?"

"Okay," she shrugged, "If you say so. Hey, who am I to judge, anyway? If you say you're just friends then I guess you're just friends."

We walked along in silence for a few minutes, then she mused, "Hey, I wonder if Jackson gets cozy with girls on *his* lap – you know, girls who are *just friends* I mean."

"Lay off, Molly, that's *not* the same thing and you know it."

"Are you serious, Leah?" She laughed. "How is it not the same thing?"

"Because *I'm* the one doing the sitting and I *know* it's totally innocent. If some girl were sitting on *his* lap, *she'd* most likely have ulterior motives."

She stopped and turned to me and another laughed escaped her. "Leah, that's the most ridiculous thing I've ever heard. It doesn't even make sense!"

"Molly, just mind your own business."

She didn't say another word about it, just put her hands up as if to say *whatever*.

▲　　▲　　▲

Thursday after class I stopped by the library to do some research for the Economics paper I'd been putting off. I set up my laptop and grabbed a few reference books, hoping I'd be able to stay awake long enough to get some work done. Econ had to be the most boring class I'd ever taken. About thirty minutes later, I felt someone standing beside me and looked up.

"Hey, bud," Chase said as he placed his backpack on the floor next to the table and sat down. "Whatcha working on?"

"Economics paper. Due Monday. You?"

"Nothing, I was returning some books and saw you. Figured I'd come over and say hi." He reached over and slid one of the textbooks closer. "Hey, what's your major anyway? Don't think I've ever asked you."

"I'm undeclared," I told him, "But thinking about going pre-law."

"Hey, I'm pre-law. My dad's an attorney and so are my brothers. My dad and my oldest brother practice corporate law for the same firm back in Ohio where I'm from. The other's a public defender." He leaned over and whispered, "He's the black sheep of the family."

I nodded. "My dad's a lawyer too - real estate - and he's been pushing me towards law since I was a kid. I told him I'd think about it, maybe take a few law courses, then make my decision."

"And are you close to deciding?"

I shrugged. "Ask me again at the end of the semester; maybe I'll know by then."

Chase laughed at my obvious lack of enthusiasm. "I'll make sure to do that." He slid the textbook back to me. "Hey, what about your boyfriend? He go to school in the area?"

Before I could answer he tapped his palm to his forehead and said, "Stupid question, I guess he must since he's able to visit you so often."

"Actually, Jackson's a musician," I told him.

"Oh cool," he said, sounding genuinely interested. "Is that his major?"

"Um no, I mean he's like an *actual* musician."

"Wow, your mom and dad must be really cool." He laughed and shook his head. "I don't know how my parents would take to my younger sister dating a musician. They're the straight-laced no-nonsense type. Anyway, Jackson seems like a decent guy; your parents must really like him."

I smiled but didn't answer right away. Was it my imagination or was Chase fishing for information? I was still working out my response when Chase said, "That's impressive, though, he must be really good if he makes a living at it."

"Well, he doesn't actually make a living at it yet but he's hoping to someday," I explained, then held in a breath, hoping he wouldn't ask what Jackson actually did to make a living. I dreaded having to say he worked half the year at a dinky ski resort and the other half pruning trees – neither of which was very impressive.

"Oh . . . well, that's cool," he said as he leaned back in his chair. "So, how much longer you going to be working here? Do you want to maybe get something to eat?"

I glanced at the stack of work lying in front of me, then at the handsome lacrosse player sitting across from me and decided it was a no-brainer.

"Sure, sounds good; I'm just about done anyway."

Getting something to eat turned into picking up sandwiches and bringing them back to his place. Then maybe we'd watch a movie afterward - 'cause friends do stuff like that all the time, right?

When we got to his place no one else appeared to be around, a fact that both excited and unnerved me. I spread the food out on the coffee table while Chase went to the kitchen and grabbed us a couple of Cokes.

"Look what I have..." he said as he reached into the cabinet and pulled out a DVD. It was *Forgetting Sarah Marshall.*

"Uh, never saw it," I admitted sheepishly.

"Get out of here! Oh, you gotta see this." He popped in the movie, then proceeded to narrate all his favorite parts to me as we ate. I don't know what was funnier – the movie or the way Chase imitated Russell Brand's English accent or Kristen Bell's much higher voice. When we finished our sandwiches, he paused the movie for a moment as we gathered up our trash and took it to the kitchen.

When we returned to the living room there was a rather large guy laying across the couch where we'd just been sitting. He was picking through the bag of leftover chips.

"Hey Chet," Chase said as he hopped onto the recliner next to the couch. "Leah, this is Chet, the best lacrosse goalie on the East Coast."

Chet nodded a "what up" at me but seemed more interested in the bag of chips.

"Chet's not a big talker," Chase chuckled as he nonchalantly reached out and grabbed my hand, then pulled me onto his lap as if it was totally natural. He clicked the remote and the movie resumed.

"Shit, this is like the best part," he said, turning up the volume. I laughed along with him as Russell Brand sang and gyrated his hips. The movie really was funny – I couldn't believe I'd never seen it.

"See, he's driving Sarah's ex crazy," Chase said, as he put the remote down on the arm of the chair. Suddenly, I felt the weight of his hand on my thigh. He started telling me some funny trivia about the movie, but I was only half-listening because his hand had started gently kneading my flesh.

This time I couldn't use the *I had too much to drink* excuse because I was stone cold sober and still making no attempt to remove his hand or to get up from his lap. The truth was I *liked* sitting on his lap and *liked* having his hand on my thigh. Was it wrong? *Hell yeah.* Was I stopping him? *Hell no.*

For the rest of the movie, his hand roamed from my thigh to my shoulder, down my arm, across my neck and up my back. I never touched him back, instead preferring to keep my hands folded in my lap and pretend I was paying attention to the movie. What I did see was good, and by the time the credits were rolling I had to agree that it was easily one of the funniest movies I'd ever seen.

"I should probably get going," I said as I made a half-hearted attempt to get up but he pulled me back down.

"But the movie's not over yet. You can't leave 'til you've seen every last credit. I think that's a rule somewhere, right?"

I laughed and said, "Hmm, never heard that one..." but I stayed on his lap a few more minutes. "Okay," I said when the credits had ended, "Now I definitely have to go."

"Okay, but I'll walk you. It's getting late," he said as he got up and grabbed a sweatshirt from the closet.

I could have been imagining it, but it seemed Chase walked slower than usual. I pretended not to notice, just as I pretended not to notice how natural it felt when he grabbed my hand. When we got to the door of my building he let his hand slip from mine.

"Hey this was fun, buddy," he said; then with a smile and a light fist-bump to my shoulder, he abruptly turned and headed back home.

CHAPTER 27 - JACKSON

"Thank God," I breathed as I pulled up to the house and saw my father's car wasn't there. That morning I'd thrown my stuff in my bag and told Beth I'd be heading home after work. She didn't ask me to leave or anything – as a matter of fact she told me I could stay as long as I wanted – but it wasn't fair to keep camping out on her couch. I knew I'd have to face the old man at some point, but I'd been hoping it wouldn't be tonight.

I slid the pizza I'd picked up for dinner in the oven to keep warm while I went up to my room and called Leah. We bullshitted for a while and then she said she had to go, something about finishing up a paper. After I hung up I went back down to the kitchen and began looking through the cabinets for a clean dish and glass. I finally gave up, settling on a paper plate and a bottle of beer.

I was barely through the second slice when I heard the garage door open. Shit. I braced myself for a showdown but when my dad came in he just tossed his keys on the kitchen counter, grunted what I thought was a greeting and went up to his room. Wasn't there long, though, and when he came back down he tossed a large brown envelope onto the kitchen table, then leaned casually back against the counter. I dropped my pizza onto the oil-stained plate, folded my arms across my chest and shot him an annoyed look.

"Another surprise?" I asked snidely.

He let out an annoyed huff. "The stuff you found in my room last week, in the box. We weren't bringing that stuff to California. This," he motioned to the envelope, "is the stuff I brought." He shrugged, "Thought you'd wanna take a look at it."

Was he serious? It was probably the first civil sentence he'd spoken to me in years. I continued to glare at him, refusing to give him the satisfaction of even a simple *thanks*. Inside, though, my mind was in overdrive.

He didn't wait for me to answer before pushing off the counter and going out to the living room. A minute later I heard the television turn on and the sound of the six o'clock news filled the kitchen.

My hunger suddenly forgotten, I reached over and slid the envelope towards me. I pulled off the tape that sealed it and slipped the contents out. It was a stack of about ten to fifteen pages of sheet music, which I quickly began to thumb through. It was much more professional-looking than what I'd found the week before in the shoebox.

I thought about waiting until he left or fell asleep to go play the music, but my curiosity got the better of me. Who cares what he thought anyway? I grabbed the beer and slipped out to the garage, then plugged my spare guitar into the amp and set the sheet music on the stand. Hands shaking slightly with anticipation, I began to play. As I continued through each song I kept waiting to be hit with that *wow* moment, but it never came. Where was the deep grit of the stuff I found in the shoebox?

I set the guitar down and picked up my beer. I found it hard to believe the West Coast had beckoned him after hearing this. Then I began to wonder - *had anyone actually heard it?* The music certainly wasn't *bad* - it had a commercial heavy metal feel to it – but to bank on a future with it seemed incredibly naïve. Then again, this type of music really wasn't my scene so maybe I was judging it too harshly.

Well, that was a letdown, I thought as I packed everything away and returned to the kitchen. Since finding out a few years back about Dad's stint in California I'd always wondered about it, but now I had more questions than before. I sat down and finished my beer before grabbing another slice out of the warm oven. That's when my father returned to the kitchen, grabbed his own beer out of the fridge and sat down across from me.

I eyed him suspiciously. Did he really think we were going to have a beer together and bullshit? After all these years he's going to sit right across from me and expect me to have a conversation with him, like a normal father and son?

He picked at the label for a moment. "Listen . . ." he sighed without meeting my eyes, but then trailed off.

I really didn't know what direction he'd planned to take this little heart-to-heart, but whatever it was I wasn't interested - at least that's what I told myself. I knew I'd sit there, stare him down a bit to show him I didn't give a shit, but in the end, it would all be an act. I'd lap up whatever morsel he threw me, then hate myself for it.

"Last week, you know, when I saw you in my room . . . lookin' through all that shit..." He hesitated as if he didn't know what he was going to say next. "Look, I just think you should know that all the shit with me and your mom and California . . . it, it didn't go down like you think it did."

I looked at him sitting across from me - really looked at him - and for the first time noticed how worn out and defeated he looked. The deep etched lines on his face, the graying hair, the near- permanent dark circles that rimmed his eyes. A better person might've felt sorry for him but I wasn't a better person, not when it came to him.

"I didn't leave her behind..." He shook his head, "...never woulda done that. Was her idea to stay; thought it'd be easier to have the baby here and then meet me out there."

"But she never did," I pointed out "Why not?"

He stood and got himself another beer from the fridge. "I came back instead." When he sat back down, he looked as if he were debating what to say next, but I cut in first.

"Wait a minute," I said, putting up a hand, "Before I hear why you came back I wanna hear what happened while you were there. Did you audition with the stuff you wrote?"

Again, he shook his head. "Never got a chance."

A long moment passed, and just when I was going to tell him to spit it out, he shrugged and said, "It was crazy out there. Things just kept getting screwed up, one thing after another. Then I got home from work one night and there was a message from my brother. He said your mom was in the hospital and she was in bad shape. They didn't know if the baby was gonna make it."

"But in the end, Mom and Beth were fine, right? So why didn't all of you go back?" I began to imagine what life would've been like for me in California.

"Because." He closed his eyes for a few seconds. "Because originally the plan was to put the baby up for adoption but in the end, we changed our minds. Mom was willing to go back once Beth got a little bigger, but I thought it better we stay here, where there was family around to help. It was the right thing to do."

Although shocked by what I'd just heard - that they'd planned to give Beth away - I couldn't help but notice that his voice sounded off when he said that last part. It told me that either he wasn't telling the whole truth or perhaps he was lying altogether. Then again what he said did add up, so maybe it was just my imagination.

"Listen, I know me and you have never really been close. I made a lot of mistakes with your mom and with you kids - especially you - but your mom and me . . ." He sighed. "Our relationship just got real complicated."

"That's bull and you know it," I shot back. *"You're* the one who got complicated, not her. Don't go trying to blame any of it on Mom, cuz it was all you. You're the one who fucked everything up."

When he stood from the table I figured the conversation was just about over. "I'm not gonna argue with you, Jackson, and I sure as hell ain't makin' no excuses for all the shit I done. Things happen in life, things get hard, and sometimes . . .. sometimes it just ain't so black and white anymore."

My father grabbed another beer from the fridge and popped it open. Just as he was about to leave the kitchen, he said, "I'll leave Mom's stuff, the shoebox, in your room. She'd want you to have it."

CHAPTER 28 - LEAH

Friday morning I felt the guilt weighing on me even before I opened my eyes. Kinda like a when you have a really shitty dream and it plagues you all the next day. Unfortunately, the events of the night before had not been scary or terrifying, but quite enjoyable. As I replayed the hours at Chase's house - the lap sitting, the back rubbing, the hand holding – I hardly recognized myself. *It was like watching another girl, the kind who steps out on a perfectly sweet boyfriend, the kind of girl I usually couldn't stand. What was I thinking?* I burrowed deeper under the covers, as if I would find the answer there.

"Leah . . . you up?" I heard Molly's gravely morning voice call from across the room.

I peeked out from beneath my cozy purple comforter. "Yeah, I'm up."

"Breakfast?"

"Ready in ten," I answered on autopilot.

The two of us walked like zombies over to the cafeteria. Me, because I couldn't shake the unease caused by the night before and Molly because she'd worked all day yesterday on her political science paper. When was she going to learn that she had to pace herself and not leave everything until the last minute?

We both got cereal and found a table way in the back.

"I didn't think I'd ever get my paper done," Molly commented as she opened her little carton of milk. "Hey, and I can't believe you were at the library so late. I was starting to wonder if you'd ever get home."

"Mmmm," I replied, suddenly fascinated with the stray Cheerio on my spoon. I'd been as quiet as possible when I came in last night, but apparently she heard me anyway. Molly always knew when I was lying so I thought it best to avoid eye contact and not commit to anything. It didn't occur to me to tell her the truth, probably because I was in no mood to hear her response.

"So, did you finish what you were working on?" she asked as she poured the milk over her Fruit Loops. Was it my imagination, or was she a little bit too curious about my work?

I took a long sip of orange juice and placed the glass down. "Um, not quite . . . I still have a bit more to do." I quickly took another sip of juice.

"Huh, that's funny, I thought the library closed at nine." She kept her eyes on the Fruit Loops. "I guess I must be wrong, though, because you got home way after nine. I think it was closer to eleven when I heard you come in."

Busted.

"Oh yeah, I, um, ran into Chase at the library. We decided to grab something to eat after it closed. No big deal."

"Oh, where did you go? Little late for the cafeteria, unless you guys got takeout." To anyone else, it would seem Molly was being subtle. I knew better.

"Yep, takeout," I confirmed.

". . . and where'd you take it? *His* place?"

I swear that girl should have worked for the FBI.

"Yes, Molly," I said with a frustrated huff, "We took the food back to his place and the reason I didn't tell you is because I knew you'd get all preachy about it."

"*Preachy?!* Why would I get preachy?" I could hear the sarcasm creep into her voice. "It's not my business what you do behind your boyfriend's back."

"How many times do I have to tell you, Molly? Nothing's going on between me and Chase! We're friends, and friends hang out, even grab a bite to eat sometimes. You're reading way too much into this."

Molly shook her head in that I'm-not-buying-your-bullshit way. "You're playing with fire, Leah, and you're going to end up getting burned. All I can say is don't put me in the middle of it."

"Oh, *please*, Molly! How can you be in the middle of something that's not even there? Chill out, will you?"

Funny, usually it was her telling me to chill out. For the second time that morning I wondered who the hell I was turning into.

We both turned back to our cereal, and for the rest of the meal the only sound coming from our table was the clanging of spoon against bowl. Pissed as I was at Molly, I couldn't totally discount what she was saying. My "friendship" with Chase had definitely crossed a few dozen imaginary lines. On the other hand, who was she to judge? I was the one who'd always walked the straight and narrow. Besides, I was perfectly capable of hanging out with Chase – I just had to cut out the handholding. The two of us were just friends – what's the big deal?

It's funny how if you tell yourself something often enough you actually start to believe it's true.

▲　▲　▲

"I can't believe you're going through the trouble of making your bed," Molly said, "It's not like Jackson hasn't seen it *unmade* before."

"Very funny," I said. "Just because he comes up all the time doesn't mean I want him to see the place a mess." I eyed the pile of books and clothes on her bed. "At least, not my side."

Normally, I was pretty neat, but school had been kicking my ass and the week just got away from me. As soon as class got out I'd run home and spent the better part of an hour dusting and folding and throwing things away.

"Well, I don't have time to clean," she quipped, "I'm resting up for the lacrosse game tonight. You know it's one of the last home games of the regular season, and then there's the tailgate..."

"Yes, Molly," I sighed as I hoisted my overflowing laundry bag over my shoulder, "You told me all about it..."

Apparently, after our little tiff at breakfast that morning, Molly had bumped into Brent. He told her about the post-game tailgate in the parking lot afterwards and even invited her to stop by. Of course, that's all

Molly needed to hear. She was *sure* tonight would be the night that he'd make his move.

My phone started buzzing just as I was shoving my laundry bag to the back of the closet. I wasn't surprised when I saw it was Jackson - he usually called before he got on the road to tell me when he'd be getting here.

"Hey!" I said, as I shut the closet door. "Are you on your way?"

"Hey, babe... uh, actually, no I'm not. I was calling to tell you I won't be there until tomorrow afternoon."

"Oh, really? How come?" I glanced over at Molly and saw she was already raising an eyebrow at me. She must have been able to tell from my end that he wasn't coming, because she sat up in bed and silently mouthed *Party!* I rolled my eyes at her.

"Something came up," he said vaguely, "but I'll definitely see you tomorrow." Jackson paused. "You okay with that?"

"Oh, no problem." I grabbed a warm can of soda from my backpack and popped it open. "We'll hang out tomorrow."

He paused for a minute, then said, "Okay, great, I'll see you tomorrow. Love you."

"Love you too!"

"So," Molly said as soon as I ended the call, "Jackson's not coming?"

"You know he's not."

"That's great, Leah!" she gushed, "Now you can come with me!"

I wanted to laugh at her abrupt change of heart. Suddenly, she was less concerned about my "inappropriate behavior" with Chase and more concerned with having backup at the party.

"Not that I care, but how come he cancelled?"

"Actually, I'm not sure why."

It wasn't until that moment that I realized Jackson hadn't sounded himself; in fact, he'd sounded a little down. And what did he mean, *something came up?* I started getting annoyed, then it occurred to me that I hadn't even asked him what was going on with him. Normally, I would have been upset that he wasn't coming; today, it was no big deal. And it really wasn't a big deal – he'd be up the next day, right? I told myself it had nothing to do with the lacrosse game.

▲   ▲   ▲

Even I had to admit it was an exciting game, especially since Chase scored the winning goal in overtime. Everyone went crazy, both in the stands and on the field – cheering and clapping and hugging. One more win meant they'd place first in their division and get top seed in the playoffs.

The team hit the locker room, then met everyone in the parking lot next to the stadium. Chase came right over when he saw me.

"Hey, bud," he said as he wrapped me in a friendly hug. "Pretty awesome win, right?" He grabbed two beers out of the cooler and handed one to me.

"Yeah, sure was," I said, unnerved by the flip my stomach did when he put his arms around me.

"Did you see how I nailed that last shot?" he said proudly, "Goalie didn't even see it coming."

"Yep," I agreed, but I was more impressed with the way his bicep flexed when he brought the beer bottle to his lips.

A few of his teammates joined us, and they kept slapping each other on the backs and high-fiving each other as they recapped the various game-winning plays. Their excitement was infectious, and I found myself having fun. Though I'd never been into lacrosse, sports had always been a big part of my life.

Every so often I'd see a girl look over at me with that *what's-so-great-about-her?* expression. After the third girl I realized it was because they thought I was with Chase. I also realized that I was enjoying their envy – maybe because I was so rarely on the receiving end of it.

"Having fun?" Chase asked as he handed me another beer.

"Absolutely," I said, "It kinda reminds me of my soccer days."

"Oh, cool, I didn't know you played soccer," he said, sounding a little surprised.

"Yeah, I played all through high school, varsity my sophomore, junior and senior years." I replied, then added, "Senior year we took the state title in double overtime. It was really something. I miss it sometimes."

He flashed me that killer smile. "I would've never pegged you as a jock."

"And why is that?" I asked in a teasing tone.

He leaned closer, then I felt his breath in my ear. "Well, let's just say you're way too hot to be a jock."

I probably should have felt insulted by what he'd said, but I didn't. Instead I felt a little self-satisfied smile tug at my lips.

He pulled back a bit and gave his head a slight shake. "Too bad we're just friends." But he was smiling when he said it. I laughed, trying to ignore that flip in my stomach. And I kept on ignoring it, every time Chase casually placed his hand on my shoulder. He's just being friendly, I told myself. Then something happened that even I couldn't shrug off. He was talking with the guys about their next game, when I once again felt the weight of his hand on my shoulder. No big deal...until the hand slowly began to slide down my back, then slipped into the back pocket of my jeans. I didn't move his hand, partly because I'd had several beers by then, but mostly because I kind of liked where it was. I was even a little sorry when he pulled the hand away to give yet another teammate a pound.

The crowd eventually started to thin and that's when I realized I hadn't seen Molly all night. I took out my phone and shot her a text. I'd barely hit send when she replied: *Ready to head out.* Judging from the curtness and immediacy, it was safe to assume things hadn't gone as planned with Brent.

"Is that Molly?" Chase asked as he motioned to my phone.

"Yeah, she's on her way over." I slid my phone into my back pocket. Sure enough, she appeared at my side a moment later, trying, without much success, to mask a scowl.

"Ready?" she asked.

"You guys are leaving already?" Chase asked, surprised. "It's still early!"

I glanced over at Molly and could tell from the set of her jaw that there was no way she was going to stay. I would've loved to hang out a little longer, but I couldn't let her leave alone. Besides, if I did stay to hang out with Chase she'd never let me hear the end of it. Smiling through my annoyance, I told Chase I'd see him next week and then the two of us were on our way.

Once we were out of earshot I turned to Molly. "Okay, out with it. What'd Brent do to get you this fired up? It's written all over your face."

"Nothing, Leah," she stated matter-of-factly, "He didn't do anything. And then after doing a whole lot of nothing he left with some red-headed bimbo."

"Ouch," I winced, "That's gotta suck."

"I just don't get it," she said as she threw her hands up, "We have such a good time when we're together. We have the same sense of humor, we both could literally *live* on pizza, he likes playing lacrosse, I like watching him play lacrosse. Tell me, what am I missing here?"

"Maybe -" I began, but she immediately cut me off.

"Do you think he thinks I'm fat? Could that be it?"

"Fat? Molly, come on! Maybe, it's just -"

"But I'm big-boned, right?" She threw her hands up again. "Damn, my mother and her giant bones! It's like a family curse; all three of us kids inherited it!"

"Molly, hold up a sec." I put a hand on her arm before she could interrupt me again. "Maybe he sees you more as a friend. Did you ever think of that? You and he have been in the friend zone since the beginning of last semester. It's possible he still sees you that way."

For the first time since leaving the party Molly didn't argue with me.

"Go on," she motioned with her hand.

"I don't know, don't be so friendly with him. Maybe let him see you hanging around with some other guys. You know, play hard to get."

She mulled my suggestion over for a few minutes. "You might actually be on to something. I mean, look at you and Chase. He's seen you with Jackson and you've told him more than once that you just wanted to be friends, yet he's still all over you like white on rice."

"Chase is not *all over me*," I snapped.

"Really, Leah," she said, ignoring my comment, "I think you may be on to something." Molly's scowl began to morph into a wide-eyed grin and I could almost see the wheels turning in her head. "I'll put my new strategy into motion tomorrow. Wait, scratch that, I'll put my new strategy into motion on Sunday, not tomorrow. I forgot Brent and the rest of the team'll be out of town checking out the competition for next week's game."

"Oh, yeah?" I asked, trying to sound nonchalant.

"Yeah. Chase didn't mention it? The coach got a bus and the whole team's leaving first thing in the morning."

"Nah, he didn't say anything. Probably just slipped his mind, what with all the excitement about their big win."

Molly rambled on about Operation Brent, but I really wasn't listening. Suddenly, I couldn't wait to see Jackson, and now that I didn't have to worry about bumping into Chase around every corner, I was looking forward to his visit a lot more.

CHAPTER 29 - JACKSON

I don't know why I didn't tell Leah the reason I didn't come up yesterday – it's not like she didn't know how fucked up my life had been. But between not hearing back from Matt about the gig in Brooklyn and the earful I'd gotten from my dad, the past couple of weeks had been particularly shitty, and I wasn't ready to rehash it, not even with her. And I would have to rehash it if I told her that I was going to Beth's, and why. Still, it felt weird to be so vague with her.

Sure, it bugged me a little that she hadn't even *asked* what was going on, but I pushed it to the back of my mind. She had her own things to worry about, and besides, I could've waited until after I got back from Leah's to talk to Beth.

My sister was surprised to find me on her doorstep so soon after I'd left.

"What's up?" she asked as she stepped aside to let me in. "Everything alright?"

I didn't answer, just scanned the room. "Brody around?"

"Nope; working late tonight. Why? Do you need him?"

I shook my head. "Na, it's you I wanted to talk to."

"Oh, okay; sit." She sat down on the couch and patted the spot next to her. "What's going on?"

"Man, I don't even know where to begin."

"Uh oh, sounds serious."

I sat all the way back on the couch and sighed. "You're not gonna believe this but I talked to *Dad* last night. Like, not just a few words either, like an actual conversation."

Beth's blue eyes widened. "Whoa, that's *really* big news. What'd he say?"

"He told me a lot of shit . . . *about Mom*. And about California and what happened."

"Oh no, not this again, Jackson . . ." she moaned.

"What do you mean *not this again*?" I asked, both surprised and annoyed by her reaction. "Christ, Beth, don't you wanna get to the bottom of what happened with them? Doesn't it bother you even all these years later that there's so much shit we don't know?"

"I know all I need to know, Jackson. *Let it go*."

"Fuck *let it go*. I'll never let it go. I wanna know everything. I wanna know every fucking thing behind what turned him into the douchebag he is today."

She went to stand from the couch, but I grabbed her wrist and pulled her back down. "For one, I betcha never woulda guessed that -"

"That what, Jackson?" she snapped as she yanked her wrist free. "That it was my fault? That if Mom hadn't kept me - that if she'd just given me away like she planned - none of this would've happened? That they would've moved out to California together and Dad would've become some famous rock star? That they would've had you and Tim and the four of you could've lived happily ever after? Is that what you were gonna tell me? Because if it is, don't bother; I'm well aware of how my arrival messed everything up."

I looked at her, stunned. Blaming her had never even entered my mind; Dad had always been the villain of the story, and the rest of us his victims.

I could see that her eyes were filling with tears and pulled her closer. "Beth, where's this coming from? Who told you all this?" All of a sudden, something dawned on me. "Wait a minute, have you been talking to Dad too?"

She shook her head and wiped the corner of her eye with her sleeve. "No . . . I, I've been spending a lot of time with Gram."

"Well, what exactly did she say?" I found it hard to believe that our grandmother would've ever led Beth to believe that she was responsible for how things turned out.

She wiped her eyes again, saw she'd gotten eye makeup on her shirt, and frowned. "She told me that Mom got pregnant the summer after graduation and that she and Dad planned to give me up. Gram was supposed to make all the arrangements for the adoption with a lawyer but she never did."

Beth reached into her purse on the coffee table and pulled out a tissue. "She said she knew that as soon as Mom saw me she would change her mind, and if for some reason she didn't Gram and Gramps were planning to take me. Gram even joked that she would've ripped me out of Mom's arms before she let her hand me over to strangers. They never told Mom that, and it didn't matter anyway because it never came to that. Just as Gram predicted, Mom took one look at me and forgot all about the adoption."

Beth turned to me, looking very serious. "And do you know what else she said? She said that it was a really difficult birth. Mom nearly *died*."

"Holy shit, Grandma told you all *that*?"

She nodded. "I go over there at least once a week to check on them and see if they need anything. You should come with me next time. Anyway, we talk a lot, about Mom, about when we were all little. I'm so glad we found them."

"But Beth, I'm sure Grandma never said she blamed you for what happened to Mom."

"No, of course she didn't." Beth sighed. "But Jackson, even you have to admit that things might've turned out a lot different if they went with their original plan."

"Maybe not . . ." I trailed off, eliciting a questioning look from my sister. "Well, what I was gonna tell you before you opened up the floodgates was that after me and Dad talked he gave me a stack of sheet music. He said it was the stuff that he brought out to California with him. After he left I went out to the garage and played some of it – actually, all of it – and it was pretty bad; well, maybe not *bad*, but totally not my scene." I shook my head. "Honestly, I can't imagine he was gonna get anywhere with that stuff if he actually played it."

"Really?" she said, sounding a little relieved.

"Yeah, really." I laughed a little, trying to make light of the situation. "Hey, you know I woulda turned out a lot worse without you there to look after me, right?"

"Who are you kidding, Jackson?" Now she was laughing. "You and Tim never listened to me. I finally gave up and started spending all my time at Brody's."

"Hah, yeah, I remember. That's when Tim started runnin' the show. Wild times."

She leaned her head on my shoulder. "I miss her, Jacks."

"Yeah, me too."

She turned to me. "You were always her favorite, you know that, right?"

"Absolutely!" I laughed.

"No, really, you were," she chuckled. "The way you used to hang onto her leg wherever we went. Always wanting to sit on her lap. It bugged the shit out of me but, man, she ate that stuff up!"

"Yep, she sure did."

Just then we heard keys jingling and a moment later Brody's burley frame filled the doorway. "I interruptin' something?" he joked when he saw us sitting so close on the couch like two collaborators. He tossed his keys on the table and then joined us.

"Nope, just talkin' about old times, right, Sis? And on that note..." I stood, "...I should probably get going. I'm headin' up to see Leah tomorrow and I still got stuff to do."

Beth stood from the couch. "How's Leah doing, anyway? I haven't seen her since . . . since Christmas, I think."

"Yeah, she's been busy with school but she'll be around for the summer." I looked between her and Brody. "Let's definitely try to get together."

"Sure, anytime," they said almost in unison.

▲   ▲   ▲

I was still thinking about our conversation the next day when I pulled into the parking lot of Leah's school. Though I still didn't have any answers about my parents, I felt good about clearing the air with Beth. Maybe I would tell Leah about it, maybe I would wait; right now, though, I just wanted to enjoy my weekend with her.

My phone started to ring just as I knocked on her dorm room door. I pulled it out of my pocket and saw the name "Matt" flashing on the little screen. I knew before I even answered it that this was *the call* – it was either gonna be the greatest weekend of my life or it was gonna totally suck.

CHAPTER 30 - LEAH

"Leah!" I heard Molly yell over the hum of my blow dryer. I twisted around and saw her sitting on her bed with one foot pulled up. She was painting her toenails the ugliest shade of orange I'd ever seen. "Someone's knocking."

I turned off the blow dryer and hurried to the door, annoyed that Jackson would see me with my hair looking like who-did-it-and-ran. He didn't seem to notice, though, as he stepped into the room with his bags in hand and his cell jammed into the crook of his shoulder.

"Hey, Jackson -" I began, but he held up his finger, signaling me to wait a minute. I couldn't tell who he was talking to but there was plenty of *uh huhs*, *mm hmms* and *yeah mans*, along with a lot of head nodding.

He followed me inside and placed his bag on my bed as he continued to listen to the caller. Finally, I heard him say, "Awesome, man; really looking forward to it. Yep, okay, I'll call you next week. Later."

He ended the call, then looked down at the phone for a moment with the hugest grin I'd ever seen plastered across his face. I was about to ask him what was going on when he grabbed me and lifted me up off my feet.

"Holy shit, babe!" he said as he spun me around.

Molly didn't say anything, but I could feel her curious stare from across the room.

"What, Jackson?" I said, laughing. "C'mon, tell me!"

"That was *the call*! The one I've been waiting for, from Matt, the guy from the band in Brooklyn!"

"Oh my gosh!" I exclaimed, "What did he say? What did he say?"

"Well," he began proudly as he placed me back down, "It looks like *you* are dating the new lead guitarist for Dirty Bushwick." He pumped both fists in the air. "Fuck! I can't believe this," he said excitedly, "This is, like, the greatest!"

"Would somebody please fill me in?" Molly groaned as she screwed the top back onto the polish and fanned her toes with her hand. "You know I hate to be out of the loop."

"Jackson got picked up by that band I told you about. You know, the one he auditioned for a few weeks back..."

She looked at me blankly, as if she had no idea what I was talking about. *Good old Molly,* I thought, *so wrapped up in herself that she didn't remember I'd told her.* Then it hit me. I *hadn't* told her; I'd been so busy with all my "Chase" drama that I'd completely forgotten to tell her about Jackson's audition.

Crap.

"Oh, Molly, you never listen to me," I said, trying to brush it off. Luckily Molly just shrugged, but I couldn't tell whether she was covering for me or she really thought it had slipped her mind.

"So, tell me about it," she said to Jackson, "Because it sounds really cool."

"Oh yeah, it totally is," he agreed, then he filled her in on all the details - the trip to Brooklyn; the disappointment when Matt didn't commit; the waiting for the phone call. I could tell from Molly's face that she was really impressed.

"So," Jackson said, still grinning, "You ladies up for celebrating tonight? I'm thinking dinner in town and then we pick up some beers and bring'm back here and then -"

Molly quickly cut him off. "*Then* we can go to the wrestling party! Yeah, the wrestling team throws the best parties and there's a huge one tonight."

I thought Jackson would decline Molly's invitation to go to the party. Although he'd gone with us before, I knew he wasn't too keen on them. I was wrong.

He walked over to the bed and offered her a high-five, which she enthusiastically matched. "A party sounds awesome! So, what time do you guys want to do dinner? Hey, and it's my treat."

"I knew I liked this guy," Molly joked as she got up and gave Jackson an exaggerated squeeze.

All I could think was thank God Chase and the rest of the team were out of town. The last thing I needed was to run into him and Brent. Although Jackson had met them and knew we were all friends, there was always the risk of awkwardness, especially considering Molly's love of innuendos.

"Whaddaya say, Lee?" Jackson asked.

I grinned at him. "Sure!"

Molly peeked over at the digital clock on her nightstand. "Well, guys," she began as she turned around and grabbed a sweatshirt, "It's just about four o'clock and being the good friend that I am, I'm going to take off and run a few errands – wink, wink." She chuckled, then opened the door and was on her way.

▲   ▲   ▲

Molly took her time running her mysterious "errands" – not that it mattered. Jackson talked nonstop about Dirty Bushwick the whole time she was gone. When she got back the three of us headed for the diner in town, and he continued talking about the band all through dinner. I ate up every word, and not just because I was going to be the lead guitarist's girlfriend. I had never seen Jackson so happy. Even Molly was into it, though she started to get antsy toward the end of the meal. On the way back to the dorm we picked up some beer, but Molly didn't open one; she made a beeline for the full-length mirror hanging on the back of the door and began fussing with her hair.

Jackson and I exchanged amused glances as we sipped our beers.

"What gives, Molly?" he said finally, "You been standing in front of that mirror since we got back." He raised an eyebrow at her. "Hot date?"

"Hopefully," Molly answered mysteriously as she moved closer to the mirror and applied some more lipstick. "I'm on the prowl tonight, if you must know."

"Uh oh, look out!" Jackson joked before downing the rest of his beer. "Hey, what about that dude Chase you had the hots for? What happened to him?"

At the mention of Chase's name, the hand holding my beer froze halfway to my lips. From across the room I saw Molly's hand did the same as she was closing her lipstick.

"Um, I think you mean Brent . . . Chase is a friend of his, but either way, I've moved on." She smirked. "At least that's the angle I'll be working tonight."

I felt myself cringing; I just wanted the subject shifted away from Chase and Brent.

"Molly, Molly, Molly," Jackson repeated as he shook his head in a mock scolding way. "It sounds like you're up to no-good."

Ignoring the comment, Molly met his eyes in the mirror. "You're a guy, right?"

"Uh, last time I checked, yeah."

She laughed. "Okay, so tell me what you think – as a guy - of this plan I have to snag the attention of a certain lacrosse player."

"Oh boy, go ahead," Jackson chuckled as he folded his arms across his chest. "This should be good."

Still ignoring him, Molly launched into her scheme. She was going to try to entice Brent by having him see her with another guy. Tonight, she would put part one of the plan into action: finding this other guy. "And I'm also going to stop being around when he calls or texts. You know, play a little hard to get. So, what do you think?"

"What do I think? Well, I think it's a great idea if you're in sixth grade and this is going to be taking place at the middle school spring social." He laughed at his little joke. "Man up, Molly! Just come right out and tell him you're interested. We guys love the direct approach; takes the pressure off." He inched closer and put his arm around me. "That's how me and this one met, right, Leah?"

"Yep," I said, remembering how nervous I was when I went up to him at that party and tapped him on the back. I had no idea what I was even going to say when he turned around.

"Best thing that ever happened to me," he said, giving my arm a gentle squeeze.

"Well, as cute as your little love story turned out, I think I'm gonna stick with Plan A – the non-direct, game-playing, make-him-jealous-till-he-screams strategy. And then if that doesn't work, *maybe* I'll try the direct approach."

Finally, she got tired of messing with her hair and grabbed a beer. The three of us continued drinking and laughing, mostly about Molly's non-existent love life. Hanging out with Jackson this way and having such a good time made me realize how much I'd missed him – really missed him – and not just because we didn't see each other all the time. Even when we were together lately, part of me had always been somewhere else. *With Chase.* I pushed the thought from my mind. That's ridiculous. It had just been a little harmless flirting. But it hadn't been harmless, because it had been going on behind Jackson's back. "Just friends" or not, the way I acted around Chase was wrong and I was going to put an end to it.

▲　▲　▲

I didn't know anyone on the wrestling team but I certainly knew enough about their parties; specifically, that they always ended with a beer-fueled brawl and sometimes a visit from the local cops. But that night, things seemed pretty tame; it was warm for March and when we got there a lot of people were casually hanging outside sipping beer from red plastic cups. Then again, it was still early.

Me, Molly and Jackson walked up the porch steps and into the house, Molly's eyes darting this way and that as she scoped the crowd for possible guys she could use to make Brent jealous.   The mild weather had provided her with the perfect hunting ground – there were just enough people in the house to make you feel like you were at a real party without being squashed in like sardines.

After hitting the keg the three of us grabbed some barstools a few feet from the sliding glass doors. That's when I saw another huge crowd of people in the backyard. Damn! No wonder these things got out of hand –

there had to be at least a hundred people there, most of them on their way to drunken oblivion.

We had barely sat down when Molly stood again and announced she was going to go "mingle." Then off she went, weaving through the crowd as she searched for a suitable victim. I glanced around the room and decided she had her work cut out for her. The guy had to be hot enough and popular enough to compete with a member of the lacrosse team. The only one that fit that bill was Jackson, especially now that he was in a real band. I grabbed his hand, glad we had some time to hang out by ourselves; besides, I knew Molly would fill me in on her ridiculous scheme later.

Conversation once again turned to Dirty Bushwick. "They practice a lot on the weekends," Jackson said excitedly, then he shot me a guilty look. "But I'll still try to make it up on Saturday nights."

"Don't go crazy trying to fit me in," I told him, "The semester will be over before you know it and I'll be home. Hey, and I can't wait to meet them!"

"Yeah, I can't wait for you to meet them too. They're really cool."

"What about Slater? He and the rest of the guys on the tree crew are going to miss you."

"Oh, I'm not leaving Slater's. Gotta pay the bills, right?"

"Oh, I just assumed the new band would be paying you."

He laughed. "No such luck. Not yet anyway. If we establish ourselves and get a following and things start to happen then, yeah, we'll be making some cash, but that's in the future. For now, Slater and the crew are stuck with me."

I just nodded. Probably naïve of me to think it was a paid gig, but he was so excited I'd just assumed.

An hour and two beers later, I stood and stretched my legs. "I'm gonna hit the bathroom. How about one more beer and then we head home?"

"Sounds good," he said as he reached out and took my cup. Then he headed for the keg and I took my place at the end of the bathroom line.

"Excuse me," I heard a soft voice behind me.

I turned to find a petite, dark-haired girl I'd never seen before. "Yes?"

"Oh, hi, my name's Lexi," she said, sounding almost nervous. "Sorry to bother you but I was just wondering if that guy you were with over there, if he's your boyfriend?"

"Uh, yeah," I said with a smirk. Barely in a band and Jackson already had a groupie!

Lexi smiled. "Oh cool, so then you're not with Chase?"

"Chase? No, um, Chase and I are just friends."

"Oh wow, I totally thought you guys were a couple. I've seen you around a lot together."

I shook my head, wondering why I was starting to get annoyed. "Nope."

"Chase is, like, so hot and I've been wanting to maybe ask him to hang out or something but I didn't want to step on anyone's toes. I'm totally not like that."

"Oh, uh, sure…" I trailed off, not knowing what else to say.

"Great! Thanks so much!" She exclaimed, then ran off, no doubt to tell her friends that she had the green light to make her move on Chase.

I turned forward again, relieved to find that there were just two girls in front of me. Did everyone really think Chase and I were a couple? *Are you really surprised, Leah? How many people have seen you sitting on his lap, or huddled in a corner at some party? Of course they were making assumptions.* Suddenly I just wanted out of there.

After using the bathroom, I headed back to Jackson. Along the way I scanned the room for Molly so I could tell her we weren't staying much longer. And that's when I happened to glance out the sliding glass doors and saw the familiar form slip through the back gate. Although it was dark and all I could see was a silhouette I knew instantly that it was Chase. *Shit.* What was he doing here? He was supposed to be out of town with the rest of the team. I never would've agreed to come here if I thought there was even the slightest chance of him showing up. He might have seen me too, but some guy started talking to him just as he was about to open the sliding glass doors.

"Long line, huh?" Jackson said, as I sat down next to him.

"Mmm hmmm." I took the beer from him and drank half of it in one gulp.

Jackson started talking about the band again but I was barely listening. I was too busy wondering how we could get out of there without Chase noticing. I stole a quick glance and saw he was now standing across the room, talking to a few guys I didn't know. I shifted slightly on my stool, hoping Jackson's body would block me from sight.

"Leah?" I heard Jackson say. I quickly snapped my attention back to him.

"You ready to head out?" he asked.

"Oh yeah, sure," I smiled.

"Okay, I'm gonna hit the bathroom quick and I'll meet you back here."

"Sounds good," I said, still smiling, then finished off my beer. When I glanced over again Chase had disappeared. Good, I thought, maybe he went back outside, or even better, had left all together. After a few minutes I figured I was safe and stood to look and see if Jackson was on his way back. That's when I felt the large, warm hand on the back of my neck. I turned quickly and came face to face with Chase.

"Oh, hi," I said, my eyes darting around anxiously. I must have looked like a lunatic. "You're back early."

His brows furrowed as his hand slipped from my neck. "Back from where?"

"The trip . . . with the team. Brent told Molly that the team was going to check out the competition for next week's game."

"Oh, that. No, I never planned on going – had to make up two assignments." I saw his eyes catch something behind me and he made a slight move backward. I didn't have to turn around to know that Jackson was approaching and the next thing I knew, Jackson was standing beside me.

"Hey, what's up, Chase?" Jackson said in a friendly tone.

"Not much, man," Chase replied casually as he slipped both hands into the front pockets of his jeans. "Just hanging out. How 'bout you?"

The two of them continued to make small talk as I stood there uncomfortably. Finally, Chase said he had to get going. Something about meeting up with a friend. *Thank God.* Jackson and I were almost to the door when I felt someone tugging on my sleeve. I whipped around annoyed, thinking it was Chase but saw it was Molly instead. She drew back when she saw the look on my face.

"Damn, Leah, what's got into you?"

"Oh, Molly, nothing. I – uh – was just about to come find you." The truth was that I had forgotten all about her the moment I saw Chase. "Jackson and I are leaving. Ready?"

"Nah, I'll stay a bit longer." She leaned in. "Mission definitely *not* accomplished."

I forced a laugh. "Okay, be careful going home."

I caught up to Jackson just as he pulled open the front door. From the corner of my eye I saw Chase with Lexi, the girl I'd met earlier in the line for the bathroom. Although I couldn't hear what they were saying I could tell by her body language that she was flirting with him. I hesitated, and in that second Chase looked up. For a split second our eyes locked, then I quickly turned my head and closed the door behind me.

CHAPTER 31 - JACKSON

I white-knuckled it the whole drive over to Brooklyn. This was my first rehearsal as an official member of Dirty Bushwick, and if I fucked up it could be my last. I was pretty sure Matt was in my corner, but Jayne and Skid had been completely unreadable at that first meeting, and the pressure was on to bring my A game. By the time I got off the Williamsburg Bridge, I was wondering if I'd even be able to play. But that's the funny thing about trying to park in Brooklyn – you get so pissed off about not finding a spot that you forget about everything else. When I finally turned off the car an hour later, I felt like l had won the lottery.

As it turned out I had nothing to worry about. I played my ass off, and aside from what seemed to be Jayne's characteristic standoffishness at first, everything went smoothly. Although I couldn't speak for the others, by the end of rehearsal it felt like the four of us had been playing together for years.

Jayne jetted as soon as we were done, but Matt, Skid and I went around the corner to Token's, the same trendy little bar where I'd first met Matt. Apparently Matt went there often, because he greeted the owners by name and they gave us the first round for free. The place was pretty packed, but we grabbed three frosty mugs of Bud and found a booth in the back. Matt told me the new owners had bought the place a year earlier and were still renovating, but they were looking to bring in some live music on the weekends in the hopes of drawing a younger, hipper crowd. One of them even asked Matt if we'd be interested in being their first live act. Matt said he told him *hell yeah,* as if there was any doubt.

Matt and I made small talk while Skid went to get us another round, and when he returned the conversation turned to the band's practice schedule.

"Hey, nothing's set in stone but I'd like to get together as much as possible on the weekends," he told me. "Maybe even squeeze a few hours in during the week. That work for you, Jackson?"

"Absolutely," I said as I finished up my beer and then placed the mug back down. That's when it dawned on me that I probably wouldn't be back up to see Leah for a while. At least she was already halfway through the semester. Besides, I knew she'd be cool about it; she knew how important this was to me. I smiled to myself. I had a really good feeling about these guys. I was still grinning hours later as I headed for home. This could quite possibly turn out to be the big break I'd been waiting for.

CHAPTER 32 – LEAH

"What's your problem?" Molly snapped when I picked up the pile of papers and books off my desk and dumped it on her bed.

I glared at her, hand on my hip. "Maybe I'm just sick of watching your crap constantly oozing over to my side of the room."

"My 'oozing crap' has nothing to do with it, Leah. You've been in a pissy mood for days. What gives?"

Couldn't argue with her there; I had been snippy all week. "Sorry, I've just been feeling so overwhelmed with schoolwork...I think I took too many credits." I shrugged. "And – I don't know - maybe I'm getting a little homesick."

Molly's face softened. "Hey, I get it. But c'mon, Leah, the semester's halfway over and then we'll be home for almost three months."

I nodded and smiled, praying she wouldn't realize that I was full of shit. I was handling my workload just fine, and as for being homesick, nothing could be further from the truth. No, my "pissy mood," as Molly so eloquently put it, began the moment I saw that girl flirting with Chase at the party. I knew it was crazy and that I certainly had no right to be angry, but I couldn't help it. I also hadn't been able to forget about it, no matter how hard I tried.

"Yeah, you're right," I conceded, hoping I sounded sincere. I opened my closet and reached for my laundry bag. "I just have to keep telling myself it's almost over."

She smiled, which made me feel even guiltier for lying.

"Be back in a bit," I said as I pulled my laundry bag out of the closet and hoisted it over my shoulder. My earbuds caught my eye on my way out and I shoved them into my pocket. Maybe some music would distract me. I got down to the basement where the laundry room was located and absently dumped my clothes in.

Someone had left an old issue of Elle lying around, but after flipping through a few pages I threw it to the side and decided to do a quick loop around campus. I told myself that I wanted to take advantage of the nice weather, but not long into my walk I found myself nonchalantly strolling past the lacrosse field. It looked like the afternoon practice was just about ending. There was no sign of Chase, which both relieved and annoyed me, so I popped my earbuds in and turned on Pandora for the walk back. That's when I felt the pebble in my sneaker. I ignored it for a bit, but after a few minutes I decided I was being ridiculous. Placing one hand on a tree, I pulled my shoe off with the other and shook it out.

Suddenly, I felt a slight tug on the wire of my earbuds. I jerked my head to the side and was delighted to find a sweaty lacrosse player smiling down at me. He was still wearing his practice gear, which made him even sexier.

"Hey, bud!" I heard him say as I pulled my earbuds out.

"Hey yourself," I replied, and immediately realized how flirty I sounded.

"Where're you headed?"

"Just getting some fresh air while my laundry's in the machine. It should be ready to throw in the dryer about now, though."

"Hey, why don't you use the dryer back at my place," he suggested. "We can order some Chinese while you wait."

"Sure, sounds great!" The words were out of my mouth before I could think about it. *What the hell is wrong with me?*

"Cool," he said as he took a few steps backwards. "I'm heading home now to hit the shower. Meet me there?"

I nodded, not trusting myself to say anything else. As soon as he was out of sight I practically bolted back to get my laundry.

Fifteen minutes later I arrived at his house. My heart was pounding, and I knew it wasn't because I'd been carrying the heavy laundry bag. I raised my hand to knock when the door flew open; it was one of Chase's roommates, who was clearly on his way out.

"Hey, Leah, come in," he said as he stepped aside to let me pass, "Chase is still in the shower; should be down any minute."

"Oh, okay," I said. I left my bag of wet laundry by the front door and took a seat on the couch.

What are you doing, Leah? I asked myself accusingly. *You should just get up now and leave.* I might have left, too, if I hadn't seen Chase sauntering down the stairs, clad only in a pair of navy-blue nylon basketball shorts. My jaw dropped, and all thoughts of leaving flew from my head. Unfortunately, the display was short-lived because he grabbed a t-shirt from the laundry basket on the dining room table and slipped it on.

"First things first," he said, eyeing my bag sitting by the door. "Let's get your stuff into the dryer and then we can get some food."

He grabbed the bag and disappeared into the basement, while I tried not to think about the fact that he was seeing my underwear. A few minutes later he returned, talking on his cell to who I assumed was the new Chinese place that had opened in town. He ended the call and then tossed his phone on the table. "Food'll be here in thirty minutes."

I nodded, wondering why I wasn't annoyed that he ordered without asking what I wanted.

He hopped onto the couch next to me and grabbed the remote. He surfed through the stations, finally settling on a basketball game.

As I sat next to him, I felt a nervous anticipation creeping up on me.

"Man, I'm beat," he sighed as he leaned his back against the arm of the couch.

"Tough practice?" I asked in what I hoped sounded like a casual tone.

He shrugged, then I felt his hands on my arms, pulling me toward him.

"C'mere," he whispered, and suddenly I found myself positioned between his legs with my back against his chest. Then, without missing a beat he moved his hands to my shoulders and began gently massaging them. He casually commented on what was happening on the TV, but though I *mmmed* and nodded at all the right places, all I could think about was how good it felt to have his hands on me again. My heart beating furiously, I reached out and put my hand on his thigh. It was a bold move for me, and Chase must have thought so too because I felt his hands stop for a beat, then begin moving again. I closed my eyes, enjoying the moment, then heard a slight change in his breath when I began to very subtly move my thumb back and forth against the hem of his shorts. We stayed that way until the doorbell rang, signaling that our food had arrived. I sighed, then reluctantly moved so he could go answer it.

We ate the lo mien and sesame chicken in the kitchen, washing it down with a few beers. I laughed as he told me about the antics that happened every time the team got together to work out. After cleaning up we returned to the living room. By that time, the sun had long since set and the only light was the glow from the television set. Chase got back on the couch but this time he laid down on his side, his tall frame taking up nearly the entire length of it. He pulled me down and positioned me in front of him, then fiddled with the remote, finally settling on an old episode of Seinfeld since the basketball game had ended.

We watched the show for a while, both laughing at the same parts, as his hand rested on my hip. About halfway through the episode I felt him gather my hair with his free hand and twist it away from my neck. I felt his warm breath against my skin, followed by his soft full lips. My eyes flew open as a bolt of electricity coursed through me all the way down to my toes. I didn't pull away, but instead closed my eyes and tried to steady my breath, thanking God he couldn't see my face.

For the next several minutes I lay there, frozen, as he continued his slow assault on the tender skin just below my right ear. When I made no move to stop him he slowly turned me onto my back, moved on top of me, and lowered his lips to mine. My heart racing, I slipped my tongue into his mouth. There was no excuse for what I was doing; it was selfish and wrong on so many levels, but still I kept on kissing him.

It was all too soon that I heard footsteps and laughter coming from outside, and I knew Chase heard it too because he pulled away and slid to the side. I turned onto my side too so whoever came in would think we were just watching TV. The laughing got louder, then I heard the door swing open. A second later, the room was flooded with light.

"Well, what have we got here...?"

I blinked in the direction of the voice and saw five guys standing there.

"Oh, there's a Seinfeld marathon on," Chase said casually.

"Mmmhmm." One of the guys held up a plastic bag. "You guys hungry?"

"No thanks, just had Chinese from Chan's," Chase said.

The guys nodded and walked into the kitchen. I turned to Chase. "I should probably get going." I started to get up but he pulled me back down.

"You don't really have to go, do you?" he said as he ran his fingers through my hair.

"I really should," I said, now feeling nervous about what we'd been doing. I sat up and began to put my sneakers back on.

He looked like he was about to argue the point, but then he sighed and said, "Okay, I'll go grab your clothes from the dryer."

"Sure, that'd be great."

A few minutes later he returned with the full laundry bag, but when I went to take it from him he pulled his arm back.

"You don't have to carry it. I'll walk you home."

We walked the short distance back to my building, talking as if nothing out of the ordinary had happened.

When we got to the front door of my building he placed the bag down and reached out and grabbed my hand. "What're you up to tomorrow?" He looked down at the bag and chuckled. "Any more laundry?"

"I think I'm good for a while," I laughed as I reached down to grab the sack.

"C'mere," he said as he pulled me over. He put both his hands on my waist and then leaned down and started kissing me again. A few minutes later he pulled back and then leaned his forehead against mine. "So . . . see ya . . . *buddy*."

▲   ▲   ▲

The next day passed in a blur. I went through the motions – going to class, folding the laundry; I even managed to field a few questions from my poly-sci professor – but not for one minute did I stop replaying the events of the night before in my head. It was like Chase still had his hands on me, still had his lips on mine. One thing was for sure, even I could no longer pretend we were just friends. There was also no denying the fact that whatever was happening between us, I didn't want it to stop. On the other hand, I couldn't imagine breaking up with Jackson. We had a history, and to throw it all away over someone that I barely knew seemed a bit rash. Jackson loved me, and I loved him...didn't I? Bottom line, what I was doing was reckless and wrong.

What I needed was time. Time to explore this thing with Chase and see if it was something worth pursuing. Of course, that meant being reckless and wrong for a bit longer, and I didn't know if I could stand it. It's not like I could even confide in Molly, though she'd surely enjoy the drama of it. Besides, it would be hard to get to know Chase – what with his busy lacrosse schedule and Jackson visiting most weekends.

Then came a phone call that made things a whole lot easier.

CHAPTER 33 - JACKSON

I called Leah as soon as I got home from work. It wasn't a call I looked forward to making, but I knew she would be cool, no matter how disappointed she was. I just had to make her understand that the situation was only temporary.

She picked up on the first ring. "Hi, Jackson," she said, sounding distracted but happy to hear from me.

"Hey, what's up?" I asked as I stretched out on my bed.

"Nothing much," she began, but then went on to dish some Molly drama and all the schoolwork she had. As always, I ate it up. Though college wasn't my thing I loved to hear about what it was like for her.

"So, listen," I said after we'd chitchatted for a while, "Looks like Matt's gonna wanna get together every weekend for a while, maybe even jam a few nights during the week too."

"Oh?"

"Yeah, so it doesn't look like I'm gonna be able to get up to see you again any time soon . . . you okay with that?"

There was a brief silence on the other end of the phone, then Leah said, "Wow, sounds like these guys are pretty serious."

"Absolutely," I said in a tone that I hoped implied both enthusiasm about the band and guilt over not visiting her. "I'm tellin' you, I really think this is it."

She hesitated again, as if mulling over what I'd said. "Well, if you really feel that way then I guess you should do whatever it takes; don't you think?"

"Totally agree, but I wanted to run it by you first," I said, relieved. "No matter what happens with the band or anything else, you know you'll always come first, right?"

". . . uh, yeah, sure."

"And this is only temporary – things'll ease up by mid-summer, the latest. Besides, you'll be home before then."

"Right, and before you know it I'll be studying for finals – I'm already going crazy with work. So, yeah, no problem, Jackson. You do what you have to do."

"Maybe we can take off for a few days this summer; go down to Florida or wherever you want. We're coming up on two years together now, right? We should celebrate – what do you think?"

"What do I think?" she repeated vaguely, "Yeah, Florida . . . sounds like fun."

"Leah?"

"Yeah?"

"You sure you're okay with this?"

"Yeah – yes," she said, and it seemed like she was returning from someplace far away. "Of course I am. Listen, I got a ton of reading to do. I'll call you tomorrow, okay?"

We exchanged the usual *I love yous* then ended the call. I stretched out on the bed again, once again filled with relief. Leah had reacted exactly as I thought she would – disappointed but cool. What a great girl, always so considerate of my feelings. I couldn't believe how lucky I was to have her.

▲　▲　▲

For once the traffic heading to Brooklyn was relatively light, and when I got to the place where we practiced Matt was the only one there. We bullshitted while I set up my stuff, then worked on finishing up a tune the two of us had started last time we were together.

"What time'll Skid and Jayne be here?" I asked.

"Skid'll be here in a few but Jayne's gonna be late, didn't say why."

Even after a few practices I still got the feeling Jayne had a problem with me. Maybe it was my imagination, or, who knows, maybe she was like that with everyone. Either way, I couldn't afford to end up on anyone's bad side so I decided to nonchalantly bring it up to Matt.

"That's a switch," I said lightly, "She's usually the first one here."

Matt nodded absently but continued to pencil in changes to the piece we were working on.

"You know, that night when I first met with you guys she kinda put out a vibe and I said to myself, *Man, I don't think that chick likes me.*" I shook my head as if to say, *crazy, right?*

What I said must have gotten his attention, because he briefly looked up and said, "She doesn't." Ignoring my look of surprise, he went back to what he was working on, but added, "But don't take it personally."

"What do you mean? Why does she have a problem with me?"

Matt shrugged. "Like I said, don't take it personally. She knows you're a talented musician and a perfect fit for the band so I wouldn't worry about it."

Obviously I was worried about it and wanted to know what her issue with me was. "So, what's her problem then?"

At first it didn't seem like he was going to answer, but then he looked up, saw the look on my face and must have realized I wasn't going to let it go. He removed his John Lennon specs and pinched the bridge of his nose.

"She had a thing with Damian, the lead guitarist you replaced. Got pissed off that he moved on. So, like I said, don't take it personally. It's not you she's got the problem with, it's Damian. Jayne's cool, though. We've been working together for a long time. She'll come around."

Before I could comment he repositioned his glasses and went back to what he was doing.

Of course I felt better after I heard his explanation, but I still decided to make a conscious effort to stay the hell out of her way. I just hoped Matt was right and she'd eventually get over her issues.

A few minutes later Skid appeared, with Jayne not far behind. We got right to work and jammed until nearly midnight.

When we were packing up to leave Matt handed me the stuff he'd been working on. "Hey, see what you can come up, lyrics-wise, with this. I've been looking at it too long."

"Yeah sure," I said. No point in mentioning that coming up with the words wasn't my strong point.

"Jayne," he called over his shoulder, "Work with Jackson on that piece. Maybe the two of you'll be able to come up with something decent."

She nodded and said *okay*, but I saw her give a slight eyeroll when she did.

"I'll see you guys the end of the week, yeah?"

"Yep. See you Friday," I said, then turned to Jayne, who was fishing through her bag for something. *This was going to be awkward.* "Um, Jayne, uh, what nights are you free this week? Any night works for me."

She snapped her bag closed and flicked her eyes towards me. "Wednesday." She stood and grabbed her sweatshirt from the hook on the wall. "Six-thirty, here? That work?"

I nodded. "Wednesday's fine but can we do it closer to seven? I'm comin' in from Ringwood - out in Jersey - and the traffic's a bitch."

"Oh, didn't know that. I'm coming in from Jersey too, not far from there. Maybe we can meet up somewhere in between."

"Sure, that works," I said and then tossed an idea out to her. "Or if you want, we can use my garage. I've got a pretty decent setup."

She shrugged. "Cool, text me your address and I'll try to get there by six-thirty."

"Sounds good," I said, feeling encouraged by her passably cordial tone. Maybe it was like Matt said; maybe she was already coming around.

▲   ▲   ▲

The next day felt more like February than early April, and I turned up the space heaters in the garage so Jayne and I didn't freeze our asses off while we were practicing. Just after sixty-thirty I heard a car pull into the driveway and looked out the window to see Jayne getting out of an older model white Toyota. I smiled to myself; from the little I knew of Jayne

I'd pictured her to have an old Volkswagen bug, maybe even a Vespa. The puffy winter coat she was wearing also seemed uncharacteristic, but I would have known that scowl anywhere. When she started up the front walk I quickly lifted the garage door and waved her in. The last thing I needed was for my dad to answer the front door.

Things between me and him had been more civil since that conversation in the kitchen, but our relationship was still lightyears from normal. Probably always would be. Sometimes it seemed like he wanted us to be closer, but then I'd remember all the times he'd acted like a douchebag, like the last thing he wanted was to be saddled with three kids. And I'd tell myself it didn't matter what he wanted, because after everything that'd happened, I had no interest in letting bygones be bygones.

Jayne slipped inside, bringing with her a gust of freezing air, and I pulled the garage door down quickly to keep the warmth of the space heaters from escaping.

"Find it okay?" I asked in what I hoped was a friendly tone since she was wearing an even bitchier-than-usual expression.

"Yeah," she mumbled as she shook off her coat and hung it on one of the rusted hooks by the door. She was wearing black leggings and an oversized gray hoodie with a faded picture of the Beatles on the front. Her long black hair was tied in a ponytail on top of her head and secured with several black bands; her pale blue eyes were heavily rimmed as always with thick black liner.

She glanced around the garage. "You ready?"

I nodded, relieved by her no-nonsense attitude. I wasn't all that comfortable around her, especially after Matt told me she didn't like me, and to be honest I was pissed that he'd suggested this little collaboration. It wasn't long, though, before I understood his reasoning. Bitchy or not, the girl had a lot of talent. And I don't know if Matt knew this or it was just dumb luck, but Jayne and I actually worked well together. I found myself bouncing ideas off her I'd never even mentioned in front of the guys and was surprised to find that she was kinda *supportive.*

About an hour in I asked her if she wanted a drink.

"Yeah, sure," she said without looking up from the pile of sheet music that had begun to accumulate.

I moved quickly around the kitchen, hoping Dad wouldn't come nosing around, then realized he was probably already passed out upstairs. Jayne barely looked up when I got back with a couple of beers, an iced tea and a few bottles of water and set them on the bench next to where we'd been sitting. I grabbed a beer while she chose the iced tea.

We sat in an uncomfortable silence for a few minutes before I asked, "So, uh, you far from here?"

"About twenty minutes," she said before taking a sip of her iced tea.

I thought this might break the ice, but I was wrong. After a few more minutes of awkward silence I tried again.

"Sometimes it's not easy..." I motioned to the papers scattered about. "I've written a lot of my own music, but a true songwriter, I'm not."

She surprised me with an uncharacteristic chuckle. "Matt's not always one either, but don't tell him I told you so."

"Hey, don't sell him short," I countered, "I think the stuff he's done is pretty awesome."

"Yeah, but it doesn't always come easy for him. Like for instance, how long was he working on this piece before he gave it to us? Weeks? Either he nails it on the first shot or he tanks and hands it off to me or Skid or I guess now you." She shrugged and took another sip. "I'm not complaining; in the end, it usually works out."

I was about to respond when my cell started to ring. Would have hit ignore too but I saw it was Leah.

"Gimme a sec," I said to Jayne as I stood and answered the call with a *hey babe, what's up*. Jayne nodded and spun around on the bench and continued with what we'd been working on.

Leah said she was waiting outside the library for Molly and as usual Molly was taking forever. From the way her teeth were chattering, it seemed Pennsylvania was even colder than Jersey. We only talked for a few minutes before she said she had to go.

"Okay, talk to you tomorrow." I ended the call, then stared down at the phone for a minute. Was it my imagination, or were my conversations with Leah getting shorter and shorter?

"Girlfriend?" Jayne asked without looking up from what she was doing.

"Yeah," I said as I tossed my cell onto the table.

"What's her name?"

"Leah."

"How long have you guys been together?"

"Comin' up on two years."

"That's cool. She from around here?"

"Yeah, not far, just a few towns over. But she's away at school in Pennsylvania."

"Oh, so it's like a long-distance thing?"

"I guess, but it's not really that far. I've gone up most weekends 'til now, but with practice and the semester's already half over anyway..." I trailed off when I realized I was rambling, like I had to explain myself. "How 'bout you?"

"How about me, what?" she asked, suddenly sounding annoyed.

"Um, are you, uh, seeing anyone?"

"No. I was seeing someone for a while, but it ended."

When she didn't elaborate I realized she was probably referring to her involvement with Damian and changed the subject. We continued to work until nearly midnight without making much in the way of serious headway, so I was surprised when she suggested we pick it up again the following night.

"I can come to your place," I offered, but she shook her head.

"You've got a better setup here and a lot more room," she said as she grabbed her coat off the hook and slipped into it. "Same time?"

"That works," I said as I opened the garage to let her out. I waited until the old Toyota disappeared down the street before closing it again.

▲   ▲   ▲

The following day I got out of work late, which meant I barely had enough time to get home and shower before Jayne got there. The water felt fuckin' great after the long day, and if it wasn't already after six I would have stayed in there longer. I reluctantly shut off the spray, then shook out my wet hair and reached outside the stall for a towel. As I dried off I found myself humming the song we had been working on – and hoping we'd get further along than we did the night before. I was still humming when I wrapped the damp towel around my waist and walked back across the hall.

"Mmmm...mmmm...mmm..." *This is the part where we always get stuck.* "Mmmm...mmm - what the heck!"

Jayne was casually leaning against the oak dresser next to my bed. She looked up at me and raised an eyebrow, but I wasn't sure if it was because I was wearing a towel or because she didn't like my humming.

"Wha - what're you doing up here?!"

"Oh, sorry," she said as she leaned off the dresser. "I got here a little early and your dad answered the door. It looked like he was on his way out but he told me to come up." She shrugged. "I didn't think it would be a big deal."

"It's not. Sorry, I didn't mean to jump at you; I, I mean I just didn't expect anyone to be in here." It hit me again that I was standing there in nothing but a towel, and I grabbed a wrinkled t-shirt off my bed and quickly slipped it on. This elicited a sarcastic eyeroll from Jayne, but I'd somehow missed the joke.

"And, hey, just a heads-up," she said as she leaned back against the dresser, "Your dad looked like he had a major bug up his butt about something."

"Why, what did he say?" I asked uncomfortably.

"Nothing really. He just motioned towards the stairs and kind of grumbled something to let me know you were up here, but he looked majorly pissed off."

"But he left?"

"Yeah, he left."

Relieved that he was gone, I asked if she wanted to get started.

"Sure," she said and pointedly eyed my towel. "You going down like that?"

"*No*," I snapped, feeling flustered, "Go ahead down, grab something to drink from the fridge and I'll meet you in the garage."

She nodded, then pushed off the dresser again and left my room.

I stood there for a minute, hands on my hips, trying to imagine Leah's reaction if she walked in right now and saw me standing around half-dressed with a girl in my bedroom. Leah was cool, but certainly not *that* cool. No one was. Man, if I ever walked in on her in a similar situation, I would have totally flipped.

Shaking off the thought, I quickly pulled on a pair of jeans, then met Jayne down in the garage.

"I grabbed you a beer," she said, motioning to the bottle of Bud on the table.

"Thanks," I said, taking the beer and popping it open.

We got right to work but an hour in we still hadn't come up with anything worthwhile.

"I feel like what we're doing is too..." Jayne paused for a minute to search for the right word. "Too *generic*." She looked at me. "Don't you think?"

I shrugged. "Maybe. But like I said last night, lyrics really aren't my strongpoint."

"I'm thinking a melody like this needs lyrics that are more on the explicit side." She thought for a minute then changed her mind. "Well, maybe explicit is too strong a word... maybe more like gritty."

Gritty. "Hey, hang here a minute, I think I might have something."

I jogged back into the house and up to my room, where I grabbed the shoebox filled with the stuff my mother had written years before. When I got back down to the garage I placed the box on the table and removed the lid.

"What's this stuff?" Jayne asked curiously as she peered inside.

"Just some old stuff written by someone I knew. Maybe we can find something that works." I handed her half the sheets and took the other half for myself.

We quickly weeded out the flowery prose in favor of the darker writings, then narrowed them down until we had one that we both agreed would be perfect. Obviously there needed to be some tweaking, but by the time we were done – it was nearing midnight – we both agreed that we'd knocked it out of the park.

"Shit, Matt's gonna go nuts when he hears this," Jayne laughed. She actually sounded giddy.

"You know him better than I do but I'd say if he *doesn't* go nuts, there's definitely something wrong."

We patted ourselves on the back for a few more minutes, then Jayne announced she was going to call it a night.

I glanced over at the rusted clock hanging over the door. Where had the hours gone? "Shit, yeah, didn't realize it was so late."

I watched as she slipped into the puffy coat, thinking that if it was anyone else I would have given them a hug, or at least high-fived them, on completing our song. Not Jayne, though; partners or not, she probably would have slugged me.

▲   ▲   ▲

The next night we met up with Matt in Brooklyn. I almost asked Jayne to ride there with me, but I figured being trapped in a car together for that long would put a strain on our newfound partnership. She must have felt the same because she didn't suggest it either. I didn't really care, though it would have been nice to have someone to distract me from freaking out about what Matt would think about the song. Turns out I was worrying for nothing because *he fucking loved it*. Not just the lyrics but what we did with the ending - how we fine-tuned it so it had a better flow.

And when the four of us played the piece for the first time we all agreed that for sure this was *the one*. The song that would catapult Dirty Bushwick out of obscurity.

CHAPTER 34 - LEAH

It was the first game in the playoff series and the first time I'd be seeing Chase since what I now referred to as "the laundry incident." I might have been torn about going, if not for Jackson calling to say he'd be too busy with band business to visit. Some people might have seen that call as a test, an opportunity to rise above temptation and be loyal to my boyfriend; I decided it was a sign from the Universe, telling me I should see what, if anything, was between me and Chase.

My plan was simple: hang out with Chase some more and try to get to know him better. And who knows? Maybe once I got to know him better I'd decide he wasn't for me after all. Then again . . . I suddenly found my thoughts drifting to that night on his couch - how it felt having him on top of me, those muscular arms around me, the feel of his hands running through my hair – and felt the now familiar hot flush spreading across my face. What if his roommates hadn't come home when they did?

Shaking those thoughts from my head, I promised myself I wouldn't do anything stupid. Obviously, I'd already crossed a line - a big one – when I made out with him on the couch and since I couldn't very well *un*cross it, I told myself that that activity was fair game so long as I didn't take it any further, right?

The rational side of me knew very well that line of thought was bullshit. That same rational side also knew that I was wrong to go behind Jackson's back *and* knew that you don't just dump a great boyfriend for some guy you barely know. This of course fed into my theory that I needed to spend more time with Chase so I could make an "informed" decision. Again, I knew this was bullshit. Maybe that's why I hadn't told Molly about it.

When it came to me and Chase, though, Molly seemed to have a sixth sense.

▲   ▲   ▲

"The game starts at eight o'clock, you ready?" Molly asked, her voice muffled by the pink sweatshirt she was pulling over her head.

I grabbed my phone from the nightstand and slipped it into my pocket. "Yep, just about."

Molly grunted unenthusiastically. She had been in a bit of funk lately, partly because she had not landed Brent and partly because she had not found some other guy worthy of using to make him jealous. I sympathized but had my own drama to deal with.

She shook out her long brown curls. "I swear, Leah, I'm done with Brent. It's just not worth it."

"Well, there's always the direct approach," I pointed out as we stepped into the hall. I closed the door behind us. "At this point, what've you go to lose, right?"

"I don't know. What if he turns me down? Can you imagine the humiliation, every time I run into him, which is, like, all the time? I just don't think it's worth it."

I wanted to remind her that she ran into him "like, all the time" because she orchestrated it. Instead I said, "Well, you'll never know unless you put yourself out there, right?"

She shrugged as if debating what I'd said but knowing Molly she'd just come up with another scheme to get his attention.

The stadium was already packed when we got there, but we managed to find decent seats mid-way down the field. Once again our team dominated (Chase scored three goals!) and as I screamed and clapped with the rest of the fans I told myself it had nothing to do with him and everything to do with my newfound love of lacrosse. *Yeah, okay Leah.* They had no sooner won the game when I got a text from Chase, inviting me to the celebration at his place. He was going to jump in the shower but said Molly and I should meet him outside the locker room and we'd all walk back together.

"Okay, this is my chance," Molly said when she heard of the plan. "On the walk back, I'll sidle up next to Brent and make my move."

"I'll believe it when I see it, Molly," I laughed, but sure enough, she made a beeline for Brent the minute he emerged from the locker room.

I mentally crossed my fingers for her, then leaned against the wall and waited for Chase. He was the last one out.

"Hey, bud," he said as he strolled towards me. He smelled of soap. "Ready?"

"Ready," I repeated as he grabbed my hand. Chase was on a high about the win – especially since he was the high scorer - and talked nonstop about it all the way to his house.

By the time we got there the party was already in full swing, at least it seemed to be, judging from the blasting music. Chase led me around to the back door but when I went to walk up the steps to the deck he suddenly stopped.

"Hey, c'mere a sec," he said as he pulled me over and laced his fingers around the small of my back. He smiled and looked down at me for a minute. "I was, uh, hoping you'd have some more laundry to do this week . . . doing laundry with you was fun."

"Well, it's always more fun to do laundry with a friend, right?" I teased.

"Friends . . . right," he drawled as he nodded his head, "I forgot about that."

He smiled down at me a moment longer, then he lowered his head and kissed me. It was almost as if he were teasing me, brushing his tongue lightly against mine. It only lasted about a minute, but he had my head spinning.

He broke the kiss and smiled down at me again. "Do you kiss all your friends like that?"

I didn't answer, just stared up at him.

"So . . . you want to go inside?" he said as he motioned with his head to the door.

I gave a slight nod, still feeling the lingering effects of the kiss.

Taking my hand again, he led me, not through the sliders but the side door. There were people hanging out in the kitchen and living room, but he bypassed both, hanging a quick left toward a narrow staircase I hadn't seen before.

I looked at him questioningly. "Where're we going?"

"Basement; I wanna show you something."

I nodded again, wondering giddily if he was taking me someplace where we could be alone. That idea went out the window when I heard voices wafting up from below, and I'd be lying if I said I wasn't disappointed.

The basement was cute, though, with a couple of small leather couches, an old fashioned, boxy TV perched in one corner and a mini fridge in another. Next to the stairs there was a door that I figured led to a bathroom. A few of Chase's teammates were hanging out and drinking, and they nodded or raised their beers in greeting. Brent wasn't with them, which made me think that maybe Molly's move had worked after all.

I looked around the room but didn't see anything special. "What did you want to show me?"

"This," he said as he reached up into a cabinet behind the TV and pulled out a bottle of liquor and a stack of small plastic shot glasses. This move elicited cheers from his friends.

"What's that?" I asked as I squinted to see the label on the bottle.

"Tequila, right guys?"

Another, even louder cheer went up from the guys. Chase explained that after a big win they always toasted with shots of tequila – it was a tradition and judging from the season they'd had I figured they'd gone through several bottles already.

Chase winked at me, then set up the little cups and poured one for each of us. The other guys immediately threw them back, their eyes flickering toward the bottle as if considering another.

"You know," he said, "Nobody knows about this but these guys, a few others, and now you. So..."

"So what?"

"So, you better not tell anyone," he said gravely, "Or I might haveta kill ya." He grinned and handed one to me.

"I can't drink that," I laughed, "I'll end up with my head in the toilet."

He shot me an incredulous look. "From *one* shot?"

I shrugged. "I've heard bad things about tequila."

"You've never had tequila?"

"Nope."

"Well," he said mischievously, "I'm glad I could be here for your *first time*." Then, oblivious to the fact that I'd turned beet read, he tossed the shot back. "Besides, it's bad luck not to toast our win."

"Says who?" I managed to say.

He shrugged. "Just made it up. You don't have to drink it, though, especially if you think it'll make you sick."

I eyed the drink cautiously, then brought the little cup to my lips. I didn't want to seem like a dud and plus I was curious.

"Well, here goes..."

"Whoa, hold up." He grabbed a beer from the little fridge in the corner and handed it to me. "You're gonna need to chase it down with this."

I took the beer from him, then tossed the shot back and immediately began gagging. I quickly chased it down with the smooth-tasting beer, then came up for air.

"Ugh! Never again!" I laughed as I put the plastic cup down on the coffee table.

"Hey, it's not for everyone," Chase said, but he was laughing too. "But thanks, we'll win the next game for sure now."

"You guys better after I just downed that nasty stuff," I joked.

We hung out in the basement for another hour or so, bullshitting with the rest of the guys. Somehow, in the middle of laughing and having a good time, I ended up on what seemed to have become my reserved spot on Chase's lap. It had become so natural that I didn't even feel guilty about it anymore. Not even when he slid his hand quietly up the back of my shirt where he kept it for most of the night. Not even when he whispered in my ear about how hot he thought I looked. Not even when his hand began discretely rubbing the inside of my thigh. Not even then.

After polishing off a few more beers, the guys started to slowly filter up the stairs to get something to eat. I didn't realize until the last one was gone that I'd been waiting to be alone with him. Chase must have been waiting too, because the minute we heard the basement door close he turned me around to face him. His hands went to my waist, but his eyes, which had a bit of a beer glaze to them, were on mine. He had this lazy smile on his face as he pulled me closer and began to kiss me. One hand slid down the back of my jeans and pulled me closer so I was pressed tightly up against him while the other hand slipped under my shirt, then inside my bra. My first instinct was to pull back but I couldn't; it just felt too damn good. I'd never get tired of having those hands on me. He removed his hand from the back of my jeans, took hold of my free hand and placed it over the button of his jeans. I was about to undo it, then froze at the sound of footsteps and voices above us. Slowly, I pulled my hand back.

"Chase," I whispered, even though we were clearly alone, "We should stop. What if someone comes down?"

"Trust me," he muttered, "If there's food up there they won't be down any time soon." Then he repositioned my hand over the button of his jeans.

"But, but they might..." I trailed off unconvincingly.

He sighed. "Would you rather go upstairs . . . with everyone else?"

I gave an almost imperceptible shake of my head.

He leaned forward and whispered in my ear, "Me neither."

I giggled, whether from nervousness or the feel of his breath in my ear, I didn't know.

Chase glanced toward the stairs as if debating something. "Hey, c'mere a sec," he said as he slid me off his lap, then stood from the couch. He took me by the hand, led me across the room to the small bathroom and pulled me inside.

Before I even knew what was happening, he had closed the door with his foot and was kissing me again. My head was swimming and the drinks were making me want to do things to him that I knew I shouldn't. Chase backed up against the sink, taking me with him. It felt so good to have those strong arms around me again. I moved my hands down the front of his snug-fitting lacrosse t-shirt before slipping them both underneath it. The hard, now-familiar muscles felt so smooth beneath my palms as they wandered from his chest to his back and up to his shoulders. He had one hand moving through my hair and the other wrapped tightly around my waist. Again, he took hold of my hand and moved it down to the top of his jeans. I hesitated, then slid my hand down and brought it along the front of his jeans where I pressed it against him.

"Leah . . ." he gasped, gripping my hand and bringing it back up to his fly. This time I didn't waver; I unbuttoned them, then grasped the zipper and slowly brought it down. His kisses became more urgent as he grasped my wrist and guided my hand inside. I took hold of him, cautiously at first, then more firmly. He moaned, then I felt him moving against the motion my fist was making. I gripped him harder, and he grasped the edge of the sink and leaned his head back so he was facing the ceiling. He hissed my name out again through clenched teeth as he continued to move against my fist.

"Fuck, Leah . . . don't stop . . . yeah, that's it."

I kept going, bringing him close then slowing down again. It was almost like a high, the effect I was having over him. He moaned again, louder this time, then his body lurched forward. I stepped back as if realizing right then and there what I'd done, the line I had just crossed. And this time there was no denying it because the proof was right there, glistening across the palm of my hand in the dimly lit bathroom of Chase's basement.

CHAPTER 35 – JACKSON

I'd heard about this kind of thing – musicians who kill themselves for years just trying to get their music heard, then – bam – out of nowhere, one thing after another falls into place. Sure, I'd heard about it, but I didn't know if I believed it and I sure as shit never believed it could happen to me. Then, within the space of such a short time, I'd joined an incredible band with people who, musically at least, were in complete sync with me. We'd written a song that was gonna blow people's minds, and if that wasn't enough, Matt had gotten a call from one of the owners of Token's, the bar around the corner. They were going to start booking live music on the weekends, even earlier than planned, and they wanted to confirm that we were still interested in being their first act. *Were we interested?* Fuck, yeah! I couldn't speak for the others, but I'd never felt like this in my whole fucking life. I was feeling...lucky.

The first thing I did when Matt told us the news was call Leah.

"Jackson, that's so cool!" she gushed, but then I thought I heard papers shuffling around in the background. "When is it?"

Was it my imagination, or did she sound distracted?

"A week from Saturday," I told her. "Listen, um, I know you're busy studying for finals and stuff but I'd, uh, I'd love for you to be there."

When she didn't answer right away, I added, "I could come up Saturday morning and bring you down. You could go to the show, meet everyone; it'd be really cool. Then I could bring you back up first thing Sunday morning..."

I could hear the pleading note in my voice. What the fuck? Not too long ago I wouldn't have even had to ask.

". . . Jackson, you know I'd love to but," she hesitated and I heard the tap-tap of a keyboard in the background. "You know, with finals and trying to decide on my courses for next year, there's just no way I could swing it. You understand, right?"

"Oh, yeah . . . sure, no problem. Just thought I'd give it a shot." I tried not to sound too disappointed. "I'm sure there'll be other gigs over the summer that you'll be able to make it to, so, yeah, don't worry about it. Next time."

"Okay, next time for sure because you know I'm dying to meet everyone and see you guys play, right?"

"Yeah, definitely."

"Okay, so listen, I really need to get going; I'm like swamped with work here. I'll talk to you tomorrow. Love you."

"Love you too, babe." Once again, I found myself staring down at the phone after the call ended. Sure, I knew she was busy, but there was still a little piece of me that hoped she'd put everything aside and surprise me. Especially for my first show with the band! I tossed my phone aside and tried to remind myself that although college wasn't something I could relate to, it was a lot of work and very important to Leah. Besides, she'd be home soon anyway, and then everything would get back to normal – even better.

▲   ▲   ▲

A couple nights later Jayne and I were back in my garage, putting the final tweaks on a song we hoped to debut at Token's. Since they'd officially booked us, we decided we'd better double up on our practice sessions to make sure we'd be ready. Though Jayne was still a little standoffish, I felt like we were settling into something of a comfortable working relationship.

"So . . . you gonna tell me who wrote those lyrics?" she asked as I returned from the kitchen with a beer for myself and an iced tea for Jayne. She said it nonchalantly, without looking up from what she was working on, but I knew she had been dying to ask. In fact, I was surprised it had taken so long. "Matt and Skid are assuming *we* did, and I'm fine with leaving it at that, but I gotta admit, I'm a little curious." Finally, she raised her eyes to mine. "Okay, *a lot* curious."

When I didn't answer right away she took it upon herself to guess. "Girlfriend? *Leah*, that's her name, right? Did she write them?"

I shook my head. "No, it wasn't Leah."

"Well, you don't have to tell me if you don't want." She chuckled. "Like I said, I'm fine with taking the credit for it."

She looked at me pointedly for a moment, then shrugged to let me know it wasn't that important to her.

"Actually," I said a few minutes later, "it was my mom."

Jayne looked up at me, her eyes wide, her usual stoicism nowhere to be found.

"Wow," she said, clearly impressed. "That's not what I was expecting. What did she think when you told her we used it? She must've been *psyched.*"

I felt my stomach clench. "She's, uh, she's dead," I replied, but kept my eyes trained on the paperwork in front of me.

"Oh, jeez, sorry; I had no idea."

I shrugged. "It was a long time ago."

"What happened?"

"Car accident. I was just a kid."

"Shit, Jackson. Sucks you had to go through that."

I shrugged again. "Like I said, it was a long time ago."

"You and your dad must be close, though, since it's just the two of you living here, right?" She shook her head. "Jeez, especially after something like that happens."

I knew Jayne was just trying to be nice, but my family had never been a favorite topic; in fact, I usually just refused to discuss them. But since I didn't want to seem rude, I just mumbled something incoherent, hoping she would let it drop.

She looked over at me, a rare almost unreadable expression on her face. Compassion? Understanding? I wasn't sure. "Hey, if you don't want to talk about it, that's cool. It's none of my business anyway."

I was sure that was the end of the conversation, but then Jayne did something that really shocked the shit out of me: she started talking about her own family situation.

"My mom's not in the picture either. She took off – barely even remember her. Haven't heard from her since I was a kid." She glanced up at me as if to gauge my reaction. "Crazy, right?"

"Yeah, that is kinda crazy," I agreed, grateful to have the spotlight off me. "So, do you have your own place or are you still living at home?"

"For now I'm with my dad; it's easier on both of us money-wise. He plans to retire soon, though, and put the house up for sale, probably in the fall."

"So, what'll you do then?"

"Matt's trying to hook me up with a place in Brooklyn."

"Wow, I gotta tell you," I said with a strum of my guitar, "I'm a little jealous. Brooklyn is the place to be."

"Yeah, and super friggin' expensive." She sighed. "Who knows?"

"What do you do? For work, I mean; don't think I ever asked."

"Guitar Center. In Paramus. You know it?"

"Yeah, sure, I've been to that one a few times but I usually go to the one in Totowa."

"They're pretty cool and they work around my schedule," she explained, "but I'm sick of driving back and forth to Brooklyn for the band stuff. It would be great if Matt came through by the time the house sells."

Jayne definitely had a point. Living in Brooklyn or even Staten Island - would be a lot easier, especially if I could land a decent paying job there as well. It was certainly something to think about if things really started to take off with the band, not to mention the added benefit of getting out of my dad's house...

I glanced up and saw Jayne watching me with a curious expression. "Yeah, Jayne, that would be great..."

Great for you, I added silently. Much as I would have liked to live in Brooklyn, it would put me further away from Leah, and that wasn't something I was willing to do.

CHAPTER 36 – LEAH

I couldn't believe it. The end of the semester was fast approaching and Molly had no clue about what I'd been up to with Chase. To be honest, I couldn't take much credit; Molly had left a ton of work for the last minute and that, along with cramming for finals, rendered her completely oblivious to what anyone else was doing. Even her infatuation with Brent took a back seat to all her last-minute scrambling.

Things had steadily progressed since that night in Chase's basement, and as much as I didn't want Molly butting in it was pretty weird keeping such a big secret from her. We had always told each other everything, and now I felt like I was cheating on her as much as Jackson.

Jackson... I tried not to think of what it would do to him if he ever found out. It certainly made it a lot easier that he was no longer coming up on weekends. Easier for me, at least. I never had to look him in the eye, and whenever he called I kept the conversation short for fear he'd be able to tell from my voice that something was up. If he did notice anything, though, he didn't let on.

Still, since I wasn't about to go flaunting it, Chase and I spent most of our time holed up in his room. It wasn't just sex, though; we really got to know each other. He told me all about his family back in Ohio and about the pressure he was under to keep his lacrosse game and his grades up. We also talked a lot about the pros and cons of being a lawyer. Like his two older brothers, Chase had always planned to follow in his dad's footsteps, but now he was starting to see just how difficult it would be. At first when he said he thought I'd make a great lawyer, I thought he was just flattering me, but after a while I began to think he was right. So, after one of our many late-night conversations I finally decided to take the plunge and major in pre-law. Chase even offered to help me out with any courses I had trouble with.

The one thing we never talked about was Jackson. Chase never brought him up and I certainly wasn't going to. It was like we were in our own little bubble where my relationship with Jackson didn't exist.

One night while we were doing homework in Chase's room, I casually asked what his plans were for the summer.

"Oh, I got that internship I applied for; the one with the law firm in Cincinnati. It's been in the works for a while. I'm not sure if I mentioned it to you."

"No," I said, trying to keep my voice even, "I don't think you did." I looked down at the textbook I'd been reading and wondered what I was more disappointed about – that I wasn't going to see him or that he didn't think to mention it to me.

"Well anyway," he said, "I'll be pretty busy with that. How 'bout you?"

I shrugged. "Hanging out with Molly; vacation with my family. The usual."

"Oh, that's cool." He shook his head. "This internship is really gonna kick my ass. With all the hours I'll be putting in, I doubt I'll be able to even think about a vacation."

"Oh, that's too bad," I said but the truth was I was too annoyed to care. I knew I was being unreasonable – we'd never discussed getting together over the summer. In fact, I'd sworn up and down to myself that things between us would end along with the semester. I'd go home to Jackson and forget all about him. Now it hit home just how much I'd been kidding myself.

Chase had become like a drug I couldn't get enough of and judging from the way I felt now it looked like the "withdrawal" was going to be much harder than I thought.

CHAPTER 37 - JACKSON

I didn't eat a thing the day of our gig - my stomach was in such knots I felt like anything I consumed would come right back up. Matt, Skid and Jayne might have been shittin' their pants too, but if they were they didn't show it, probably because they'd had a few gigs like this before. The only live audiences I'd ever played in front of were high school kids sneaking drinks at backyard parties. By the time I picked up my guitar they were usually drunk off their asses – an easy-to-please crowd for sure. Token's was full of twenty-somethings paying for their drinks and expecting a lot more from a live band.

When Matt told me our set would only be a half-hour, I didn't know whether to be relieved or more stressed. It was the first time Token's was having live music and I guessed the owner wanted to see how it went over. I saw his point, and in a way it took the pressure off, not having to play all night; on the other hand, we wouldn't have much time to win over the crowd. A few days earlier we'd chosen four songs we unanimously decided were our best, and I'm not gonna lie – I thought it was fuckin' awesome when Matt suggested we close with *Anna's Leash*, the song Jayne and I had collaborated on. We'd come up with the title quite accidentally in my garage one night, after a particularly long jam session and a few beers that left us exhausted and punchy.

"What'd your mom name it?" she'd asked after we played the song for the umpteenth time.

"Annalise," I said absently, thinking she'd asked what my mom's name was.

"*Anna's Leash...?*" she said curiously, then, before I could correct her she added, "I like it. In fact, I'd say it's perfect. *Anna's Leash* it is."

I didn't bother correcting her because I agreed; it was perfect.

Finally Saturday night arrived, and good thing, too, because by that time I was coming out of my skin. When we took the stage, the crowd was sparse and their response lukewarm, but that was to be expected. I mean, it's not like we had a following. They stood around in small groups, drinking and talking, their eyes occasionally flicking our way. They didn't seem to hate us, but they clearly weren't enthralled either. We were background noise.

It wasn't until we neared the end of our very short set that I noticed that people here and there had stopped their respective conversations and were watching us. They seemed to be not only listening to the music but genuinely enjoying what they were hearing. There were even a few bobbing heads, which was pretty cool.

We finished the set with *Anna's Leash* and left the stage to the sound of scattered applause. But when I heard a few whistles coming from the back of the bar, my face split into a shit-eating grin. It was no standing ovation, but in that moment it felt just as good.

After packing up our equipment the four of us gathered at the bar to throw back a few beers and pat ourselves on the backs. It felt great when two bartenders and one of the waitresses came over to say how they really dug our music, but I was dying to know what the owners thought. They were there – I had seen them before the set – but they hadn't spoken to us since. The patrons were also still hard to read; no one said anything, but I thought I saw a few of them glancing over at us. No matter, I told myself, I was glad I'd made it through the set without yacking.

A couple hours later, it was just me and Skid sitting at the bar. Matt and Jayne were around somewhere, though I hadn't seen them in a while. Skid and I had since moved on to shots and were talking about what had gone right with the set and what we could do better next time. I had just raised a shot of Hornitos to my lips when over Skid's shoulder I saw two girls approaching. They were both attractive, with similar slim builds and the same long dark hair.

"Hi," I heard the taller of the two say, "You guys were really great." She stuck her hand out. "I'm Amanda," she said, then jerked her thumb toward her friend. "This is Callie."

Callie gave us a shy little wave.

"Hi," Skid and I said almost in unison. "So, you liked the show?" I asked, itching for some real live feedback.

"Oh, *yeah*, definitely," Amanda said, "I didn't even know this place had live music."

"It's something new they're trying out," I explained.

"Oh, well if the rest of the bands are as good as you guys then I'd say it'll be a success." She smiled in a flirty way and I couldn't tell if she was being sincere or just blowin' smoke so she could "meet the band."

"You girls want a drink?" Skid asked as he signaled to the bartender.

"Sure," they said and pulled over two stools. They really did look alike, and I briefly wondered if they were related but decided I didn't care enough to ask. Skid had enough interest for both of us - touching Amanda's arm when he asked if she wanted another drink or flashing a suggestive grin at Callie - and I couldn't tell which one he was after. Maybe it was both. Judging from the way the girls were responding to him, it seemed anything was possible.

Now starting to get bored, I glanced around to see where Matt and Jayne had disappeared to. My stomach did a little flip when I saw Matt standing near the entrance with one of the owners. Were they trying to work out another date for us to play? With fingers crossed, I turned back to Skid and the girls.

"So, you guys want to go back to our place and hang out?" Amanda's eyes flickered from Skid to me and back again. "We're not far from here."

Before I could think of what to say, Skid said, "Sure, lead the way." Then he stood from his stool, turned around and threw a few bills onto the bar.

Obviously, I wasn't going with them but before I could think of a good enough excuse, a great one sidled up from behind me.

"Ready, babe?" I heard Jayne ask as her arms wrapped around me and she planted a big wet kiss on the side of my neck while Skid looked on curiously. "Sorry, got tied up with some stuff in the back, you want to head out?"

I stood up quickly, hoping the surprise didn't show on my face.

"Uh, yeah, just about," I said, noting the girls' puzzled expressions. "Uh, Jayne, this is Amanda and, um, Callie."

"Hi!" Jayne said in an overly friendly tone I'd never heard her use before. "Were you guys here for the show?"

"Oh yeah, it was great!" Callie gushed, while Amanda just nodded nervously.

It took all I had not to burst out laughing.

"Cool," she said, then turned to me. "Matt says he got us in again for next Saturday." She turned back to the girls. "Come back again next week if you're around, bring some friends. We could really use the exposure. Nice meeting you."

She grabbed hold of my hand and led me toward the back room where our equipment was. Once inside, she let go of my hand and closed the door, then turned to me with a strange expression on her face. It was almost...*flirty*. I'd thought she was just fucking with Amanda and Callie, but now I had to wonder, had Jayne been *serious*?

"Um, Jayne," I said, the heat rising to my face, "I'm, you know, flattered, but, uh, you know I'm with Leah so um . . ." I trailed off.

She looked at me as if I had three heads, then started to laugh. And not just a chuckle, but a full-fledged fit. When she came up for air she wiped her eyes and put her hands on her hips. "Man," she said, still giggling, "you need to Get. Over. Yourself."

I just looked at her, embarrassed, relieved and more than a little annoyed.

"Did you *actually* think I was making a *play* for you? Gimme a break, I saw the look on your face when those two asked you to go back to their place. You looked like you were about to panic...though not nearly as badly as you panicked when I got you in here."

"Fuck off, Jayne," I shot back. She'd been messing with me, no doubt about it.

"*Fuck off Jayne*, really? Is that how you want to play this? Okay, well how about next time I let you come up with your *own* lame-ass excuse for why you're not gonna leave with two hot girls who were obviously into you. *Oh, sorry girls, I can't 'cause my girlfriend might get mad at me.* Yeah, real cool."

She took a step back now, looking just as pissed as I was. "Better get used to it," she said, as she started packing up her keyboard, "Gonna happen all the time in clubs like this."

I now felt like the biggest asshole on the planet. In one fell swoop I'd managed to completely sabotage the already shaky friendship I'd built with her. I had to say something to fix it or we'd be right back to the barely concealed hostility from when we first met.

I fidgeted for a moment, not sure how I was going to handle it. Finally, I figured since Jayne was a straight-shooter I'd be one too.

"Okay," I conceded, "Maybe I was a little tongue-tied at first, but I was far from *panicking* over it. I'm sure if you hadn't *swooped in* I would've come up with something smooth to say to them."

She spun around on her heels, a smug grin on her face. "Ha! I knew it, loser!"

I quickly grabbed her into a playful headlock. "Loser? Call me loser again and you're a dead woman!"

She straightened up, trying unsuccessfully to mask her smile with a scowl. "But all kidding aside, this kind of thing is gonna happen - more often than you think when we're playing in places like this. It just goes with the territory." She shrugged. "But hey, if that's what you're into then go for it; no one really gives a shit what you do on your own time."

I rolled my eyes at her. There was no way I would ever cheat on Leah. Sometimes I still couldn't believe a girl like her was into me – I sure as hell wasn't going to do anything to fuck it up. Just the thought of having to deal with girls at every gig was extremely annoying. Flattering, but annoying.

"No, that's not what I'm into," I began as I toyed with the notion now forming in my mind, "In fact, I'm thinking maybe we can make a deal..."

"A *deal?* Okay, I'm intrigued." She motioned with her hand to go on as she sat on the corner of the desk by the door.

"How about during gigs you let me pretend that we're, uh, together, so if a situation arises, I got an easy out. You know, like what you did tonight."

"*Okay.* And what do *I* get out of the deal?"

I shrugged. "Well, I'll do the same for you if you want."

She laughed. "I don't need a beard, Jackson, I can handle myself just fine. But sure, you can pretend you're with the hot rocker-chick."

"Okay, so . . . we're good?" I asked.

"Yeah, we're good." She hopped off the desk and continued packing her stuff. "So, hey, when am I gonna meet this mystery woman of yours? I'm beginning to think you just made her up."

"Soon, maybe next week," I said.

"It's funny, 'cause I have this picture of her in my mind and I'm wondering how close I'll be," she mused.

"Okay, now *I'm* curious," I said as I hopped onto the desk she'd just vacated, "Let's hear what you've got."

"Hmm, let's see..." She tapped her chin with her index finger. "Stand up a sec; let me take a good look at you."

"But what does that have to do with -?" I began, then decided to go along with the game. I stood and folded my arms across my chest as she gave me the once-over. "Seen enough?"

"Yeah. You can sit."

I returned to my seat on top of the desk.

"Okay, so, I'm going to stick with my first instinct. I'm guessing since you're about average height that she's probably on the smaller side, tiny even. You know, 'cause guys always like to feel big."

I rolled my eyes at her.

"She's got long hair, light brown or maybe even blonde...?"

I kept my face carefully blank. So far she was describing Leah to a T.

"Not flashy," Jayne continued, "dresses more on the conservative side. And I'm guessing she comes across as very straight-laced and polite, you know, the 'please and thank you' type."

"That's bull," I said as I shook my head. "You must've seen a picture. Either in my garage or maybe on my phone."

"Ha! So I nailed it, right?"

"Wait a minute, you were in my room that time. You must've seen a picture of her there."

"Oh, yeah, that's it," she began sarcastically. "I tore through your room because I just *had* to know."

I narrowed my eyes suspiciously. "So how were you able to describe her almost exactly then?"

"Simple. I just described what I thought your type would be, that's all. And by the way, you're not so unique; what I described is most guys' type."

I found myself annoyed because she was basically calling me and Leah stereotypes and I didn't see us that way at all.

"So, what about you then? What's *your* type?"

"My type?" She paused for a minute, as if she'd never considered the question before. "Well, I'd like to think I don't have a type *per se,* that I'm open to giving everyone a fair shake." When she saw my eyebrows raise she quickly added, "Scratch the image from your perverted mind - what I meant to say was I'm open to giving every *guy* a fair shake."

I laughed because that was exactly what I was thinking.

"I'll tell you this, though, as a rule I don't date musicians."

I raised an eyebrow at her. "Oh, really? And why's that?"

She shrugged. "Most can't be trusted. They're too into themselves and the idea of becoming the next rock icon with a different girl in their bed every night. I guess some people can deal with it and look the other way, but not me. I'm not into that scene."

For a minute I thought about calling her out on her bullshit. She'd obviously broken her "rule" for Damian — or maybe she'd made the rule because things hadn't ended well between them? Either way, she wasn't going to tell me about it and I wasn't going to force the issue. What would it accomplish, other than pissing her off again?

"Well, *I'm* a musician," I countered, "and if you ask Leah she'd tell you I'm nothing like that."

She smiled as if she knew something I didn't. "Maybe not yet, but give it time..."

I shook my head because she didn't get it and, really, how could she? She'd never met Leah so she hadn't a clue what the two of us had together.

"No way. Me and Leah are tight, real tight. You'll see when you meet her; we're the real deal."

CHAPTER 38 – LEAH

I'd been so focused on getting through the semester, I hadn't given much thought as to how I would feel when it ended. It wasn't until nine a.m. that Friday, when my mother called to say they were five minutes away, that it hit me: I was going home. I hurried around the room throwing toiletries and other last-minute items in a bag and realized I still didn't know how I felt.

Molly was overly dramatic as usual. After greeting my parents and little brother, she stood solemnly watching as Dad decided which boxes should go out to the truck first. She helped us carry things down, all the while alternately sighing and shooting me sad looks, as if I was abandoning her. She was acting ridiculous; I would see her within a day or so of being home and then we'd be hanging out all summer. She would have ridden home with us, but there was too much crap – most of it hers - to fit in one vehicle, even if it was a Suburban. Her own parents would be there in a few hours to get her.

Finally, after what seemed like a million trips back and forth, my father announced that we were ready to roll. He said he wanted to beat traffic, but I knew he was probably just dying for a cup of coffee. I turned to tell Molly I would call her later and found myself wrapped in a tight hug.

"Bye," she whispered.

"Seriously, Molly...?"

"Well, it's sad that our freshman year is over." She sniffed. "Of course, you don't care – all you care about is getting back to *Jackson*."

"Okay, okay, sorry," I said quickly so she wouldn't see the deer-in-the-headlights expression on my face. The truth of it was, I *was* torn about leaving school, and it had very little to do with Jackson.

The night before, Chase and I had said our goodbyes at his place – his bed, to be specific.

"C'mere," he'd said as he pulled me up next to him. "So, you gonna miss me?"

"Maybe..."

He laughed. "Right. I bet you'll forget all about me as soon as you pull out of the parking lot." He paused. "Outta sight, outta mind, right?"

Since he was giving no indication that he would miss me, I certainly wasn't going to go there.

"Nah, it'll take me, oh, I don't know, a few days to forget about you. Maybe even a week."

We both laughed at that one, but the joke was on me. I figured by the time I "forgot" about Chase I'd be coming back to school. I just had to pray I didn't give myself away to Jackson in the meantime.

"This place has good coffee..." I told my dad as he approached the small sandwich shop not far from my dorm.

"They better," my father replied as he pulled over, "Just look at that line."

"I'll take a hot coffee – large," I said, then leaned against the truck to wait while the three of them went inside.

Can't believe it's summer, I thought, mentally listing all the things I wanted to accomplish over the next few months. My most ambitious goal was to get the darkest tan of my life, followed closely by catching up on the TV shows I'd missed while studying. My gaze wandered over to across the street, and that's when I saw Chase and an older-looking carbon copy of him, standing in front of the campus bookstore.

"That's gotta be his dad," I said, and just then he looked over and saw me too. We exchanged waves, then he turned to his father and said something before they both began walking towards me... just as my parents and brother emerged from the deli.

"Hey, long time no see," Chase joked as my parents looked on questioningly.

He looked toward his dad and said, "This is my friend Leah, the one I was telling you about."

Chase told his father about me?

"Oh, yes, the future lawyer." His dad flashed the same killer grin Chase had. It was weird. "My son says you've got quite a head on your shoulders, young lady."

I smiled modestly as I extended my hand. "Nice to meet you, Mr. Wagner; I've heard a lot about you."

Behind me, I heard my dad loudly clear his throat. "Oh," I said as I stood back. "Mr. Wagner, Chase, these are my parents."

My dad nearly knocked me over as he stepped forward, his hand outstretched. After shaking with both of them, he introduced my mom and brother, then proceeded to make polite, if awkward, small talk. At least it was awkward for me. My brother, who had recently begun playing lacrosse, saw Chase's team t-shirt and struck up a conversation about it. Chase was more than happy to answer questions about his favorite topic, though every now and again he'd glance over at me and smile. The last smile was accompanied by a sly wink that made me blush because it reminded me about what we'd been doing the night before.

After what seemed like an hour, the two dads wrapped it up with another handshake and an exchange of business cards. My brother whined in protest because he wasn't done grilling Chase about his best moves. As they said their goodbyes, Chase high-fived him and told him to keep up with the practices if he wanted to make varsity by senior year.

"Nice meeting you all," Chase said, then tossed me a *Take care, bud* which was of course was accompanied by that sexy grin of his.

"William, I'll be in touch," his father added as he held up my dad's business card; then the two of them headed back across the street. They even had the same confident walk, I realized.

We'd no sooner climbed back into the Suburban when my mom started fishing for information.

"So, Leah," she began, trying unsuccessfully to sound nonchalant, "How come you've never mentioned Chase before?"

I shrugged. "He's just a friend."

My mom glanced over her shoulder from the front seat. "Well, my goodness, he's certainly handsome, and so well-spoken. Did I hear him say he was studying law?" She turned to my father. "William, did you hear him say that?"

"Yes," Dad replied as he slid the Suburban into traffic, "and his father mentioned that his two older sons are also lawyers." He glanced in the rearview mirror. "How long have you known this boy, Leah?"

"Oh, since last semester, I think."

"Last semester!" my mother exclaimed, "And we're just hearing about him now."

"I told you, Mom, he's just a friend. There was nothing to tell."

Actually, there was a quite a bit to tell, and I almost laughed out loud, thinking how I would have laid it out for my proper mother. *Oh, by the way, Mom, I'm cheating on my boyfriend who may be unacceptable to you but is actually pretty wonderful. Oh, and P.S. I have no idea how this "handsome, well-spoken" guy even feels about me, because we spent most of our time screwing.*

"Well, he certainly seemed to be quite taken with you, Leah. I saw the way he kept glancing over at you and smiling."

Of course she had noticed that, but though my radar shot up I refused to take the bait.

"What time'll we be home?" I said pointedly, "I'm meeting *Jackson* later."

That comment caused my mom's smile to droop into a small frown – just the reaction I'd hoped for – and she turned back towards the front without another word.

"Shouldn't be long, the traffic seems pretty light for a Friday."

They didn't bring up Chase again for the rest of the ride home, but I knew it wasn't likely they'd let the subject drop for good. It was just a matter of time.

▲   ▲   ▲

"Are you sure we'll be able to get in?"

I took my eyes off the road just long enough to glare at Molly. It was the third time she'd asked and we hadn't even made it to the George Washington Bridge yet. At this rate I'd have to hear the question at least three more times before we got to Brooklyn.

"Really, Molly? I told you, Jackson said it wouldn't be a problem."

We were on our way to see Jackson's band play at Token's, the bar in Brooklyn he was always talking about. Though I wouldn't admit it to Molly, I too had a hard time believing we would get in, but what was I supposed to do? Jackson had been asking me since before school ended to go, and until now I'd never been able to. I figured worst case scenario we'd get turned away at the door and just drive back to Jersey, but of course Molly had to up the drama ante. She had this crazy notion that the two of us would be arrested in some kind of sting operation. I told her she watched too much TV and that the cops had bigger fish to fry than weeding out two underage Jersey-ites slipping into a bar.

"I just don't need my parents being called down to the station, that's all," she huffed.

The station, jeez. I snickered under my breath – or so I thought - when I heard that.

She shot me an annoyed look. "You *know* what I mean, Leah. Your parents would flip too if they knew we were here."

"I'm not worried. Jackson wouldn't have asked us to come if he thought it would be a problem..."

"Oh, well, I'm glad you can trust him," she said curtly.

I glanced at her again, eyes narrowed. Had she just given me a dig? Sure sounded that way, but about what I wasn't sure. An awkward silence settled between us, then I handed her my phone, which was opened to the directions Jackson had texted me earlier.

"It gets a little confusing once we get over the bridge – can you read this to me?"

"Sure." She took the phone from me, then said, "Leah?"

"Yeah?"

"Do you think they'll let us in?"

My head whipped towards her, then saw the sly grin on her face and bust out laughing.

"You're nuts."

Forty-five minutes and a few wrong turns later we finally found Token's. I was pleasantly surprised when I found a spot down the block - Jackson had warned me about the parking in Brooklyn – and proud of myself when I got into the spot after only two tries. He must have been waiting for my text because less than a minute after I sent it he was outside.

"Hey!" he said as he wrapped me in a hug.

"Hey yourself." I put my arms around his neck and stood on my tiptoes for a kiss. His hair smelled of that shampoo he used. I always meant to ask what brand it was and always forgot. It smelled good, familiar.

He let me go, then went over to Molly and gave her a peck on the cheek. "This way," he said, grinning from ear to ear as he led us to the door. The bouncer waved us in, but Jackson told us not to go to the bar just to be on the safe side.

"I'll get you guys sodas before we go on stage," he added, the grin broadening as he said the words *on stage*.

His excitement was contagious, and after months of – let's face it – being completely self-absorbed, I found myself looking forward to the show and meeting the rest of the band.

I also noticed the predatory glint in Molly's eye as we grabbed a table and waited for them to get started.

"I've never met a real live band before. Do you think they'll be cute?"

"From the way Jackson described them I don't think they're your type," I laughed. "And one of them is a girl."

As soon as the words were out of my mouth, I realized my blunder.

"A girl? Really?" She sounded intrigued. "Huh, I don't remember you ever mentioning that."

"Well, I did," I said quickly to hide my annoyance. Jackson had told me about Jayne from the beginning, and it wasn't a big deal. I, however, had not mentioned it to Molly because I knew she'd *make* a big deal out of it, just like she made a big deal out of everything lately. She had deemed my friendship with Chase "inappropriate" long before it became well...really inappropriate. Jeez, she'd gotten so judgey with me lately, thank God I had never told her what really went on.

She thought for a minute and then shook her head. "Nope, I definitely would've remembered that nugget."

"Well, it certainly wasn't a secret," I lied. Lying seemed to have become my number one pastime. "I mean, you surely would've noticed the minute they came on stage, right?"

She just shrugged it off. "True..."

Molly was quiet for a few minutes; almost too quiet. Like she had something to say but was waiting for the right opening.

Finally she spoke. "Hey, can I ask you something?"

"Yeah, what?"

"Now, don't jump down my throat or anything but I'm curious . . . do you feel the least bit guilty about how close you and Chase have gotten?"

I froze. *Did she somehow find out that I'd been sleeping with Chase?*

"I mean, all the late nights at the library, the sitting on his lap, the joking around . . . I know you say it's all innocent . . ." she trailed off.

I let out the breath I'd been holding. Before I could answer my mind drifted back to the previous afternoon. It was a few hours after I'd gotten back from school and Jackson was coming to pick me up.

As soon as the doorbell rang I braced myself for the guilt I was sure was going to stab me right in the gut the moment I saw him. But oddly, no guilt hit me. Not when I opened the door. Not when he lifted me off my feet and hugged me so tight I thought I'd burst. Not even when he looked into my eyes and told me how good it felt to have me back in his arms again.

I reasoned that maybe I *did* feel guilty but it was overshadowed by the fear that he'd be able to tell just by looking at me what I'd been up to. Or maybe it wasn't that complicated after all. Maybe it was as simple as me having been able to totally separate the two, like I was living two completely different lives. Then I started feeling guilty for *not* feeling guilty. Thank God Jackson didn't pick up on any of it.

"No, Molly," I said as I slipped off my jacket and hung it on the back of the chair. "I have nothing to feel guilty about; Chase and I have always been just friends."

Really, really good friends.

▲　　▲　　▲

Molly and I were on our feet and screaming as soon as Dirty Bushwick took to the stage. Jackson smiled and nodded toward us, and that's when I realized that we were the only one's yelling. I looked around the bar and saw the crowd was kind of sparse and except for a couple of polite smiles, didn't have much of a reaction. I'm sure Molly noticed it too, and I didn't look her way as we sat back down. I'd had visions of a packed house with hundreds of cheering fans and honestly, how could I not have thought along those lines? The way Jackson went on about it you'd think he was playing Madison Square Garden.

My disappointment with the turnout evaporated the minute they began to play. I had always loved Jackson's music, and though I had never heard the others play it almost sounded as if they had adopted *his* style. Maybe this was naïve, but whatever the case it was as if they had been together for years rather than a few months. Still, I had to wonder if I was the only one who felt that way – each time a song ended, I'd look around to see the same thin, unenthusiastic crowd. Thank God for Molly, who cheered and whistled and woo-hoo'd alongside me. Her need for attention, while annoying, really came in handy at times.

They certainly were an odd-looking bunch, though. Both guys – Matt and Skid - had long, lanky physiques and wore faded jeans and t-shirts, but that's where the similarities ended. One had olive skin and very long, very dark hair pulled back in a ponytail, and the other had shoulder-length, shapeless blonde hair and blue eyes that peered out from behind small, round wire-rimmed glasses.

But Jayne was the weirdest of all. She was thin almost to the point of scrawny, and tall - a good four inches taller than me - with jet black hair teased on one side. And her outfit was a nightmare - black skinny jeans with several tears cut across each thigh and a sleeveless white t-shirt with a rock emblem, layered over a black tank top. Even if I was worried about Jackson meeting with her alone, the sight of her would have put those fears to rest.

When the set was over, some people – mostly Token's staff – briefly paused in their conversation or drink pours to applaud them, but Molly and I kept going until the four of them had disappeared from the stage. Jackson appeared at our table a few minutes later looking happier than I'd ever seen him. The first thing he did was reach over and hug me.

"I'm so glad you're here," he whispered into my hair.

"You sounded great!" I said excitedly.

"Yeah!" Molly said. "Like real live rock stars!"

"Thanks, Moll." He high-fived her, then glanced over at the bar. "I want you to meet the others."

I followed his gaze and saw the two guys from the band sitting there with frosted mugs of beer in front of them.

"I'll be right back," he said, then walked over to them. I saw him pointing toward our table, then after he ordered his own beer, the three of them came over. I wondered vaguely where Jayne was, then remembered Jackson saying she was pretty standoffish so maybe she'd taken off.

Jackson placed his beer on the table, then slipped his arm around my shoulders. "Skid, Matt, this is my girlfriend, Leah."

The two looked even odder up close. When Skid (seriously, was that his real name?) reached out to shake my hand, I noticed that his right arm was completely covered in a colorful tattoo sleeve. I also noticed that his eyes were so dark you could barely make out the pupils. He was actually spooky.

"And this," Jackson said, "is our friend, Molly."

Skid turned to her, and I had to stop myself from laughing at her wide-eyed expression.

The other one, Matt, was a strange duck too, but not at all ominous-looking. In fact, if he got a haircut and traded the jeans and tee for a suit and tie he'd have fit right in on Wall Street.

Once I got past their looks, I had to admit they were both extremely nice and seemed genuinely interested in meeting me and Molly. Matt was soft-spoken and seemed quite intelligent, and Skid's grin, when he chose to show it, was electric.

Two sodas and half of Jackson's beer later, it was time for me to make a trip to the ladies' room. When I returned, Skid and Matt were gone and Jayne was sitting at the table talking with Jackson and Molly. Even from a distance, I could see from her posture and the set of her brow that she had a rather intense way about her.

I made my way to the table and slid into the chair next to Jackson. When he introduced us, Jayne stared at me for a beat, then held out her hand. Her skin was extremely pale, but perhaps that was the look she was going for, because other than the awful thick black eyeliner she wore, she had on very little makeup.

"Nice to meet you," she said, her voice surprisingly pleasant. Maybe I was being bitchy, but from the looks of her I expected something deeper, bordering on coarse. She also seemed nice enough, though aside from asking what we thought of the music she didn't really have much to say.

A little while later, Matt, who had returned to the bar, signaled for Jackson to come over. As soon as he was gone, Jayne turned to me and said, "Jackson's told me a lot about you. It's really nice to finally meet you . . . and you too, Molly."

"Yeah," I replied, "he's told me a lot about you guys too. It's nice to put faces to the names."

"Hey, Jayne," Molly interrupted, "What's it like being the only girl in the band? Do you, like, meet a ton of guys?"

I rolled my eyes in Molly's direction. With her it always came down to one thing: male attention.

Jayne laughed. "You'd think, right?"

Molly looked at her, dead serious. "Yes, I'd definitely think."

Jayne laughed again but didn't really answer, which led me to believe guys weren't exactly breaking down her door.

We chitchatted for a bit longer – mostly about the songs they were working on for the next gig - then Matt came looking for her. After saying again how nice it was to meet us, she slid off the chair and went off with him.

Molly looked at her watch. "We should get going, Leah; I have to be in work by eight tomorrow morning."

"Okay," I said, scanning the room, "let's just find Jackson and let him know." He was standing with Skid, talking to two men I didn't recognize. I managed to catch his eye, then pointed to the front door to indicate that we were headed out.

"We have to get going," I said when he came over. "Molly's got work tomorrow morning."

"Shit, yeah, okay; I'd tell you to hang around and I'd take you home myself but I might be a while."

"It's okay," I laughed, "Molly'd never be able to find her way back home on her own."

"That's true, Jackson," Molly confirmed, "I have no sense of direction."

"I hear you," he said as he walked us to the door. "The first few times I came over here it felt like one big maze."

Once we got to the door Jackson slid his arms around my waist and said, "Thanks again for coming, babe; it really meant a lot having you here."

"I'm glad I was finally able to come," I said, and I meant it, "You guys were really great."

"So . . . tomorrow? I get you the whole day, right?" he asked, then gave me a sly look. "And we're only coming out of my room to eat... deal?"

"Deal," I agreed and then stood on my tiptoes and kissed him.

"So, what'd you think?" I asked. My eyes were trained on the rearview mirror as I carefully inched the car out of the tight spot I'd managed to maneuver into earlier. "They're pretty good, right?"

"Oh my God, they were great!" Molly gushed. "And they're not cookie-cutter, either - their music has a really unique sound..."

I glanced her way as I shifted the car into drive, pulled up a little bit, then reversed again. She sounded sincere.

"Yeah, I think so too." I smiled. "I thought I may just be the biased girlfriend."

"No, they definitely have something. But *Dirty Bushwick*? Where'd they come up with that name?"

"I don't know; they had it before Jackson joined and he's never said." I laughed. "If you ask me it suits them; the three of them are pretty dirty-looking."

She thought for a minute, then shook her head. "I wouldn't say that; I think 'edgy' is a better word."

"*Jackson's* edgy; I don't know about the other three."

"Well, *dirty* is pretty harsh." She gave me a sideways glance. "I like their look; it's cool. Like they don't give a crap."

We drove in silence for a while, then as I eased the car onto the ramp to the GWB she asked, "What about Jayne? Do you think maybe she's with Skid or Matt?"

I raised an eyebrow. "Why, you interested in one of them?"

She vehemently shook her head. "Definitely not."

"Didn't think so," I laughed as I changed lanes so I'd be able to get off on Route 4.

"So, do you think she's with one of them?" she asked again. "I didn't get the feeling she was but you never know."

I shrugged. "Don't think so. And anyway, Jackson mentioned she used to go out with the guitarist they had before him."

"Huh, that's interesting." She fished through her purse for a minute, then pulled out a pack of gum. She handed me an unwrapped stick.

"What's so interesting about it?" I took the gum and popped it into my mouth.

"Well, if she dated the last guitarist maybe she's got like a thing for them." She laughed, then added, "Hey, you never know, she may try to swoop in on your man."

I rolled my eyes and laughed quietly. "I'm not worried."

CHAPTER 39 - JACKSON

I'd never been one to throw the word "epic" around, but there was no other word to describe this summer. Not only did we get two more dates at Token's, Matt was also able to line up a few gigs in similar places in and around Brooklyn. They weren't jam-packed, but so what? They certainly weren't empty either, and the way I saw it, it only took one person – the *right* person – to hear us play. But the absolute *best* was the all-day, outdoor concert he'd lined up for us in Overpeck Park. Apparently Matt knew the promoter, who'd offered to let us play a few songs if we stuck around to help keep an eye on the crowds and do anything else that had to be done. I translated "anything else" to mean "clean up," but it didn't matter. Several well-known local bands would be playing that day and Dirty Bushwick would get exposure to their very loyal fans. Matt put it to a vote, and it was unanimous - a no-brainer. I didn't tell the others, but part of the reason I was so amped was the location. Brooklyn may be the hotspot, but it was nowhere near as cool as playing in Jersey. Isn't that where Springsteen and Bon Jovi got started?

"You need to *caaalm* down, cowboy," Jayne joked one night after a particularly long practice. It was a few days before the concert in the park and three beers in I was still bouncing off the walls.

"Calm down?" I shook my head. "Not possible."

"Seriously, Jackson, you need to take a breath, because – and I hate to burst your bubble here - this isn't the big break you think it is. Sure, it's exposure and any exposure is good, but if you're thinking the next step is a recording contract you're going to be majorly disappointed."

This wasn't the first time Jayne had given me this speech and I knew it wouldn't be the last.

"*But*," I countered, "This weekend will be the first time we're selling the CDs, right?"

Ever since we learned about the gig in the park the four of us had been working on a CD to sell there. It had only six songs on it, but they all sounded incredible. Between the music and the cover art Jayne had designed, the whole thing looked and sounded like it'd been done by a professional record label.

"True -" she began, then stopped herself. "Heck, I give up, Jackson. I love your enthusiasm."

I just smiled at her and took another sip of my beer. Nothing Jayne or anyone else said could have brought me down from the high I was on about this concert. *Heck, there was going to be thousands of people there.* So what if those thousands weren't actually there to see *us?* It would still be the closest I'd ever gotten to the big time.

I wasn't the only one – Leah was so excited about the concert you'd have thought she was dating one of the Stones. Actually, I'd been feeling like a rock star ever since she came home. I hated to admit it, but things had been a little off those last few months she was at school. Nothing I could put my finger on, just a feeling that went away the moment we saw each other again. These days, we were closer than ever.

Leah had come to most of our shows, usually with Molly in tow. I'd even enlisted the two of them to help set up and man the CD table. Surprise, surprise, Molly had completely taken charge with what she called her "marketing expertise."

When I questioned Leah about it she just laughed and shrugged. "The only marketing I've seen her do was for our Girl Scout troop's cookie sale outside the grocery store when we were nine." She thought for a minute. "Come to think of it, though, she did win the prize for selling the most cookies."

Beth and Brody were also coming, along with a "surprise guest." After a half-hearted, unsuccessful attempt to find out who it was, I decided to go with the flow.

"Bring as many surprise guests as you want," I told her, "So long as it's not Dad."

I hadn't seen much of Beth lately, hadn't seen much of anyone except my bandmates. Even the one-on-one stuff Jayne and I were working on had been put on hold so we could focus on practicing for the concert and our other gigs. We had decided we should play what we felt most comfortable with; when things slowed down after the summer we'd get back to writing new stuff. Strange as Jayne was, I might've missed hanging out with her if I hadn't been so busy. If I wasn't working, I was practicing; if I wasn't practicing, I was with Leah. It was nuts. Then again, it probably would have been hard for me and Jayne to get together anyway. A month earlier, she'd moved to Staten Island, where a buddy of Matt's had a two-bedroom. I was pretty sure Staten Island wasn't her first choice, but these days it was the only affordable borough in New York; plus the apartment was right over the Verrazano Bridge from Brooklyn, which made it a hell of a lot easier to get to gigs and the Guitar Center on Flatbush Avenue, where she now worked. I just hoped she'd still be willing to drive to my house for our practice sessions because they'd really helped me up my game.

Jayne's new roommate was a guy named Eddie, who I'd never met but who Matt had vouched for. Personally, I didn't think moving in with someone you barely know was a good idea, no matter who vouched for them, but I didn't say anything. Jayne seemed happy enough with the arrangement, so what was the point of me getting all big-brotherish?

The night before the concert at Overpeck I didn't sleep a wink. It wasn't until I saw the sun coming up in the cloudless sky that I realized how worried I'd been about the weather. Though the concert was technically rain or shine, a crappy day would mean a fraction of the crowd. But as usual I was freaked out for nothing. Instead of the usual blistering heat that tended to plague Jersey in late July, the forecast called for low humidity and a temperature that hovered just around eighty degrees. As I hopped in the shower and tried to calm my nerves, I decided to take it as a good sign.

By eleven o'clock I was pulling into the staff parking lot to meet up with Jayne, Skid and Matt. Though the music wouldn't start until much later

— we were the first act and scheduled to begin at two - there were already a lot of people milling around, buying t-shirts from vendors, playing the carnival-style games, and munching on fried dough from one of the many food trucks. It was nowhere near as packed as it would be when *Rabid Fox*, the headliner, went on that night. It sucked that we wouldn't have anywhere near the crowd they were going to, but I guess it went with the territory of being the opening band for the opening band's opening band. In the meantime, I was going to spend the early part of the day trying to sell as many CDs as I could. Leah and Molly had agreed to come at noon to help with that effort.

A few minutes later Matt, Skid and Jayne rolled up and we began unpacking our equipment from Matt's truck and carrying it to the stage. Once everything was set up, I grabbed the box of CDs and went back to the entrance to find Leah and Molly already there with a small card table and two folding chairs.

"Right on time, ladies." I grabbed Leah's hand and gave it a squeeze, then high-fived Molly. "Thanks a lot for doing this for us, it's a big help."

I could feel the smile on Leah's lips as she leaned up and kissed me. "Glad we could help." She looked around. "Wow, this place is packed."

"This is nothing, wait'll you see it tonight."

"Hey, boss," Molly chimed in as she held up the box. "Where do you want us to set this up?"

I looked around. "I guess as close to the stage area as -"

Molly cut me off, "I'm thinking towards the back, that way we snag them on their way out, *after* they've heard you play. What do you think?"

I was about to answer when the "marketing expert" interrupted me again. "Trust me, it's the way to go."

I laughed and gave her a mock salute. "Yes, ma'am!"

Leah shook her head. "I told you she'd take charge, didn't I?"

Pushy as she was, I couldn't deny that Molly had a good eye. She'd created a detailed poster, which she propped up next to pictures she and Leah had taken at some of the other shows. Whether there'd be any sales remained to be seen, but either way both of them had done a great job.

"This is incredible, thanks, guys." I said as I squeezed Leah's hand again. "I guess I should get back to Matt and the others. I'll see you in a bit."

I was heading back toward the stage when my phone beeped. It was a text from Beth, letting me know that she and Brody were at the front gate. I was about to reply when she texted again, wanting to know where they should stand to get the best view of us. I laughed when I read that one – did she think it would be so mobbed that she wouldn't see the stage? I was about send a reply to that effect, then decided not to be a dick. She was, after all, there to show sisterly support, so I sent off a *Be there in a sec* and started walking toward the gate.

The crowd had grown even thicker by then, and "a sec" turned out to be several minutes. As I approached the gate, I saw Brody's tall bulky frame first, then Beth...then...I stopped dead in my tracks when I saw the tall, gray-haired man standing beside them. Next to him, a frail elderly woman sat in a wheelchair.

I picked up the pace until I was standing right in front of them. "Holy shi - I mean, crap, holy crap! What're you guys doing here!"

My grandmother struggled to her feet with the help of Brody. "We weren't going to miss our grandson's big day." She turned to my grandfather. "Right, John?"

"That's right, Jackson; when Beth invited us we told her we wouldn't miss it for the world."

Beth nodded. "That's true, Jacks."

"Let me take a look at you, sweetie," my grandmother said as she held me at arm's length. "Would you look at that, John? Still the spitting image of Anna."

My grandfather's eyes misted up as he looked at me. "Yep, always was."

As I reached out and hugged her, a wave of guilt rose up in me. It had been far too long since I'd visited them, and I made a mental note to change that in the future.

"I'm so happy you guys are here," I said, pulling back from her surprisingly strong embrace. "Hey, and I hope you like the music. I know it's probably not your thing but you never know; you might end up really liking it."

"Nonsense, I'm sure we'll *love* it!" She smiled as she lowered herself back into the wheelchair, then motioned around the park. "And, my word, look at all these people who've come out to see you; they must love your music too."

I didn't have the heart to tell her that no one was there to see us, so I just nodded.

"Is Leah here, Jackson?" Beth asked. "It's been forever since I've seen her."

"Yeah, she's here." I told her about the CD table, then turned to my grandmother. "Hey Gram, do you wanna say hi to Leah? You remember Leah, right? She was over at Christmas?"

"Yes, I certainly do remember," she said, "Such a dear girl."

We weaved our way through the growing crowd to where Leah and Molly had set up shop.

When Leah saw my family, she jumped up and ran over to hug them. You would have thought it was her own grandparents standing there.

"What have we got here?" my grandmother asked as she put her glasses on and read the sign on the table. She looked up at me in amazement. "Goodness, Jackson, you've made your own record album?"

Before I could answer she opened her purse and said, "I'll take two, girls."

"Gram, put your money away." I wagged my finger at her, "No charge for family."

"Nonsense," she said as she pulled out a thick, worn leather wallet. "I'll need one for the hi-fi at the condo and one for the car."

I was about to protest again but the look of pride on her face stopped me.

"Oh, okay."

We chatted for a few more minutes, then I told them I had to go get ready for the show. They all wished me luck, then just as I was about to disappear into the throngs of people I heard Brody belt out in his deep voice, "Break a leg, Jacks!"

▲　　▲　　▲

I made my way over to the backstage area, where I found Matt, Skid and Jayne hustling around with some last-minute details.

"Nice of you to join us," Jayne joked as she tossed me the cord for my amp.

I laughed. "Sorry, I was busy courting some new fans."

"You guys almost ready?" I heard Al, the concert promoter, shout from up top the stage, "You're on in a few minutes."

"Hell, yeah," Matt called out, but Jayne looked at me, eyebrow raised.

"You sure you're ready? 'Cause you look a little nervous."

I was about to echo Matt's enthusiastic shout, then shrugged instead. "I dunno; this is fucking crazy, right?" I looked out at the crowd, which was large and growing by the minute, and felt the start of sweat under my arms and on my upper lip. "I mean, do you see how many people are out there? What if . . . I mean can you imagine if . . . if they hate us?"

She waved me off. "So, if they hate us, they hate us. It's not like they're gonna start booing and throwing rotten fruit at us."

"Yeah, I guess you're right," I sighed. "It's just . . ." I trailed off.

"Just what?"

"I don't know, I guess I just *really* want them to like us."

"They're probably not gonna *really* like us, Jackson. To those people out there..." She motioned with her hand to the crowd, "we're just background noise . . . but that's okay. For now."

"What do you mean?"

"I mean that we may be just background noise to them *now* but it doesn't matter because I *know* we're gonna make it. Just give it time because I believe down to my soul that our music is *that* good. Those people out there, they just don't know it yet."

▲　　▲　　▲

The four of us stood in the wings of the stage - and not some crappy "makeshift" stage either - waiting for Al to finish his rundown of the day's events. The PA system was blaring, but to me it sounded like his voice was travelling through a tin tunnel and from a million miles away. My heart was racing and my stomach was doing flips. I'd thought I was nervous before that first gig at Token's, but boy, did that seem like a fuckin' joke now.

Suddenly, through the fog in my head, I heard the uptick in Al's voice.

"Okay everyone, time to get the party started! And there's no better band to do that than the one about to take the stage. Now, it's their first time playing this side of the Hudson..." - I thought I heard a few good-natured boos and found myself smiling in spite of myself; I was, after all from, Jersey - "...so put your hands together for..."

I looked over at Jayne to find she was staring at me, brow furrowed in mild concern. If I looked anything like I felt, she probably was worried I'd keel over in the middle of the set.

". . . Brooklyn's very own..."

Her eyes locked on mine and she slowly nodded that it would be okay. To my amazement, it helped a little. Still, my heart was racing when I heard Al cry out:

"...DIRTY *BUSHWICK*!"

I'd like to say we took to the stage amidst thunderous applause, but I'd be lying. The first part was true enough - the four of us bounced out to the stage and grabbed our respective instruments as if we were headlining at the Meadowlands — but aside from my little fan club, there was little applause. I tried to block out the fact the no one was even paying attention to us and just concentrate on the music.

I'd like to say we wowed the crowd, who begged us to keep playing, but again I'd be full of shit. We played our asses off too — a six-song set ending with *Anna's Leash* — but nothing much changed where the crowd was concerned. My "fan club" cheered of course, but they were all but drowned out by the other activity going on.

We'd barely left the stage before Al was back at the microphone introducing the next act. No one applauded them either, which both comforted and annoyed me.

Matt seemed completely unaffected by their lack of enthusiasm.

"Great job, guys," he said as he mopped his brow with the sleeve of his t-shirt, "We sounded better than ever."

"Ditto," Skid said as he high-fived Matt, then Jayne and myself.

"So, I'm gonna change and get something to eat," Matt said. "What do you say we meet back here in an hour or so and see what Al needs us to do."

We all agreed, and Jayne grabbed her backpack from the table beside her.

"I'm gonna change and get cleaned up, then check out what's around; I'll catch you later." Her brow furrowed again. "You okay?"

"Yeah, yeah," I said a little too quickly. "It was great."

Her brow raised dubiously, then she was gone.

I spent the next two minutes changing my shirt and another ten talking myself out of my disappointment. How could the others play time and again to such a lukewarm reception? Better question – how could I grow the same thick skin? I would certainly need it if I was to have a shot in this business. *Suck it up, Jackson,* I told myself, *six months ago you would have killed for this gig, applause or not.* Then, pasting a smile on my face, I headed out to find my cheering section who was once again gathered around the CD table.

They all made a huge fuss over me, especially my grandmother. She went on and on about "my group" as if we were the twenty-first century equivalent of The Beatles.

"Thanks, Gram," I said as I bent down and kissed her cheek.

"We're going to be on our way, honey, I'm starting to get tired." She patted me on the arm. "Beth and Brody are coming for dinner, would you like to join us?"

"Wish I could, but I have to help out around here until everything ends. Next time, though."

"Okay, sweetie, another time," she said, then turned to Leah and Molly, "And you too, girls."

"We'd love to," Leah said, and Molly nodded in agreement.

She reached up and gave me a peck on the cheek, then returned to her wheelchair. I could tell by looking at her that the day had really worn her out.

"See ya, man, great show," Brody said as he slapped me on the back, then Beth hugged me and said congratulations.

I watched as the four of them headed toward the exit, then turned back to Leah and Molly. "You were amazing up there, Jackson," Leah said as she hugged me.

"Yeah!" Molly agreed. "It's so cool to actually know someone on that stage!"

"Thanks," I said, then motioned to the table, "You guys have been a big help. Any sales?"

They looked at each other, then Molly said, "Uh, yeah . . . three; we sold three."

"Three?" I asked incredulously. I don't know why I was surprised, considering the lack of interest when we were playing.

"Yes, Jackson, *three.*" Molly smiled.

"And would that be *including* the two my grandmother bought?"

"Let's not split hairs here, Jackson," she countered. "Three is three, right?"

I stared her down for a moment, then shrugged and said, "Fair enough." The fact that we sold even *one* to someone not related to me was pretty cool. I glanced around. "I guess you guys can close up shop."

"Okay," Leah said, "What time will you finish?"

"I'm here 'til the end, but don't hang around; it'll probably be after midnight."

"Oh, okay," she said, in that unreadable way she had sometimes, "if you think you'll be that long then I'll just go home with Molly. We can hang out tomorrow."

"Sounds good," I said, then I handed her the box of CDs so I could fold up the table. I helped them carry everything to the parking lot where we loaded everything into the trunk of Leah's car.

"You were really great today," she said as she slipped her arms around my waist.

"You think?" I never got tired of hearing her say how much she loved my music.

"Without a doubt," she nodded. "So, I'll see you tomorrow, right?"

"Yep, tomorrow for sure," I said as I leaned down and kissed her.

"Let's go, guys," Molly yelled impatiently from inside the car then tapped the horn.

"You better get going," I laughed. "Looks like Colonel Molly wants to cut out."

She laughed too, then slid into the driver's seat. I stood there watching until the car disappeared from sight.

▲　▲　▲

By the time I said goodbye to the girls I had to go straight to meet the others, which meant I couldn't even grab something to eat. That pretty much sucked because I'd been too nervous to eat before the show and now I was starving. Then I found Matt, and what I saw made me forget all about my hunger. He was talking to a girl with dark hair pulled back into what my sister used to call "French braids." She was wearing a blue tie-dyed tank top, cutoffs and a pair of very worn yellow rubber flip-flops and couldn't have been more than sixteen. I shook my head and smiled to myself. What do you know? DB's first little fangirl. Looks like maybe there *had* been a few people watching us.

I figured I'd hang back and let them finish but when Matt caught sight of me he waved me over. He had a bewildered look on his face.

"Why're you just standing there?" he asked as I approached. Disappointment hit when I realized the girl talking to him wasn't a fan after all, but Jayne. She was dressed in ordinary clothes with her face scrubbed clean of any makeup, including the black shit she usually wore around her eyes.

"You tryin' to get outta cleanup duty?" she asked.

"Who me? Never," I laughed. "I didn't realize it was you; thought Matt was talking to an actual fan and didn't want to interrupt."

"I wish," Matt said, then changed the subject. "Hey, Al says he won't need us for at least another hour so we're free to hang out until then. Skid had to take off for a while, but he'll be back." He pulled his phone from his pocket and glanced at it. "I need to make a few calls so I'll catch you guys in about an hour."

"Great," I said, already thinking about the juicy-looking burgers I'd seen them grilling under the tent near the entrance, "'Cause I gotta eat." I looked at Jayne, still unable to believe how different she looked. "You wanna come?"

She shrugged. "I already ate but I'll take a walk with you."

The burger was even better than it looked, especially with the greasy fries and an ice-cold cherry Coke. After I wolfed down my feast, Jayne and I decided to take a loop around the park. Jayne couldn't stop talking about how awesome she thought we did. It was unlike her to chatter so much - it was as if in dressing differently she had taken on an entirely different persona. I was enjoying myself, though, not only the topic, but because she seemed to be completely unaware of the fact that she was turning the heads of quite a few high school guys who probably thought she was their age. Without her usual Goth clothes and heavy eye makeup, she could easily pass for sixteen or seventeen. I cast a sideways glance at her and laughed to myself but decided not to mention it. Sometimes the oddest things could piss her off.

As we walked, I found myself noticing the crowds of people milling about. There were groups of guys hanging out, young parents with little kids, groups of giggling teenage girls, older couples enjoying an afternoon out. The same kind of people who'd been here for our set. I began racking my brain for a way we could've better engaged them. What would've made them stop what they were doing and just *listen*?

"*Hello?*" Jayne said as she snapped her fingers in my face. "Earth to Jackson."

"What?" I said as I swung my head toward her. I hadn't even realized I'd zoned out. "You say something?"

"What's with you? I feel like I'm talking to a wall." She sounded annoyed. "I was *saying* that Matt said he's gonna talk to Al about working out the same deal for us at the Labor Day Festival. He said that one usually draws an even bigger crowd."

"Awesome, that's great news!" I could already feel my anticipation brewing.

"Hey, we should head back." Jayne checked the time on her phone. "We've been gone nearly an hour."

I tried to pay attention to what she was saying, but as the two of us meandered back to where we were to meet Matt and Skid I found my focus once again shifting to the people walking by. I noticed many of them had on concert t-shirts for various bands – Led Zeppelin, The Eagles, Bon Jovi, Aerosmith, The Rolling Stones – and suddenly something struck me. I debated a minute whether or not to mention my idea to her but finally decided *what the heck.* She was still chatting like crazy, though, so I had to wait a few minutes for her to come up for air.

"Hey, check this out," I began, "All these people chose to spend their Saturday afternoon at an outdoor concert, right?"

"Uh, yeah, so?"

"*So,* it means that obviously they like music, correct?"

"Correct, professor."

"Okay, so the question is – how do we get these people, who obviously like listening to music, to take a chance – you know, like step out of their comfort zone and listen to something new? And by something new, I mean *our* shit, of course."

"I don't know," she shrugged, "I guess keep doing what we're doing. Playing clubs and places like this and hopefully people start to take notice."

"Well, what if instead of waiting around for people to step out of their comfort zone and take notice, we do something to coax them out?"

"So far I'm not following you, but please, go ahead..." She motioned with her hand as if rolling out the red carpet for me, "Bestow your wisdom on me."

"Okay, so the way I see it, people stop and listen when they hear something familiar; something, you know, that they like. So -"

Jayne's hand immediately shot out, stopping me in my tracks. "Whoa, hold it right there. I know what you're getting at and you can *forget* it. Matt'll never go for it."

"But -"

"No buts, Jackson; *no way*." She shook her head fervently. "Matt would *never* go for it. I've known him a lot longer than you and believe me he is adamant about not playing anything but our own stuff."

"I know but -"

"Matt never wants Dirty Bushwick to become a cover band -" She looked at me with something like disdain, "and you shouldn't either."

"I'm not talking about turning us into a cover band, Jayne." Now I was getting annoyed. "I'm just saying we cover one song to get their attention; then maybe they stick around, give our stuff a shot."

"Believe me, I get where you're coming from, really I do, but it's a slippery slope. You cover one tune then it's another and then another and the next thing you know you're just one of many in a long line of cheap knockoffs."

"Whatever," I said, shaking my head. "Forget it, forget I said anything. It was just an idea."

I decided to let it go for the time being. Jayne did have a point and I got it, but I couldn't help thinking it was worth a shot.

CHAPTER 40 – LEAH

I brought the sweating glass of ice water to rest on my forehead and sighed. It was brutally hot, too hot to lay out, but I wasn't about to waste a tanning day. Neither was Molly, who lay on the lounge chair next to me, seemingly unaffected by the heat. Boiling or not, we planned to spend every sunny day right here at her pool. I was just glad it hadn't been this hot at the concert yesterday. Neither Molly nor I had spoken much about the concert, other than to agree that they sounded great.

"Hey, just curious," she said as she squeezed some sunscreen into her palm, "Did Jackson ask you who bought that third CD?" She rubbed her palms together and carefully applied the lotion to her shoulders.

"Yes."

"And . . . what did you tell him?"

"What do you mean *what did I tell him?* I told him the truth. That it was a young girl who bought it."

From the corner of my eye I could see her raised eyebrow. "She was young alright."

I shot her a look, but she was already laying back down with her eyes closed. Was Molly really going to make an issue of this? Should I have told Jackson that the girl couldn't have been more than five or six and was only interested in the colorful artwork on the cover? That her mother had said no at first, then gave in to avoid a meltdown?

"Listen," she continued, "I would've done the same thing. I feel bad for him – for them. I don't understand it. We think their music is great but I'm beginning to think we're the only ones. Judging from the reaction – or should I say *lack* of reaction - of the crowd, they better not quit their day jobs."

I couldn't argue with her there. "Yeah, I know. He puts in so much time and works so hard and he's not making a dime from it."

She turned to me, eyes wide. "You're kidding! He doesn't make *anything*?"

"I kid you not." I flipped over onto my back so I would tan evenly. "But what can I say – it's his dream."

"It would be so cool if they were like really popular and became famous and then people would be pointing at you and saying *Hey, that's the chick that dates the lead guitarist for Dirty Bushwick.*" Molly sat up and turned to me, suddenly looking very excited. "You two would be on the cover of magazines, maybe even followed by the paparazzi! Girls would copy your style because they'd want to dress just like Jackson Foxx's girl so they could land a famous rock star too."

"Oh my gosh, Molly, do you hear yourself? You sound crazy." I laughed, partly because she was being silly and partly to hide the fact that I thought it would've been kind of cool if things turned out that way.

Molly wasn't fooled. "Don't deny it, Leah, you'd love the attention you'd get if he actually made it."

"You live in a fantasy world, Molly," I said as I tossed my sunglasses aside and grabbed a t-shirt to shield my face from the sun.

"Yeah, I guess I do." She laughed. "It's funny, though..."

"Mmmm hmmm..."

"There you were, walking around the concert grounds with the lead guitarist from one of the bands and no one paid a bit of attention to either of you, right?"

She didn't wait for me to answer before continuing.

"*Yet* whenever you walked around campus with Chase, girls were eyeing him up and down and staring daggers at you. Imagine what it'd be like if you were actually going out with him!" She shook her head. "Sheesh, then the claws would really come out."

I kept silent. I'd never admit it to her (shit, I barely admitted it to myself) but I did love the envious stares I got from girls when I was hanging out with Chase.

"Oh, hey, speaking of hot lacrosse players, I forgot to tell you...Brent texted me last night, after you dropped me off."

My eyes shot open beneath the shirt that was thankfully covering my face. "Oh really?" I said nonchalantly, "What did he have to say?"

"Nothing really. He just asked what's up and how my summer was going. Isn't that weird though?"

I kept my voice neutral. "Yeah, that's weird."

"What about Chase? Have you heard from him?"

"No," I answered, but realized right away that I'd said it too quickly. "But I didn't expect to."

"Why not? I'd think he'd at least touch base, see how your summer was going..."

I slipped the t-shirt off my face. "Why would you think that?"

"I don't know," she shrugged. "I guess I just figured that since you two were so chummy at school you'd keep in touch over the summer, that's all."

"Nah, we weren't *that* chummy, and besides, he's got a lot on his plate with that internship he has." I felt as if I was making excuses for him, and it got me thinking – would it have killed him to text and see how I was doing?

"Oh, yeah, you're probably right. Sometimes those companies make their interns work crazy long hours." She paused. "You should text him, though, see how it's going."

I didn't answer. Text him? Was she crazy? I almost asked her as much, then remembered she didn't know anything. When I left school in May, I'd decided to put everything that'd happened with Chase behind me. I chalked it up to an "experimental fling," something I wasn't proud of but needed to get out of my system.

If I texted him he'd think I wanted to start things up again and I definitely did *not* want to do that.

Or did I?

▲　▲　▲

Molly had no idea that our poolside conversation had struck a nerve with me — several nerves, in fact. I knew I was being bitchy — it wasn't her fault Jackson's band seemed to be on the fast-track to nowhere. I mean, if he said *it takes time to get a following* one more time I was going to scream. And how could he continuously be on such a high when playing to such unenthusiastic crowds? Yesterday was the worst yet because yesterday the *entire* crowd *completely* ignored them. It was actually painful to watch. At least when they played at bars there was some scattered applause from the staff.

The other topic — Chase — really wasn't Molly's fault, since she didn't know the extent of our relationship, but it bugged me just the same. I was in a shitty mood when I got home, and it was about to get worse.

"Leah," my mom called up the stairs. "Can you come down here a minute? I want to talk to you before you go out."

I rolled my eyes because I could tell from her tone that she was in lecture mode and I had neither the time nor the patience to listen to her. Jackson was picking me up and we were going to get something to eat at a new place that had opened in town. Afterwards we were going back to his house to hang out.

"Be right down," I yelled back, then grabbed my phone and headed down the stairs. When I got to the living room I looked around but she wasn't there.

"I'm in here, honey," she called out from the kitchen — it was her preferred lecturing spot.

Sure enough, when I went into the kitchen I found her sitting at the table, sipping a cup of tea, a purposeful expression on her face. "Have a seat," she said.

"I can't, Mom, Jackson will be here any minute. I don't have time to sit and chat."

"It'll only take a minute." She reached over and pulled out a chair for me. "And besides, Jackson is what I wanted to talk to you about."

I let out an exaggerated huff as I yanked the chair the rest of the way out and plopped myself down into it. "What is it now?"

"Listen, honey, the reason I wanted to talk to you about Jackson is -"

I quickly cut her off. "Mom, we've had this conversation like a million times and I'm sorry you feel the way you do but it doesn't change anything. Jackson and I are staying together and there's nothing you can do or say that's going to break us up so you might as well forget it. Jackson's here to stay. End of discussion."

She looked annoyed, just like I'd hoped she would. "Are you finished?"

"Yep." I folded my arms across my chest.

"Leah, you've made it clear how you feel about Jackson and the fact that he's who you want to be with, so far be it from me to interfere anymore."

"What do you mean?" I asked, suddenly confused. Had she just deviated from her usual script?

"What I'm saying is that you're an adult and it's your choice. Although he wouldn't be my choice for you, I guess it could be worse." She spooned a little more sugar into her tea and stirred it before continuing. "He's actually a very nice person and he does seem to adore you so I think it's time your father and I take a step back and let you live your life." She took a sip of tea then returned it to the table. "I'm sure you'll end up being a very successful lawyer if you put your mind to it so I see a comfortable life ahead of you, no matter who you end up with. Besides, lots of women today are the breadwinners in the family. You're lucky; it wasn't like that when I was your age."

I threw my hands up. "There you go, marrying me off again."

"Don't be silly. I'm not marrying you off, I'm just being realistic. It doesn't hurt to look ahead."

"Are you done?"

"Yes, I'm done. Go ahead, enjoy your night," she said as she shooed me from the table.

Just as I pushed the chair back in, she added, "I mean, if that Chase couldn't pique your interest then I'd say no one is going to come between you and Jackson. So handsome and polite, I wouldn't think there'd be a girl alive who could turn that boy away. Guess you're the exception..."

"That's right, Mom. I told you, Chase and I are just friends."

"Maybe so," she said as she shook her head and reached for her mug. "But something about the way he was looking at you made me think he would like it to be more."

▲   ▲   ▲

I felt a little guilty when Jackson and I walked into the restaurant – it was one of those chichi places where you pay fifteen bucks for a hamburger and I knew he couldn't afford it, not that he would ever let me chip in. I felt even guiltier when my mind kept wandering through the entire meal. I tried to pay attention to what he was saying, really, I did, but my thoughts kept returning to the conversation with my mother. Suddenly she and my father approved of Jackson? How did that happen? I should've been happy, right? I had won, which I suspected was part of the problem. Part of Jackson's allure was that his presence really pissed them off. Then there was the comment she'd made about there not being a girl alive who'd turn Chase away. It really got under my skin, especially after my earlier conversation with Molly.

Jackson didn't seem to notice my distraction, though, because he was too busy going on about the concert. I think he was still on a high from the whole experience. The way he was talking you'd think there were tons of screaming fans and people hounding them for autographs. He seemed to forget the fact that I was *there* and that aside from me, Molly and his family there were no screaming fans. Actually, there were no fans, *period*.

"So, I'm thinking, if things keep going the way they're going I may have to cut back on my hours with Slater next summer. Maybe even quit altogether."

Now he had my attention. "Really? Do you think that's a smart move?"

"I don't think I have a choice. If I wanna move forward with this then I gotta give it my all. This is my shot, Leah. I can't blow it for a job that's basically there just to pay the bills."

Was he serious? "Yeah, but you still have to pay the bills, right?"

Suddenly I saw my life flash in front of my eyes: me coming home from the office every night to find Jackson sitting on the living room floor tinkering with his guitar – probably minus a sock. Oh my gosh, suddenly the whole scene seemed so . . . depressing.

"Well, I guess I'm just gonna havta wing it and hope it works out."

Wing it. It seemed like all he did was wing it. His life was one big crapshoot. I reminded myself that it was one of the traits that had once drew me to him, but now it seemed so irresponsible ... so immature.

If he sensed my disapproval, he gave no indication, just signaled for the check and said he'd be right back, then headed for what I assumed was the men's room.

I watched him disappear from sight, then leaned my head against the back of the booth. His passion for his music was admirable but at some point he'd have to realize that it was just a pipe dream. And then what? He'd have to start from scratch with no prospects of a job. Working for Slater wasn't exactly a career but at least it was something.

For the hundredth time that day I thought about Chase. What it'd be like to be with him – I mean *really* be with him – and not just holed up in his room. Chase had it all – looks, money, goals, ambition. He was the whole package – so what was I doing still here?

Without even realizing it, I found myself fishing through my purse for my phone. When I found it, I pulled it out and stared at it for a long moment, then scrolled through my contacts until I came to Chase's name. My finger hovered over it as I debated texting him. The next thing I knew my fingers were tapping out a quick *hey, what's up?* I sent it before I could change my mind.

Just as I put my phone down next to me, Jackson returned carrying a small lavender gift bag tied at the top with curly white ribbon. He sat down and placed it in front of me, his upper lip curled slightly.

"What's this?"

"It's just a little something. I was hoping to give it to you if we went away this summer, you know, for our two-year anniversary." He pushed it across the table toward me and smiled. "Open it."

I reached for it, already feeling a nervous anticipation as I undid the daintily tied bow. *Or is it guilt*, I wondered as I peered inside, then pulled out a small black velvet box. I glanced at Jackson, then slowly flipped the box open to find possibly the most striking ring I'd ever seen – shiny silver and molded into the shape of a guitar. I'd seen plenty of spoon rings like that, the kind where the spoon wraps around your finger, but never one like this. Leave it to Jackson to remember that I loved them, though I'd probably only mentioned it one time, way back when. I took the ring out and held it in my hand.

"Jackson, it's . . . it's beautiful."

His face lit up. "Flip it over," he said, "Read what it says inside."

I turned it over in my hand and read the inscription - *Livin' it...together* - as a tear welled in the corner of my eye. I looked over at him and saw him smiling proudly.

He shrugged. "Hey, so I'm no poet, but as you can see, I didn't have much room to work with. I just wanted to say how lucky I am to have you – always sticking by me, you know, believing in me and my music. And one day, when all this hard work pays off, you'll be right there with me. *Livin' it* seemed to cover that." He laughed. "Like I said, I'm no poet."

"Jackson, I . . . I don't know what to say. I love it."

"Here, give it to me," he said as he reached for it then slipped in onto the ring finger of my right hand. "Hey, look at that, a perfect fit."

I continued staring down at the shiny silver ring as he held onto my hand.

"You mean everything to me, you know that, right?" he said as he gave my hand a gentle squeeze.

I nodded my head, unable to speak past the lump in my throat. It was the first time the full weight of what I'd done hit me. What was I thinking? Most people can go through an entire lifetime without ever finding what I had with Jackson, yet here I was, ready to give it all up.

Just then my phone began to vibrate. I knew even before I glanced down that it was Chase calling. I looked back at Jackson, then reached down and hit *ignore*.

CHAPTER 41 – JACKSON

At first, I didn't understand it. Here I was, having the best summer of my life – I was finally playing in a band; shit, I'd even gotten a raise at work – and yet there was this anxious feeling gnawing at me. It was there when I woke up in the morning and when I went to sleep at night. What the fuck? Then it suddenly hit me – the summer was coming to an end, which meant Leah would be headed back to school. And things had been so great between us, too, though lately I'd gotten that off vibe from her again. Probably just nervous about getting back to the books – she'd acted the same way at the end of last semester, when she was studying for finals. Plus, I'm sure it bothered her that I wouldn't be able to get up to see her very much. I was certainly going to miss having her and Molly at our gigs, and I wasn't the only one. It had been nice having real live fans cheering us on.

And to that end, I'd decided to go against Jayne's advice and approach Matt about covering a song or two at one of our upcoming gigs.

"Well, if you're really going to bring it up to him then I want to be there to witness it," Jayne said smugly when I told her of my plans.

"Witness what?" Skid asked.

"Jackson here wants to run an idea by Matt," she said, "But wait'll you hear it."

He raised an eyebrow. "What is it?"

"He wants us to become a part-time cover band."

"That's not what I meant, Jayne, and you know it," I interrupted before Skid had a chance to comment.

I turned to Skid. "All I said was that we cover one song – *one song* – in the middle of our set. Something that people know. They stop and listen, then after we finish we go right into one of our own and, who knows, maybe they hang around."

We both eyed Skid, waiting for a response.

"Hell, if this were a year ago I'd say *no fuckin' way*." He shook his head. "I think our stuff's great, but, man, we're gettin' nowhere fast, so I say *fuck it*. I'm willing to try anything at this point – even stoop to the level of cover band if that's what it takes."

Jayne glared at him as if he were a traitor, but he gave it right back to her.

"Don't give me that look. He's got a point."

She held his gaze. "Well, I still say Matt'll never go for it."

Skid shrugged. "Hey, you never know, he may surprise you."

▲   ▲   ▲

I approached Matt the following night after a particularly long practice session. With the summer winding down we'd shifted our focus to writing new stuff, which always meant hours of trial and error and arguing back and forth. I was friggin' exhausted but wanted to say something before I lost my nerve. And since there was no way I was doing it in front of an audience, I also had to wait until Jayne and Skid were gone. Luckily, they were as tired as I was. Matt, though, never seemed to run out of steam; even now, he was thumbing through the music we'd been working on.

"Hey, Matt, you got a minute?"

"Yeah sure, Jackson," he said, glancing up at me, "What's up?"

I felt nervous so I glanced over to the table in the corner. "You wanna sit?"

"Sit? Uh, yeah sure," he said as he slid the papers into a folder, walked over to the table and pulled out a chair.

"So . . . um, I had an idea," I said as I sat across from him. "It's just a thought and if you're not down with it I'll totally back off, no problem."

He looked intrigued. "Jackson, I like to think we have a level playing field here. I mean, I may have started the band but we all contribute equally so if you have an idea that you think would help, by all means, share it."

I paused for a moment, Jayne's warning echoing through my mind, then decided, fuck it – what did I have to lose? True to form, Matt sat quietly without interrupting while I explained my idea and the reasoning behind it.

"What you're proposing is nothing new," he said after I'd finished. "Bands do it all the time. The problem with what you're suggesting – and I've seen it so many times – is that bands start to get lazy. Let's face it - it's a lot easier to play someone else's music than write your own. Not to mention the fact that you've suddenly got people stopping and listening. What band doesn't like playing to cheering crowds? It feels good, but in a way it only reinforces the idea that people don't want to hear your stuff."

"Okay, no problem, Matt. It's just something that's been rattling around my head since Overpeck and-"

He held up a hand. "Whoa, you didn't let me finish. When I said we were all equal I meant it." He shrugged. "Let me think about it."

My eyes widened. To hear Jayne tell it, he would have not only refused to consider the idea – he'd have lost his shit altogether.

"You look surprised," he commented as he smiled and stood from the table. "I like to think I'm pretty reasonable."

"Totally," I said, "And thanks, Matt."

"No problem. I'll see you tomorrow."

I was glad Matt at least heard me out, though I couldn't tell if he was really open to it or was just paying me lip service to keep the peace. Either way, I was glad I'd brought it up and even gladder that he listened.

▲   ▲   ▲

There were two surprises waiting for me when I got to Brooklyn the next night, the first being that I found a parking spot after just one trip around the block, which never happens. The second was that Jayne was there already (I saw her shitty white car illegally parked across the street), which also never happens. Don't know why I was surprised about that one – she'd been blowing up my phone all day, wanting to know what had happened with my sit-down with Matt. Of course she'd assumed he'd laughed me right out of the garage – she just wanted me to cop to it.

I walked in to find her leafing through the latest issue of Rolling Stone. "Phone dead?" she snickered. It was a reference to the many texts I'd ignored throughout the day.

I shrugged. "Where are the guys?"

"They'll be here." She looked back at her magazine, a small smile playing on her lips. "Told ya he'd squash it."

"Yup," I said as I fiddled with my guitar case. She was really enjoying this.

Just then, Matt walked in, followed a minute later by Skid.

"Group meeting," Matt announced as he set down his guitar. Jayne still had the small smile as she closed her magazine and looked up at him expectantly.

"Jackson and I talked last night about the gigs this summer...where the band is going...and he suggested we cover a few songs." He looked pointedly at Skid and Jayne. "You two know how I feel about cover bands, but I gotta admit I'm actually considering the idea..."

I slid my eyes to Jayne – her expression was priceless.

"... I'm thinkin' for now we keep things as they are for the smaller gigs but have something prepared for the Labor Day Festival."

Before anyone could object Matt held up a hand. "That's not to say we've gotta do it. We see what the vibe of the crowd is and then go from there." He looked at the three of us. "So, what do you guys think?"

It took some effort but I managed to keep the shit-eating grin from my face. "Sure, sounds good."

Skid hesitated a moment and I thought he was gonna object, but then he just nodded in agreement. Not the case with Jayne.

"Are you serious, Matt?" she asked incredulously with her arms folded across her chest. "What happened to *cover bands suck* and *we'll only ever play our own shit*?"

"Relax Jayne, it's not a lock and even if we decide to go with it, it's only one song." He looked over at me and chuckled. "And, hey, don't go blaming the new guy. He's got a point; maybe we need to take a chance, mix things up a bit."

I couldn't even look her way for fear I'd bust out laughing. She was so pissed off.

"Fine, whatever," she said, her eyes flicking over the three of us, "but I want to go on record as saying I'm totally against it." She then spun on her heels and retreated over to her keyboard.

Matt nodded once. "Duly noted, Jayne." He turned to me and Skid. "Okay, now that that's settled, let's get to work."

After another long practice session, I went over to Jayne, who'd done her best to ignore me for most of the night. I leaned against the wall next to where she was packing up her stuff.

"I don't know what you're so pissed about," I said, after making sure Matt and Skid were out of earshot. "It's not that big of a deal."

"Easy for you to say, but to me it *is* a big deal. The reason I was so drawn to Matt is because he was always about making it with our own stuff." She glared at me. "Now, thanks to you, that's gonna be shot to shit."

"You're being ridiculous. One song doesn't make us a cover band."

"It's fine, Jackson. I said I'd do it and I will." She zipped her bag closed and swung it over her shoulder. "But that doesn't mean I have to like it."

Then she tossed a *see you later* over her shoulder and headed out the door.

⁂

We didn't have practice the next couple of nights, and I didn't hear from Jayne. At first I laughed it off – she just couldn't stand to be wrong – but somewhere along the line it stopped being funny and started to bug the shit out of me. In fact, it always bugged the shit outta me when Jayne was mad at me, probably because I didn't want it to be uncomfortable to work together. When my *hey, what's up* texts were ignored, I knew I'd have to find another way to fix it.

The opportunity presented itself at our next practice, when Matt asked us to suggest some covers.

"If we're gonna do this, it should be a classic," Skid said.

"Agreed," Matt said, "Something recognizable to everyone." Though he didn't elaborate, the meaning was clear: if we were gonna sell out, it had to be with a song that was going to attract more listeners. "Right, Jayne?"

She looked at him for a moment, then shrugged. "Right."

I glanced over at her. Boy, she wasn't going to let this go.

"What about we put our own stamp on the song?" I suggested, "That way, we can still showcase Dirty Bushwick...?"

I looked over at her again and saw the smallest flicker of interest. Of course she didn't say anything, not even when Matt and Skid said what a good idea it was. I knew she was full of shit, though. What musician in their right mind wouldn't jump at an opportunity to put their own personal stamp on a classic?

To sweeten the pot Matt told Jayne she could have the final say on the song, so long as it jived well with *Anna's Leash*. It had to since *Anna's Leash* would be the song we'd go into right afterwards. Jayne gave a resigned grunt, then we spent the next half hour throwing songs out. I don't know who suggested Free Bird, but as soon as it was out there, it was a no-brainer. For one, it's sound was right in line with *Anna's Leash* and two, well, who doesn't love Free Bird?

Jayne quickly took charge, putting in her two cents about subtle ways we could make it ours without taking too much away from everything that made it great in the first place. By the end of the night Jayne had completely taken over - surprising for someone who'd been dead set against it from the get-go. I didn't care, though, because at least now things between us were getting back on the right track.

CHAPTER 42 – LEAH

"Can you even *believe* we're back already?" Molly asked, eyes wide, as she twirled around in her new desk chair.

I shook my head. "Crazy, right?"

I felt like just minutes ago our parents had picked us up for the summer, and here we were, the Friday before the official start of the fall semester, settling into our *sophomore* dorm. It was much nicer than the freshman dorms, with a lot more room and more windows that made it much brighter.

By ten that morning —and after a lot of micromanaging by our parents about how to set up the room - Molly and I were left alone to do as we saw fit. By one o'clock we agreed it was perfect and that we now had the whole weekend to hang out and maybe even check out a few parties before the stress of classes started.

"Okay, now I'm starving." Molly brought the chair to a sudden stop. "Cafeteria?"

"Sure," I said, trying to play it cool as I slid my phone and ID card off the desk, "I could eat." The truth was I was dying to check out the cafeteria, and not because I wanted an order of their grease-soaked fries. We walked through the quad, where small clusters of students had gathered to bullshit about their summers and compare schedules. Even as we waved to this one and called a *hey, what's up* to that one, my eyes were darting back and forth, scanning the faces for Chase. The truth was, I wasn't sure whether I wanted to see him or not. I mean, it was bound to be awkward – me texting him, him calling me right back, only to have me blow him off... It was messed up. But what was I supposed to do after Jackson gave me the ring – go home and call the guy I'd cheated on him with? Even I wasn't going to sink that low. One day had turned into two, after that it just felt too weird to return the call.

I continued my surveillance as we entered the cafeteria and headed for the food line. Molly was of course completely oblivious to my furtive glances – she was too busy chattering about did I see so-and-so's new haircut and how what's-her-name had shed the freshman fifteen, and I yessed and nodded in all the right places. It didn't matter though because Chase was nowhere in sight. I followed her to a booth in the back, relieved that I could eat in peace. As I unwrapped my Italian hero and took a bite, my thoughts once again returned to the night he'd called. Much as I wanted to think it was loyalty to Jackson, there was another reason I hadn't gotten back to him.

His message had been short - saying his internship was busy and he hoped I was having a good summer – but he sounded . . . off . . . distracted . . . just not himself. There was no *give me a call back* or *talk to you later* – just that he would see me in a few weeks. Maybe he was really busy, but of course, it got me wondering: Had he met someone over the summer? There was no need to remind myself that Chase was a hot commodity and certainly not sitting around counting the days until he saw me again. Not that it mattered anyway because I was officially over him. I had a great boyfriend and had no plans to ever stray from Jackson again. I glanced down at the silver ring wrapped around my finger and smiled. So maybe he'd never be rich or successful, but so what? He was sweet and loved me and that was so much more important, right?"

"Leah, will you wipe that stupid grin off your face?" Molly laughed, "Sheesh, the way you're staring at that ring you'd think it was a five-carat diamond."

"Huh?" I looked up at her just in time to see Chase and Brent enter the cafeteria. I felt my heart skip a beat. Molly turned to see who or what had caught my attention and when she saw who it was she immediately jumped up and started waving them over.

Shit, shit, shit.

Brent waved back, then nudged Chase in the ribs. I saw his lips stretch into a smile when he saw it was me and then the two of them began to walk toward us.

"Oh my gosh, Leah! Brent's on his way over!" Molly smoothed the front of her shirt down then ran a hand through her curls. "How do I look?"

"Well, of course he's on his way over," I said, harsher than I intended, "you made enough of a scene getting his attention."

Molly whipped her head around and eyed me curiously.

"Just sayin', we just got back and I wasn't really in the mood... Anyway, you look fine." She still looked suspicious, but there was no time to get into it now. I turned back toward Chase, striding confidently toward me. How was it possible that he looked even better than I remembered? Was it the deep tan? Was it his hair, which was now sun-streaked and just a tad bit longer than the last time I saw him? Was it the way his t-shirt seemed to cling perfectly to his muscular chest?

"Hi girls," Brent said, "How was everybody's summer?"

Molly quickly began a play-by-play of her entire summer, barely letting either of them get a word in edgewise. She always spoke quickly when she was nervous or excited and my guess was that Brent showing up caused a little of both.

Chase looked down and shot me that sexy grin of his. "Scoot over," he motioned with his hand for me to make room for him. "Looks like she's not gonna be stopping any time soon." He slid in next to me, just close enough that I could feel the warmth coming off his body.

"So...you have a good summer?"

"Oh, yeah, it was great," I began, trying to sound breezy, unlike Molly who was talking so fast she sounded like a loon. "It was too short, though; could've used another week or two." I figured I'd be vague about what I'd done since most of my summer was spent doing things with Jackson. "How about you?"

"Worked a lot but I was able to squeeze in some fun here and there." I thought at first he was opting to go the vague route as well, but then he spoke about a couple of weekend camping trips and the few days he'd spent visiting family in Kentucky.

Throughout the conversation I found myself feeling very conscious of Jackson's ring. Although I kept my hand in my lap, I kept nervously twirling the ring around my finger with my thumb. Then, almost without realizing it, I nonchalantly slipped the hand wearing the ring under my thigh so it was out of sight.

"Leah," I heard Molly call across the table, "I'm gonna go grab a cookie; you want one?" She didn't wait for me to answer. "Brent, come with me," she said as she latched onto his arm and began steering him to the dessert section.

"Wow, a cookie's the last thing that girl needs – she's like bouncin' off the walls."

I laughed. "I guess she's just happy to be back."

He looked at me a moment. "What about you? You happy to be back?"

"I guess I'm on the fence," I answered noncommittedly. "I mean I'm definitely not looking forward to all the work. I've got a few really tough classes this semester."

"Yeah, tell me about it. I've already got a tutor set up for organic chemistry – that class is gonna be a killer."

"*Organic chemistry*," I asked, nearly spitting out my iced tea, "Since when do pre-law students take that?"

He laughed. "They don't. When I started out I thought I might want to go into the pharmaceutical industry. Guess I'm just hedging my bets."

"Phew," I said, "Thought I might have to rethink my own career path."

Neither of us said anything for a minute, then Chase reached under the table and put his hand on my thigh. "So, what are you up to tonight?" he asked. "You should come over; we could hang out."

I figured I knew what he meant by "hang out" and instantly the response I'd rehearsed so many times popped into my head - *Chase, I think I'm going to have to say no. A lot has happened over the summer and I don't think it's a good idea for us to continue with the way things were last semester.*

Unfortunately, just as I was about to speak those exact words I felt his hand inch a little higher up my thigh and before I knew it, *Sure, that sounds great*, popped out of my mouth instead.

I was rewarded with yet another sexy grin as he gave my thigh a gentle squeeze. "Cool, I'll see you later."

Molly, who had just returned to the table, caught that last line. "*See you later?* A party already? It's only our first night but heck, I'm in."

"Yeah, excellent idea, Chase," Brent chimed in just as excitedly as he pulled out his phone, "Party at our place – I'll text the guys."

I knew that wasn't what Chase had in mind, but I silently thanked Molly anyway for unknowingly swooping in to save my ass. Just another momentary lapse in judgement, I told myself, but sometimes that was all it took to screw everything up.

⚔ ⚔ ⚔

Molly was beyond giddy as she got ready for the party. She was fussing and primping so much you'd think she was Cinderella on her way to the ball.

"I really wish you'd change your mind and come." She turned from the full-length mirror to give me a suspicious look. "You seemed fine this afternoon."

"Well, I *was* fine this afternoon but now I feel a headache coming on," I lied. "And the loud music will only make it worse. The last thing I need is to be knocked off my game the first week of classes."

No, Leah, the last thing you need is to mix Chase with alcohol. Didn't matter much, though; even completely sober I lost all sense of reason when I was around him. First day back on campus and I'd already said I'd "hang out" with him.

"Fine, whatever, but I think you're being ridiculous. I wouldn't miss this party for the world." Molly smirked at her reflection. "*Especially* since I'm going to get to hang out with Brent."

"I thought you'd given up on Brent," I said. "At least that's what you said at the end of last semester. What gives?"

"It's a new year," she replied as she pulled her mascara from her makeup bag. "It's like all slates are wiped clean and everyone starts brand new." She swept the wand over her lashes, widened her eyes, then added another coat. "I've got a good feeling about me and Brent; I think this is going to be our year."

"Your *year*?" I laughed. "Your year for what?"

She turned around to face me. "This is going to be the year that Brent and I finally take our relationship to the next level, if you get my drift."

I wanted to say that from where she and Brent started, there was nowhere to go but up. She'd spent two semesters chasing him and he barely gave her the time of day.

"And what makes you think things'll be different this year?"

"Well, Leah, if you must know," she began, sounding almost mysterious, "I've been reading *Cosmo* all summer and let's just say I've got a few tricks up my sleeve."

"*Cosmo*, wow," I said because I didn't know what else to say. I couldn't imagine what "tricks" could magically change things, but if Cosmo had the answers to romantic dramas, I figured I ought to start reading it.

"So," she began excitedly. "How do I look?"

"Great, Molly." It was the first truthful thing I'd said all afternoon. "You'll knock his socks off tonight!"

"Thanks." She grabbed her phone and key and headed for the door. Just as she pulled it open, she looked at me, winked and said, "Don't wait up."

"Ha, ha," I said, then flopped onto my bed. This certainly wasn't how I'd envisioned spending my first night back at school.

▲　　▲　　▲

After she left I called Jackson but he didn't answer so I left him one of those mushy I-miss-you-already messages that did nothing to ease my guilt. With a sigh I changed into shorts and a t-shirt and turned on the TV. *So I'll have a quiet night. No big deal. Doesn't mean I'm a geek or anything.* I surfed through the stations several times before finally settling on an old episode of "Friday Night Lights" that had just begun a few minutes earlier.

My phone rang just as the final credits began to roll. I figured it was Jackson calling me back, so my heart skipped a beat when I saw Chase's name on the caller I.D. I hesitated for a moment, then against my better judgment, accepted the call.

"Hello."

"Hello yourself," he said. "We're missing you over here; Molly said you're sick?"

"Nah, just have a headache, that's all."

"A headache? You blew me off for a *headache*," he joked.

I laughed. "Hey, gotta be in tiptop shape when classes begin on Monday, right?"

"This is true," he agreed. "But, just wanted to say your presence was missed."

"Thanks, Chase," I laughed again and as I did there was a knock at the door. At first, I thought it was Molly, but I'd seen her take her key, and besides, it was way too early for her to be back... unless things hadn't gone well with Brent. I chuckled to myself at the thought of her using her Cosmo tricks – whatever they were - on him.

"Hold on a sec, someone's at the door." I padded over to the door and pulled it open to find Chase smiling down at me. He pressed "end" on his own phone and slid it into his front pocket.

CHAPTER 43 – JACKSON

When Leah left I'd figured I was going to be miserable – luckily, my schedule with Dirty Bushwick was even busier than ever. In addition to regularly getting together with DB, Matt suggested that Jayne and I get back to a bunch of stuff we'd put on the backburner. I offered to go to her place in Staten Island but she thought my setup was better. No shock there – Jayne always had to say and do the opposite of everyone else...or at least the opposite of me.

"Besides, I could stay at my dad's place and spend some time with him," she reasoned. Her father had recently sold the house and for the time being was renting the top floor of a small home in Wanaque, right in my neck of the woods.

We also spent a lot of time working on Dirty Bushwick's rendition of Free Bird, and even I was surprised by how much I enjoyed it. There was something really cool about taking an existing piece of music – especially such a famous one – and figuring out how we could put our own signature to it. It was oddly freeing, and though Jayne would never come out and say it I knew she felt the same way. It made it all the more fun to bust her balls about it.

"Shit Jayne, for someone who was *so* resistant to doing covers you sure are putting a hell of a lotta effort into this one." It had been another late night in my garage, most of which had been spent on Free Bird, even though we had plenty of other shit to do.

She ignored me at first. "Listen, if we're gonna do this we're gonna do it right. We need to be prepared - I don't want us fumbling around like idiots on stage."

"Oh, we're prepared alright." We had been kicking ass, and I had my fingers crossed that Matt would give Free Bird the green light at the concert this Sunday.

After another hour of working on it I'd finally had enough. "Jayne, I'm done. Let's move on to something else. You know as well as I do the fucking thing's perfect."

"Fine," she said, but she sounded annoyed. "How 'bout we work on that psychedelic number that Skid loves so much."

"Great, perfect, anything but more Free Bird. I love it, but I'm starting to sing it in my sleep."

We worked on the other piece for a bit but kept coming up empty. I suggested a soda break and grabbed a couple of Cokes from the kitchen.

"Hey," she mused, "Would it be cheating if we looked through the stuff in the shoebox again?"

I took a sip of my Coke. "You mean my mom's stuff? You think there's something else we might be able to use?"

"Sure, why not?" She gave me a sideways glace. "Would you mind?"

"No, not at all. I'll go get it." I stood from the table and headed back into the house, but just as I was about to close the garage door I heard Jayne start to play Free Bird again on my acoustic. I shook my head; there was no denying we'd done a phenomenal job.

When I got up to my room I looked around for the box, finally remembering that I'd stored it in the top of my closet. I reached up and grabbed it, but instead of going right back down to the garage with it, I opened it and started leafing through the contents.

All these writings must've been so important to her at some point, when she was young and happy. A carefree teenager with her whole life ahead of her. I wondered sometimes what my mom would've thought about hearing her words put to music. I smiled to myself; she would've fucking loved it.

I never used to let myself think about her, it was too hard. Lately, though, maybe because I had my life on track, I'd allowed myself to wander back to those early days. The long lazy summer afternoons spent swimming at the lake. Making her watch as I made endless haphazard dives off the dock and her clapping and cheering after each one. Claiming I was too tired to walk home so she'd carry me while pulling our cart filled with beach towels and sand toys. The smell of her long hair as I rested my head on her shoulder and pretended to sleep the entire three blocks to our house. The faded yellow sundress she always wore around the house in the summer because I said she looked so pretty in it.

"Make it twirl, Mommy!" I'd say, and she'd spin around the kitchen floor with her bare feet, her hair whirling as the dress fanned out around her. The two of us would always laugh ourselves silly over things like that.

Then there was the tense look she'd mask with a nervous smile whenever she heard the garage door open - a signal my dad was home.

"What the fuck, Anna?" I remember him saying. "What the hell are you wearing? I told you, you look like fuckin' trailer trash in that thing." He'd laugh humorlessly. "No wonder I barely come home after work anymore."

I remembered the look of defeat that would shadow her features the rest of the night, even as she pretended to be upbeat, never wanting us kids to know how sad she really was. I don't know how she did it. She was so young, not much older than Beth was now. How was she able to deal with all Dad's crap and still be able to make our home such a happy place for us kids?

Whenever I thought about my life, it was always clearly defined by *before* and *after* - before the accident and after it. I'd often wondered what path I would have taken if she hadn't died. Would I have gone to college? Studied music? I bet she'd be Dirty Bushwick's number one fan! What about Tim? Would he still have enlisted? I doubted it. Shit, I hadn't seen my brother in years.

Suddenly my cell rang, pulling me back to the present. It was Leah calling. "Hey, what's up?" I said as I shook the thoughts of the past away.

"Nothing much, just want to say hi," she said.

We spoke for a few minutes — mostly about her first week of school - then she said she had to go and I said I did too. I ended the call and then gathered up the box. *Jeez, Jayne's gonna be wondering what happened to me.*

When I got back down to the garage, she was looking through a pile of old record albums.

"Where'd all that come from?" I asked as I tossed my phone on the table.

"They were in a box down the basement." She answered without looking up.

"What were you doing down the basement?" I asked, then adopted a joking tone to cover up that fact that I thought it was odd. "Surprised you made it out in one piece. It's a shitstorm down there."

"Oh, I wasn't down there, your dad brought them up and -"

I quickly cut her off.

"My *dad* brought them up? What do you mean?" Where had my father even come from? Usually I heard the son of a bitch lurking around but tonight the house was quiet.

She looked up when she heard the annoyance in my voice. "Well, yeah. He came in – I guess he heard me playing Free Bird when he was passing outside. Anyhow, we started talking and I told him about the cover we were doing, which by the way he didn't seem to know anything about – hey, don't you two talk?

I just looked at her, too annoyed to speak or even give her my usual shrug.

"Anyway, he said he had a lot of old record albums and that he thought he had the album with the live version of Free Bird on it and did we want to take a look." She looked at me strangely, like she couldn't understand what I was so upset about.

"What the fuck, Jayne?" I snapped.

"What do you mean, *What the fuck?*" she snapped back. "Jeez, what's the big friggin' deal?"

"The big friggin' deal is that I don't need him up in my goddamn business." I was fuming. "Christ, what the hell else did you spout off about?"

"*Spout off?* What are you talking about?"

I didn't say anything, just glared at her with a look of utter contempt.

She glared back a me a moment, then said, "Fuck this," and began tossing stuff in her backpack. When she was done she threw it over her shoulder and said, "I'm outta here. Call me when you get your head outta your ass." She stormed out of the garage and slammed the door behind her.

I stood there for a minute and then furiously slammed my fists down on the table. *What the fuck was he doing in here? And why the fuck was Jayne talking to him?*

Suddenly it dawned on me. She had no clue about my relationship – or lack thereof – with my father. How could she? I'd never spoken to her about it.

Fuck. I ran outside but was too late. Her car was already halfway down the block.

▲   ▲   ▲

The traffic to Brooklyn was so bad I felt like leaving my car on the side of the expressway and walking the rest of the way, but even that didn't piss me off as much as the thirty-minute search for a parking spot once I got there. Three times I thought I had one, only to see it was a fire hydrant or a driveway or a tow zone for some ridiculous fucking reason. When I eventually did find one it was five blocks away and I was nearly a half-hour late to practice. The real reason for my shitty mood, though, was that I was dreading dealing with Jayne. I knew I should have called to explain why I'd gone off on her, but I figured she'd just ignore my call or hang up on me, and I didn't feel like dealing with that crap either. It seemed like when it came to Jayne I was always doing some kind of damage control.

"Don't ask," I said as I walked in and saw Matt pointedly glance at the clock on the wall.

As I put my stuff away and got out my guitar, from the corner of my eye I could see that Jayne was giving me the bitchy stare-down. Nothing new there. I ignored it all through practice, but when we finished I pulled her aside.

"Hey Jayne, can I, uh, talk to you a minute?"

She let out a huff. "Fine, but make it quick. I have things to do, can't be hanging around here all night."

274

I hesitated. "Listen, I just wanted to talk about last night, what happened. You know, with my dad. I shouldn't have come down on you like that."

She was quiet for a beat, but her expression had softened.

"*And...?*" she said finally.

"*And* what?"

"*And*, since I don't want to end up in the middle of your little family feud again, you might want to clue me in on the basics so I know who I can and can't talk to. Get it?"

"Fair enough," I agreed, then motioned with my head to the door. "How 'bout we take a walk down to Token's, get a drink and I'll give ya the lowdown."

She mulled it over, then checked the time on her phone. "Okay, but just one, it's getting late."

Token's was pretty empty but we grabbed a booth in the back anyway. I ordered two Coors but Jayne never touched hers so I ended up drinking it myself.

"So..." I began, but she cut me off.

"Listen, Jackson, whatever's going on between you and your dad is none of my business. If you want to talk about it, I'll listen, but please, don't feel like you have to. I've been through a lot of shit myself and believe me I don't go shouting about it from the rooftops, so I get it."

She grabbed a pretzel from the bowl in the center of the table. "But just for the record, your dad didn't seem like such a bad guy."

"Yeah, well he's a fuckin' scumbag." I took a long sip of my beer.

"Listen, I'm not discounting what you're saying. *I'm* just saying he didn't come across that way at all." She grabbed another pretzel. "Hey, and he mentioned he used to be in a band. No wonder he came in when he heard me playing." She chuckled, "From the looks of those albums he showed me, though, I'm guessing he was a real headbanger back in the day."

"Yeah, I know. Totally not my – *our* - scene."

I ordered another beer and then we sat in silence a bit as I debated how much, if anything, I should tell her. She didn't press me, though, which was maybe why I started to talk. She never said a word, never stopped me to ask a question or to clarify anything. I just kept talking until several more empties lined the table and I had nothing left to say.

"Wow," she said when I was finished, "Sounds like you guys really got a raw deal."

"Yeah, tell me about it," I slurred, as the effects of the alcohol took hold.

"Well, it sounds like things turned around for you, though. I mean you have a job, the band's doing well, you have a girlfriend."

Leah. Even she didn't know anything about my dad other than the obvious. I'd never wanted Leah knowing any of that shit. I never wanted her to know just how different we actually were.

"We should go," I finally said.

"Yeah, it's getting late."

I walked Jayne to her car but when we got there she said, "Get in. You're not driving home like that. You can crash at my place."

Before I could object, she stopped me. "Sorry, not up for discussion; climb in." She reached over and unlocked the passenger side door.

I was too tired to argue with her, not to mention the fact that in the state I was in I was never getting out of my parking spot.

▲   ▲   ▲

I knew before I even opened my eyes the next morning that I wasn't at home – there was far too much street noise outside for my boring-ass neighborhood. Beyond that I didn't have a fucking clue where I was. I sat up and looked around, and that's when it came back to me. Too many beers. Jayne's couch. She had given me some pillows and a very soft blanket then disappeared into her room. I glanced at the cable box near the TV and saw it was only 6:45 –way too early. I laid back down and though it wasn't cold, pulled the blanket over me. When I woke again, two more hours had passed. On the coffee table next to me sat a small bottle of water and two Advils.

This place has pretty good service, I smirked to myself as I sat up and opened the bottle of water, drinking half of it in one gulp. Other than being parched I felt pretty good, which was surprising considering how many beers I'd had, but just to be on the safe side I downed the Advil anyway. Suddenly, I was hit with the smell of homemade pancakes and...was that *bacon* I smelled? *Jayne* was cooking me *bacon*?

"Hey, you're up," she said cheerfully as she padded into the room carrying plates and silverware. She set them down on the table on the other side of the room, then turned to look at me. Her dark hair was pulled back in an uncharacteristically neat ponytail and her blue eyes were scrubbed clean of the trademark black makeup she usually wore. Like after the last outdoor concert she was almost unrecognizable. "And just in time; breakfast is just about ready."

"Cool. Mind if I hit your bathroom first?" I asked, but I was already on my way down the hall.

After a quick shower, I towel dried my hair as best I could and put back on the same wrinkled clothes I'd slept in. I strolled out to the kitchen only to find her already eating and having what looked like a very playful conversation with a blonde dude wearing nothing more than a pair of red plaid flannel pants and a baseball cap perched backwards on his head. *The roommate?*

"Hey, Jackson," Jayne said when she saw me come in, "Grab some food and pull up a chair. Oh, and this is my roommate, Eddie." She turned to Eddie. "Eddie, my friend Jackson."

"S'up?" he said, jerking his chin toward me.

"Not much," I said coolly as I eyed him, "*S'up* with you?"

The two of them continued talking as I filled my plate. Apparently, I'd ended up in the middle of their Saturday morning routine which consisted of them taking turns cooking a big breakfast. They'd eat together and catch up with what they'd done all week. With their conflicting schedules, it was the only meal they shared.

"Jayne here's got me beat when it comes to her perfectly crisp bacon, but I got the corner on the waffle market. Right, Jaynie?"

Jaynie? If there was one thing Jayne was not it was a "Jaynie."

I sat and ate with them but I couldn't help but feel I was intruding. Their easy banter made me think that they knew each other pretty well, especially since they hadn't lived together very long. It was almost like they were brother and sister...sort of; I couldn't put my finger on it. It was just weird 'cause I never thought of Jayne as having a life outside the band – she never talked about anything but music and, occasionally, her dad. Now, as I listened to their conversation, I heard her casually mention three different apparently close friends and a couple of parties she'd been to recently.

"Shoot, look at the time," she said, as if suddenly realizing I was there. "We should get a move on, Jackson. Matt wanted us in by eleven." She glanced from me to Eddie, an excited look on her face. "Big day tomorrow."

"Oh right," Eddie drawled, "I forgot, the big concerto is tomorrow."

"I'm just gonna change and get ready," she told me. "Give me fifteen minutes, tops." She turned to Eddie. "Don't forget, you're on cleanup duty."

"I didn't forget," he said but she was already on her way to her room. He waited until her door was closed and then turned to me, eying me up for a minute. "So, you're in the band with Jaynie?"

"Uh, yup," I said as I speared another forkful of pancake.

"Cool," he said, nodding slowly, then grabbed the sports section of the newspaper lying on the table.

He didn't say anything else so neither did I. When I finished I cleaned my plate and coffee mug in the sink and set it on the rack to dry. Thankfully Jayne emerged a few minutes later. I didn't think I could take another awkward minute.

Eddie looked up from the paper. "Hey look, Jaynie's back in rocker-chick mode. High-five bat-girl."

Jayne gave him a playful eyeroll but high-fived him anyway. She turned to me, "Ready?"

"Hell, yeah." I followed her into the living room to grab my keys and phone.

"See ya later, Jaynie," Eddie yelled as he turned back to his newspaper and then almost as an afterthought said, "See ya 'round, Jack."

Jack? What the fuck? Was it my imagination or was this guy a total douche? I turned around and eyed him but he never looked back up from the paper. I shook it off, maybe it *was* my imagination.

"Hey, thanks a lot for letting me stay here last night," I said once Jayne and I were settled in her car. "You were right, I was in no shape to drive."

"Anytime." She maneuvered out of the parking spot and pulled onto the road. "I remember how much it sucked driving back and forth to Jersey."

We drove for a while in silence, then I finally said, "So, it looks like things are working out with your, uh, roommate situation."

"Oh, Eddie? Yeah, Eddie's great. It's working out well."

"So, he's a frienda Matt's?" I asked because Eddie didn't seem like someone Matt would hang out with.

"Actually, he's a friend of a friend. Matt doesn't know him all that well but he knew I really needed a place so he put some feelers out and came up with Eddie. We have like totally opposite schedules, plus, he's a total gym-rat so when he's not at work, he's working out. I don't see him all that much. But hey, he did say he'd come on Sunday and bring some friends so we might have a cheering section. That'd be cool."

"Yeah, really cool," I lied as I stared straight ahead.

Total fucking douche.

▲　　▲　　▲

We only practiced a couple of hours because Matt wanted everyone to be rested and in top form for Sunday. Fine by me. I still had a slight hangover, plus the shower I took at Jayne's didn't quite take since I didn't have a change of clothes and I needed another, pronto. Dirty threads aside, I left with a really good feeling about this concert and not just because of Free Bird, which Matt hadn't officially greenlighted - yet.

My good mood got even better when I got to Overpeck the next day and Matt told us we weren't the first band in the lineup. Two bands were going on before us, which brought us closer to a three-p.m. start time. The later we played, the more people would be around to hear us. After telling us to be back by two-thirty, Matt sauntered away as if he didn't have a care in the world.

I was nervous, of course, but not nearly as nervous as last time. I knew what to expect, and I knew what *not* to expect – in other words, I wouldn't be disappointed when there were no screaming fans.

I drove around for a while thinking it would clear my head, then forced myself to eat something, but I soon realized that killing time was only making me more anxious. So I headed back to Overpeck and found Jayne and Skid already there. Guess they didn't have anything else to do either. We got set up and before we knew it, it was a quarter of three and Al, the same concert promotor from last time, wandered over and said everything was going according to schedule and that he'd introduce us at a little after three. As if on cue, Matt came in right behind him.

"This is it, guys," he said as he walked over and grabbed his bass guitar. "Everybody ready?"

"Yep," we all said, practically in unison. We had been waiting for hours and now it was time to get the show on the road.

"Let's go," Matt said, then led us up the stairs to the wings of the stage.

My stomach dropped a little when I heard Al's deep voice booming through the microphone. "Okay everyone, this next band is our first returning act of the day. They rocked the house back in July so put your hands together as we welcome back Brooklyn's very own . . . DIRTY BUSHWICK!"

Once again the four of us bounced out to the stage like we were headlining at the Meadowlands, and once again there was woefully little applause. It stung – always did, but I did my best to ignore it and just concentrate on the music. But when we got through the first four songs with no change in the crowd, Matt gave the signal for us to go with Free Bird next. I looked over at Jayne and smiled as she gave me the thumbs-up.

Jayne started out on her keyboard and then the rest of us joined in. At first the audience was lukewarm at best, but little by little I felt a change in the vibe. People were beginning to stop and take notice, and by the time Matt started singing we had the attention of nearly the entire crowd. Suddenly, it was like living out a fantasy – or pretty damn close to it. No wonder musicians fell into the trap of only doing covers – they'd do anything to hear that cheering crowd.

We all knew we had to do something dramatic if we were going to have any shot of holding onto the crowd, so just as we finished the last note of Free Bird we launched right into *Anna's Leash*. Although not everyone hung around, a big portion of them did and that was good enough for us. By the time we finished *Anna's Leash* the crowd was still decent and judging from the sound of the applause they really liked it.

I couldn't speak for the others, but I knew that if I lived to be a hundred I'd never forget the high I felt on the stage that day...and it was about to get even better. When we made our way to the back of the stage where the other bands were waiting to go on there were actually a few people waiting to meet us – *meet us*! It was so fucking cool. There was an old dude who said he was out in Oakland, California back in '77, where he saw Free Bird performed live. He just wanted to tell us that our performance brought back some great memories for him. There was also a young girl who wanted to meet Skid. She said she liked his tattoos. The best was the couple in their thirties who asked if we played anywhere local on the weekends.

"Hey, you guys wanna grab a few beers? Something to eat?" I didn't want to leave, didn't want the excitement to end.

Skid's eyes immediately flickered to his newfound groupie, so I knew he was going to bail, but Jayne nodded.

"Just let me go change first."

"Me too. Meet you back here in twenty?"

When I got back Jayne wasn't there yet, and I wondered whether she was scrubbing all that black shit from her eyes. That's when I saw Matt, talking to some well-dressed dude I didn't recognize. They talked for a while and then shook hands. The guy smiled and handed Matt his business card before turning and leaving. I briefly wondered what the exchange was about but didn't have time to think about it because just then Jayne reappeared.

"Ready?"

"Yep, and hey, let's hit that burger stand by the parking lot. I'm starving." As we turned to leave I glanced over my shoulder just in time to see Matt toss the man's business card into a nearby trashcan.

▲   ▲   ▲

The first time it happened, we were on line waiting for our burgers. I thought it was my imagination, but then it happened a few more times - someone would glance at us and do almost a doubletake, like they recognized us. I didn't know if Jayne even noticed it, but it took my high to a whole new level. This was fucking awesome.

After devouring our burgers and Cokes, Jayne and I decided to check out the other bands. We found a spot in the back where we could just hang out and listen to the competition.

We were there only a few minutes when Jayne nonchalantly nudged me in the ribs with her elbow.

"Hey, don't look now studly, but I think you have some admirers."

"No way," I said without turning to look.

"Yes, way...and here they come."

Jayne reached over and quickly snatched my hand then laughed. "Don't worry, I got you covered."

"Uh, I think I'm good," I laughed, though I didn't pull away. I knew she was just goofing around because our "deal" pertained to clubs, not outdoor family friendly concerts in the park.

Before I knew it, three girls approached and started talking to us about the concert. We chatted for a bit, but they didn't stay long. I couldn't quite tell if they were interested in more than just meeting the band, but either way Jayne's performance made short work of any ideas they might've had. I could hardly keep a straight face as she looped her arm around mine, kissed my shoulder, even reached up and adoringly brushed my hair back with her fingers until they finally left.

The encounter was flattering, no doubt, but unlike Skid I had no interest in going in that direction.

The two of us were still laughing and Jayne's arm was still locked around mine when I heard a familiar voice.

"Hey, look, it's rock chick!" We both looked up to find Eddie and a crew of three other guys approaching. "Great show, Jaynie," he smiled and put up a hand to high-five her. I felt my arm automatically clamp down on hers as she met his hand with a slap of her free hand.

"Thanks, Eddie! I can't believe you came, this is great!"

"Hey, told ya I would." Eddie turned to his friends and jerked his thumb towards me and Jayne. "This is my roomie." He eyed my arm clamped onto hers and smirked as he added, "and this is her, uh, friend, um, *Jack*, right?"

"Jackson," I said then nodded a *what up* in the direction of his buddies.

They continued talking and if Jayne thought it was weird that I wasn't letting go of her arm she didn't let on. What was Jayne doing living with this jerk anyway? Jayne, who didn't take shit from anyone and could certainly take care of herself. Still, I hoped she could see through all his "Jaynie" bullshit because I would've hated to see her get taken advantage of by this douche. Jayne needed to meet a decent guy – or at least find a decent roommate.

When they finally walked off, Jayne yanked her arm free of my grasp. "What're you doing?" She sounded annoyed as she rubbed her arm where I'd had it crushed to my side.

"Just returning the favor, pal," I joked as I gave her a friendly slap on the back. "Ready to head back?"

She looked at me for a moment, then nodded and the two of us headed back to see what was up with Matt and Skid.

▲ ▲ ▲

The Labor Day Festival was our last big gig but we had plenty of smaller ones lined up, and not just in Brooklyn. We'd branched out into a couple dive bars in Manhattan and rumor had it that Matt was working on getting us a gig in Pennsylvania – Philly to be exact. It would be Dirty Bushwick's first road trip.

It seemed like overnight things were beginning to happen for us. More people were showing up at our gigs, which in turn meant that we were getting more gigs. We had CDs available every time we played and we averaged selling maybe one or two a night – not platinum, but a hell of a lot better than the two we sold to my grandmother back in July! We continued doing one cover per show – sometimes Free Bird and sometimes other classics, and most times the response was positive.

Things with Slater would be winding down for the season soon and I had to make a decision – do I work the winter at Powder Peak or do I bag it and concentrate on the band? I knew I had enough money saved to coast through the winter so in the end I decided it was a no-brainer. I'd concentrate fully on the band and writing new music and keep my fingers crossed that in the end it would pay off.

Granted, we were still small potatoes where the music scene was concerned, but there was no denying that things had begun to pick up. But nothing – I mean *nothing* - could've prepared us for what was about to come next.

CHAPTER 44 – LEAH

I didn't even know what to say to Jackson anymore. I mean, what do you say when your boyfriend has completely lost touch with reality? Telling me that Dirty Bushwick had not only developed a small following, but were selling CDs and had gigs lined up in Manhattan and Philadelphia? I might have believed it if I hadn't seen the reaction – or lack thereof – at their gigs over the summer. Now, two months later, things had done a one-eighty? I highly doubted it. Not that I thought he was lying – sometimes I thought it would have been easier if he were. It sounded to me like he was reading way too much into things. The "small following" was probably friends of Beth and Brody. The CDs they were supposedly selling were probably purchased by other little kids who liked the fancy artwork on the cover. And those gigs in Manhattan and Philly? Let's face it, they were probably booked in some kind of cheesy battle of the band's lineup. That's not to say I didn't think they were good because I totally did, but since when did being good equal commercial success in the music business? It took a whole lot more than that, and whatever it was, Dirty Bushwick clearly didn't have it.

I knew he was delusional when he told me about Free Bird. How many times had he said he wanted to move on from Blow Torch because they were "just a cover band?" Now he was talking as if Dirty Bushwick was the only band in history to "put their own signature" on a cover song. Give me a break. Jackson acted as if this move was going to get them to the next level, whatever that meant. To me, it reeked of desperation.

I'll admit there were a few times when I thought, *heck, maybe*, but then he would inevitably hit me with a reality check that left me unable to say anything but, "Sounds great, Jackson." I didn't want to give him false hope, but I wasn't going to be the one to crush his hopes either.

"Holy shit, Leah, you're never gonna believe this..." he said when I answered the phone one night.

I barely managed to hold back a groan. Lately far too many of our conversations had begun this way, and when one did I knew there were a lot of "Sounds great, Jacksons" in my immediate future.

I sat there and listened while he told me this crazy story about how Matt was approached by a "suit" – his word, not mine - at the outdoor concert they played over Labor Day weekend. Supposedly the guy was working on some indie film and was looking for a band with original music that he could use for the soundtrack.

When I casually asked him why it took him so long to tell me – I mean, Labor Day was a while ago – he said that at first Matt had blown the guy off. Even threw away his business card because he figured it was a scam. But the guy kept calling and eventually convinced Matt to look at a rough trailer for the film. He'd even sent over some sort of contract.

"I've seen it, Lee," Jackson said, "Seems totally legit." He paused. "Do you think your dad would mind looking over the contract, you know, translate all the legal bullshit?"

That's when I rolled my eyes and turned on the TV (I kept the volume down low, of course. I wasn't a total bitch). Actually, I felt sorry for him. He tried so hard and wanted it so bad that he was buying into this craziness, and from the sound of things it sounded like Matt, Skid and Jayne were too.

"Ummm, I can ask him..." I said carefully, "I know he's been swamped..." Other than the thing with Chase, it was the only time I'd lied to him. But there was no way I was going to bother my father with this.

"No problem," he said and then chuckled, "Besides, once I quit Powder Peak, I'll have plenty of time to do a little legal research on my own."

My first thought was, *So now you think you're a rock star and an attorney?*, but that actually didn't sound as ridiculous as the other thing he'd said.

"Did you say *quit your job*? How will you pay your bills?"

"I've got some money saved," he said nonchalantly, "so I'll be okay. Besides, I've got a really good feeling about the direction the band is headed; I think we're finally on the right track."

At this point, I couldn't even muster a *Sounds great, Jackson.*

There was a time when I would've been totally on board, doing the whole supportive girlfriend thing, but there was no way I was going to act like it was okay to go and quit his job over a pipe dream. I cared about him too much to do that.

Who are you kidding, Leah? This has nothing to do with Jackson, or his bills.

Chase and I had resumed our relationship exactly twelve hours after I arrived back at school. In fact, we'd ended up in bed the same night I'd bailed on the party, claiming to have a headache. I'd tried to do the right thing, but it turned out my resolve didn't survive Chase's unexpected appearance at my door. Since then I hadn't even entertained the thought of giving him up. Jackson's band fantasies had only made Chase seem more appealing in comparison, though clearly he didn't need any help in that department. In *any* department, if I was being totally honest.

I knew it was only a matter of time before Molly caught on. She had to be suspicious of all the time I suddenly spent "at the library" and all the unexplained texting when we were together. Fortunately, she was so busy with her own drama she didn't bother trying to delve into mine. She had once again officially given up on Brent - on lacrosse players altogether - after getting chummy with one of the distance runners on the cross-country team. Apparently they were in a couple of classes together. Now all she wanted to do was hang out at the "track house." At first she bugged me to go with her and I went a few times, just to keep her off my back. Every now and then, I'd casually let it drop that I was hanging out with my "friend" Chase (if I'd learned anything from this experience it was that the best lies had a little bit of truth to them) but other than an innuendo here and there Molly hadn't said much about it.

I don't know if it was because she was so distracted or because I'd become such a good liar, but somewhere along the line I'd gotten too comfortable, and that's when I screwed up. I mean, how stupid could I be, telling her I was hanging out at Chase's so much because it was easier to do my laundry there? As soon as the words were out of my mouth I knew it was a mistake, but Molly had just given me an odd look and went about her business. Safe! Or so I thought.

One night I returned to the dorm just after one a.m. to find Molly furiously typing away on her laptop. Clearly she had put off another paper for the last minute.

"Oh, you're still up..." I said, suddenly very conscious of the fact that I'd told her I was going to Chase's to do laundry but was coming home empty-handed. I'd expected her to be in bed and none the wiser. "My clothes were taking forever so I just decided I'd go there tomorrow and-"

I cut myself off when I saw that Molly had stopped typing and was just staring at me, her face unreadable. Then she raised an eyebrow and not-so-subtly flicked her eyes to the pile of dirty clothes on my bed.

Busted.

I let out an annoyed huff. "Molly, if you have something to say, just say it."

"Say? What could I possibly have to say, Leah?" She managed to sound sarcastic and bewildered at the same time as she returned to her laptop.

"Oh please, Molly, skip the dramatics."

She glanced at the digital clock on her desk, an annoyed look on her face. "Leah, it's the middle of the night. *Laundry?* Really?"

I looked at her for a minute, then shrugged. "What do you want me to say?"

"Nothing, Leah," she sighed. "If you want to continue spinning tales of clothes that seem to need constant washing then go ahead. I give up, and besides, I'm too busy with Aiden to care anymore."

"Who's Aiden?" I asked as I kicked my sneakers off.

"Well, if you actually gave a shit about anyone other than yourself you'd know that Aiden is the guy from the cross-country team I've been hanging out with. He and I are *a thing*, you know." She hesitated a beat, then under her breath I heard her say, "Well, almost."

Molly was right; she and I had become, well, just *roommates*. We had zero classes together and most of my classes were in the morning whereas most of hers were late afternoon. Even on weekends, we often went our separate ways. I was so busy sneaking around with Chase that I hadn't paid much attention to what she was doing or who she was doing it with. And even when I wasn't with Chase, I was so consumed with him that I'd nearly shut her out completely. There'd been so much lying, cheating and sneaking around my head was spinning, and if I didn't start to reign myself in I knew things – our friendship included - would quickly begin to unravel.

"Fine," I blurted out, "You win."

"I...win?"

When I didn't answer she slowly turned her desk chair around and said, "Did you just say *I win*?" She let it sink in a minute. "So...there really is something going on between you two?"

My silence was all the confirmation she needed.

"Since, since when?"

Again I just shrugged, not wanting to admit how long I'd been lying to her.

"Shit, Leah, I guess I can't really say I'm surprised, but, wow, hearing you admit it, I don't know what to say." She let it sink in a minute before the obvious hit her. "Oh my gosh, Leah...*Jackson*. How could you do that to him?"

"I know, I know, I'm a horrible person." I lowered my eyes to the ground. "I kept thinking I could keep it innocent, you know, some harmless flirting, but then...I don't know... then it *wasn't*."

"Holy crap, Leah." She shook her head, and I thought I heard a hint of disgust. "So, what are you gonna do? You can't keep bouncing between the two of them."

"Yeah, tell me about it," I sighed, "but I don't know what to do. I thought Chase was just a phase, something I had to get out of my system, but Molly...." I sat down on the edge of my bed before continuing. "Molly, this thing with me and Chase, it's no phase."

"You mean it's *serious*?"

"Yeah, it's serious; I think..." I glanced around the room and then brought my voice down to a whisper, as if someone was in the dorm room with us. "I think he's in love with me."

"Holy shit! Did he actually say that?" She sounded surprised.

"Well, no, not exactly, but I can tell."

"Wow, that's nuts," she said, then saw the look on my face and clarified. "I just mean it's hard to believe a guy like Chase would be so serious with a girl he had to share with another guy."

I ignored her comment, not wanting to admit that I'd often wondered the same thing. "Molly, I don't know what to do. I can't keep this up."

"You're right, you can't keep it up. Leah, you're going to have to break up with one of them because it's not fair to either of them – especially Jackson." She looked thoughtful for a minute. "You know, for a long time I was dead set against your relationship with Jackson, but over these last six months or so, I gotta say he's really grown on me. He's a great guy and doesn't deserve what you're doing to him, not by a longshot." She stood and came to sit next to me on my bed. "But whatever you decide, I got your back." She smiled, but her voice was serious. "Just *don't* put me in the middle of it."

🔺　🔺　🔺

I didn't normally consider Molly the voice of reason, but this time she was right. Here I was accusing Jackson of living in a fantasy and I was doing the same thing. How long did I really think I could pull this off before it blew up in my face? Unfortunately, this reality check did nothing to change the fact that *I wanted Chase.* Chase was the whole package – looks, money, brains, ambition and on top of all that he was an unbelievably talented athlete. He was easily the most sought-after guy on campus and I ate up the attention I got when we were together. Not to mention the fact that someone like him, who could pretty much have any girl he wanted, had chosen *me.*

But that was only part of it. I could actually see me and Chase having a real life together – I mean, a real post-college life. Jackson, on the other hand, was just spinning his wheels, never really getting anywhere. Yes, he was a nice guy and he was even hot in a grungy sort of way, but the more I hung out with Chase, the more Jackson began to seem like a loser. The whole band thing, which I used to think was so cool, now seemed childish. He might even end up holding me back, even become an embarrassment at some point. Imagine ten years from now showing up at my law office's Christmas Party with *Jackson* in tow. Oh my gosh, what would people think?

I knew I had no choice; I'd have to break up with Jackson. But, really, did I have to do it right away? Jackson never came up here anymore, not with his "hectic band schedule," so he'd never find out on his own. Plus, we hadn't seen each other – or slept together – in forever. Basically we were a couple in name only, so why hurt him? That was part of it; then there was the other part - that I loved having two hot guys fawning over me – and who wouldn't? Molly acted like she was so superior but I knew for a fact that if she were ever lucky enough to be in my shoes she'd be eating it up just the same.

Sure, it would have to end, and I would take care of it... eventually.

CHAPTER 45 – JACKSON

I don't know when I first realized that something was wrong between me and Leah. It started out as a feeling in the back of my mind, a hint of anxiety, maybe even a little dread. In the beginning I didn't even associate the feeling with Leah; I assumed it was about the band, that I was fooling myself thinking I might actually have a shot at a career in music. But that wasn't it; in fact, things were so busy with Dirty Bushwick that I hadn't even had a chance to visit Leah at school. I felt like shit about it too, especially since I'd always assured her that our relationship would come first, and that's when it hit me: she hadn't even asked when I'd be coming up. She sometimes didn't return my texts right away and she rarely picked up the phone when I called. The times she did pick up she seemed distant, even distracted. At first I chalked that up to the fact that she was readjusting to school, but a few weeks went by, then a month, and it only seemed to get worse. I started thinking maybe she was mad at me. Didn't she know my time wasn't my own anymore? That I had to either devote every waking moment to the band or kiss my dream goodbye?

Ever since Matt broke the news about the movie, things had been kind of crazy. I'd been eating, breathing and sleeping Dirty Bushwick and I still couldn't believe it.

When I first heard about Russ Decker – that was the guy who'd approached Matt – I refused to even consider the possibility that he was on the level. The others were even more skeptical – they didn't think it was a scam, exactly, because what could be gained by scamming poor musicians? They just thought this guy probably had even less going for him than we did and was talking out of his ass.

I'll never forget the day Matt showed up at practice and announced that, as far as he could tell, Decker was legit. "He's from Jersey – Alpine, to be exact – and apparently his father's a real fat cat. He ponied up the cash Decker needed to get the project started." Matt paused for a minute to take in our shocked expressions. "He's shopped the script around and found a few more backers, even landed a producer..." He grinned. "...so it sounds like it's definitely moving forward."

Matt was a pretty mellow guy, but even he seemed keyed up about it.

"And the kicker is," he continued, "Decker was about to leave the festival – was actually walking *out the gates* – when he heard the start of Free Bird and did an about-face. It's one of his favorites."

I felt Jayne's eyes flicker toward me and I fought the urge to gloat about pushing so hard for a cover song.

"Wow," I began, "That's really -"

Matt held up a hand, his grin widening. "I'm not finished. Apparently Decker was so impressed by what we'd done with Free Bird that he decided to hang around and see what we played next." He locked eyes with me. "When he heard *Anna's Leash,* he said he knew he'd found the sound he was looking for."

Now I did turn to Jayne and allowed myself a small smirk. It was just like I'd said all along: we just needed the right person to hear our stuff because I knew it was *that* good, and the best way to get the right person to listen to us was to nail a popular cover. If Decker did use our music for his film, and if it did well, it could be our ticket out of obscurity. Of course, those were still pretty big ifs, but still I couldn't help but think that in some small way it could also be my mother's chance to be heard.

"Listen," Matt said, interrupting my thoughts, "This is still in the early stages. We need to put it out of our minds for now and concentrate on writing new stuff and getting as much exposure as possible at the club level. Remember, building our following, even locally, can only help us."

We tried not to get our hopes up, at least on the surface. When the four of us were together we didn't even bring it up. It was like nobody wanted to jinx it. I did tell Leah, but she didn't have much of a reaction, except to say that her dad might be too busy to look at the contract.

Needless to say, by the time Jayne and I got together to practice I was ready to burst. I didn't plan on talking about it, figuring she'd be pissed if I did, but she tore into my garage looking like a kid on her first trip to Disney World. We played the "what-if" game for at least a half-hour before finally getting down to work. It turned out to be one of the best sessions we'd had so far.

"A chance like this only comes along once in a lifetime," she said after we finished up for the night. She was lying along the bench in my garage with her knees pulled up, gazing up at the garage ceiling as if she were lying in a meadow staring up at the stars. "Can you imagine if it really panned out?"

I set my guitar aside and popped open a beer. "You mean *when* it pans out. Gotta think positive."

She ignored my comment. "Imagine...thousands of people are going to be listening to our music. How cool is that?"

"Pretty fucking cool."

"Hey, what's the hold up with the contract? I thought Leah's dad was going to look it over." She sat up and looked at me. "That's really important, Jackson."

"Oh, yeah..." I said, averting my eyes, "He was just finishing up this big case he's been working on. I'm going over there tomorrow to talk to him."

Truth was, there was no "big case." I'd just been too embarrassed to tell the others that Leah had never mentioned the contract to him, that she'd had zero interest in the movie deal, or anything else concerning the band, since returning to school.

Of course, I didn't know this until I called her father a few days earlier and it quickly became apparent that he had no idea what was going on. Actually, he was scared shitless that something had happened to Leah, because why else would I be calling him when she wasn't even home? After swearing up and down that she was fine, I asked him when it would be a good time to drop off the contract.

"Contract?" he asked, clearly confused. "Sorry, Jackson, but I don't know what you're talking about."

It took another several minutes – several humiliating minutes – to explain about the movie deal. Once he understood, he was very nice, telling me that he wouldn't be home but I could just leave it in the mailbox and he would take a look. Good thing, too, because I was too annoyed at Leah to face him. I was still annoyed when he called the following afternoon and set a time for us to speak about it.

"Don't drag your feet." Jayne said, sounding annoyed. "It's important we know exactly what we're getting into so we don't get screwed."

"Relax, Jayne. I said I'm going over there tomorrow."

"Good." She looked at her phone and then stood up. "I'm gonna hit the road. Eddie just texted me that he's ready."

"Ready for *what*?" I said, harsher than I'd intended.

"He had an issue with his car and asked if I could pick him up. Jeez, is that okay with you, *Dad*?" She tossed her phone back into her bag.

I glanced at the clock on the wall behind her and shrugged. "Whatever, if you gotta go, you gotta go."

She looked at me for a moment, a peculiar expression on her face. "You don't have a problem with Eddie...do you?"

"No," I said defensively, but I knew right away I'd said it too quick.

"You do. I *knew* it." She started to laugh. "It's because he called you Jack, isn't it?"

"Get the fuck outta here," I laughed it off, "That's crazy."

Sure I didn't like the guy, but it had nothing to do with him calling me Jack, though that definitely hadn't helped his case. I didn't like him because I could see right through him and all his phony "Jaynie" bullshit. Guys could always spot a dirtbag a mile away, even if girls couldn't, and it wasn't hard to figure out that he had his sights set on turning Jayne into a "roommate with benefits." I was still debating whether I should share my thoughts on this when she quickly changed the subject.

"Hey, Matt's going out of town and won't be back until Sunday night. Did you still want to get together?"

"Na, I think I'm gonna surprise Leah with a visit." I smiled just thinking about the look on Leah's face when I showed up at her door. I was planning to take her out to dinner someplace nice over the weekend - the swankier the better. Despite what she had done – or not done – with the contract, she was worth it. I needed to do something to smooth things over.

"Leah, jeez, it seems like it's been ages since you've seen each other. I guess outta sight outta mind doesn't apply to you two."

"Definitely not."

"That's okay, maybe it'd be good we take a few days off, start fresh next week. Eddie's been bugging me to hang out with him and his friends anyway."

I rolled my eyes. Jayne, who prided herself on being such a tough girl, couldn't spot a con right under her nose. It was unbelievable.

"Did you just roll your eyes at me?" she asked accusingly.

"Yeah, I did," I said, my voice taking on a big-brother tone. "What the fuck, Jayne? You, Eddie and all his buddies? In what universe does that sound like a good idea? Are you really that naïve?"

"Whoa, hold up a minute," she said, holding up an index finger, "Did you actually call me *naïve*?" She took a step back and placed her hands on her hips. "Wow, if that's not the pot calling the kettle black." She snorted incredulously. "*Naïve*. This, coming from the guy who hasn't seen his 'girlfriend' in months, who's said 'girlfriend,' by the way, spends every weekend hanging out with a bunch of drunken horny colleges guys."

"What the fuck are you saying?" I said, my eyes narrowing at her.

"*What the fuck am I saying*? I'm saying maybe you should look a little closer to home before you start lecturing me."

She'd just totally crossed a line and I'm sure by the look on my face she damn well knew it. I was just about to rip her a new one when she put her hand up to stop me.

"Sorry," she muttered, "totally shouldn't have gone there."

"Damn straight you shouldn't have gone there."

"Hey, I said I was sorry, but you really pissed me off. If there's one thing I'm *not*, it's naïve." She glared at me. "And for your information, I know exactly what Eddie is. I've seen a lot of shit over the years and believe me I know how to take care of myself; I know how to I play the game."

"Game? What game?"

"The game where I pretend *not* to know what Eddie is. I don't know if I told you, but my dad wants to move to Florida and I know he'll never go unless he's sure I'm settled somewhere. Eddie's place was cheap, available and close to work and practice. I *need* it until I can afford my own, so I play along. Eddie likes living with "Jaynie," so you know what? I'll be Jaynie, play nice and keep a fucking lock on my bedroom door. No big deal."

I didn't know how to respond since I was still really pissed off about what she'd said. Maybe Jayne had it tougher than I thought, though. My dad may be a douche but I rarely saw him. So long as we stayed out of each other's way, I had a pretty decent setup.

"So...truce?" she asked.

"Yeah," I nodded reluctantly, "Truce."

"Now I really do need to get going." She grabbed her bag and moved toward the door. "See you next week?"

"Yeah, next week."

She grabbed her sweatshirt off the hook by the door, then pulled it open. She didn't look back, but just before she slipped through said, "Listen, I don't need anyone looking out for me, but it's nice to know someone's got my back just in case."

⋀   ⋀   ⋀

When I got off work Thursday all I wanted to do was go home and go to bed – it had been a long day and I was still tired from a long practice session with Jayne the night before. The *last* thing I wanted to do was go to Leah's parents' house to pick up the contract for the movie deal. But I had promised Matt and the others that I would get it looked at – we needed a professional eye and there was no way we could afford a lawyer.

I pulled into their driveway but didn't turn the car off right away; I just sat there, trying to summon a genuine-looking smile. It wasn't that I didn't want to see her parents – I appreciated her dad's help – I just couldn't believe how this had gone down, that Leah hadn't even mentioned it to him.

I saw movement in the house and turned off the ignition before they decided I was a total freak, then headed up the walk. Her father was already opening the door.

"Come on in, Jackson," he said, pulling it wider so I could enter, "and have a seat on the couch. I'll grab the contract and join you in a second."

"Thanks, Mr. Miller. I really appreciate you doing this for us," I told him, "Legal language is like Greek to me."

"It was no problem, no problem at all." He offered me a small, perhaps sympathetic smile, then disappeared into his office while I sat down to wait.

Her father returned a moment later with an envelope in his hand. "From what I could see everything seems to be on the level. That being said, this isn't really my field of expertise so I want you to get in touch with a colleague of mine who's an entertainment attorney." He handed me the envelope, then reached into his pocket and pulled out a business card. "I already gave him the heads-up you'd be calling. If you're serious about this, he'd be a better person to speak to."

"Oh, man, that's awesome, Mr. Miller," I said as I stood up from the couch. "Thanks so much for doing this for me - for us."

"No problem, Jackson." He stuck out his hand towards me. "Everything else okay with you?"

"Yeah, I mean, yes, Mr. Miller, everything is great."

"Okay, well, let me know if I can do anything else for you."

We said goodnight and I walked back to my car feeling as high as a kite. So it had slipped Leah's mind – she was just busy and, besides, everything had worked out in the end. In fact, it seemed like every time I turned around something else was going my way. I shook my head and smiled; I could really get used to this. Once again, I was feeling...*lucky*.

▲ ▲ ▲

By Friday night I had pretty much moved past the whole thing with Leah and her dad. I mean, sure, it still stung a bit, but everything had worked out in the end. Matt and the others were psyched about Mr. Miller's take on the contract; the fact that he had referred us to the entertainment lawyer was just further proof that this whole movie thing was really happening. Still, I was more convinced than ever that what Leah and I needed was face time, and a visit this weekend was just the thing. I'd even packed my bag the night before so all I had to do when I got out of work was shower. First things first – I had to call Leah and make sure she'd be around without it looking suspicious. I really wanted to surprise her.

She picked up on the second ring.

"What's up babe?"

"Nothing much Jackson. No practice tonight?"

"Yeah, I'll be heading in soon," I told her, barely able to contain my excitement about seeing her later. I chitchatted with her a while longer to make it look good, then told her I had to get going and would talk to her later.

I ended the call with the smile still on my face. Soon after, I was on my way.

I headed south on Route 287 with The Stones blasting from the speakers. About twenty minutes into the ride I hit some traffic so I texted her like I usually did when I was at practice – *wats up 4 2nite?* She answered right away: *The usual. Dinner with Moll, then hang out in dorm room & watch a movie.*

I smiled. Everything was going according to plan.

I texted her twice more when I hit different pockets of traffic. The first time she said they were heading back from dinner and the second time she said they were laying around watching The Gilmore Girls, which also made me smile because although it was way too girly for me I knew it was one of her favorites. That's when I put my phone away – didn't want her getting suspicious about all the texts.

I pulled into the lot outside her new building, which was on the opposite end of campus from where she'd lived last year. It took some poking around but I was eventually able to find her room. Before knocking on her door, I set my bag down next to my guitar and pulled out my phone to shoot out one last text. *Practice ending early, heading home soon. How bout u?* A minute later her response came through: *Movie over, in bed, early nite.*

I knocked twice then stood back, ready to catch her when she jumped into my arms, but the door was opened by a very surprised looking Molly.

"Jackson! Wow, long time no see," she said, her eyes flicking down the hallway. "I didn't know you were coming!"

"Came to surprise my girl," I said as I moved passed her only to find the room empty. My eyes quickly flashed to Leah's bed, which was still neatly made. *What the fuck?*

I heard the door close behind me, then Molly said, "Oh, she's, uh, not home yet; late night cramming in the library." Molly seemed nervous. I felt the hairs on the back of my neck go up, even as the bottom dropped out of my stomach.

"Oh, uh, no problem," I said, trying to sound nonchalant as I looked at the desk clock and then at Molly. "I'm sure she'll be home soon."

I put my bag and guitar down and sat down on her bed while Molly took a seat on her own bed and proceeded to make small talk.

"Yeah, I'm sure she'll be home any minute," she said as she reached for her phone which was on the nightstand between the two beds.

On instinct, I reached over and placed my hand over Molly's phone then slid it towards me. I knew what she was trying to do, but I wasn't about to let her text Leah with a heads-up.

"Hey, I see you got the new iPhone...mind if I take a look?"

"Oh, uh, no, go ahead." Molly seemed *really* nervous now. She looked pale and even a little sweaty.

"Cool," I said as I looked it over then placed it at my side and pulled out my own phone. I shot out one last text to Leah: *Almost home. U guys still up?*

She answered quickly, *Yep, still watching tv but Moll's passed out.*

I lifted my eyes to Molly then lowered them back down to my phone, unable to believe what I was seeing. She was *lying* to me? Where the fuck was she? Suddenly, the argument I'd had with Jayne the other night began to echo in my ears. *Was Jayne right? Was I the naïve one?* It couldn't be. I was still trying to convince myself that there *had* to be another explanation when I saw it. Lying amongst a pile of stretched out hair ties, a broken earing and a crumpled receipt was the silver guitar ring I'd given Leah over the summer. Molly watched as I picked it up and stared at it for a moment before placing it on the tip of my pinky and twirling it absently. Could she have forgotten to put it on? Sure...but that's not how it looked. Instead it looked like it had been left there on purpose. Discarded like a piece of junk.

I felt Molly's eyes on me as if she was waiting for me to explode. But I wasn't going to, not yet. I still felt numb. Leah, who I would've trusted with my life, had been lying to me. Was she possibly lying to cover up the fact that she was...screwing around? I didn't want to admit it — I *wouldn't* admit it — not until I saw her face and looked her square in the eye.

I don't know how much time passed before she got back. All I know is I was still stretched out on her bed, ring in hand, when I heard her key in the lock.

CHAPTER 46 - LEAH

"Jeez, is that Molly *again*?" Chase asked as I reached for my phone on the nightstand next to his bed. Holing up in Chase's room had become somewhat of a Friday night routine for us. It beat any party on campus, and although I couldn't speak for Chase I got the feeling he felt the same way, or at least he had until tonight. Jackson had been blowing up my phone and as annoying as it was, I couldn't just ignore his texts. On the other hand, I wasn't about to tell Chase who it was either.

"Yeah," I lied as I skimmed another message. "More Aiden drama."

"Tell her she's killing the mood," he joked as he rolled onto his side.

"That should be the last one," I said. "She said she's going to bed." I was about to return my phone to the nightstand when a cold chill crept up my spine. Something felt off. I didn't know what it was, but I could feel it.

"What's wrong?" Chase asked when he felt me shudder.

"Oh, uh, nothing," I said, trying to convince myself as much as him, "Just feel a little cold, that's all." I returned the phone to the nightstand and turned to face him. "Now..." I gave him a suggestive smile. "...where were we?"

"C'mere, and I'll show ya," he said slyly as he pulled me on top of him. I felt a gentle pressure on my shoulders and, still smiling, wiggled down between his thighs. He folded his arms behind his head and sighed. "Uh, I think when we left off you were just about to make me a *very* happy guy."

▲   ▲   ▲

Chase might have been happy, but I couldn't get that nervous feeling out of my mind. In fact, I couldn't wait to get out of there, which was

302

weird because ever since Molly found out about me and Chase I'd taken to spending a couple of nights a week at his place. Chase looked at me like I had two heads when I stood up and started pulling on my clothes. I babbled some bullshit story about wanting to make sure Molly was okay, and he seemed to actually believe it. I guess I'd become a much better liar than I gave myself credit for.

I texted Molly as soon as I left Chase's but she didn't answer, which wasn't like her. The whole way back to the dorm I kept glancing over my shoulder, like I'd find the answer there.

I was sure I'd feel better once I got inside my building, but I didn't. The hallway was quiet, almost eerily so, and my footsteps seemed to echo loudly off the walls as I got closer to my room. I could see the light on under the door. If Molly was up, why hadn't she replied?

I put my key in the lock, turned the knob and pushed the door open. "What's going on, Moll – I -" I stopped speaking when I saw Molly sitting on her bed, looking like a deer caught in the headlights. Her gaze flicked toward to my bed, and that's when I saw him, sitting upright at the head of my bed with his back against the wall. He had his arms folded across his chest and his legs were stretched out in front of him as if he'd been there a while. His face was unreadable, but his green eyes bore into mine as if searching for something.

CHAPTER 47 - JACKSON

I don't know what time it was when she finally got back; I'd stopped looking at my phone after that last text. All I know is that I'd had plenty of time to think, but from the looks of her wrinkled clothes and messy hair it wasn't hard to figure out what'd been going on. She'd been screwing around - right under my fucking nose.

I'm not gonna lie; I knew when she first left for college she'd be hanging out with other guys and I also knew she'd get hit on. I didn't like it, of course, but I brushed it off because I thought Leah was above all that. Not that "kind of girl." What a fucking fool I was. And what killed me was I could've easily fucked around on her and she wouldn't have had a clue. Like any other musician I'd had plenty of opportunity, especially over the past couple months, but the truth was I had no desire to be with anyone else. She was all I ever wanted, and I always assumed she felt the same.

But the bullshit just kept on coming.

"Jackson, wow, what...what a n-nice surprise." Her voice sounded phony, but not nearly as phony as the excuse she came up with. "I was, um, cramming at the library. I, uh, must've fallen asleep. They have these really comfy couches there and..." She trailed off. I guess she realized how lame she sounded, especially after all the texts she'd sent earlier.

"Really, Leah?" I gave her an incredulous look as I swung my legs over the side of the bed and stood up. "I'm gonna ask you once and don't fucking lie to me." I hesitated a beat as I stared her down. "Where. Were. You."

I waited for her to say something, anything, but she just stood there with this scared-shitless look on her face like she was afraid I was gonna beat the crap outta her or something. It really pissed me off.

"Wow, nice," I nodded sarcastically, "Not even gonna try to cover your ass?"

Still, she had the nerve to stand there like a fucking mute. Finally, I gave up, deciding that her silence was all the confirmation I needed.

"I can't fucking believe that after all this time you'd do something like this. Who...who *are* you, Leah? Just man-up. If you didn't wanna be with me anymore you should've told me to fuck off. Hell, I would've had a lot more respect for you than finding out like this. So, tell me, I'm curious; how long? How long have you been making an ass outta me?"

That's when the tears started. The fucking *tears*. I was about to rip into her again when fortunately for her my phone rang. I briefly looked at it but when I saw it was Beth, I hit ignore.

Finally, between her pathetic little sobs she choked out, "Jackson, I, um, I'm...I'm so-"

"What? *Sorry*? Is that what you were gonna say? Well, save it."

I turned to Molly, who had been sitting there in stunned silence, and tossed her phone backed to her. She missed it and it landed with a thud at her feet.

I glared at her and turned back to Leah. "You know what, Leah? I'm gonna make this real easy for you." I picked up my duffle bag and guitar and began moving toward the door, but stopped when I reached her. "Just remember one thing...you fucked up – big time – 'cause you'll *never* find someone who'll love you like I did. I fucking guarantee it."

I moved past her, but just as I was about to go through the door I stopped, reached into my pocket and said, "Oh, hey, I think this is yours." Then I pulled out the silver guitar ring and tossed it at her feet. "Found it laying with the rest of your trash."

Before she could respond, I was gone.

⏶　⏶　⏶

I barely remembered driving home – it was as if I'd just suddenly appeared in my driveway. By that time I was numb. How in hell had I not seen this coming? I cursed my stupidity at having been so fucking blind. Of *course* this relationship was never going to last. My whole life had been one big disappointment after another and I'd been fooling myself to think this would turn out any different.

If someone like Leah could pull this shit on me, then anyone could. It was over, and I was done trusting anyone – other than Beth, of course, because my sister was true-blue. She'd stand behind me no matter what. *Beth.* That's when I remembered she'd called when I was in the middle of the shitstorm with Leah and twice more on the ride home. All three times I'd ignored the calls. It wasn't like her to call so late. I grabbed my phone off my bed and checked it but there were no voicemails, just a text that said *call me* in caps. I shook my head, feeling annoyed and a little nervous as I placed the call, but then figured things couldn't possibly get any worse, right? When she picked up I knew right away by the commotion I heard in the background that something was wrong, and I had a sinking feeling that things *were* about to get worse. I braced myself, but even after everything I'd been through with Leah earlier nothing could've prepared me for what she was about to say. I never thought that another piece of my world would be shattered so soon.

CHAPTER 48 - LEAH

"**M**olly, please, can you give it a rest?" I glared at her from across the cafeteria table, "Or at least keep your voice down?"

It had been nearly a week since what Molly referred to as the "episode" and she still couldn't talk about anything else. I was sick of it.

Less than a week – that was all it took for my life to turn into a mess. And as if I didn't feel crappy enough about it, Molly took every opportunity to remind me. I couldn't argue with her - she'd been telling me to end it with Jackson ever since she'd found out about Chase. Obviously she'd been right.

I still cringed when I thought about that night, the awful look on Jackson's face. Never in a million years had I envisioned him finding out like that. I'd told myself that at some point, I'd break it to him easy, say something like *I just need some time to myself* or *let's take a break*. I even toyed with the idea of blaming it all on him by saying, *You don't have time for me because you're just too busy with the band*. Sure, they were all bullshit clichés, but they certainly would have been preferable to getting caught in such an awful lie.

"So, have you spoken to him?" Molly asked for what must have been the thousandth time.

"You know I haven't."

"What about Chase? Does he know about the episode?"

I rolled my eyes. "No, Chase doesn't know, and would you please stop referring to it as 'the episode'? You make it sound so dramatic."

"Well it *was* dramatic. Don't forget, I was there. And if you ask me, you got off pretty easy. It was probably the tears," she mused, as if noting it for future reference, "Guys can never handle tears, no matter what a girl's done to them."

I shot her an annoyed look.

"What? Come on, Leah, what you did was pretty low, and you know it. He kept his cool better than most, that's for *damn* sure."

"Kept his cool? Are you kidding? Did you hear how he spoke to me? And that look in his eyes, it was scary."

"I don't know...a few curse words, the evil eye, tossing a ring at you? Coulda been much worse."

"Are you done?" I huffed. She was really pissing me off.

She leaned back in her chair. "For now."

I checked the time on my phone. "I gotta get going or I'll be late for class." I stood from the table. "And don't wait for me for dinner, I'm gonna grab something with Chase."

She nodded. "Okay, see you tonight."

I grabbed my books off the table and headed out of the cafeteria.

▲　▲　▲

After class I took the long way to Chase's place. By then it was late afternoon and chilly, but I didn't care; I just needed to be alone and think and I certainly couldn't do that with Molly around. A couple times during the week I'd dialed Jackson's number but could never bring myself to complete the call. I didn't know what to say to him or if I should say anything at all. Nothing could make up for the way I had hurt him, especially since I didn't even know why I had acted the way I did. Was it that Chase was so great, or that I had simply outgrown Jackson and his pipe dream? Until I answered those questions for myself there was no point in calling him.

I was no closer to figuring things out when I reached Chase's place; all I knew was that I couldn't wait to see him.

"Finally," he said as he pulled open the door, "I thought you'd blown me off." He was smiling, though, at least he was until he saw me. "My God, Leah, you're shivering. Are you okay?"

"Mmm hmmm," I said with a few rapid nods, "Just cold."

He opened the door wider so I could walk through. "Hold on a sec – I'll go get you something to throw on."

A few minutes later, we left the house again, dressed in matching hoodies. By that time it was around seven and the cafeteria was starting to clear out. As always, people called out to him, but Chase just waved and grabbed a table for two in the back. Since the semester started we'd been eating there at least twice a week, then we'd usually head over to the library to do homework before going back to his place. We'd never officially "gone public" but of course people noticed we were together. Chase was so attentive it was easy to forget that he was basically a celebrity on campus – then I'd get that *what's-so-great-about-her* look from some girl and remember that I had become the object of scrutiny, envy and, in some cases, intense dislike.

We bullshitted over roast beef sandwiches and potato salad, then he said, "Hey, you wanna forget the library tonight and just go straight back to my place? There's a couple new shows on Netflix I wanna check out."

I grinned at him, then nodded slowly, and not because I felt like binge-watching something. No matter how much time I spent with Chase, I never got tired of him, and I certainly never passed up a chance to be alone with him. We made it back to his house in record time.

We were just getting comfortable on his bed when we heard a commotion outside his room.

"Hang on a minute," he said as he went to check it out. I heard a lot of laughing and banging before he came back.

"What was that all about?" I asked.

"Nothing, just Brent and Chet back from happy hour in town," he said as he climbed back onto the bed next to me.

"Brent, wow, I haven't heard much about him since Molly moved on." I chuckled. "How's he doing?"

"He's fine, more than fine, actually." He laughed. "Molly's better off."

I shrugged. "Maybe Molly just wasn't his type."

This time his laugh came out more like a snort. "*Every* girl is Brent's type."

"Oh really?" Maybe I was being naïve, but I'd never thought of Brent as a player.

He shrugged. "He's still into riding the wave of sports groupies, that's all."

Sports groupies? Shit, did people think I was a sports groupie? Did Chase think I was?

"I don't know anyone on the team who *hasn't* ridden the wave," he continued, then, as if reading my thoughts, he added, "But it gets old fast – it did for me, anyway." He reached for my hand. "I'm more of a one-guy-one-girl sorta person, but I'm guessing you already know that."

Though his tone wasn't accusatory, I felt a stab of guilt. It had been obvious he wasn't seeing anyone else, and just knowing I *had* been made me squirm a little. At least, I reminded myself, Chase had always known about Jackson.

"Chase, I, uh, want to tell you something..." I began.

"What's that?" he asked as he put his arm around me, then pointed the remote at the TV.

"I, uh, just wanted to tell you that I'm not seeing Jackson anymore. Actually, I haven't been seeing him for a while." This wasn't really a lie. Sure, we were technically a couple until a week ago, but I hadn't seen him since the summer."

"Shit, Leah, I'm sorry." He turned to face me. "I had no idea. I just assumed you guys were still together."

It wasn't exactly the reaction I was expecting.

Suddenly a look of realization came over him. "It's not because of me, is it?"

I wanted to say, *Well, of course it's because of you*, but I stopped short when I saw how genuinely concerned he looked.

"Oh no," I said, a little more emphatically than I had intended, "We just, you know, sort of grew apart, that's all."

"Oh, okay," he sighed, seeming almost relieved. "Because I'd hate to be the cause of you guys breaking up. Besides, I always assumed you guys had some sort of arrangement."

"Arrangement? What kind of arrangement?"

"You know, like a don't ask, don't tell sort of thing," he chuckled. "Or a what-happens-on- campus-stays-on-campus scenario." He turned back toward the TV and started flipping through the stations. Then, almost as an afterthought, he added, "Like Missy and I have."

I felt my stomach clench, but somehow managed to keep my voice even. "Missy?"

"Yeah, Missy, my girlfriend back in Ohio." He turned toward me, his eyes searching my face. "You knew about her, right? Her picture's right here on my dresser."

"Oh, yeah, of course I knew," I said, even as I glanced toward the dresser. "I, uh, just didn't know her name, that's all." My gaze came to rest on the brown frame. I had seen the picture before, just never paid attention to it. It was of a group of people sitting around a campfire, and Chase had his arm around a girl. She was kind of plain-looking and I'd just assumed it was his sister. I never even bothered to ask because *how could he have a girlfriend when he'd been sleeping with me for months?*

"I don't talk about her much," Chase continued, still studying me. "It just seems a little weird to talk about your girlfriend at home to the girl you're seeing at school. That's why you never talked about Jackson, right?"

"Oh, yeah, totally." I swallowed past the lump that had formed in my throat.

"But, hey, if you guys aren't together anymore I guess we can be more free on campus." He laughed as he pulled me onto his lap and kissed my neck. "Although, lately we've been pretty free anyway, right?"

"Uh, yeah...right." I laughed too, but it sounded hollow. How could I have been so stupid? To think the star of the lacrosse team was single and wanted to be exclusive with me, of all girls...I *had* to be stupid. Not as stupid as Missy, I told myself spitefully. Only a truly desperate girl would let her boyfriend run around on her.

"So, uh, tell me about this arrangement. Whose idea was it?"

"Missy's," he said as he picked up the remote and lowered the volume. "And I gotta admit I was against it at first. I mean, who wants to think of their girlfriend sleeping with other guys, especially when said girlfriend had never been with anyone other than yours truly?"

It just gets better and better, I thought as I rolled my eyes and pretended to pick some imaginary lint off my leggings. "So what made you change your mind?"

"Missy insisted." He shrugged. "Wouldn't take no for an answer. She said she didn't want me to have any regrets later that I'd missed out. Thought I should get it all out of my system before, you know..." He shrugged again as he trailed off.

I assumed *you know...* meant she wanted him to get everything out of his system before they got married, but to hell if I was going to come right out and ask.

I knew I was being a glutton for punishment, but I had to know everything there was to know about this girl who I *hated* even though I'd never even met her.

"Does she play lacrosse too, or something else?"

"Missy? Lacrosse?" He laughed and shook his head. "No way. She's not into sports *at all*."

"Bookworm?"

Chase laughed again, an affectionate laugh that made me slightly nauseas. "Nope; not really into academics either." He thought for a minute. "Actually, she's sort of 'artsy'." He playfully nudged me with his elbow. "And she's into music too, kinda like Jackson. But she plays the cello, not the guitar."

"Where does she go to school?" I asked, hoping it was Alaska or Hawaii or *Italy*, someplace far away. No such luck.

"She stayed local; doesn't even dorm. She's a bit of a homebody."

Okay, I'd had enough. I knew I had to get out of there before I lost it on him – something I knew I had absolutely no right to do.

I made a point of stretching, then sat up and threw my legs over the side of the bed. "Well, I'm going to head out. I have a ton of work to do and I left the books I need in my room."

"Really?" He was studying me again. "You alright?"

"Oh, yeah, I'm fine. I just have a ton of work to do and like I said the books I need are in my room."

"Okay," he said, looking genuinely disappointed, "I'll walk you out."

That was the last thing I wanted, but I knew it would look weird if I told him no so I just smiled and said, "Sure."

I waited until I was outside and he'd closed the door behind me, then I let out the breath I'd been holding. What the *FUCK*! He'd had a girlfriend all this time...? If so, I guess that made me ...*the other woman*! No wonder he never brought up Jackson and no wonder I didn't hear from him all summer. Well, that was it! It was over. There was no way in hell I was going to continue being his piece on the side.

▲   ▲   ▲

By the time I got back to my room I was ready to explode. Though I had taken the direct route, it had been more than enough time to run through every single thing Chase had ever said and done to make me think I was important to him, that I was his girl, not just his *girl at school*. I pushed the door open, about to let loose with an expletive-laced rant about what an asshole he was but stopped short when I saw Molly lying in bed with a book in her hand. She looked up at me with a friendly smile, but all I could picture was the smug expression she'd have when I told her what had happened.

"Hey, what are you doing here?" she said as she put her book aside. "Didn't get enough studying done on your 'studying date'?" She wiggled her eyebrows at me.

I forced a laugh. "Some...but I just have too much to do."

Most people would be happy with that explanation, but not Molly. She was like a bloodhound, and my only hope of avoiding a third-degree was to throw her off the trail. "Oh, and I saw Brent tonight. Wait no, I stand corrected, I *heard* Brent tonight."

Her ears perked up at the mention of his name. *Mission accomplished*, I thought smugly. "He and Chet were in the hall outside Chase's room, and they were *so loud*. Apparently, they were trashed from another happy hour."

"Oh, so you didn't actually talk to him?" She sounded deflated. *Over him, my ass.*

"No."

She looked disappointed but didn't question me any further. I stretched my hands over my head. "Well, gonna take a shower, try to wake up, so I can do more work."

Molly peered at me suspiciously and for a minute I thought the bloodhound had returned. Then she just nodded, and I went about the room gathering my things for the shower.

I stood under the water longer than usual, hoping it would wash away the anger before I had to face Molly again. It didn't, but by the time I was done, Molly was passed out, her book lying on her lap. At least I wouldn't have to pretend to study, because my head just wasn't in it. I slipped into bed and lay there for what seemed like forever, staring up at the ceiling as my mind went over everything I'd found out tonight. And it wasn't just the girlfriend, though that had been the biggest shock. It was the fact that somewhere along the line, while I was busy running around on Jackson and lying to Molly, I had also been falling in love with Chase. I had also been assuming that he felt the same about me, that he was just waiting in the wings until I got rid of my boyfriend. What a jackass I was.

Who was this *Missy*, anyway, and why was he with her? He obviously had a lot more in common with me than with her. She was almost like... the *anti-me*.

My first instinct was to end it - I had never been one to compete over a guy. But then I started thinking. If I broke it off, there'd be a line of girls a mile long waiting to take my place and I'm sure there'd be more than a few who wouldn't mind playing second fiddle. No, giving up wasn't the answer. I'd work extra hard to make Chase see that I was the one for him, not *Missy*. I smiled to myself in the darkness. By the time I was done he wouldn't even be able to remember her name.

CHAPTER 49 - JACKSON

I sat quietly, my lower back pressed up against the coolness of the tombstone, my head resting on my knees. I felt a hand gently nudge my shoulder but brushed it off.

I felt the hand again but this time it stayed resting on my shoulder. When I looked up Jayne was standing over me. She was different, somehow. Softer.

"C'mon, Chief." She motioned with her head. "Your sister and grandmother are waiting at the car."

How had she even found me? I'd quietly slipped away right after my grandfather's service and found myself at my mother's graveside. After everything that'd happened this week I just wanted to be by myself.

When I left Leah's that night, I didn't think it was possible for me to sink any lower. *Wrong again, Jackson.* Though I was barely able to understand Beth over all the noise in the background, it quickly became clear that she was at the hospital and something had happened to my grandfather.

"I'm on my way," I'd said, already beating myself up for not answering my cell the first time she called. I drove like a lunatic to the hospital, but it was for nothing. I ran through the emergency room door to see a doctor talking to Beth, Brody and my grandmother. I stopped short in front of them when I saw him shake his head. I knew the news wasn't good.

"There was too much damage to his heart," I overheard him say. "And there was nothing we could do." He reached over and took my grandmother's hand. "I'm so sorry."

Her eyes glistening with tears, Grandma squeezed the doctor's hand as if she were comforting him. So typical of her. She then turned to hug Beth, who was wiping away her own tears with the sleeve of her sweatshirt. Brody put his arm around both of them.

My feet felt cemented to the floor as I watched the scene in front of me. I knew it was crazy, but I felt if I joined them it would be real. My grandfather would really be gone. That's when Beth looked up and saw me standing there.

"Jackson," she said as I closed the distance between us, then pulled me into a tight hug. "I can't believe this," she whispered. I nodded against her, then, too choked up to say anything, I withdrew and bent down to hug my grandmother. She felt so frail, like a little bird; I couldn't imagine how she was going to make it without him.

Beth must have thought the same thing, because she insisted on staying with my grandmother at her condo. We all went back to get her settled and while Gram phoned some relatives to break the news, Beth filled me in on what had happened. Gram had invited her and Brody over for dinner, and as soon as they walked in they knew something was wrong.

"He just didn't look right, Jacks; his coloring was off and he couldn't seem to catch his breath." She grabbed a tissue from the box on the kitchen counter and blew her nose. "He kept insisting he was fine, but after we ate and were clearing the table he just...just collapsed."

"Shit, Beth." I shook my head. "I can't believe this."

"I called the ambulance and Brody tried CPR, but it took them forever to get here. They kept working on him in the ambulance and in the hospital but I guess..." Her eyes filled with tears again as they darted around the room. "I guess it was just too late."

The days leading up to my grandfather's wake and funeral were still a blur. Matt, Skid and Jayne came to the wake, but only Jayne came to the funeral. I told her it wasn't necessary, but she wouldn't hear it.

"How'd you find me, anyway?" I asked.

"Your sister. She thought you might be here." Jayne knelt down next to me. "You gonna get up? They're going to the diner."

The diner. I'd forgotten we were going there after the service.

"Tell them I'll be there in a minute."

She stood up reluctantly, as if she didn't want to leave me. "Okay. I'll meet you at the car."

I watched her walk away then slowly got to my feet, brushed off a few stray leaves clinging to the cuff of my pants. I turned and gently touched the top of the headstone. I didn't come here often, I couldn't; it was too hard, because when I did it made me feel like I was seven years old again, standing in the drizzling rain holding tightly onto my grandfather's hand. I remember feeling too scared to even cry.

It was my grandparents who got us through those early days, making sure we got back to our routines as soon as possible. My dad sure as hell wasn't in any shape to do it. They put their own grief at losing their only child aside to help me, Beth and Tim deal with the unimaginable. And thanks to my father, in the end, they had lost us kids too.

I took one last look at the inscription on the front of the stone, then turned and made my way back toward the car.

▲   ▲   ▲

We grabbed a booth in the back of the Stateline Diner, just a few miles from the cemetery.

"Jackson, dear," my grandmother began after we'd placed our orders, "You should have invited your friend from your rock and roll group to join us. I wouldn't have minded."

"Na, Gram, Jayne had to go to work," I lied. Actually, I wasn't sure whether Jayne was working or not, but I figured it'd look weird that she was here and Leah wasn't. Beth had already asked me earlier that day if Leah was coming to the funeral, and though she seemed to buy my bullshit excuse - that Leah had an exam she couldn't miss - I didn't want to invite any questions. Eventually, I'd have to tell them what'd happened between me and Leah, but I didn't feel like it yet, not when the whole thing was still so raw.

"Well, it was nice Jayne came to the funeral," Beth said, then gave a small smile. It was the first time I'd seen her smile all week. "She wasn't at all like I expected, judging from her, uh, *stage persona*."

I smiled back, but it was an empty one. How could it not be, when I felt so hollow inside? She was right though, Jayne was nothing like the character she portrayed on stage, once you got to know her.

I was relieved when our food came, ending the conversation. As we ate, Beth and Brody asked my grandmother about the various people they had seen at the funeral, which had been filled with friends and even a few relatives from out of state who had come to pay their respects. Beth and I had never met any of them, another thing to blame my father for. While my grandmother explained who they were, my thoughts returned to Leah. With the death of my grandfather, I'd pushed all the shit that happened with her to the back of my mind. I had to, otherwise I wouldn't have been able to get through this week. Now that everything was over, though, it was already starting to creep back in. I still couldn't believe what she had done to me, how she had lied. Should I have seen it coming? Maybe, but I didn't. Not by a fucking long shot.

▲　　▲　　▲

I spent the rest of the day holed up in my room, feeling like shit and wondering if another shoe was about to drop when there was a knock at my bedroom door.

I sat up, but before I could say anything, the door creaked open. "Knock, Knock," I heard Jayne's voice as she peered in.

"Hey," I said, too exhausted to express my surprise. "What're you doing here?"

She moved a pile of dirty clothes from the chair beside my bed and sat down. "Came to see if you're okay. I called, but your phone went straight to voicemail."

I reached over the side of my bed and grabbed my phone. "I guess it's dead," I said listlessly as I tossed it back to the floor then ran my fingers through my unruly hair.

"Were you, um, planning to come to practice tonight?" She asked. "'Cause we could really use you; we're working on some new stuff." She watched me for a moment, then added, "Hey, Matt heard from Decker again, about the movie. Production starts next month."

"Really?" I said, perking up in spite of myself. I guess since everything else in my life had turned to shit, I'd figured this was bound to also.

"Yeah, really, so come on, let's go." She stood, then reached over and pulled off the comforter that lay across my legs. "Hurry up, go take a shower - I'll wait for you here."

Twenty minutes later I was riding shotgun in Jayne's Toyota, heading into Brooklyn.

"What were you doing still in town, anyway? I thought you left right after the funeral – and by the way, thanks for coming." I turned and glanced out the window for a minute, then turned back to her. "You didn't haveta do that, you know."

"I know, but I wanted to. We're friends, right?" She glanced over at me and smiled. "Sometimes, anyway." She eased the car onto the highway before continuing. "Besides, I spent the rest of the day at my dad's; he needed help packing for his move to Florida. I'm going back there tonight, so I can give you a lift back."

I nodded and went back to staring blankly out the window. It was nice to be in the passenger seat for once.

▲　▲　▲

It never failed to amaze me. I could be going through the worst shit of my life - feeling like my head was about to fucking explode - then I'd pick up my guitar and know everything was going to get better. Like tonight - my first practice since the shit hit the fan. The others seemed to know I didn't want to get into it, because aside from mumbling "Sorry, man" in reference to my grandfather they were business as usual. Maybe Jayne had warned them – I wasn't sure, but I left there feeling better than I had in a while. I should have known it wasn't going to last.

It was close to midnight when Jayne and I headed back to Jersey. We'd just pulled onto the highway when she turned to me and asked, "So, what does Leah think about the contract? Has her dad mentioned anything else about it?"

Instantly, my mood turned dark. I mumbled a kind of non-answer and tried to change the subject, but it was too late. Just hearing Leah's name brought me right back to that moment she walked into her dorm and found me sitting on her bed. I could still see the look on her face go from shock to panic, then guilt.

"Jackson?" Jayne said, pulling me back from my thoughts.

I turned toward her but before she could say anything else, I said, "Hey, you mind dropping me off in town?"

"In town? Where?" She sounded confused as she glanced at the clock on the dash. "It's late, nothing's open."

"I don't feel like going home," I shrugged. "Just drop me off at Dunes; it's always open."

"Why don't you just go home," she suggested, "You've had a long day."

"I'm fine, Jayne," I snapped, "Christ, you don't have to hold my fucking hand."

She looked hurt but didn't say anything, which pissed me off even more. Since when does Jayne not give it right back? I knew I wasn't being fair because if she had known what had happened with Leah she surely wouldn't have brought her up. I wasn't about to tell her, though. Not yet anyway.

We fell into an uncomfortable silence, punctuated only by my curt directions. A few minutes later we were sitting in front of Dunes, a small, shitty bar not far from my place.

"Thanks," I said without looking at her as I reached for the handle. "I'll see you during the week." I didn't look back but I know she didn't pull away until I had slipped inside.

The place was nearly empty, and after a quick scan of the room for familiar faces – the last thing I needed was to make conversation with some guy from high school - I took a seat at the sparsely-filled bar that lined the back wall. A second later, the bartender – a twenty-something girl in a tight white Dunes t-shirt – asked me what I wanted.

"I'll take a Bud and a shot of Jack," I said, then pulled out a wad of cash and plunked it on the bar, "And keep'm coming."

She raised an eyebrow as if to say, *Are you gonna be a problem?* then shrugged and got my drinks.

I immediately threw back the Jack, enjoying the feel of the bitter amber whiskey as it travelled through my veins, warming my body and dulling my senses. I had a ways to go, though; I planned on drinking until I was barely able to stand, until I barely knew my name.

"You from around here?" the bartender asked as she poured another shot of Jack and placed it in front of me. "I don't think I've seen you here before."

I stared blankly at her, vaguely noting that she wasn't my type but attractive in a slightly trashy way.

When I didn't respond she shrugged and stuck her hand out toward me. "Well, my name's Gina. Let me know if you need anything else."

I nodded, then grasped her hand and said, "Jackson."

"Nice to meet you, Jackson," she said, then walked off to help another customer. As soon as there was a lull she was standing in front of me again. "So, Jackson, what is it you do for a living?"

I opened my mouth, about to say *nothing.* The season was over with Slater and I'd quit Powder Peak to concentrate on the band. But instead I heard myself say, "I'm...a musician."

"No shit!" she said excitedly. "My boyfriend's a musician; he plays drums for a band called Meddle Cube. Ever hear of them?"

"Nope," I said as I took a long swig of my Bud.

"Well, they're just starting out but they're *really* good." She sounded proud when she said it, kind of like how I'd always imagined Leah sounded when she spoke about me and Dirty Bushwick.

"What's your band called?"

"Dirty Bushwick."

"Huh, never heard of you guys."

"You will," I said, with a cockiness I didn't necessarily feel and not caring in the least that I sounded that way.

She smiled and handed me another beer. "On the house."

I watched as she placed the sweaty bottle in front of me then scooted off to help another patron. She seemed awfully friendly for a girl who claimed to have a boyfriend. Is that how Leah acted when I wasn't around? A week ago, I would've said no way, but now I wasn't so sure. I wondered whether the guy Leah was fucking knew about me. If he did he obviously didn't give a shit. I glanced over at Gina, took in the way the tight white t-shirt clung to her chest, and decided I wasn't gonna give a shit either. I gave her a half-smile as I cocked my head, signaling for her to come back over.

She smiled back and happily obliged.

I looked her over, slow and deliberate. "So, your boyfriend don't mind you working here?" I glanced around. "A girl like you must get hit on quite a bit in a place like this."

She blushed. "Sometimes, but he doesn't worry. The guys who hang out here are no threat." Suddenly, she met my eyes and smiled. "Most of them, anyway."

I chuckled to myself, thinking it had never been this easy to meet girls. I guess all you needed was a few drinks and a cheating bitch of a girlfriend. "Hey, what do you say we hang out at my place after you get off? I can play you some of my music and you could let me know how it measures up to *Meddle Square*."

She pretended to mull over my offer for a moment. "Sure, sounds like fun...and it's Meddle *Cube*, not square." She glanced up at the clock hanging over the bar. "I get off in about twenty minutes."

"Cool," I said as I downed the last of my beer.

While I was waiting for her to finish up, I heard a familiar voice a few stools down ask Gina for a beer. I turned just as she said, "Sure, Keith. The usual?"

There, a few feet away, stood my father. He must have felt my stare, because he turned and looked at me, clearly surprised. He took the beer from Gina, threw some cash on the bar and then moved toward me. I had been wrong before when I checked out the bar. *This* was the last thing I needed.

"Never seen you here before," he said as he took the stool next to me.

"It was the only place open."

Just then Gina came over with her purse and jacket in hand. "Ready, Jackson?"

"Yup," I said as I staggered to my feet. It was the first time I'd gotten up all night and hadn't realized how drunk I was.

She looked between the two of us and noting that he was sitting on the stool right next to me, innocently asked, "You guys know each other?"

I glanced briefly at my father as I gripped the side of the bar to steady myself, then turned back to Gina and said, "Nope."

We left through the side door since she said her car was parked around the back.

"Keith, the guy who was sitting next to you," she began, "he's a regular; comes in all the time. A real sweetheart. Doesn't say much, though." She reached into her purse and pulled out her keys. "Always seems sad. Someone said his wife was killed in a car accident years ago but I don't know how true that is." She unlocked the car door then turned toward me. "That's long before I started working here, and anyway -"

I backed her up against the car and kissed her because I couldn't stand listening to what she was saying. I wasn't mad at her or anything, but I didn't want to hear another word about Keith the "sweetheart" and his sob story.

A couple of minutes and cheap feels later and we were pulling out of the parking lot. Once back at my place I grabbed a couple beers from the fridge, then took her up to my room where she asked to hear some of my music. We listened for a while and drank a few more beers. I guess she liked what she heard because it didn't take much coaxing afterwards to get her into my bed.

When I next opened my eyes, the room was still dark and my head throbbed with a dull ache. I groaned and glanced at the clock. Just after five a.m. I was about to close my eyes again when I remembered Gina. *Shit.* I reached gingerly toward the other side of the bed and sighed with relief when I realized she had gone. She seemed okay, but I wasn't looking for anything more from her than what I'd already gotten. I felt like a douche for about two seconds, then remembered the boyfriend she obviously had no qualms about cheating on.

As I swung my legs over the side of the bed, everything seemed to hit me at once. Leah...my grandfather...and the one thing that always came back to haunt me when things went south...my mom, and what my life would've been like had she not died. I don't know how long I sat there with my head in my hands, sobbing like a fucking little kid. All I know is that the sun shone bright in the sky when I finally passed out, exhausted.

▲   ▲   ▲

Eight hours after Gina's departure I woke up again with a nasty headache, a mouth full of cotton, and a desire to stay in bed for about a week. I would have too, but I had practice in a few hours and I wasn't about to fuck up the last good thing left in my life. A hot shower and a big plate of spaghetti went a long way to making me feel better, and if it didn't take care of my foul mood, well, I figured that would improve as soon as we started playing. I drove to Brooklyn with the window down, letting the cold night air clear the last remnants of Jack Daniels from my brain.

I hadn't heard from Jayne since my awkward departure the night before, but I hadn't expected to. What I *had* expected, though, was for her to bust my balls about it the minute I walked in. I was all ready to fire something right back at her about minding her own damn business, but she didn't say a word. In fact, it was almost like she was, not exactly avoiding me, but more like walking on eggshells. Matt and Skid were acting normal, only Jayne seemed to be pussyfooting around me. I pretended not to notice, but it really pissed me off.

It was the same thing when we played at Token's the following night. She tried to act like everything was cool between us but she wouldn't even look me in the eye. *What the fuck?* I decided to ignore her. I didn't have time for any shit, especially since the crowd was really into our new stuff. I had to stop worrying about other people and start focusing on bringing my A game to Dirty Bushwick.

I held onto that attitude after the show, when we all went to the bar and I broke my vow to cool it on the drinking. It was hard with people coming up and buying us shots and telling us how awesome the set was. I was actually having a great time, but then I'd look up and catch Jayne watching me with slightly furrowed brows, like she was worried about me. It was starting to get on my nerves so I moved to the other end of the bar to get out of her line of sight. I wasn't there long when I was approached by a girl who'd I'd seen at a few of our other gigs. She'd clearly had a few too many and judging from her body language she was definitely interested in a lot more than *meeting the band.* I bullshitted with her for a while, though I had no intention of leaving with her. It would've led to a shitstorm of questions about Leah. I don't know why I just didn't tell the others what had happened. It's not like I was the first guy to get dicked over.

After about twenty minutes I was ready to jet. The girl had just downed another shot and was getting sloppy. I was thinking of an exit plan when Jayne sidled up next to me and slipped her arm around my waist. It was something she'd done plenty of times to help me out of a situation I didn't want to be in, but for some reason it really pissed me off this time.

I gave a long, cold look, then slipped out of her grip and stepped over to the girl. "Hey, Jayne, meet -" I stopped short and glanced at the girl. Shit, I didn't even know her name.

"Cassie," she said, slurring slightly, then smiled as she moved closer to me. I threw my arm around her.

Jayne looked stunned, a rare sight that I thoroughly enjoyed. I didn't know why I was being such a douche to her, because she really hadn't done anything wrong. I guess I just wanted to be a douche to someone and at the moment Jayne was the easiest target.

Quickly recovering from my little stunt, she shot me an annoyed look, then turned and began chatting with Cassie. Jayne, making small talk with some drunken groupie? I nearly laughed out loud when I saw that one.

Jayne waited until Cassie turned to order another beer, then leaned in toward me. "Hey, I know you're upset about your grandfather," she whispered, "but you're gonna feel *ten* times worse if you end up leaving with her." She jerked her head toward Cassie. "Don't be stupid, Jacks.

Think about what you're doing...Leah's not one to fuck around and neither are you - so *don't*."

Her words had lit a fuse, and if Cassie hadn't turned around just then I'm sure I would've blown. I must've shot her a murderous look, though, because Jayne drew back as if startled.

"It was nice meeting you, Cassie," she said as she glanced down to check the time on her phone. "I'm gonna cut out," she said to me, "I'll see you during the week."

I nodded, still seething, then watched her disappear into the back room. She reemerged a short time later with her jacket on and bag in hand. She never looked back my way as she said goodbye to Matt and then slipped out the side door.

▲   ▲   ▲

It was just before dawn when I quietly snuck out of Cassie's apartment, careful not to wake her. I shivered in the early morning cold as I stood on the sidewalk and tried to remember where I'd parked my car. *Great, Jackson, now you're picking up strangers* and *driving drunk*. I flipped up the hood of my sweatshirt, shoved my hands in my pockets and walked further down the block. Ten minutes later, I found my car, illegally wedged between a fire hydrant and driveway. I should've been grateful that I didn't have a ticket, but I was too desperate for a piss and a cup of coffee to care. As I headed back to Jersey, my thoughts returned to the events of the night before.

Jayne had no sooner left when I turned to Cassie and said, "You wanna get outta here?"

She had looked at me in surprise, probably because in the past I had made it clear that I had a serious girlfriend. Then she just smiled, placed her beer on the bar and said, "Sure."

I hadn't even thought to ask where she lived, but luckily it was only a few blocks from Token's. She talked the whole way there and didn't seem to notice when I just nodded or gave one-word answers. Is this how it had been with Leah? Was she all up on some guy's shit, some guy who didn't even care about her? Who just tolerated her attempts at conversation until he could try to get her into bed? I wondered how hard I'd have to try with Cassie, but that question evaporated a minute after we entered her apartment and she jumped my bones.

I knew leaving with Cassie had been a mistake, and I placed the blame squarely on Jayne's doorstep. It seemed every time I turned around lately she was either bringing up Leah or staring at me like I was a time bomb, ready to have some kinda fucking breakdown. It was *her* fault I'd ended up with this chick. *Fucking Jayne.*

I was still pissed when I pulled into my driveway and let myself into the house. It wasn't until I had crawled into bed that I realized I hadn't seen my father's car. *Asshole's probably sleeping it off in the Dunes parking lot*, I mumbled, then drifted off to sleep.

▲ ▲ ▲

I sat up and stretched, noting the slight throb of my head, the slight queasiness in my gut. Could be worse, I thought. Correction: *has* been worse. I glanced at the clock – three p.m. – and sighed. Waking up in the late afternoon with a hangover was becoming my new norm. I looked around for my phone, finally spotting it lying on the floor next to my bed, and reached for it. There was a text from Beth, asking me to stop by before practice. I sent her back a "K," then slid out of bed to complete the ritual – a long, hot shower followed by a nuked plate of leftover spaghetti.

I pulled up to Beth's the same time she did.

"Got outta work late," she explained as she got out of her car. "Brody's not home yet."

I nodded, glad it would just be the two of us. Brody was cool, but it had been ages since I'd hung out with my sister alone.

"You want something to eat?" she asked as we walked into the house. "I'm just going to change clothes and then I can fix you something."

"Nah, just ate." I sat on the couch, threw my legs on the coffee table and turned on the TV. I was still mindlessly flipping through the channels when she returned.

"So..." She took the remote from me and muted the TV. "I wanted to talk to you about Thanksgiving."

My stomach clenched, and not because I was stressed about the holiday menu.

"I'm thinking of having it here this year. I know Gram usually puts on a big spread, but..." She paused, and for a minute I thought she was going to cry. "...with everything that's happened, I think it's just too much for her." She sat down next to me on the couch. "We'll do the cooking together, and I'll invite Brody's parents and his brother. I just wanted to know if you and Leah will come for dinner. I know you usually eat with her family and just come for dessert, but it would be nice if we were all together."

There it was, the reason for the stomach clench. I'd known it was only a matter of time before I'd have to tell Beth and now was as good a time as any. I picked up the remote and unmuted the TV. "I'll come for dinner," I said, staring at the screen, "but I'll be solo."

"Solo?"

I let out a sigh and turned to her. "Yeah, solo. Leah and I split."

Her eyes grew as big as saucers. "Holy shit, what happened?"

I shrugged, turning back to the TV.

She grabbed the remote and turned it off. "Jackson, what *happened*?"

"She...was screwin' around."

"*What*?!"

"You heard me."

"Leah? Screwin' around? Are you serious?"

"Shocked, are ya?"

"Uh, *yeah*."

"Well, not as shocked as I was." I proceeded to give her an abridged version of the whole fucked up night. Beth didn't interrupt, just sat there in stunned silence.

"So, that's the story," I said when I finished. "And, yeah, it pretty much sucks to be fucked over like that, but it is what it is." My insides were in knots at having to relieve the whole ordeal, but I put up a good front. I had to; Beth had enough to deal with without me adding to her stress.

"Shit, I'm sorry, Jacks. I know how tight you guys were and -"

"Yeah, well...." I cut her off as I stood. "I should probably head out; don't wanna get stuck in rush hour traffic."

"Yeah, sure," she said as she followed me to the front door. "You sure you're okay?"

"Yes, Beth," I huffed as I pulled the door open, "I'm fine."

She held me at arm's length and looked me over as if she were trying to see through my façade. My sister knew me well.

"Okay," she said finally as she wrapped me in a hug. "I'll talk to you during the week."

"Sounds good," I said, not meeting her eyes as I stepped outside.

▲ ▲ ▲

It was one thing to tell Beth about Leah; Jayne was another story entirely. The whole thing was just so fucking humiliating, and she was already looking at me like I was some pathetic thing. If she heard about Leah, the pussyfooting would get twice as bad, and that I couldn't take. It was hard enough acting like I was fine when I most definitely *wasn't*. Inside I was a fucking basket-case and I didn't need Jayne or anyone else knowing it. I'd deal with it myself – *my* way – just like I'd done since I was a kid: tuck it away and try to forget.

Of course, forgetting was best achieved with large amounts of alcohol, which was convenient since most of our gigs were at local bars. It never occurred to me that my efforts would only bring everything to a head... and make me cross a line so deep I feared it would be nearly impossible to uncross.

▲ ▲ ▲

"Keys!" Jayne shouted over the music as she extended her palm.

I looked down at her, smirking at the way she had one hand on her hip and the other flipped out toward me. Over my constant and often angry objections, Jayne seemed hell-bent on trying to save me from myself, but what she failed to realize was that I didn't need saving – not by her or anyone else.

I tossed her my keys anyway, because even I had to admit I was in no shape to drive all the way back to Jersey. How could I be? I'd been drinking nonstop since our set ended at Token's three hours earlier. It was some set too; I was *still* on a high from it...or was that the whiskey? I didn't know and frankly, I didn't give a shit.

She caught the keys and slipped them into her pocket. "I'll come find you at closing."

"Can't wait," I muttered as I watched her thin form disappear into the crowd. I turned back to the bar to find a full sweaty bottle of Heineken in front of me. The bartender saw my curious expression and jerked his head toward a blonde a few stools away.

I smiled and lifted the beer in gratitude, and lo and behold, a moment later she and her perfect double-Ds were walking toward me.

I fuckin' love being in a band.

The blonde (I never caught her name) and I were engaged in conversation (meaning I had established that she lived nearby and was about to ask her if she wanted to get out of here) when Jayne appeared at my side again.

Shit. I had forgotten all about her.

"Ready," she said, but it was more of a statement than a question. Her eyes shot daggers at the blonde, who quickly scurried away.

"Yep," I huffed, rolling my eyes at Jayne. As I stood I had to grab the edge of the bar to stop myself from swaying.

"Drink enough?" she asked sarcastically as she reached out to steady me.

"Almost."

"Almost my ass - you're *done*." She took my arm, then led me through the crowd and out the front door. "Where'd you park?"

I hesitated, looking up the street and then back down.

"Shit, Jackson, don't tell me you don't remember where you parked; it's freezing out here." She flipped up the collar of her jacket.

"Relax," I slurred, "It's...it's thataway..." I pointed to the spot where I'd squeezed my Nissan behind a box truck. The truck was still there and nearly blocking the car from sight. I shrugged and added, "So sue me," eliciting an annoyed look from Jayne.

Once again, I felt her hand gripping my arm as she hustled me down the block. When we reached my car, she propped me up against the side and with shivering hands unlocked the passenger side door. I watched silently until she dropped the keys, then burst out laughing.

"You're funny," I said.

"Yeah, and you're an asshole," she snapped, then shoved me inside and ran around to the driver's side. "You do know I'm not driving you all the way back to Jersey, right?" She turned the ignition, then rubbed her palms together, trying to get warm. "You can crash at my place and drive back in the morning."

"Cool," I mumbled, then reclined the seat because lately I never felt like going home. "Hey," I said as I turned to her, "Where's your car, anyway?"

"Battery's dead; Eddie dropped me off," she said as she maneuvered out from behind the box truck. "Shit!" she said suddenly as she stopped short, pulled out her phone and placed a call. I heard the short conversation between her and Eddie explaining that he didn't have to pick her up. I leaned my head back and rolled my eyes because in my book Eddie was nothing but a prick with an agenda.

At this hour there wasn't much traffic on the BQE, so we got to Staten Island in no time. When we walked into her apartment, *the prick with an agenda* and two of his buddies were in the living room watching a replay of an earlier football game. Immediate buzzkill.

"Hey, Jaynie, what's up?" Eddie shouted over his shoulder. "How was the concert?" He turned and saw me standing there. "S'up, *Jack*?"

I hated when he called me that, and judging from his douchey grin, he knew it. I eyed him right back but said nothing. No sense in starting trouble for Jayne. I stood by, half-listening to her go on about the night.

"...so, anyway," she said, "Jackson's gonna crash here tonight."

His eyes flicked back to me as Jayne went to hang up her jacket in the hall closet. She shut the closet door then turned to me and whispered, "You can hang out in my room 'til they leave." I knew exactly what Eddie was thinking so I gave him a subtle smirk as I followed Jayne into her room.

Once there, I laid back across the foot of her bed and said, "You know your roommate's an asshole, right *Jaynie?*"

She laughed. "Maybe sometimes, but, hey, thanks for letting his 'Jack' comment slide. I know it drives you crazy when he calls you that."

She went into the closet, grabbed an extra pillow and some blankets, and tossed them to me. "His friends'll leave soon; you can crash on the floor 'til then."

I grunted in response, watching as she moved over to the dresser, pulled out some clothes and slipped into the hallway. While she was gone I glanced around the small, sparsely decorated room. Other than a small framed photo on her dresser of her and someone I assumed was her dad there really weren't any other personal things. I was lying flat on my back, so I might've missed something, but I was too comfortable and wasn't about to move.

Jayne returned with her face scrubbed clean and her hair tied on top of her head in a messy ponytail. She looked oddly hot in her flannel pajama pants and black Beatles t-shirt. Funny, because I never thought of Jayne as being hot, although it could've been the alcohol that was making me see her that way.

"Okay, Eddie's friends are gone so the couch is free." She laughed as she climbed into bed. "And believe me, it's much more comfortable than the floor."

"This is fine," I said. Suddenly my body felt too heavy to get up.

She laughed as she nudged me with her foot. "Sorry, bud, but there's a couch in the other room with your name on it."

I got up and grabbed the pillow and blankets. "Can you at least help me set it up...please?" I said as I held up the blankets.

"Fine," she said sounding annoyed as she whipped the navy-blue comforter down and hopped out of the bed.

"Give it to me," she said, holding out her hand like she had done with the keys. I handed her the blankets, but when she pulled open the door I put my palm against it and closed it again.

"What are you doing?" she asked, confused, as she yanked the door again, but again I held it closed.

She whipped around. "What the fuck, Jackson?"

"C'mon, you really want me to sleep out there?" I slurred as I motioned with my chin to the room on the other side of the door.

"Uh, *yeah*."

Before I knew what I was doing I pushed her back against the door and kissed her. I couldn't even say whether I enjoyed it, because a split second later the worst pain I'd ever felt was radiating from my crotch. I bent over, gripping my thighs and gasping. Damn, I'd seen guys get kneed in the balls before, but I had never imagined it could hurt this much.

"What the fuck, Jayne!"

"What the fuck, *Jayne*? Are you *serious*? What the fuck's wrong with you, Jackson?"

"Well whaddaya expect?" I said, trying to stand, "You lure me back here, parade around in that sexy outfit -"

She cut me off. "*Lure you back here? Sexy outfit*? If you think flannel pants and a t-shirt equates to 'sexy' you probably need to get out a little more. And as for *luring you back here*, you were drunk off your ass and probably would've ended up wrapped around a tree if I hadn't taken your keys, so you're welcome, *asshole!*"

"Oh, gimme a break, Jayne," I said, then let out a humorless laugh. "I know all about your *thing* for guitarists."

"My *thing* for guitarists?" she snapped back.

"Yeah, your thing for guitarists," I repeated. "It's no secret you were fuckin' around with that guy, Damian, the one I replaced, so I figured *what the fuck*, I'd give it a shot."

She looked as though I'd slapped her. "*That* was a low blow, Jackson."

I just shrugged, already wishing I could take it back.

"You know, Jackson," she began, her voice surprisingly calm. "I've been trying to cut you some slack ever since you lost your grandfather 'cause I know how hard it's been on you and your sister, but I am *done*." She took a couple of steps back.

I'd never seen her so angry.

"What the fuck happened to you, Jackson?" She shook her head in disgust. "I really thought you were different, hell, I even considered you a friend, but shit, I don't even *know* you anymore. What I do know, though, is that Leah oughta dump your sorry ass because she is *way* too good for a piece of shit like you."

Even through the booze and the ache in my balls, her comment about Leah cut into me like a knife.

"Now, get the fuck *outta* my room and get the fuck *outta* my apartment. And you sure as hell better sober up 'cause I am *done* giving a shit about what happens to you."

"Good," I hissed back at her, "'cause you know what? I don't need you givin' a shit about me. So, fuck you, Jayne and fuck Leah too; the two of you can go to hell for all I care."

She didn't have time to respond because at that moment I yanked open the bedroom door and stormed out through the living room, thankful Eddie wasn't there to witness the scene.

Once out on the street I headed straight for my car, but as soon as I got behind the wheel I knew I was still too fucked up to drive. Damn, it was freezing. That's when I remembered the old blanket I kept in the trunk. I went and got it, then I climbed into the back seat.

It was only then, as I lay curled up with my face pressed against the cold vinyl, that I slowly began to comprehend the magnitude of what I'd done. My life was more fucked than ever, and this time I had no one to blame but myself.

▲　▲　▲

I woke at the crack of dawn the next morning, the ache in my back rivaling the ache in my head. I slowly pulled myself up to a sitting position and for a moment stared bleary-eyed through the front windshield. That's when the events that landed me sleeping in the back of my car came crashing back. My hands on Jayne, pinning her against the door as I tried to stick my tongue down her throat, then the overwhelming agony of her knee in my nuts. I cringed, setting off the jackhammer at my temple. What *the fuck* was I thinking, trying to kiss Jayne like that?

In all the time I'd known Jayne I'd never thought of her as anything other than a friend – sometimes not even that. There was only one excuse for my idiotic behavior and it was one I'd been using way too often lately. Alcohol and my rage at the entire fucking world made for a lethal combination.

Putting the moves on her wasn't even the worst of it. I'd never forget the look on her face when I made that crack about Damian. It was a shitty thing to say, and ironic, considering my own track record with relationships.

The whole fucked-up scene played on a loop in my mind as I awkwardly climbed into the front seat, fished the keys out of my pocket and turned the ignition. The windshield immediately fogged and while I waited for the car to warm up I reached over the steering wheel and wiped it with the sleeve of my sweatshirt. By the time I pulled out of the parking spot, I'd graduated to replaying the scene with alternate and definitely more favorable endings. If only I'd stopped after a few beers... if I'd just gone to the couch when she asked... if only I'd just kept my fucking hands to myself and my fucking mouth shut. Coming up with these scenarios was ridiculous, but it was better than thinking about how I'd handle seeing Jayne again later that night.

By the time I got home I was mentally exhausted. As I walked up the path to my front door, I heard the crunch of tires on the gravel driveway and turned to see my father's car pulling behind mine. *Where the fuck has he been,* I thought as I threw him a curt nod then continued inside. Suddenly it struck me that maybe dear old dad and I had something in common after all. I cringed again, then just as quickly shook the thought off as I trudged up the stairs.

It seemed before I knew it I was headed back to Brooklyn, but this time the excitement I usually felt about jamming was replaced with pure dread. I didn't know what to expect, but I doubted Jayne was going to let my actions slide. Heck, I wasn't even sure I wanted her to.

Any question about Jayne's reaction was answered the minute I saw her. She was borderline hostile to me - but in a weird, passive sort of way - the entire night. It was extremely uncomfortable, but I just sucked it up and prayed Matt and Skid were too focused on the playing to notice. It seemed that way at first, but then a few nights later Matt asked me and Jayne to hang back after practice so we could "discuss" something. *Fuck*. As practice came to a close I felt my stomach clench. What if he wanted us to work together on something? I didn't know how that was going to happen, not when Jayne and I hadn't really spoken since the night of my colossal fuck-up.

As usual, Matt got right to the point. "Listen," he began as he looked from me to Jayne and then back again. "I don't give a shit what you two do on your own time; it's none of my business. But when it starts to affect the band it *becomes* my business. I can cut the tension between you two with a knife so either straighten out your issues or we're gonna have a problem."

I should have known Matt would notice. Nothing got by him. I was quick to try to apologize, but he was quicker to put his hand up and cut me off.

"Hold up Jackson, I'm not blaming you." He turned to Jayne. "I'm not going through this again, Jayne; so, straighten it out or some major changes'll have to be made."

If I thought Jayne looked mad the week before at her apartment, it was nothing compared to the way she looked now. If looks could kill, Matt and I would've been toast. I kept my feet planted and waited for her to throw my sorry ass under the bus, because I knew I deserved nothing less.

Matt looked pointedly at Jayne. "Am I making myself clear?"

That's when I knew if I wanted a future with Dirty Bushwick – and I damn well did – I needed to step up.

"Wait a minute Matt," I said as I put my hand up, "It's...it's not Jayne's fault."

The two of them turned to me.

"It's me; it's not Jayne, it's totally my fault. I've been under a lotta stress since my grandfather died and..." I trailed off, tempted to just leave it at that. No, I decided, it was time to come clean. "And...uh...Leah, we're, uh, not together anymore. Things are, um, really fucked up for me right now and Jayne just kinda got caught in the crosshairs. Like I said, it's not her fault, it's totally me. This band is everything to me and I'll...I'll definitely get my act together."

If Matt was surprised by my confession, he didn't show it; he just sized me up for a moment as if gaging my sincerity, then he nodded. "Okay. This band is obviously everything to me too." He looked between the two of us again. "And I'd hate to have it crash and burn over something like this, not after we've come this far."

I let out the breath I'd been holding but didn't say anything else.

"Okay, so I'll see you guys day after tomorrow, yeah?" Matt said, then grabbed his buzzing cellphone off the table to take a call.

I kept my head down as I gathered my stuff, unable to look at Jayne, but she slipped out pretty quickly so it wasn't even an issue. I kicked myself the whole ride home for letting my personal shit with Leah get in the way of the band. Why did I still give a shit about her anyway? The fact that she would do what she did proved she wasn't the person I thought she was. I was *done*. From now on, fuck any*one* or any*thing* that tried to come between me and my music.

▲　　▲　　▲

The whole next day I did nothing but work on new guitar riffs; it was the only thing that could keep my mind off the shitstorm I'd brought down on myself. When I finally put my guitar aside, my fingers were raw and my stomach was growling. I went into the kitchen and poked around the refrigerator for a few, finally deciding it would be easier to just go out and pick something up. Just as I shut the fridge door, the doorbell rang. I padded to the front door, mentally running down the short list of people it could be – mailman, census taker; we didn't get too many visitors. I never imagined I'd find Jayne standing on my stoop.

We stared at each other for an awkward moment before she finally said, "You gonna invite me in?"

"Uh, yeah, sure," I said as I stepped aside to let her pass.

Another awkward moment passed between us before she noticed my guitar in the corner. "What are you working on?" she asked, motioning to it. It was a simple question but enough to break the ice. I grabbed my guitar and the two of us headed out to the garage, my hunger forgotten.

An hour later it had returned with a vengeance, and we took a break to order some pizza.

Jayne waited until I had a mouthful of peperoni before she asked, "So why didn't you tell me about Leah?"

I made a big show of chewing as I mentally formulated my answer. How many times was I going to have to relive this?

Finally, I shrugged and said, "Not much to tell. She was screwin' around." I tried to make it like I'd totally moved on, like it didn't matter anymore.

"Screwin' around? *Leah*? Holy shit."

"Yeah, well..." I trailed off.

"Jeez, no wonder you were so messed up. First your grandfather and then *that*. Shit, that's a lot of crap for anyone to deal with at once."

I sat down on the wooden bench by the table, trying to get up the nerve to say what I knew had to be said if we were ever going to get things back to the way they were before. "Listen, I, um, I just wanna apologize for...you know...for the other night."

"Oh, you mean for your extreme lack of judgement in trying to lock lips with me?" she said in a half-joking manner. "Don't worry about it. Hey, I guess I never realized how well I rocked flannel pants and a t-shirt. Consider it forgotten."

Maybe she meant it, or maybe she was as good as I was at acting like shit didn't matter.

"That's, uh, actually not what I meant, but, yeah, um, sorry about that too. I was, uh, talking about what I, um, said, you know, afterward...about you and Damian. That was a real douche thing to say. I don't even know why I said it; I didn't mean it."

She didn't say anything at first and I thought maybe it would've been better if I'd just let it drop.

"Yeah, it *was* a real douche thing to say," she deadpanned, then just stared back at me, which of course made me feel even worse.

"Listen," she said after a minute, "I'm gonna give you a pass this once, okay? But talk to me like that again and the way I knee'd you in the balls is gonna seem like a picnic compared to what I'll do to you next time. Get it?"

I nodded, relieved that she was willing to accept my apology. "Got it, boss."

She came over to where I was sitting. "Jackson," she began "I've been playing with Matt since I was sixteen and we've never been closer to making it as we are right now." She placed a hand on each of my shoulders and stared down at me. "Like I told you back in July, I believe down to my *soul* that our music is *that* good. We are on the cusp of something big... bigger than anything either of us could've imagined. So, you know what I say?"

I felt like I was in a trance staring back at her, waiting for what she was going to say next.

"I say, to *hell* with Leah and to *hell* with Damian because nothing is gonna stop us, *nothing* and no one." She paused. "And that includes you too, Jackson. Matt doesn't give a lot of second chances. Fuck up again, and it won't matter how good you play. You'll be out on your ass so fast it'll make your head spin."

CHAPTER 50 - LEAH

I slowly packed my things, wishing I could blink and have the winter break behind me. Thanksgiving was bad enough and that was only a long weekend; how was I going to deal with not seeing Chase for over a month? Actually, being apart from him wasn't bothering me nearly as much as the fact that he'd be spending all that time with *her*. *Missy*. Not that he talked about it; actually, he rarely mentioned her at all. But that hadn't stopped me from becoming completely obsessed with her, even stalking her on Instagram on a daily basis. There really wasn't much to stalk, though, since most of her posts were pictures of her artwork, which if you ask me wasn't very impressive. Didn't stop me from looking, though, much as I promised myself every night that I wasn't going to do it anymore. I had turned into one of those pathetic girls I despised, but I couldn't help it. I had to find out what her appeal was and why Chase was with her.

I knew I'd hit rock bottom when I finally broke down and told Molly everything. I had to. I needed a sounding board to vent my frustrations. Her initial smug reaction was no surprise, but after the shock wore off, she too became obsessed. Not so much about Missy, but about the drama of it all.

"Maybe this sort of thing is common in the Midwest," she mused one rainy afternoon. It was the last week before break and already the school was clearing out. Molly and I were supposed to be studying for finals but instead had treated ourselves to a lazy afternoon of laundry and a Gilmore Girls marathon.

"You think?"

"I don't know, maybe." Molly said as she folded a pair of flannel pajamas pants. "I mean, from the few pictures she has of herself on Instagram she doesn't seem to be some country bumpkin." She shrugged. "Maybe open relationships are all the rage out there."

"Well, I think it's a desperate attempt on her part to hang onto him any way she can," I argued. "She knew he was bound to meet someone else at college so she offered to let him have his cake and eat it too."

She tossed her empty laundry bag back into the closet then turned to me and sighed. "I don't know, Leah. I think you're fooling yourself. Maybe it's exactly like Chase said and she didn't want him to have any regrets. Maybe it's even *more* than that. Maybe *she* didn't want to have any regrets either. Maybe it was something that just *worked* for them. He really has no reason to lie." She chuckled. "Heck, it's not like *you're* going anywhere."

I shot her an annoyed look which she pretended to ignore.

"Hey, I've told you before, if it's bothering you so much, just end it. It's not worth the stress. Besides, look around," she swung her arm in front of her for effect. "It's not like there's any shortage of guys here."

End it? Was she serious? At this point I was in far too deep to just pull the plug. My stress levels may have been in overdrive knowing that Chase was going home to *her*, but even so, I still wasn't ready to give up. And besides, we spent so much time together this semester he was bound to miss me, right?

⟁　⟁　⟁

Wrong.

Winter break came and went without a peep from Chase – not even a *Happy New Year* text at the stroke of midnight. I couldn't even enjoy the party Molly dragged me to - thrown by one of her old high school crushes – because I was so busy checking my phone all night. I felt like that's all I did these days, stare at that stupid thing, willing it to *ding* with a message from him.

Not that I had reached out to him. Sure, I thought about it each day – a hundred times a day – but each time I reminded myself that he needed a chance to miss me. To compare me to her and presumably find her lacking. But his radio silence made me question that decision, and by the third week of January I couldn't wait to get back to school. I kept telling myself to take it easy, to give it a day or two to collect my thoughts before seeing him. And that was my plan, right up until he called to tell me he was back and did I want to come over? What an asshole, I muttered, even as I grabbed my keys and left the dorm.

When I got to his place one of his roommates let me in.

"Hey there, Leah!" he said, giving me a quick hug.

Well, at least he treats me like Chase's girlfriend, I thought nastily.

After a few minutes of small talk about winter break, he said, "Chase is in the shower – why don't you wait in his room?"

"Sure, thanks." I gave him a smile I didn't feel, then headed up the stairs, let myself into Chase's room and reminded myself to play it cool. After a quick perusal of his dresser for new photos of her – there were none – I sat down on the bed to wait. A few minutes later Chase waltzed in wearing nothing but a dark gray towel wrapped around his waist. His damp hair was neatly slicked back and there were little beads of water still clinging to his shoulders. My irritation about not hearing from him over winter break quickly waned as I drank in the sight. He really was perfect.

He noted my admiring stare and shot me that sexy grin of his.

"Should I bother getting dressed?" he asked as he moved closer.

"That depends..." I said coyly. *Why could I not say no to this guy?*

"...on what?" His hands were already at the towel as if to pull it off.

"Well, it depends...did you miss me?"

Still smiling, he took hold of my hand and moved it inside the towel. "What do you think?"

We spent the next few hours in bed, more than enough time for my anger to melt away. The respite wouldn't last long, though.

"Looks like we're too late for the cafeteria," Chase said as glanced at the clock. "You hungry?"

I shrugged. "I could go for something."

"Yeah, we worked up quite an appetite, didn't we?" he chuckled. "How 'bout Chinese? I think the menu for Chan's is in the kitchen." He didn't wait for me to answer, just slipped on a pair of sweats and said he'd be right back.

As soon as he was gone I laid back on the pillows and smiled dreamily as my mind replayed the amazing sex we'd just had. Maybe I'd been too harsh. Winter break wasn't really *that* long and I think he'd mentioned way back that his dad wanted him to spend some time clerking at his law firm while he was home. So, between that and visiting with family I guess I could understand him not having much free time.

Still smiling, I turned onto my side to grab my phone, which I'd left in the pocket of the crumpled jeans on the floor. I reached downward and that's when I saw it – the picture frame I had missed earlier because it wasn't on the dresser with the others. My stomach tightening, I dropped the phone and leaned in for a better look. It was Chase and Missy, standing in front of a Christmas tree. They were wearing matching Christmas sweaters and huge grins on their faces, like they knew how dorky it was to be wearing matching sweaters but didn't care because they are just *that* into each other.

Maybe it was an old photo, I thought, but I knew even before I saw the timestamp in the bottom corner that I was grasping at straws.

WTF?!

I got off the bed and slipped into my clothes, intending to leave right then and there. Then I thought about how weird (and possibly pathetic) that would look, so I sat back on the bed and took a couple of deep breaths. By the time I heard Chase's footsteps on the stairs, I was laying back against the pillows, smile in place.

"I ordered us lo mien and sesame chicken," he said as he shut the door behind him. "It'll be here in thirty minutes." He looked at me and smirked. "You got dressed? What for?"

I forced a laugh. "I didn't feel like eating naked."

He shrugged, then climbed back onto the bed next to me and picked up the remote. He flipped through the stations before settling back to watch a basketball game.

"Chase…" I began, not really knowing what I was going to say.

"Yeah?" he said distractedly.

"Can I, uh, ask you something?"

"Sure. Shoot," he said, his eyes still glued to the screen.

"When we first met, what was it about me that made you...you know... want to get to know me better?

"Huh?" He sounded bewildered as he turned to me.

"Well, let's face it," I said as I reached over and pressed mute on the remote. "There's a lot of girls on campus, really pretty girls, so I guess I just wanted to know...why me?"

"Are you kidding?" he laughed lightly, "You are fucking *hot*, Leah." He pulled me onto his lap. "And yeah," he shrugged, "there're a lot of hot girls here, but it wasn't just that."

"Well, then what else was it?"

"Hmm, let's see..." He tapped his index finger to his chin as if he were really contemplating the question. "Well, I thought you were a genuinely nice person and I really dug hanging out with you. You're smart as a fuckin' whip, that's for sure, and, oh, did I mention you're *smokin'* hot?" He shrugged again. "I don't know, I guess you were the whole package."

I looked pointedly over his shoulder at the picture of him and Missy. "The whole package, huh?"

He glanced back to see what had caught my attention. "Leah...where're you going with this?"

"Where am I going?" I repeated, then chose my words carefully. "Well, I guess I'm just wondering why, if I'm the 'whole package,' you're still seeing her." I motioned with my head toward the photo. "Missy."

He sighed. "Shit, Leah, I thought you were cool with it. Just like I was cool with you and Jackson. That's why I never gave you any crap about it; I figured we were on the same page."

"The same page?"

"Listen Leah, like I said, you were a lot of things – hot, nice, smart, fun..." He paused for a beat, then added, "...and you were *attached*."

"Attached?"

"Yeah, *attached*. That was what, you know..." He seemed to struggle for the right words, "...sealed the deal for me."

"Sealed the deal?" I couldn't believe what I was hearing.

"Yeah, I figured it was the perfect setup for both of us. You backed off at first and I didn't pressure you, but then, I don't know, it seemed like you wanted to hang out so I figured you and Jackson must've made some sort of arrangement. You know, like me and Missy have."

"Huh," was all I could seem to muster, along with a curt nod.

"Leah, c'mon; you *know* I'm crazy about you. And we've got a good thing going; let's not mess with it."

"Well, yeah, *you've* definitely got good thing going, that's for sure," I said with just a touch of sarcasm. After my weeks of angst, I was proud of how cool I was handling this.

He sighed.

"Chase, I think...I think maybe I need a little time to rethink our... *situation*."

"Leah...."

"When we're at school things are great but then you go home for break and it's like I don't even exist. Then you come back and expect us to pick up right where we left off. You've got this whole other life that I can never be a part of so long as..." I waved my hand dismissively toward the photo. "...so long as *matching sweater Missy* is still on the scene."

"Leah, *come on-*" he began again, but I quickly cut him off.

"Chase, don't..." I said as I got up from his bed, pulled on my boots and grabbed my jacket from the floor. "I just...I just need some time."

▲   ▲   ▲

"You coming to the cafeteria?" Molly said, her voice muffled by the sweater she was pulling over her head. "I'm starving."

"No time," I mumbled from under the covers, "I have some reading to do before I go to class."

"Right," Molly replied with a dubious tone in her voice. I couldn't tell whether she was just being her nosy self or could actually tell that I was lying, which of course I was. There was no reading to do; I wasn't going to the cafeteria because a) the nervous knots in my stomach made the thought of breakfast revolting, and b) I dreaded the thought of Molly grilling me, which she would surely do if we were sitting across the table from one another.

I lay there, just listening as she gathered up her books and grabbed her jacket from the closet. "Okay, well, I'm out. See ya later."

"See ya," I replied, then sighed with relief when I heard the door close behind her. I hated being around Molly when I wanted to keep something to myself, which lately was all the time. She definitely would have something to say if she knew the reason for my anxious gut - the conversation I'd had with Chase last night.

She'd probably say I should've kept my mouth shut about Missy, and the truth was she was right. As much as I hated that he went home to her, I still loved the fact that when he was here, he was all mine. All anyone on campus knew was that Leah Miller had landed the most popular guy on campus and that made my stock pretty high.

I laid around most of the morning, flipping through the channels and trying unsuccessfully to stop obsessing. Just when I had convinced myself I'd blown the whole thing, I got a text from Chase asking if I would meet him in the cafeteria later that afternoon. Immediately, I felt my mood begin to lift; in fact, I was pleased with myself for having stood my ground. After all, I was a catch – or as Chase put it, "the whole package" - and certainly worthy of more than playing second fiddle. The knot in my stomach began to relax, and I got dressed and headed for my noon class.

A few hours later I headed to the cafeteria, where I found Chase waiting for me outside. He actually looked *nervous*.

"Hey, what's up?" he said as he reached for his backpack and hoisted it over his shoulder. "Hungry?"

I nodded. "Starved." That was an understatement. I hadn't eaten since dinner the night before. We walked inside, grabbed some sandwiches and sodas, and found a small table near the back. As we ate we made small talk, mostly about classes, and if Chase noticed I was scarfing down my sandwich he didn't say anything. It wasn't until we were finished that I sensed something was off. I couldn't put my finger on it; he just seemed uncomfortable. Never in a million years, though, was I prepared for the grenade he was about to drop.

"So, listen..." he began, "...about last night...."

"Yeah?" Instantly I felt my gut twist up again.

"Well...I, uh, thought a lot about what you said and..." He hesitated, then rubbed the back of his neck as if wrestling with what to say next. "... And I think maybe it's best if we didn't see each other anymore."

I stared at him, speechless, because this was *not at all* what I was expecting.

"Yeah. It's just that I get the feeling you want more outta this than I can give you right now...and it's, it's not really fair to you."

"What? No, Chase...I...we're great together and -"

He quickly cut me off.

"Yeah, it is great, but it's not like what Missy and I have together, and to be honest, I don't think I could ever have that with you."

"Wha...what do you mean?"

"Well, I know me and Missy's arrangement may not sound ideal to most people, but for us it was a middle ground. Neither of us wanted to break up but we were also realistic. At first, I'd just assumed you and Jackson had done the same, but after you told me you guys broke up I got the feeling that he had no clue what'd been going on behind his back." He leaned way back in his chair. "He didn't know, did he." It was more a statement than a question.

I didn't answer.

"Yeah, that's what I thought." He leaned forward and started fiddling with the straw in his empty glass. "Leah, like I told you, you're smart, fun, nice and hot as fuck, but this relationship could never be anything more than what it is right now, because, for one thing, I *love* Missy. But even if for some reason me and Missy split, I could never picture a future with you. Hell, if you'd screw around on someone who, from what I could see, is a decent guy like Jackson, who's to say you wouldn't do it to me? Bottom line, Leah, I could never trust you."

I was afraid to speak. Afraid that my voice would give away how totally desperate I felt at that moment.

After what seemed like the most awkward silence of my life, he said, "I guess I should probably get going." He pushed his chair back and stood, then reached down to grab his backpack. "Still friends, though, right?"

I nodded – three quick jerks of my head.

"Okay, so, I guess I'll see you around then." He smiled, then just when I thought it couldn't get any worse, he put up his hand for a fist bump.

I stared at his fist for a moment, then slowly raised my own toward it. With another flash of that killer grin, he headed for the exit, only to be stopped by a table of freshman girls. It was nothing new – girls were always calling him over. They had just never done it right after he dumped me. Completely different experience. There was a brief friendly exchange, then he was on his way, leaving the girls giggling and whispering amongst themselves.

After he was gone I sat there for another five minutes trying to get my shit together. No such luck – my legs were still trembling when I stood and grabbed my bag from the floor beside my chair. As I walked purposely across the cafeteria, I couldn't help thinking about the table of girls and wondering if one of them would end up being my replacement.

▲　　▲　　▲

I must've looped the campus a dozen times before finally returning to my room and Molly's inevitable inquisition. I figured I could put off telling her for about five minutes, but after that she was bound to hear from someone that Chase and I were no longer together. Then I'd have to deal with her inquisition and her hurt feelings about my lying to her...again.

By the time I bit the bullet and returned to the dorm, my toes were nearly frostbitten. Unfortunately, the emotional numbness I'd felt for the past two hours was starting to wear off. Molly was working on homework at her desk when I quietly slunk in.

"Hey, why so late? Out with lover -" She glanced from the clock and to me, cutting herself off when she saw my face. "Oh. Trouble in paradise...?"

It was the moment I had dreaded. Best friend or not, it wasn't easy to admit that some guy had cut you loose. Especially a really hot guy and in the middle of a crowded cafeteria. But once I started, the words – and a few tears – started spilling out. I even told her about the giggling bitches at the other table.

"Wow," she said when I finished, "Never saw that coming." She shrugged. "Well, you gotta give him points for honesty, that's for sure."

I didn't say anything. Instead I just laid on my bed and stared up at the ceiling.

"Do you think he did it in a public place so you couldn't freak out on him?"

Actually, the thought *had* crossed my mind, but I certainly wasn't going to admit it to Molly. "Who knows?"

"So, what are you going to do now?" she asked. I could feel her eyes studying me.

"What do you mean?" I snapped. "Nothing. What, you think now I'm gonna start stalking him like some pathetic loser? Blowing up his cell with endless text messages?" I was talking too fast and knew I'd better slow down before she caught onto how upset I really was. I paused for a breath. "Anyway, you know the old saying, plenty of fish in the sea, right?"

"True," she nodded. "And there're so many parties every weekend. Hey, I heard the football team just got a new quarterback. He's a junior, transferred from Nebraska *and* I heard he's really hot." She was actually starting to sound excited as she stood and started pacing. "Okay, I think you should get your feet wet Friday night at the track house. The parties there are usually pretty mellow. And there's a wrestling party most Saturday nights that's always loaded with hunky wrestlers and-"

I had to cut her off or she was never going to stop. "Okay, I get it Molly, like I said, plenty of fish."

She nodded. "Yep, plenty of fish." She looked away and just when I thought she was done, she said, "Hey, I'm, uh, just curious, what about the fish you threw back?"

I turned toward her. I should've *known* that was coming. "I assume you're referring to Jackson."

"Yeah, too bad you burned – or should I say annihilated – *that* bridge."

"Give me a break, Molly. Chase or no Chase, that was over." I meant it, too. Jackson and I might have broken up over Chase, but it was way more than that. I had outgrown him and his ridiculous dead-end dreams and I'm sure I would've broken it off sooner or later anyway. Chase had just sped up the inevitable.

"Maybe, but it's ironic when you think about it," she mused. "All your lying and sneaking around behind Jackson's back was done for someone you never really had in the first place."

Molly was trying to coax me into an argument so she could say *I told you so,* but I stayed silent.

"That reminds me, the other day I heard this song on the radio that sounded a lot like Dirty Bushwick." This was one of Molly's favorite methods – when someone wasn't taking the bait, attack from a different angle. "It wasn't them, but it really did remind me of them."

"Yeah, right," I scoffed, "Like they'd ever be on the radio."

"Hey, you never know. Their stuff was good enough to make it. You know it was."

I chose to stay silent once again, even though I agreed with her. Dirty Bushwick *was* good enough to make it, but so were a lot of bands. The ones who became famous also had other things going for them – things like looks, stage presence, connections - that from what I could see DB was definitely lacking. I had no idea what would become of Jackson and the band, but I did know one thing: it was no longer my concern.

CHAPTER 51 - JACKSON
One Year Later ...

I was stopped at a light when I heard my cell go off in the passenger seat next to me – not with a call, but with one of those annoying little noises to let you know you have a text or an email, or in this case, a tweet. If someone had told me a year ago that I would even *have* a Twitter account, I would have said they were fuckin' nuts. Now I felt a familiar thrill as I grabbed the phone and looked down. Sure enough, there was a new tweet from @JayneGotGoth:

Where Brooklyn at? Jenks in Point Pleasant this Saturday #DirtyBushwick

Fuckin' Jayne, I thought, but I was smiling. It was her third tweet today, but it wouldn't be her last. When Matt put her in charge of the band's social media accounts, she'd acted like he was asking her to shine his shoes. A few months and five thousand followers later, she still pretended it was a chore, but who was she kidding? She loved it, and, more importantly, she was good at it. That tweet would soon be retweeted and retweeted again, and hopefully would translate into a packed house this weekend.

I did my part and clicked the retweet button, then set the phone down on the console between the seats. While I enjoyed reading Jayne's tweets and her followers' reaction to them, I had yet to master the clever one-hundred-forty-character response. Given my natural aversion to social media, I wasn't even sure I wanted to master it.

The light changed and I eased onto the service road that would take me to the New Jersey Turnpike and eventually, to Brooklyn for rehearsal. Traffic was at a crawl – something that used to aggravate me to no end but these days I couldn't even summon the energy to complain. How could I, when things were going so good? Gone were the days of playing to near-empty bars, or even worse, crowded bars where everyone ignored us. Over the past year Dirty Bushwick's fan base had grown, not to a huge following, but a respectable one. It was also a *loyal* following, with a lot of familiar faces showing up at each local gig.

Now we were all praying the release of *Die Tryin'* would take Dirty Bushwick to a whole new level. Production on the movie had wrapped and, fingers crossed, the director hoped to premier it at the Tribeca Film Festival in April. From the little footage I'd seen it looked pretty decent, if a little low budget. There were no big-name actors, but rumor had it that the lead guy, who I'd never even heard of, had already been offered a major part in some upcoming action flick. We figured some of that buzz had to increase the hype surrounding *Die Tryin'* – and by extension, Dirty Bushwick. That's when the producer suggested we expand our social media presence, which we found pretty fucking funny, because we didn't have a social media presence at that point.

The gist of the movie was that this seriously talented and very fucked up rocker overdoses just before the release of his band's first album. The album ends up going double-platinum and the remaining band members then have to decide if they want to go on without him or go their separate ways. If you ask me it sounded pretty cliché, but, hell, so long as they were using our music as the soundtrack, I sure as shit wasn't gonna complain.

Whatever else happened with the movie, it had forced me to get my shit together, though if I was being honest that night at Jayne's apartment had just as much to do with it. Since then, I rarely drank, except for an occasional beer or two after a gig. I was relieved Jayne had forgiven me for what she jokingly called my "dark night of the soul." She even busted my balls about it from time to time, which coming from Jayne was a sign that things were back to normal.

And speaking of dark times, I didn't miss that lying cheating bitch at all. I did miss *Leah*, though, and by that I mean the girl I met that summer at the party, not what she turned into later. Sometimes I wondered whether the person I loved had ever existed at all. I mean, shit, how does someone do a complete one-eighty like that? Whenever my mind started to go down that road, I tried to remember all the times we spent together, the girl who stood by me when *no one* was listening to my music, and who loved it almost as much as I did. The girl who, though I never said it out loud, I'd planned on spending the rest of my life with. That's the girl I missed, sometimes so much it hurt, though I never talked about her and everyone – including Jayne - knew not to ask.

There had been some pretty big news on the home front as well. For one, last spring Brody had finally popped the question. Yep, my sister was getting hitched and I couldn't have been happier for her. I didn't see as much of Beth these days - when she wasn't working or planning the wedding, she was with Gram, taking her shopping or helping out around the condo. Beth had been trying to get her to move in with her and Brody, and although Gram had so far resisted, she was starting to slowly come around to the idea. I hadn't even realized how much my grandmother's loneliness had been weighing on me until Beth and Brody stepped up.

The biggest surprise, though, came one night just before I left for rehearsal. I was having my usual dinner of spaghetti with marinara sauce and glancing through the newspaper. On the other side of the table sat a stack of mail, including two thick white envelopes that could only be Beth and Brody's wedding invitation. *So, she'd decided to invite the old man after all.*

I was just about to open my invitation when I heard the knock at the door. I groaned when I got up to answer it, thinking Dad had forgotten his house key again. I pulled open the door, ready with a nasty comment, when I saw *Tim* standing there. I hadn't seen my brother in nearly four years and honestly if I'd seen him anywhere but on our doorstep I don't think I would've recognized him. He was much bigger and broader than I remembered, and his hair was cut into an uncharacteristic buzz cut, not to mention the fatigues and big black army boots he was wearing.

"Holy crap!" I exclaimed, but before I could hug him he stepped forward and twisted me into a friendly headlock.

"What's up, little bro," he said as if we had seen each other the week before.

"Fuck man, what're you doing here? Last I heard you were in the Middle East somewhere, then radio silence."

Tim was in one of those units you see in the movies – they were sent into places no one else would go and took part in operations only people with high level clearance knew about. Sometimes I think he joined up just so he couldn't hear what was going on back here. I didn't blame him one bit. "You out for good?"

"No way; already reenlisted, but they transferred me Stateside – Texas, to be exact." He pulled out a kitchen chair and sat. "Gotta be at Fort Hood in a couple days but I wanted to stop by and surprise you guys." He glanced around the kitchen. "So, where's the old man?"

I shrugged. "Fuck if I know. I keep outta his shit, he keeps outta mine. Nothin's changed on that front."

Tim ended up coming with me to Brooklyn that night and listening to us jam. He even hung out afterwards and had a few beers with everyone. The next day, we went to visit Beth. Boy, did she freak out when she saw Tim standing there – she threw herself at him so hard she nearly knocked him to the ground. For him, the biggest shock was finding out we'd reconnected with our grandparents. He was bummed when he heard Gramps had passed but wanted to head right up to Rockaway to see Gram. We ended up staying at the condo late into the night, just sitting around reminiscing, making sure to stick with the good times and avoiding the bad.

A few days later, Tim left for Texas, but not before promising he'd be back for Beth's wedding. She'd asked both of us to give her away, because Dad sure as shit didn't deserve to do it. Although I didn't say anything to Beth, I doubted our father would even show up. It was pretty humiliating to be invited to your own daughter's wedding as nothing more than a guest, but I was staying out of it.

The day after Tim left I got the letter opener out of the kitchen drawer and neatly slit open the invitation. The inner envelope had "Jackson Foxx and guest" printed across the front. *And guest.* I hadn't planned on bringing a date since I wasn't seeing anyone seriously – or not seriously, for that matter. Don't get me wrong, I met a lot of girls – girls who were only too willing to hook up with someone in the band - but to be honest I was still a bit gun shy about getting too involved since the whole Leah fiasco. Shit like that'd make anyone think twice. And besides I was too busy working on my music.

Matt hadn't let up on us for a minute – in fact, since the movie wrapped he'd been pushing us even harder. The rest of us bitched a little – with all the gigs we were playing we were exhausted – but when he said it would be a good idea to have enough new stuff in case things took off after the movie release, we shut up. Wishful thinking? Maybe, but we wanted to be prepared for the best-case scenario and for us that meant a recording contract.

I tossed the invitation aside and started poking through the fridge for something to eat before Jayne arrived. The new stuff we'd been coming up with lately was nothing short of awesome. It was weird, but after we came out of the rough patch brought on by my bullshit we had been more attuned than ever. The ideas never stopped flowing, and we'd often look up at the clock to see it was three a.m. We didn't talk about it too much because we were so afraid we'd jinx it.

I heard a knock on the kitchen door. *Speak of the devil.*

"Hey, what's up," I said after opening the door for Jayne.

"Usual," she answered as she shook off her jacket and hung it by the door. "Ready?"

"Yeah, gimme a few; just want to grab something to eat. Sit down."

"Hey, is that your sister's wedding invitation?" she said as she eyed the envelope on the table. She pulled out a chair and sat. "Wow, that came up fast. Seems like yesterday you were telling me they got engaged."

"Yeah, right? It did come around quick," I commented as I grabbed some leftover wings out of the fridge. As I arranged the wings on a plate and popped them into the microwave, I had a thought. "Hey, how'd you like to be my plus one?"

Before she could answer, I added, "You know Beth and Brody and you've met my brother so what the hell? It'll be fun."

She hesitated, and I knew by the way the smile was slowly stretching across her face that she was shifting into ball-busting mode.

"Huh, well, I dunno...I clean up pretty good, you know, and I wouldn't want to be accused of, you know, trying to, um..." She hesitated as she pretended to search for the right word, "...*entice* you."

It had been a while since she busted me about that night in her apartment and as much as I tried to keep a straight face, I couldn't help but laugh. This was a fairly new development – for months I'd felt my face flushing a hot, beet red every time she brought it up.

"Ha ha, very funny. Go on," I motioned with my hand, "get it all out." I stood for a moment with my arms folded across my chest.

"Couldn't help it," she laughed. "You stepped right into that one."

"So, you wanna go or what?"

She shrugged. "Sure, I'll go; it'll be fun. And, hey, it'll be worth the price of admission to see you do a solo."

"I'm still not sure about that. I gotta talk to Brody, see what he thinks."

I'd really wanted to do something special for Beth and the idea I had was perfect, but since it was their day I wanted to run it by Brody first.

"I'm sure he'll be fine with it," Jayne said, while I made a mental note to give him a call during the week.

"Ready?" I said as I grabbed my plate of wings from the microwave and a beer from the fridge before the two of us headed out to the garage.

We had a productive night but ended early - Jayne had work the next morning and had to drive all the way back to Staten Island. It had been much easier when her dad had the house a few miles from me – she'd just stay over there on the nights we worked together. Now he had moved to Florida, and I think she knew from my half-hearted offers to let her stay in Beth's old room that I was still uncomfortable. The wedding was a different story, though; as much as I hated to admit it, the thought of going without a date had bugged the shit out of me, almost as if Leah – the evil, two-timing Leah – had won.

▲　　▲　　▲

We got word in early March, just before Beth and Brody's wedding, that *Die Tryin'* had been selected to premier at Tribeca. That's the day it hit me

— there was a really good chance that we *were* gonna make it. We all had our fingers crossed that the audiences would love it because if the movie caught on the exposure for Dirty Bushwick was gonna be huge.

"Hey, guys," Matt said after the news had sunk in, "I think this means we'll be walking the red carpet at the premier."

"Red carpet!" Jayne exclaimed. I glanced her way and noticed she looked anxious, but I brushed it off. Jayne never got nervous over anything. "That means photographers, reporters, the works, right?"

We all kind of shrugged and then Matt said, "Yeah, I guess it does."

Matt looked into it and found out it was true. Red carpet, cameras, reporters. Holy fuck, this was really happening!

"So, listen up guys," Matt said the next night when we arrived at the Brooklyn garage for practice. "Since Tribeca is classy event, I say we follow suit and go black-tie all the way. Agreed?"

We all nodded. Abso-fuckin-lutely.

"Okay, so we got about a month before the film festival, maybe a little more. At this point we have nothing left to do but show up, so let's put it aside and concentrate on the task at hand – polishing the new music we've done so it's ready in case..." He trailed off.

We all just nodded, and by unspoken agreement, let it go. As I said, nobody ever wanted to jinx it.

᛭   ᛭   ᛭

Tim and I stood at the doors of the little stone church, waiting for the limo carrying my sister, her five bridesmaids, and our grandmother to arrive. We glanced back through the glass doors at Brody, a sheen of sweat clearly visible on his forehead as he nervously pulled at the knot of his tie. Poor dude was nervous as shit, though I didn't quite understand why – he and Beth had been together forever.

Tim leaned over and whispered, "You think he's gonna make it?"

I laughed. "He'll be fine."

"Hey, you seen Dad yet?" Tim asked as he glanced around.

I shook my head. So far, Dad was MIA, though according to Beth he'd sent his response card saying he was coming. I didn't say anything to her but I highly doubted it. I just prayed that if he did come he'd arrive sober and stay that way. Better my sister be disappointed by a no-show than have her wedding ruined by a sloppy drunken mess.

Just then Tim nudged me with his elbow and whispered, "Whoa, check *her* out."

I followed his line of sight until my eyes stopped on a girl at the far end of the parking lot. She was wearing a short dark blue dress with thin sparkly straps that reflected the sun's rays and fit her like a glove. Black high heeled shoes showed off toned calves, and her long dark hair hung way down her nearly bare back. At her side she clutched a small silver purse. I laughed because if I remembered correctly, she was exactly Tim's type.

"Probably a friend of Beth's," I told him, but no sooner were the words out of my mouth when the girl turned around and I realized it was Jayne.

"Nooo, don't do that," Tim joked as she draped a black coat over her shoulders.

"That's Jayne..." I said as I squinted in her direction, "...from my band. You remember, you met her when you first got back to the States."

"No shit," he said as he narrowed his eyes and continued to stare in her direction. "Hey, she cleans up pretty nice."

"Yeah," I said slowly, "She sure does."

I laughed to myself, remembering how not too long ago Jayne had said the exact same thing about herself. As she turned toward the church, I put my hand up and waved her over.

Tim gave a low whistle as she approached.

"Shut up," I muttered, eliciting a chuckle from him.

"Didn't think I'd make it on time," she said as she gingerly climbed the church steps, "Huge accident on the Goethals Bridge." She looked between me and Tim. "Ooh, don't you two look swanky in your tuxes."

"Yeah, like twins," I said, and just then Beth's limo pulled up.

"Uh oh, looks like the show's about to start," Jayne said as the chauffeur got out, walked around to other side of the limo and pulled open the door. "I better grab myself a seat."

She scooted inside and down the aisle with Tim staring after her. When he turned back around the bridesmaids had already started getting out of the limo.

"Holy crap," he said, "One's better looking than the next."

"I think you need to get out more," I joked, but he was right. Beth's friends were pretty hot – shit, I'd had crushes on all of them at one time or another – and today they looked especially good in their matching sapphire blue dresses. But none of them could hold a candle to my sister. Sounds sappy, but when the driver helped her out of the limo I felt my eyes get watery. Not only did she look stunning in her traditional white wedding gown; she looked just like our mother. I caught Tim running a finger under his eye and knew he was thinking the same thing.

Thankfully we didn't have too much time to be sad about it. As soon as Beth's white ballet slippers hit the sidewalk, a flurry of activity that would've rivaled backstage at any concert began. Any lingering guests scrambled inside to take their seats and the bridal party lined up in the vestibule. As soon as everyone was settled, Tim walked up to Gram and gallantly offered her his arm. As the two slowly made their way down the aisle, I didn't know which of them looked prouder – Gram, on the arm of her soldier grandson, or Tim, for having the chance to escort such a dignified woman. I couldn't help but notice, though, that of the many rows of guests, she was our only relative.

Fuckin' Dad.

After seating Gram in the front, Tim looped back around to join me and Beth in the vestibule. "You ready?" he grinned down at her. She nodded, then as the last of the five bridesmaids proceeded down the aisle, she poofed out her skirt and held out an arm to each of us. Tim took her left arm, while I stepped to her right.

"We got this," I whispered as the organist began to play the Wedding March and the three of us slowly began our walk down the aisle.

A hundred pairs of eyes followed us, a fishbowl-type sensation I'd never felt onstage. I spotted Jayne smirking at me from the middle of a row and threw her a wink, then found myself fighting back tears again when I looked ahead and saw Brody. The nervousness was completely gone, and he was staring at my sister like she was an angel. Finally we reached the altar and Beth went to stand beside Brody while Tim and I joined the rest of the groomsmen. The service was short but moving, and before I knew it Brody was kissing his bride. The whole church erupted in cheers as we were headed back up the aisle. I was nearly to the door when, from the corner of my eye I spied my father sitting at the far end of a row in the back of the church. He was dressed in jeans and a sweatshirt, and I knew right then and there that there was no way he was showing up for the reception.

After what seemed like the world's longest photo session, first at the church and then at a local park, we finally got to the hotel to find the cocktail hour already in progress. I plucked a Swedish meatball from a waiter's tray, then quickly located Jayne who was standing at the bar with a glass of wine in her hand. She looked very comfortable, considering the only people she knew had been gone most of the day. When she saw me, she waved me over and handed me a beer.

"Thanks," I said as I took it from her and downed half of it.

"Whoa, slow down," she laughed, "You're a lightweight these days."

"Good thing, too. I gotta get a buzz going if I'm gonna make it through my two-and-a-half-minute-one-man-show."

"Brody gave you the greenlight?"

"Yeah," I said, then downed the rest of the beer. "He told me to go for it."

"Well, I'd be lying if I said I wasn't looking forward to your solo debut."

We had a couple more drinks, then I took Jayne around and introduced her to some of Beth and Brody's friends. Considering how standoffish she could be, I was pleasantly surprised to see Jayne laughing and joking with everyone. She was actually kinda *fun*. I soon realized, though, that I wasn't the only one enjoying this softer side of Jayne. First, I noticed the way the guys we were talking to were looking at her; then I glanced around the room and saw more of the same. It seemed everywhere I looked there was some dude giving her the once over. I really couldn't blame them; shit, a guy'd havta be *dead* not to notice the way she looked in that dress. There was one guy a few feet away who was practically leering at her. After a few minutes it was starting to piss me off so I reached over and draped my arm across her shoulders. I did it very nonchalantly, though, and timed it perfectly with a little chuckle so it would look to Jayne like a friendly spontaneous gesture. I knew she wouldn't appreciate what she called my "Neanderthal overprotectiveness," but I figured she'd appreciate getting eye-fucked by some dirtbag even less.

The guy got the hint pretty quick and moved on, but I kept my arm where it was for a few more minutes just in case, then slowly slid it back to my side. Jayne had enough ammunition to bust me with - no sense in handing her any more.

I was glad when it was time to head into the reception – my buzz was starting to wear off and I couldn't deal with the small talk totally sober.

"Wow, this place is gorgeous," Jayne said, gesturing around the ballroom. I took in the orchid centerpieces and beautifully glowing candles and nodded in agreement. My sister had certainly outdone herself.

Jayne and I stopped to pick up her name card, then I walked her to her table. For a while, at least, I'd have sit at the head table with the rest of the bridal party.

"This'll be kinda awkward for you," I whispered, "but I'll come get you as soon as everyone's settled."

Jayne shot me an incredulous look. "*Awkward* for me? I'm not some social outcast, Jackson." She shooed me away with her hand. "Go; do your usher duties. I'll catch you later." Then, before I could even say okay, she was already pulling out a chair and introducing herself to the couple sitting next to her.

I hustled myself back to the head table, ignoring Tim's raised eyebrow as he glanced from Jayne to me. The rest of the bridal party was already seated, so as soon as I arrived Brody's brother gave a traditional best man speech then slipped me the microphone. I slowly stood, my palms already beginning to sweat.

I nervously walked over to the edge of the dance floor, where the DJ had his equipment set up. I cleared my throat as I lifted the microphone, wondering why, after all the gigs I'd played over the past year, I was so nervous now. Every eye in the room was on me, but all I could feel were Beth's.

"Hey, folks," I began, hating the tentative sound in my voice. "Uh, for those of you who don't know me, I'm Beth's brother, Jackson." I heard a couple good-natured hoops and hollers from the back of the room. "I'll make this quick 'cause I know everyone wants to get to the partying, but, uh, I couldn't let this day pass without doing something special for my sister. She's done a lot for me and Tim over the years, and believe me, the two of us weren't the easiest brothers growing up, especially once we hit high school." I looked over at Tim, who was nodding and chuckling to himself.

"Anyway, most of you probably don't know this, but my sister," I pointed toward Beth with the microphone, "was actually named for a song recorded way back in '76. The tune's called *Beth* and, honestly," I chuckled as I shook my head, "Beth, Tim and I always thought it was pretty lame. But over the years I've come to see the song differently and now I actually think it's pretty cool. I'm also guessing it probably held a lot of meaning for our mom." I felt myself choking up so I hesitated a beat. "So, *Beth*," I said as I grabbed my acoustic that the DJ had stored for me, then returned the microphone to its stand, "this one's for you."

The song lasted all of about two and a half minutes, but it felt a whole hell of a lot longer, and when I finished you could've heard a pin drop. A few seconds later Brody slowly put his hands together and little by little everyone followed suit until the entire room was on their feet applauding. I set my guitar down and when I turned back Beth was standing in front of me with tears in her eyes.

She grabbed me, hugged me tightly and quietly said, "*You* are *freakin' awesome!*"

"So are you," I whispered, not bothering to hide my own tears. We stepped apart just as Brody joined us and the DJ yelled something over the microphone. Within seconds, loud music was playing and the dancefloor was packed, but I headed straight for the bar and ordered myself a beer and a shot of jack. I downed the shot, still unable to believe how nervous I'd been up there. Maybe I still wasn't used to being sober.

"Hey, since when did you become such a crooner?" I turned to see Jayne take the spot next to me at the bar. "Seriously, what the hell was that? You were amazing."

"Ya think?"

She laughed. "Yeah, I do; I think you stunned everyone into silence."

"Was my voice shaky at all?" I asked.

She shrugged. "Not that I could tell."

"Good, I guess all my practice paid off."

We ate, mingled, drank a bit more. A lot of people came up to me and complimented me on the song, which was pretty cool.

After we finished dinner, Tim dragged me and Jayne onto the dance floor. I wasn't the best dancer but considering the drunken state of most of the other guests I doubt anyone noticed.

After about ten minutes the DJ switched to a slow song and our group began to disband.

"Hey, where're you going?" I said as I grabbed Jayne's hand and pulled her back. "You're not gonna leave me high and dry out here, are ya?"

"Well," she laughed, "I *was* going to get myself another drink, but -"

"*Another* one, wow," I joked, more than a little surprised as we moved together on the dancefloor. If there was one thing Jayne was not, it was a drinker. "That's not at *all* like you."

She was about to come back at me with what was sure to be one of the smartass comments I'd come to expect from her and now even enjoyed, when I saw her eyes flick behind me. Then I felt a tap on my shoulder and turned to find Tim standing next to me, smiling ear to ear.

"Mind if I cut in, bro?" he asked.

"Oh, uh, no," I said, caught off guard and for some reason feeling more than a little annoyed. "Go ahead."

"Dance?" he said to Jayne.

"Absolutely sergeant," she joked as she took his hand, "Gotta support the troops."

I watched as he took Jayne's hand and guided her into the sea of swaying couples, not wanting to admit that for the first time I hadn't been ready to let her go.

▲　　▲　　▲

I woke the next day with a pounding head, a mouthful of cotton and not the foggiest idea where I was. A moment later, it came back in a series of flashes: Beth and Brody at the altar, my shithead father cowering in the back of the church, my hit solo and far too many drinks at the reception, then staggering to my hotel room after. I sat up to look at the clock, the movement making my stomach clench in revolt. *Shit, haven't felt like this in a while.* Slowly, I reached over and grabbed the Advil and the bottle of water I'd placed on the nightstand in a moment of foresight before going to sleep. *Old habits do die hard,* I thought as I popped a couple of pills and chased them down with the water. Good to know I could still keep up, though; I'd matched Tim shot for shot. Speaking of Tim... I glanced to the other side of the room and realized the other bed had not been slept in. I smirked. Last time I saw my brother he was at the hotel bar, pounding back shots of who-knows-what with two equally hammered bridesmaids. *Looks like Tim got lucky.* I wondered vaguely which one he'd hooked up with. Maybe both of them. Well, he'd better get himself together – it was nearly noon and he was booked on a six p.m. flight to Dallas, or was it Houston? I wasn't sure.

I reached for my phone and sent a quick text to Jayne asking if she made it home okay. It was a bit overdue – by now she'd probably been at work a few hours – but I figured better late than never, right? A minute later her response came through: *Yeah, pops, safe n sound.* I chuckled to myself as I tossed my phone to the side. Musta sucked for her, having to drive all the way back to Staten Island that late.

I stretched lazily, then reached for the remote. Just a few minutes of TV, and then I really needed to haul ass. I had to get Tim to Newark, then be in Brooklyn by seven, and if I didn't throw a load of wash in at some point in between I'd be wearing my rented tux to practice.

Tim staggered into the room just I was getting out of the shower, and from the look on his face it had definitely been both bridesmaids.

"I don't wanna know," I said, eliciting a chuckle from him, "Let's just get going."

A half-hour later, we walked into my house.

"You want something to eat?" I asked Tim, but he grimaced and shook his head.

"Wake me up when it's time to go to the airport," he mumbled, then went to his old room to pass out.

I scarfed down a bagel and coffee, then got to work on the mountain of laundry. So far, everything was on schedule. I was sorting through the pile of clean socks and t-shirts strewn across my bed when my phone rang. I figured it was Jayne, reminding me about practice, so I was surprised to see Beth's name flashing on the screen.

"Hey, what's up? I thought you'd be on your way to sunning yourself in Cancun by now."

"Jacks, thank God I caught you," she said, her voice sending a jolt of panic through me. It was the same tone she'd had when she called to tell me our grandfather had been rushed to the hospital.

"What's the matter?" I asked anxiously. "Is it Gram?"

"Gram's fine," she assured me. "Listen, I don't want to get into it over the phone, you just need to get over here right away, and bring Tim."

"Okay, okay, we'll be there in a few." I ended the call, then went down the hall to find Tim already awake and headed for the shower.

"Beth wants us over at her place; says it's important."

Tim held up a towel. "I gotta shower, man. I reek. What's she still doing here, anyway? Shouldn't she be in Mexico by now?"

I shrugged. "I guess they're not leaving 'til tomorrow. Hurry up, though, she seemed upset about something."

"Okay, okay," he said, then closed the bathroom door. A second later, I heard the water running and ran back to my room to get changed.

When we got to Beth's place she hustled us into the kitchen where there was a small shoebox sitting on the table surrounded by discarded wrapping paper.

"You rushed us over here to show us your gifts?" Tim asked when he saw the box.

She looked between the two of us. "Yeah, but this isn't just any gift." She reached across the kitchen table and pulled the box closer. "This gift is from *Dad* and it's not just one gift, it's *three*." Again, she looked between the two of us. "There's one for each of us."

Tim and I looked at her incredulously.

"Did either of you see him at the reception? The gift was sitting with all the others. Was he there?"

We both shook our heads, but then I said, "I didn't see him at the reception, but I did see him in the back of the church. He must've gone to the hotel and dropped it off before anyone got there."

"So...what was in the box?" Tim asked as he peered inside.

"This..." she said as she held out her hand to reveal a key.

"What's it for?" I asked as I took a closer look.

"The *house*, Jacks. He gave me the fucking *house*."

"Holy shit," I said as I took the key from her and examined it. "Are you sure that's what it's for?"

"Yeah, and there's a letter too with contact information for a lawyer. I'm supposed to go see this lawyer and sign a few things and then it's mine."

"Jeez, what else was in there?"

"Two more envelopes – one for each of you." She handed each of us an envelope.

Tim opened his, which contained a much smaller key – one for a safe deposit box at a bank. Along with the key was information about the bank and box number, along with contact information for the same lawyer.

"Open yours, Jacks," Beth urged.

I carefully slit open the envelope, but all that was inside was a short, handwritten note saying that he'd left something for me at the house. I'd find it in his room.

"What's it say?" they asked at the same time.

I handed them the note, which they both quickly scanned.

"What the heck's going on?" Beth asked as she handed back the note. "Where is he?" She turned to me. "Jacks, when's the last time you saw him?"

"Other than the church yesterday..." I thought for a minute, "Come to think of it, he hasn't been around lately." It was true, he'd barely been home the past month or so.

"You don't think he..." Beth trailed off.

"What? Offed himself?" I scoffed as I glanced between the two of them. "Let's cut to the chase...that's what you're both thinking, right?" Neither of them said anything. "Well, forget it; there's no way."

"Well, where is he then?" Beth asked.

"Shit if I know, but I'm sure he'll show up sooner or later." Even as I said it I wasn't sure I believed it. Just another fucking mystery to add to the pile.

"So, what do we do?" Tim asked.

"Do? Nothing for now. The bank's closed today and you can't get in touch with the lawyer until Monday." I turned to Beth. "Tim's flight leaves in a couple hours and yours leaves first thing tomorrow, so we'll just haveta wait." I turned back to Tim. "You can call the lawyer Monday morning about the box, but I don't know how much info he'll give you over the phone."

Beth opened her mouth as if to argue, then she just nodded. I knew it was going to be near-impossible for her to enjoy her trip with this shit on her mind – *thanks, Dad* – but there was nothing more we could do at the moment.

On our way to the airport, Tim and I ran through a million and one scenarios about where our father could be, what he was thinking and if he was planning on ever explaining. I wondered if any of the answers lay with what was waiting for me at home.

I pulled up to the airport without much time to spare and got out to help Tim pull his bags from the trunk.

"It was great seeing you again, bro," Tim said as he reached over and hugged me. "Next time you and Beth gotta come to Texas. I'll give you the grand tour and you can check out army life."

"Sounds good," I said as I stepped back. "You better get going or you're gonna miss your flight." I walked around, opened the car door and got in. I was about to pull away when Tim knocked on the passenger side window and signaled for me to roll it down.

"What's up?" I asked.

"Hey, call me later and let me know what Dad left at the house for you."

"Will do," I said, but as I was putting the window back up he stopped me.

"Yeah?" I said through the half-opened window.

"Hey, what's the deal with your friend, Jayne? She, uh, seeing anyone?"

I was about to say no, then stopped myself. "Uh, yeah, I think she is."

He looked at me as if he wasn't sure he believed me, then he shrugged. "Too bad, I woulda liked to get to know her better."

▲   ▲   ▲

I couldn't concentrate for shit at rehearsal. All I wanted to do was get the hell outta there and back home to see what was waiting for me in my father's room.

When we finally finished up Jayne pulled me aside. "What's up with you tonight? It's like you're a million miles away."

"You're not gonna believe this," I whispered, glancing to make sure the guys couldn't hear. I wasn't ready to air my family's dirty laundry to them. I then quickly told her the whole story – the house, the key, the mystery waiting for me at home.

"Holy shit," she said. "The *house*? Your dad left her the *house*? That's unbelievable! No wonder you were so distracted all night." She thought for a minute. "Any idea what he left for you?"

I shook my head. "No fucking idea."

▲   ▲   ▲

I was actually grateful when I crossed the Goethals Bridge and saw the sea of brakes lights on the Turnpike. Seemed as soon as I left practice, all my curiosity about my father's "gift" drained away, leaving only anxiety. What the hell was it and why had he kept it separate from Beth and Brody's? It was not lost on me that out of the three of us I had the shittiest relationship with him. I spent the stop-and-go of the late-night construction traffic blasting the radio and thinking of excuses not to go home, and when I gave the finger to the jerkoff in a Beemer who made me miss my exit it was more habit than heartfelt.

By the time I got off at the next exit and circled back, another half-hour had passed. When I finally pulled up to my house, I was relieved but not surprised that my father's Chevy wasn't in the driveway. The vision of his disheveled appearance at the church the day before flashed through my mind, but I pushed it away. He hadn't really been around for years; this just made it official.

The house was dark and eerily quiet as I climbed the stairs to his bedroom. As soon as I flipped on the light I saw the envelope leaning against the lamp on his nightstand, my name scrawled across the front.

I sat down on the edge of his bed, then picked up the envelope and stared at it a minute before finally slitting it open. Inside was what looked to be a rather lengthy letter. When I slid it out and unfolded the pages, a photo went fluttering to the ground. I fought back tears when I saw it was the black and white of my parents sitting on the hood of an old Camaro, each holding a bottle of beer. They were both laughing, and my dad had one arm around her and the other raised up in salute.

I stared at the picture a moment, then pulled my cell phone from my pocket and silenced it before settling down to read.

Jackson,

You probably noticed there's only this letter and the photo attached. Please don't take it as a slight cause it isn't meant to be. I gave Beth the house cause I know how hard it is starting out, and I don't want her to have to struggle like me and your mom did. And I gave Tim the cash to help him get on his feet when he leaves the military.

You sure don't need no help from me cause I been listening to you practice out in the garage and up in your room for years and I got no doubt you're gonna make it fine on your own. You got that raw talent I never had – that most musicians only dream of – and it's gonna take you places. Whatever you do, don't waste it cause what you got's a gift.

Anyway, I know the only thing you ever really wanted from me was an explanation – the truth – but first you gotta understand one thing. Your mom meant EVERYTHING to me. The two of us, we planned that move to California for damn near two years. Anyway, circumstances changed and we both agreed I'd go on my own and she'd meet me later on, only it turned out to be nothing like I expected. I assumed the auditions I set up were just for me but that wasn't the case. All of them were open auditions with hundreds of other musicians. I was disappointed but still had myself convinced I had a shot. I can't remember how many times I was sent packing before I was finally taken aside and told flat out that I had the look but not the talent and that I might want to reconsider a career in music. Hearing that pretty much wrecked me, and I finally had to admit that maybe I wasn't as good as I thought. Going home and facing your mom as a failure wasn't an option, especially after all the hype. You gotta understand, she was my biggest fan, thought there was nothing I couldn't do. I bullshitted her for as long as I could, telling her how great things were going, but the pressure, it got to be too much so I started avoiding her calls. It was just easier. The few times I did pick up, I acted like a real dick and eventually we had a huge argument and she stopped calling. At first I was relieved, but with money running low and no prospects I knew I couldn't stay much longer. That's when I got the call from my brother saying that Mom had the baby and both of them were in bad shape. I panicked and got right on a plane back east. When the plane landed, I didn't even stop home, just took a cab right to the hospital. I took one look at your sister, so tiny and helpless, hooked up to all those machines. Shit, all I wanted to do was hold her and take care of her and your mom. That's when it hit me, I had an easy out, a way where I'd come out the hero. It was the coward's way, but you know your old man. I never told her the truth about California, and when she talked about going back I brushed her off and told her that for the time being we should stay near family and that there'd be plenty of time to think about going back later. She agreed and we got married. Even though those early years were tough, they were the best. We were so fucking happy with Beth and Tim and then you. Then, somewheres along the line, things started to change. I started to think maybe I left L.A. too soon. I started lying to myself, saying that maybe if I'd given it more time I might've made it. The easiest scapegoat was your mom. I started blaming her, telling myself she'd tricked me, that she never wanted to go to California, which wasn't true. She wanted it just as much as I did, but it was easier blaming her than admitting I never had what it took. It got so that every time I looked at her I was reminded of what might've been. I was a shitty husband and an even shittier father — especially to you. After she died I could barely look at you. Beth and Tim, when those two were kids, they were all me. But you, you were all her. With those green eyes of yours, every time I looked at you it was her I saw looking back at me, so I stopped looking. You were the biggest reminder of how I'd fucked up. I know I was awful to you as a kid, the way I always put you down, but I want you to know, Jackson, that it all came from the guilt I felt over your mom. I'm not trying to make excuses for what I done and I'm not asking you to forgive me cause I know what I did was unforgivable. I robbed you of your mother and I robbed you of your childhood and there ain't no making up for that. Just know that I'm truly sorry for the way things turned out and also know that I'd do anything to be able to go back and do it all over again. You, Beth and Tim don't need me around and I know damn well that I don't deserve to be part of your lives. But please know I'm there for you if you ever need anything.

Dad

P.S. The picture was taken the night we found out I'd scored the first audition in California. The two of us were out celebrating with our friends. My writing on the back is too faded to read, but it says, "Anna – Livin' out the dream! Luv ya, Ace." Keep it and know that there were lot of great times between your mom and me and that I loved her a whole hell of a lot.

I looked down at the letter for a moment, completely numb. This was what I'd wanted, right? To know what had happened between them? So why didn't I feel any better? I turned back to the photo a moment longer, and though I had seen it before it felt like the first time. Slowly, I folded the letter and returned both items to the envelope, then reached for my phone to call Beth.

▲   ▲   ▲

Weeks later, and despite my best attempts to forget it, I was still trying to come to terms with the letter. I debated calling my father, but what was the point? He'd been pretty clear about what'd happened with him and my mom, but the fact that he clarified why he'd been a dick didn't make him any less so. I guess it felt good to have him admit he thought I had talent, but that wasn't going to change anything either. Too much time had passed and too much shit had happened to go back and start over. When I called Beth and Tim that night to tell them about the letter, they said they felt the same. We'd even joked that he'd probably changed his cell phone number – never mind his I'm-there-if-you-need-me bullshit.

A few days later Tim called the lawyer, but like I thought, he couldn't get much info over the phone. The lawyer claimed he didn't know how much cash was in the safety deposit box, or if there was anything else in there; Tim would have to come back and go to the bank himself the next time he got leave.

Beth, on the other hand, met with the lawyer the day after she and Brody returned from their honeymoon. The lawyer told her everything was in order for her to take possession of the house - all she had to do was sign a few things. That's when she found out Dad had taken an early retirement and moved out to Arizona, where his brother Ronnie lived. Personally, I think the lawyer slipped, that Dad didn't want us to know where he went, but I didn't dwell on it. No matter where he lived, how many letters he wrote or how much shit he gave away, he'd never be able to make up for all the pain he caused.

▲   ▲   ▲

I'd never paid much attention to the Tribeca Film Festival before; to me, it had always seemed like a bunch of artsy-fartsy actors and wannabes cheesing for the camera. That all changed the minute I found out we were going, and in the weeks leading up to the premiere I'd devoured every article, post and – to my embarrassment – hashtag about it. Plus, it was my only diversion from the latest bomb my father had dropped on us. Since we'd opened those letters, Beth, Brody and I had divided our time between rehashing the past and moving their shit into the house. It seemed if I wasn't at rehearsal I was unpacking boxes of clothes and kitchen utensils or on the phone talking to Tim about it. Suddenly, the big day had arrived and I was slipping into a tux for the second time in a month. I was dying to down a beer or two, but I had to drive to Brooklyn where a limo – courtesy of the director – was picking us up.

I was the first to arrive at Matt's place, where I was greeted by Mia, his blond, anemic-looking on-again, off-again girlfriend. I'd only met her a handful of times since they seemed to be more "off" than "on." Tonight, she had poured her stick-thin self into a pink dress that left little to the imagination.

"Jacks!" she said, pulling me into a hug as if we were lifelong buds. Mia would fit in perfectly at the Festival.

"Hey, man," Matt called out from the bedroom, "Grab a beer. I'll be out in a minute."

He didn't have to ask me twice. I was on my second Heineken by the time Skid and his girlfriend du jour – a flashy-looking groupie whose name I didn't catch – arrived ten minutes later. I was just about to ask where Jayne was when the buzzer rang again. As she walked into the apartment, I couldn't suppress a double-take. Somehow she looked even hotter than she had at my sister's wedding, in a simple sleeveless black dress and shiny black heels that added a good four inches to her slender frame. Her makeup was dramatic, in contrast to her long hair, which was pulled back into a simple, sleek ponytail.

"Hey," I said, feeling slightly uncomfortable as I watched her accept a beer from Mia and settle herself onto a chair. In response, she raised the bottle and offered me a small smile.

Things had been different between us ever since the wedding. Not that we'd really spent any real time together. We couldn't practice at my place, what with Beth and Brody's shit all over the garage, and it seemed like when we practiced with the band everyone scattered to the four winds as soon as it was over. And when I did see her, she was quiet – not like in the past, when she gave me the cold shoulder, but almost shy. I couldn't quite put my finger on it. I wanted to ask her what was up, but ever since I'd fucked up in her apartment that night I'd been afraid to do or say anything stupid. I woulda chalked it up to some typical moody girl bullshit, but Jayne wasn't like other girls. For a moment I thought maybe she'd started dating that douche roommate of hers, but that took my mind to places I didn't want it to go, so I headed to Matt's kitchen and grabbed another beer.

I'd just popped the cap when Matt's phone went off.

"Limo's here," he called out, grinning. "Ready for our debut?"

He was as chill as could be. Didn't this fuckin' guy ever get nervous?

Once we'd all piled into the spacious limo, Skid popped open one of the four bottles of champagne that were in the back and poured everyone a glass.

"To DB and everything to come," he toasted and we all clinked glasses.

It's less than seven miles from Bushwick to Tribeca, but as usual that didn't mean shit. The limo driver pulled onto the Brooklyn Bridge and proceeded to creep along at a snail's pace. We didn't care, though, we were all enjoying the ride too much. We chattered about the movies being premiered that night and the stars we expected to see, and thanks to my recent research I was able to hold my own. Only Jayne wasn't talking. She also looked paler than usual, and I wondered if she wasn't feeling well.

Suddenly, we felt the limo pull up to the curb and roll to a stop. Everyone paused mid-sentence and scooted over to one side to peer out the darkened windows. Of the photos and video clips of the red carpet I'd googled, not one did it justice. A mob scene of the hottest people I'd ever seen milled about in gowns and tuxes, smiling and hugging and doing that kiss-kiss-on-both-cheeks thing. Cameras flashed from every direction, trying to capture the big stars and up-and-comers alike. Behind them, Spring Studios rose up from the sidewalk, a huge structure of glass and steel, and from what I'd read, with one hell of a rooftop deck. As the driver came around and opened the door, I thanked God we weren't performing that night, because I didn't think I could even hold my guitar, let alone play it. One glance at the others and I knew they felt the same. Even Matt looked a little peaked.

It seemed we took a collective deep breath, then climbed out onto the sidewalk – that is, all except Jayne.

"What're you doing?" I asked as I poked my head back into the car, "Everyone's waiting."

She looked at me blankly for a moment.

"Jayne, you okay?"

"Yes, yes, I'm fine," she said dismissively, then eased herself out of the car.

"Look, there they are," Matt said. I followed his gaze to the spot where the director of *Die Tryin'* was being interviewed by a reporter. A few feet away, the cast and crew stood chatting with some action movie star, I couldn't remember his name. Matt, Skid and their dates walked over to join them, and a second later Matt was laughing and joking with the reporter like he'd done it a million times before. Jayne and I followed and introduced ourselves to two actors who played the musicians in the movie. One shake of their clammy palms and I realized they were as nervous as I was.

A few minutes later, as if by some unspoken cue, the entire crowd began making their way toward the entrance of the theater. I held my arm out to Jayne and we walked behind the actors along the red carpet.

We were almost to the door when I felt Jayne's fingertips digging into my arm. When I glanced over, I noticed her wide eyes and a thin sheen of sweat on her brow.

"What's with you?" I whispered.

"I don't know...all of a sudden all these eyes are on us and I feel like I'm freakin' out."

I felt the same but seeing Jayne like this was a surprise.

"You're kidding, right?" I laughed. "We're on stage playing three or four nights a week with just as many eyes on us; this is no different."

"Yes, it definitely *is* different. I feel so...so exposed. I don't even feel like myself...you know, dressed like this and without my keyboard in front of me."

Suddenly, it made sense. Even in all the selfies she'd tweeted she was wearing her usual heavy black eye makeup and gothic garb; it was her armor, just as my guitar and a cold beer were mine.

"I get it," I said, meeting her eyes. "But we're gonna do this...together. Besides," I chuckled, "nobody's interested in us – they all wanna see the movie stars."

She nodded and took a tentative step forward, but I could actually feel her shaking as we walked into the theater. I thought it might be more relaxed once we were inside, but there were even more cameras. Mostly people wanted shots of the actors and actresses, but they took a few of us too. After a while I barely noticed the flashes, and even Jayne loosened up enough to smile for a few pics.

A few minutes later we were being shepherded again, this time to the screening room. Almost without thinking, I grabbed Jayne's hand and led her to the row reserved for the band. When we got there Matt, Skid and their dates were already there, so Jayne and I scooted across to the first empty seats and sat down. When she glanced down at my hand still locked on hers, she slowly pulled it back.

I waited for her to hit me with some kind of sarcastic comment about holding onto her hand too long, but instead she very softly said, "I...I think I'm okay now."

I nodded, relieved that the lights were dimming. More than anything else about this evening, Jayne was stressing me out. I spent the first twenty minutes of the movie with eyes darting around the room, trying to scan the faces for a reaction. But then I heard the music, *our music,* begin to play, and they all just faded away. For the next hour and a half, I forgot about Jayne, my father, and just about everything else. It wasn't because the movie was so great – I mean, it wasn't bad but it wasn't going to win any Oscars – but how fuckin' weird it was to see Dirty Bushwick's songs coming from four total strangers. I told myself this was how John Cafferty must've felt when Eddie and the Cruisers came out. The movie was way before my time but I'd caught it on HBO, and I'd even seen the Beaver Brown Band when they played in Atlantic City a few years earlier. Difference was, they were already established before Hollywood got involved, whereas we were hoping the movie would launch us.

Before I knew it, the end credits were rolling and I heard the sounds of polite applause echoing in the theater. I glanced around again, but it was impossible to gage the reaction to the music in this kind of setting. It's not like this chichi crowd was going to boo and throw shit at the screen if they didn't like it.

I stood from my seat and saw Matt inching down the row toward me, a huge grin on his face. "Fuckin' surreal, huh, man?" he said as he grabbed my shoulder.

"You can say that again." I glanced around at the rapidly emptying theater. Next to me, some woman was talking to Jayne about the movie, and hopefully, giving props to the soundtrack. "So, is the limo going to take us back to Brooklyn?"

"Back to Brooklyn? Are you kidding? We're going to American Cut, baby!"

"American – huh?"

"American Cut... fancy steakhouses a few blocks from here...?" Matt paused. "For the afterparty...? Jacks, you really have to get out of Jersey more."

"I know what an afterparty is," I said, trying not to sound annoyed, "I just didn't know we were going."

Matt grinned again. "It's the most important part of the night – where all the real networking happens – and besides, I'm starving."

Twenty minutes and a few blocks later, we were squeezing through another thick throng of people whose outfits cost more than I made in two years. Everywhere I looked there was some late-night talk show host or some other familiar-looking face. Matt and the others had melted into the crowd, so I grabbed Jayne's hand and headed toward the nearest bar. When we got there it was three-deep, so Jayne left me there to wait and headed off to the ladies' room.

I was just about to catch the bartender's attention when I heard a voice behind me say, "'Scuse me, are you from Dirty Bushwick?"

My head whipped around to see this edgy-looking dude with jet black hair shaved on one side, his hand outstretched toward me.

"Yeah, um, yes, I am," I replied, completely taken off-guard. He introduced himself, then started asking about the band and our history, even said he dug our "cool, distinctive sound." I answered every question on autopilot, because once he said he was from Rolling Stone Magazine, I couldn't think of anything else. Fucking *Rolling Stone*! I wouldn't even have remembered his name if he hadn't pressed a business card into my hand.

"I'll be in touch," he said, then disappeared into the crowd before I could even ask how he would be in touch; I hadn't given him my number.

I looked down at the card. His name was Robbie Smith. Like everything else, it seemed familiar. With so many famous people milling around, it was like the whole night had been one big déjà vu moment.

Jayne returned a moment later. "Sorry," she said, "The line was a mile long." She peered at me. "You okay? You look dazed."

I handed her the card.

"Jayne," I said slowly, "I'm a hell of a lot better than okay."

▲ ▲ ▲

I tried not to be too disappointed the next morning when I read the reviews for Die Tryin', most of which were mixed at best. A few called the story unoriginal, which I couldn't argue with, though I did think the acting was better than the cast was given credit for. I snorted in disgust. *What did you think, Jackson? That some movie was going to launch the band?*

I had just set the phone down on the table when it started to ring. Jayne's name flashed across the screen and I figured she was calling to commiserate.

"Hey – I know, I just saw-"

"Oh my God," she screamed in a tone I'd never heard before, "Is this unfuckingbelievable or what!?" She then began to ramble so quickly I couldn't make out much – something about *trending*.

"Huh? Jayne wait, slow down."

She proceeded to tell me that her Twitter account was blowing up about Die Tryin' – how the lead actor was so hot - blah, blah, blah - but more importantly how amazing the soundtrack was. Some guy even compared it to *Almost Famous*, which I thought was pushing it but who's complaining? For the first time, I truly understood the benefits of social media.

Though the movie would end up with a limited release, thanks to the Twitter buzz it did garner a bit of a cult following, mostly because of Dirty Bushwick.

True to his word, Robbie Smith had been "in touch," which for him meant a full-page spread featuring up-and-coming indie bands in New York. Though the article didn't center around us, it did dedicate quite a bit of space to "the band behind the band." That, along with the attention generated by the movie, helped us land a recording contract with Sony.

Turns out Matt had been right about the afterparty — it *was* the most important part of the night.

He was a little slower when it came finding us a manager, something we apparently should've done as soon as we were approached about the movie. Luckily, we weren't screwed over by the film company, and now with the recording contract we couldn't afford to wait any longer. When the following week he announced he'd found someone he liked — an industry guy named Artie Reynolds — we immediately agreed. We trusted Matt completely.

Once Artie took over, things started to quickly snowball. By the first of June we were on a plane to L.A. to record our first album. Artie put us up in a sweet four-bedroom house on the beach, and though we were too busy to really enjoy it, it was a fuckin' rush to wake up to the sight of the ocean every day. Wanting to ride the momentum from the movie and the article, he also set up a string of dates in some local clubs and college campuses. I don't know how he did it, but every single campus concert was completely sold out, and later we heard a couple of the clubs had to turn people away at the door. For every one of those shows I was even more nervous than when I first joined the band.

What was supposed to be a two-week trip turned into a month when Artie announced he'd added a few shows in the Bay Area. I guess there weren't any houses available so the record company put us up in a hotel instead. I was expecting to be squashed into a room with Matt and Skid, so when the bellman escorted me to my own suite and carefully placed my ratty suitcase inside, I almost wept with gratitude.

♦ ♦ ♦

A couple nights later, I'd just slipped into bed to watch TV when I heard a knock on my hotel room door. *Sonofabitch.* We'd just finished back-to-back shows at one of the colleges and all I wanted to do was decompress for a bit. The trip had been great — better than I had even imagined — but I was exhausted.

I grunted in annoyance as I flung the sheet off me and padded to the door. Probably someone from the front desk, I thought, though what they could possibly want with me at one in the morning, I couldn't imagine. I pulled open the door and was surprised to find Jayne standing there with a bag of Cheetos in one hand and a deck of cards in the other.

"Feel like company?" she asked, waving the bag of Cheetos back and forth. She was wearing flannel pajama pants and a t-shirt, her long hair wet and twisted into a ponytail-slash-knot thing on top of her head.

"Absolutely," I said as I stepped aside to let her in.

I watched as she crossed the room, sat down at the edge of the bed and tore open the Cheetos. She held the bag out to me. "Cheet?"

I sat down next to her, took a handful from the bag and popped a few in my mouth. "So, what's up with the late-night visit? Couldn't sleep?"

She shrugged then picked up the remote and started flipping through the stations. "Something like that."

I reached into the bag of Cheetos and grabbed a few more.

"Nothin's on," she commented as she muted the TV. "You wanna play some cards?" she asked, but she was already opening the deck.

"Sure. How 'bout Spit?"

"You're on," she said as she tucked her legs underneath her and started dealing. "But I'm warning you, my nickname is *Lightning* in the local Spit circles."

"Uh...Spit circles?" I asked, raising an eyebrow. "I didn't know there was such a thing."

She didn't answer, but I saw the hint of a smile tug at her lips.

I turned to face her on the bed, crisscrossing my legs in front of me. I began to gather my cards and tried to figure out a strategy to make *Lightning* eat her words. Once we started to play, though, I realized that I wouldn't be needing much of a strategy after all since *Lightning* barely made a spark. I briefly wondered if she'd ever even played at all.

"Jackson..." she began as she gathered up the cards after another loss. "Can I ask you something?"

"Yeah, Lightning," I snickered. "Shoot."

She didn't seem to notice my attempt at humor. "Are you...scared?"

"Scared? Scared of what?" It seemed such a random question.

"Of all this..." She motioned around her. "Of everything that's happening."

"Like what?" I asked, my brows furrowed. "You mean like with the band or is this some kind of philosophical question and you mean like with the world in general?" I chuckled, but I honestly didn't know what she was getting at.

"I'm being serious, Jackson." She sounded annoyed. "I mean with the band; with all of us. It's all...all changing so fast."

"Yeah...but...that's a good thing, isn't it?"

She sighed. "I used to think so but now, I don't know, now I'm not so sure."

"What the heck are you talking about? The changes, they're all for the better. And hey, I was talking to Reynolds last night and he said there's a lot of buzz going around about us and..." I gave her a cheesy grin as I imitated Artie's voice, "You can't beat buzz, right?"

She smiled, and repeated, "Yeah...can't beat buzz," but without much enthusiasm.

"Hey..." I put my hand on her knee, half-expecting her to swat it away. She didn't. "I know it's gotta be more than our 'great buzz' that's got you so wound up, so spill, what's really bothering you?"

"You're right," she admitted as she picked at the remains of her chipped black nail polish, "It's more than that."

"So...what gives?"

She let out another sigh. "It's just that I don't want to lose sight of who I am – who *we* are, as a band. I guess I don't want us to ever, you know, sell out. Shit, maybe I'm getting ahead of myself. I mean, we haven't even released our first album, but I can't help it. This is the kind of shit that keeps me up at night." She turned and looked up at me. "Do I sound crazy?"

"Um, maybe a little, but, hey, everybody's got their hang-ups." I reached behind me, grabbed the nearly empty bag of Cheetos and scooped out the last few. When I finished, I said, "You know, I used to always say to L-" I stopped myself before I could say Leah's name and quickly rephrased it.

"Used to always say to myself that I didn't care if I was playing to crowds of hundreds of people or just a handful, so long as they loved the music as much as I did. To me, it's never been about fame, it's always been about the music. The four of us work well together because we all feel the same way, right? *So*, that being said, I don't think you have to worry about any of us selling out."

"It's just that I've been doing this for so long and now that we're so close, it just, I don't know, just feels scary."

"Hey, you know what feels scary to me?" I didn't wait for her to answer. "The last few shows we did I swear I saw my dad in the audience, like he's haunting me. Now *that's* crazy."

She laughed. "Yeah, that's pretty crazy."

"So, see, we're all a little crazy in our own way."

"I guess so," she sighed, but I could see her mood had lifted a bit. "And another thing," she blurted out, suddenly shifting gears. "I hate these friggin' hotel rooms. I liked it when we were in the house with all of us together. Shit, I'm actually starting to miss Eddie."

"*Eddie?*" I said a little harsher than I'd intended even though I knew she was kidding.

She laughed. "Just trying to make a point." She picked up the remote and unmuted the TV. "Feel like watching a movie?"

"Yeah, sure. That's what I was gonna do before you got here with your bag of Cheetos anyway."

She started clicking through the list of on-demand choices and exclaimed, "Hey, Pulp Fiction!"

"Never saw it."

"You're kidding," she said as if it were the craziest thing she'd ever heard. "How is that possible?"

I shrugged. "I don't watch a lot of TV."

"Pulp Fiction isn't TV; it's a *classic*," she said as she scooted to the top of the bed and grabbed two of the extra pillows I'd requested at check in. "And Travolta at his finest, I might add, so sit back 'cause you're in for a wild ride."

As the movie started she continued chattering, something about Uma Thurman in a Twist contest. I was just about to tell her to stop giving things away when she fell silent.

"Hey," I said a few minutes later, "This is a pretty cool -" I stopped myself when I looked over and saw Jayne was sound asleep.

I watched the movie for a few more minutes but soon I too was fighting to stay awake. So much for the wild ride, I thought as I clicked off the TV. For a moment I debated waking her so she could go to her own room, but she looked so comfortable I didn't have the heart. I carefully pulled the two extra pillows out from under her head so she wouldn't wake with a stiff neck. Then I pulled the sheet and blanket up over her since I had the air-conditioning cranked up, and, finally, lay down beside her. She was probably going to be pissed when she found me there, but the only alternative was to sleep on the floor and I wasn't about to do that.

As it turned out the joke was on me because when I woke the following morning she was gone. I was actually a little disappointed since I was looking forward to busting her about being in my bed.

I'd even planned out what I was going to say... *Uh, Jayne, I just wanted to apologize for last night. I mean, I guess I didn't realize when I answered the door in my t-shirt and sweats how, uh, enticing I looked. But, wow, never expected you'd be so overwhelmed that you'd go so far as to climb into my bed!*

She'd turn beet red for sure. Yep, Jayne could definitely dish it out, but I doubted she'd be able to take it.

While I was lying in bed snickering about my clever plan gone awry, I heard my phone go off with a text. It was from Jayne: *Picked up bagels, I'll be over in 5.*

As soon as I saw the word bagels I realized how hungry I was; except for the Cheetos I hadn't eaten since the previous afternoon. Jayne knocked on the door just as I was finishing a quick shower. I briefly toyed with the idea of answering the door with just a towel wrapped around my waist and a wink, but decided I'd be pushing my luck and instead pulled on shorts and a t-shirt before opening the door. Jayne was standing there with a bag of bagels in one hand and awkwardly balancing two bottles of Snapple in the other. I grabbed the Snapples from her and stepped aside to let her in.

"Cool," I said, "Breakfast in bed; well, almost."

"I was up early; figured, why not?" she said as she placed the bag of bagels on the little round table by the sliders that lead to the balcony.

I pulled out a chair and sat down as I popped open my Snapple. I could barely keep the smile from my face as I unwrapped the soft poppy seed bagel and took a bite. *Not bad for California.*

We bullshitted a few minutes about the changes Matt wanted to make for the show that night and what we were going to do that afternoon. Turns out we both planned on taking it easy and hanging by the pool. I was just about ready to start my little good-natured tease when she said something that made me hesitate.

"Hey, listen," she began, not meeting my eyes as she picked at the label of her Snapple. "I, uh, just wanted to thank you for last night."

"Thank me? Thank me for what?"

"For, you know," she shrugged, "Just listening. Sometimes I get these crazy thoughts running around my head and I start to freak out a little. Talking to you really helped clear my head. So, uh, thanks again for listening."

She actually had me momentarily tongue-tied with her very out-of-character speech; then quick as a wink she shifted gears again.

"Hey and by the way, Mr. Lightweight," she said, sounding all full of herself. "You fell asleep during the movie last night. I figured I'd leave before you woke up and started accusing me of trying to entice you again."

My eyes went slightly wide and just as I was about to call her on her bullshit, I stopped myself because oddly enough I couldn't tell if she was *actually* bullshitting me or if she really *did* believe what she was saying – that I was the one who fell asleep first. Whatever the case, I decided to let it go. As much as I might not have wanted to admit it, I liked having her in my room last night and was suddenly afraid that if I called her on it she wouldn't come again.

The following night was our last show and then we'd be heading back east in the morning. So far there was no word on a release date for the album, but when we met with Artie he assured us it would be within the next couple months. He also assured us that most likely there'd be a much lengthier tour scheduled for soon afterward.

"Rest up, guys," Artie said, "Because if this tour is any indicator of what's to come I'd say your album's gonna do pretty well." He shook his head in disbelief. "Heck, my guess is that you guys are headed for some pretty big things."

As it turned out, Artie was a little off-base because, although no one could've predicted it at the time, Dirty Bushwick was poised to explode onto the music scene with a force like *no one* could've imagined.

CHAPTER 52 - LEAH

I stretched out across my bed, cell phone still in hand. Two minutes earlier I'd hung up with Molly after trying, unsuccessfully, to talk her out of coming over "pronto" (her word, not mine). That meant I had about ten minutes to close my eyes before she was ringing the bell.

"You don't understand, Leah," she'd said with that on-the-edge-of-hysteria tone she used so often these days. "I have major gossip that needs to be discussed *in person*."

I rolled my eyes. "No, Molly, *you* don't understand. I've just spent ten hours going through deposition transcripts and all I want to do is sleep before I have to do it all over again."

The truth was, just hearing Molly's voice was enough to make me wish I was back in the office. Considering how I felt about my job, that said a lot about my interest in her latest drama.

It was my second summer interning at my Uncle Kevin's law firm in Morristown, which was one summer more than I needed to realize I *hated* law. That left me with just one year of college left and no idea what I wanted to do with my life, but at least I'd figured out in enough time to dodge a bullet, right? *Wrong.* When I told my dad I'd decided against law school, he flipped; basically told me to start studying for the LSAT now or my free ride would end with college graduation. What happened to the man who'd always said I could do whatever I wanted with my life? I didn't know, but that guy was long gone, replaced by one of those parents who just want their kids to follow in their footsteps.

Sometimes I wondered whether I'd really wanted a legal career or if it had just been something to bond with Chase over. Lotta good that had done me. After that day in the cafeteria, it was as if I didn't even exist to him. He wasted no time replacing me, though. Two weeks later, Molly rushed home from a party to "break the news" that he was making out in the corner with some freshman soccer player. I tried to play it off but it was like getting kicked in the gut. I hated the girl - who I'd never seen or met – until the day I walked into the cafeteria and saw them having lunch. In the brief moment before I hightailed it out of there, I saw the adoring look on her face, the same one I'd had every time I was with him. This girl probably didn't even know about Missy and their bullshit open relationship. And, as it turned out, it wasn't open very long. When we got back to school after this past Christmas break, I learned - again, courtesy of Molly – that he and Missy had gotten engaged. *Engaged*! Missy might've been fine having her *boyfriend* run around on her, but obviously had no intention of affording her *fiancé* the same freedom because Chase wasted no time in dumping the soccer player, a tidbit Molly had gotten right from the teary-eyed girl herself.

Not that my dating life was much better. After things ended with Chase I went on bit of a bender, going out nearly every night to one party or another. I figured since I'd landed the captain of the lacrosse team – aka the hottest guy in school - I'd have no problem finding someone else. But as I quickly found out, most college guys aren't looking for much beyond drunken weekend hookups, and those who *were* got snatched up pretty quick. That's when I finally realized what an idiot I'd been, assuming that Chase and I were exclusive. When he graduated in May and returned to Ohio, I felt nothing but relief.

Through it all I hadn't thought much about Jackson. Actually, if I was being honest, I hadn't thought about him at all. It was almost like our relationship never happened, and if not for my alcohol-fueled blowout with another athlete, it might have stayed that way.

Corey Turner and I had been seeing each other for a few weeks, ever since Molly dragged me to a soccer game. He was on the team, and though I really didn't give a crap if they won or lost I did love watching his well-defined quads as he ran or kicked the ball. Turned out they did win, so after the game we headed for his dorm, where they had a celebratory keg waiting. Corey stuck mostly to a small band of loyal followers, but I accidently on purpose bumped into him on a trip back from the bathroom and struck up a conversation. He asked me to hang out the following night, and that was that. He was hot and funny, and I was just starting to think it might actually be a fun semester after all.

One Saturday, we made plans to meet up a party. I was looking forward to it – even agreed to go an hour early because Molly was worried she'd miss her latest crush. As we walked in, I prepared myself for the boring small talk I'd have to make until Corey showed up. A few shots of tequila helped, and I was feeling good as I followed Molly through the crowded living room as she searched for the object of her affection. That's when I saw Corey, sitting on the couch with some bimbo cheerleader on his lap. He didn't even blink an eye when he saw me. Actually, if I remember correctly, he even patted the spot next to him as if to say *why don't you join us*. I let loose with a few choice words, which didn't seem to bother him but made me feel better.

On the way back to our dorm, I raged first about Corey then the rest of the assholes I had hooked up with recently. As Molly nodded and mmm hmmmed alongside me the thought *Jackson never would have done this to me* ran through my mind. Jackson was a decent guy – more than decent, he was a great guy. It really was too bad that he was such a loser because if he weren't, things could've ended up a lot differently between us. Maybe I was being too harsh calling him a loser. It wasn't his fault that all his hard work had gotten him nowhere.

It was water under the bridge, anyway, so there was no sense rehashing it. I may have gone about it in a shitty way (who was I kidding, I had been a total bitch), but it'd been the right thing to cut my losses. The way things were headed, I would've ended up having to support Jackson and his hobby and I definitely would have wound up resenting him for it.

The sudden knock on my bedroom door pulled me from my thoughts.

"C'mon in, Mol," I said as I stretched.

Molly walked in, her expression a mix of apprehension and nervousness. She gave me a tight wave then sat down on the edge of my bed.

I laughed. "What is it *now*?"

Lately it seemed she was always worked up over some stupid thing, so despite her facial expression I had no reason to suspect that she was about to drop the mother of all bombs.

"What's up?" I asked when she still hadn't answered.

"I think maybe you'd better sit down for this," she began in true dramatic Molly fashion.

"I *am* sitting Molly," I said impatiently. "C'mon," I motioned with my hands, "Spit it out; what fire do you need my help putting out now?"

"This is not a *fire*, Leah, it's more like an *inferno* and it's not mine, it's all yours."

Though I didn't quite believe her, my stomach clenched anyway.

"What is it, Mol?" I asked nervously.

"Get your laptop; you're gonna want to see this for yourself."

I grabbed the laptop from the night table and brought it over to Molly. "Okay, now google *Die Tryin'*," she instructed.

"Die Trying?" I asked, "What's that?"

"*Tryin'*," she corrected. "Just do it."

I did what I was told and was relieved when a movie ad popped up. Obviously this had nothing to do with me. "Yeah, so?"

"Read it," she said as she motioned with her eyes to the screen. "The whole thing."

"Fine," I huffed, already thinking how quickly I could get rid of her so I could take a nap. *Up and coming band, blah blah blah, lead singer overdoses, blah blah blah.* I skimmed the rest and was about to tell her to just spit it out when the words *Soundtrack by Dirty Bushwick* stopped me dead in my tracks.

"Soundtrack by..." I mumbled, "What. The. FUCK?"

Suddenly my mind flashed back to a conversation I'd had with Jackson way back. He'd babbled on about a movie and some contract he wanted my dad to look at, but I'd barely listened. Then I remembered how preoccupied I'd been with Chase at the time. I turned to Molly, my mood quickly darkening.

"How...how did you find out about this?"

She opened her mouth to explain but I held a hand up. "Hold on a minute," I said, as I marched across my room and swung open the door. "Dad!" I yelled down the stairs.

A moment later I heard him at the bottom of the stairs. "Yes, Leah, what is it?"

"Did Jackson ever come see you about -" I began, but he cut me off.

"Who?"

"Really, Dad? *Jackson*. My ex. It hasn't been that long."

"Yes, yes, of course. Sorry, hon."

"Did he ever come talk to you about a movie? Or a contract having to do with a movie?"

"No," he said, but then quickly corrected himself. "Yes, he did have me look over a contract, but I referred him to a colleague because it wasn't really my area of expertise." He scratched his head. "Whatever happened with that?"

I was furious as I yelled down the stairs to him. "Jesus Christ, Dad! And you didn't think to tell me about it?"

"Watch your mouth, Leah. I probably just assumed you knew."

My mother heard the yelling and came to his side. "Don't you speak to your father like that," she called out, then turned to him. "Honestly, I don't know why you let her get away –"

I slammed the door and turned toward Molly, who had a shocked look on her face. "How did you find out about this?"

"The actor, the one who plays the lead - Trevor Marlan - you know, the super-hot guy that's going to be in that new action flick with Vin Diesel...?"

I nodded impatiently. You had to be living under a rock not to have heard of Trevor Marlan.

"Well, anyway, I googled him. I was just curious to see if he'd done anything else and that's when I found out about *Die Tryin'*."

I thought for a minute. "Well, I guess the movie didn't do very well. I mean I've never heard of it; have you?"

"No, I'd never heard of it either, but..." She trailed off.

"But what?"

"There's more."

"More?"

"Yeah. After I found out about Dirty Bushwick doing the soundtrack, I googled the band. Leah, they're all over social media – Twitter, Instagram, Facebook, you name it." She hesitated a beat. "Judging by the tweets, seems they've been pretty busy. There was even mention of them working on an album." She paused, obviously to let it sink in before she dropped the next bomb. "Oh, and I also found this." She was typing something into the search and then turned the laptop towards me.

I looked at the page of images she'd pulled up for a moment before I realized what it was I was looking at. There in front of me was Jackson and the band all decked out at what I assumed was the premier of *Die Tryin'*. When I saw the caption – *Dirty Bushwick at the Tribeca Film Festival* – I actually felt nauseas.

One of the pictures taken in front of the theater had Jackson walking arm-in-arm with a stunning girl. I zoomed in on it to get a better look and when I did it left no doubt in my mind. By the way he was looking down at her they were definitely a couple. I knew that look well, as it was a look once reserved only for me.

"I wonder who that is," I said to myself, or so I thought.

Molly looked at me. "Leah, are you serious? Take a closer look...that's *Jayne*."

"Jayne?" I repeated as I looked closer. "Holy shit! That bitch!"

"Bitch?" Molly chortled. "You're kidding, right?"

I ignored her. "I betcha she had her eye on Jackson from the get-go. Probably even poisoned him against me as she waited in the wings ready to swoop in when he was at his most vulnerable."

"Oh my God, Leah. You can't be serious. You *do* realize that you're the one who dumped *him*, right?"

"That doesn't matter," I said, not willing to admit that Molly was right. "And anyway, who knows when this began? Maybe he was cheating on me all along with that tramp."

"Uh, no...if I remember correctly it was *you* who was cheating on *him*. So...I guess that makes *you* the tramp."

"Fuck off, Molly."

"*Fuck off, Molly?* Really? Hey, save your little hissy-fit, Leah, *I'm* just the messenger." Molly stood and started walking toward my bedroom door. She had her hand on the knob when she turned her head and added, "You made your bed a long time ago, Leah, so don't turn around now and try to blame anyone else."

⋏　　⋏　　⋏

I woke up the following morning feeling groggy after a long night of trolling the internet. It started with a simple post about *Die Tryin'*, which led to another article and another link and a thread of comments and so on. Before I knew it, it was well after midnight and I hadn't even gone near their social media accounts yet. As I started wading through their tweets and Facebook and Instagram posts, I told myself I was only checking how well the band was doing; it wasn't until I signed off that I realized I hadn't seen one thing about Jackson being involved with anyone. It wasn't until then that I also realized it was what I'd been looking for all along.

As I rolled over to hit snooze, the events of the previous evening came flooding back, namely, the argument with Molly. Over the years we'd gotten into it a few times – well, more than a few – but we had never talked to each other the way I had to her. I had been a complete bitch, and all because she'd hit a nerve about Jackson and how badly I'd messed up with him. Crazy as it sounded, whenever I thought of him I'd pictured him exactly where I'd left him – in a band that was on the fast track to *Nowheresville*. I'd even imagined him pining away for me, like at any moment I could've snapped my fingers, cried a few crocodile tears and gotten him back. It was a thought that made me feel better whenever some guy I was seeing turned out to be another noncommittal loser. Finding out the band was doing well, and that Jackson had probably moved on, was a bitter pill to swallow, especially considering the state of my own life at the moment.

I knew I'd have to call Molly and apologize, but not yet. I needed aspirin, at least two cups of coffee, and a little more time to process everything without her two cents added to the mix.

Half an hour later I emerged from the shower and walked over to the closet to find something to wear to work. That was my intention, anyway, but it seemed I could do little else but stare at several pairs of boring dress pants and polyester shirts. Suddenly, I found myself across the room, pulling open the top drawer of my nightstand. There it was, the guitar-shaped ring Jackson had given me. It seemed like a lifetime ago. I ran my index finger along the intricate design before slipping it onto my finger. It really was a beautiful piece.

That's when I noticed my cell lying on top of the nightstand. Might as well get this over with, I thought as I reached for it.

"Yeah?" Molly answered on the second ring. Her tone was extra snippy.

"Hey, it's me."

"Listen Leah, I don't have anything to say. I'm still pretty pissed off about yesterday and -"

I cut her off with an apology before she could say another word. I knew Molly couldn't possibly stay mad at me long, especially when she was surely dying to discuss the "Jackson debacle," as she called it, in greater detail. I was right, too; just seconds after I uttered the words *I'm sorry* she'd forgotten all about how angry she was.

"So, what are you gonna do?" she asked.

"*Do?* Nothing." I shrugged as I twirled the shiny silver ring around my finger. "I mean, really, there's nothing I could do at this point, right?" Truth was, I had already considered calling Jackson and dismissed the idea just as quickly. What would I even say at this point?

"I guess not," she conceded. "Hey, I don't want to be the one to say it -"

"Then *don't.*"

She ignored me. "I *told you so*, Leah. I don't mean to sound like a bitch, but it's true. Right from the start I said to break up with him, but no, you had to keep sneaking around behind his back. Didn't you ever consider, even for a minute, that it might blow up in your face?"

"Are you done?" I huffed.

She wasn't.

"You didn't even have to tell him about Chase; you could've just said something lame like you needed some space. Yeah, he would've been upset, but he'd have eventually accepted it and at least that way you wouldn't have completely burned your bridges."

I bit back an angry retort, not only because I didn't want another fight with her, but because I knew she was right. There was certainly no denying the fact that where Jackson was concerned, my bridges were toast.

CHAPTER 53 - JACKSON

The angry sound of the car horn jolted me from my thoughts. I glanced in the rearview mirror to see the guy behind me – why were the biggest tools always driving Beemers? – gesturing wildly.

"Alright, alright," I muttered, but I was smiling as I inched a car-length forward. It's not like it would make much difference in bumper-to-bumper traffic on the BQE. How many times had I made this trip, screaming at everyone to *just fuckin' move* so I wouldn't be late to practice?

Today, though, I found it hard to summon even the tiniest bit of anger. Today, I didn't care about the traffic, didn't care if it took me four hours to get to Brooklyn. Because today, I wasn't just headed to practice. I was headed home.

The lead on the apartment had come courtesy of Matt just before we left for the month-long tour of the West Coast college circuit. He'd seen the place himself - apparently, one of his many friends with benefits lived there but was moving to Chicago for a new job. It was on the small side, he told me, but in an area on the cusp of regentrification, which was to say it was still relatively reasonable and on the verge of being cool.

The first time I looked at the place I literally laughed out loud. *On the small side? Really, Matt?* The place was a glorified closet! Then I looked again and couldn't deny the place had a certain charm. It was on the third floor of an older building and had two big windows that faced the street, which meant it got lots of light. The wood floors needed polishing, but the appliances in the nearly non-existent kitchen seemed fairly new and in good condition. Best of all, it was only a few blocks from the garage where we practiced.

The car horn beeped again, the tool's equivalent to the last word. I half-heartedly held up a middle finger, but it was more out of habit than rage. Smiling, I looked in the rearview mirror to see the guy screaming in response. Ahh, Brooklyn.

Sure, I got a serious case of sticker-shock when I heard the rent, but I told myself to get over it. Things were going amazing. We'd only been back from L.A. a couple of days when we got word that Sony was pushing up the release date for our album - self-titled "Dirty Bushwick" – to the first of November - a full month earlier than expected. The tour had far surpassed everyone's expectations, and that, along with the "buzz" – Artie's favorite word - already generated from *Die Tryin'* was why Sony had decided to move up the release date.

Living close to the action wasn't the only reason I wanted to move to Brooklyn. As it turned out, my living situation in Jersey was about to get a lot more crowded. Beth had finally convinced Gram to sell her condo and move in with her and Brody. Gram insisted that since she was going to be living with them that they take the money from the sale of the condo and put it towards fixing up the house. Beth finally agreed, but decided the first thing they'd do would be to add a bedroom and bathroom to the first floor so my grandmother wouldn't have to deal with the stairs. Anything left over they'd use to update the kitchen. And, there was even bigger news - my grandmother wasn't going to be the only new resident at the house. I'd arrived home from L.A. to Beth's announcement that she and Brody were expecting a baby. I couldn't have been happier for all of them, but I was sure glad I had the apartment lined up. Heck, it was one thing living with Beth and Brody but it was quite another thing entirely living with the two of them, my grandmother *and* a baby.

CHAPTER 54 - LEAH

About a week later Molly and I were roaming around the lush green campus of Ramapo College waiting for the first in its series of four summer concerts to begin. Though the college was in Mahwah, just a ten-minute drive from my parents' house in Franklin Lakes, it was the first time I'd ever been there. As we walked along the quiet paths between the beautiful collegiate brick buildings, I couldn't stop thinking about how different my life would've turned out had I chosen to commute to a place like this rather than live away.

"You've gotta let it go, Leah," Molly said, interrupting my thoughts. "Chalk it up to a lesson learned and *move on*."

No doubt she was sick of my responding to every attempt at conversation with little more than a nod or a one-word answer. Hey, I'd told her I didn't want to go tonight, but as always, Molly wouldn't take no for an answer.

"You're right, I know you are, but I just can't help thinking of what might've been if I hadn't messed everything up with my crazy infatuation with that asshole Chase."

"What might've been?" she said with a chuckle, "I'll tell you *what might've been*. It would've been *you* strolling the red carpet with that hot-as-hell rocker and it would've been *you* jet-setting around the country with the band." She stopped herself and turned to me, suddenly full of excitement. "Hey, imagine you had to drop out of school because you were being stalked by the paparazzi!"

"That's overkill, don't you think?"

She shook her head. "Actually, I don't. I mean, have you read Jayne's Twitter feed?"

I snapped my head to her. "Don't tell me you actually follow her."

"Are you kidding? *Of course* I follow her – Twitter, Instagram, Facebook – you name it. I like being able to say *I knew them when.*"

"Does she know you're following her?"

She laughed. "I doubt it; they've got *thousands* of followers." She looked at me curiously. "You're telling me you haven't checked out their social media?"

"I've glanced at it a couple times," I admitted, "But I don't obsess about it."

She kept her eyes trained ahead as she mumbled a *yeah, right* that I pretended not to hear.

"Who are you waving to?" I asked when I saw Molly's hand suddenly shoot up.

"I told you I was meeting a few people here."

I didn't recall her telling me that, but then again, my mind had been on other things. I followed her line of sight until it landed on a small group of people, a couple of whom I recognized from high school. They went to Ramapo and presumably had told Molly about the concert – some local up-and-coming band.

We milled around the crowded lawn as we waited for the show to start, finally settling on a spot not far from the stage. About ten minutes later I told Molly I was going to find a bathroom, which I prayed was an actual bathroom and not some gross port-o-potty.

No such luck. I spied the row of blue plastic structures with the words *Royal Flush* painted on the sides. For a moment I thought about leaving, but the idea of waiting out the concert with a full bladder was not an appealing one. I held my breath and slipped inside, my hand already on my zipper.

When I came out I didn't feel like going right back to Molly and the others. They kept asking all those questions that everyone asks when you run into them post-high school. I decided to loop around in the opposite direction and check out what else was going on.

I was about halfway to the other side of the stage when I saw him standing not twenty feet from me. My mind said, *It can't be*, yet my body was stopping dead in its tracks and my heart was slamming against my chest. Holy shit, it *was* Jackson. If he turned just a little he would see me standing there like a deer caught in the headlights. Glancing this way and that, I saw a group of guys huddled around a large cooler of beer a few feet away. I quickly stepped back behind them, where I would be able to watch him unnoticed.

There was something different about him, and it wasn't necessarily the way he looked, though I did notice he seemed a bit broader and his hair was a tad bit longer than I remembered. But it was more than that. His stance...the way he gestured when he spoke...the way he held his head - it all exuded a confidence he hadn't had when we were together.

I watched as he turned and said something to the guy next to him. Must have been funny, too, because the guy burst out laughing. At first I thought it might be one of the other guys in the band, but then he turned my way and I realized it was Brody, Jackson's sister's boyfriend. Was the rest of the band there, I wondered, and by the rest of the band I meant Jayne. Immediately, I felt my hopes rising; maybe I'd been wrong about them being a couple.

I was about to back away and head back to my friends when I saw Brody lightly tap Jackson's arm then walk away. I didn't know where he was going or how long he'd be gone, but before I could think too much about it I had squeezed past the guys and was inching toward Jackson as if my legs had a mind of their own. Suddenly I was barely ten feet from him. I saw him reach into his pocket and pull out his phone. He briefly glanced at it then returned it to his pocket. I paused for a beat, wondering if this was just one more in a long line of huge mistakes on my part. Maybe it was, but there was no way I was going to leave the concert without talking to him. I moved closer so that I was right behind him, then slowly reached out and tapped him lightly on the back without the faintest clue what I was going to say when we came face to face.

CHAPTER 55 - JACKSON

When Brody took off to grab a slice, I slipped my phone out of my pocket to see if Jayne had texted that she was on her way. We were always eager to check out new bands – something we rarely got to do now that things had begun to take off with Dirty Bushwick. Even tonight she hemmed and hawed because it was a hike to come all the way from Staten Island; but she'd heard good things about these guys and she wanted to show her support for the drummer, who was a good friend of Brody's.

Just as I was slipping my phone back into my pocket, I felt a light tap on my back. A small smile played on my lips because every once in a while, something really cool happened – I was *recognized*. It didn't happen often, but when it did, man, it was so friggin' awesome. It was something I still hadn't gotten used to and probably never would. If I was being honest, I really didn't want to.

I put a big smile on my face and got ready to greet my fan, but when I turned, there, standing right in front of me was *Leah*. Stunned, all I could do was stand there, eyes wide and mouth hanging open like a moron. I couldn't believe that after all this time I was looking right at her and it wasn't the lying cheating bitch looking back at me. It was *Leah*.

"Hi, I, uh, thought that was you," she said nervously as she shifted her weight from one foot to the other. "How...how are you?"

You mean, besides feeling like I've seen a ghost...?

A million and one thoughts raced through my head, though, oddly, none of them involved me reaching over and strangling her for what she did to me.

400

"Uh, good, I'm good," I said finally as I slipped my hands into my front pockets. "You?"

She nodded. "Me, oh, yeah, I'm, uh, good…" She gestured around. "You, uh, checking out the competition?"

"Nah, just here for the free beer," I said as I reached down and grabbed a Bud from Brody's cooler. I cocked my head toward the stage and added, "The drummers' a friend of Brody's; they went to high school together, I think."

"Oh…." she nodded again.

This is getting super fucking awkward.

"So, uh, who ya here with?" I asked as I looked around because I didn't really know what else to say.

"Molly, yeah, I'm here with Molly and a few other friends."

"Moll's here, cool. How's she doin'?"

"As dramatic as ever. She's good, though."

I chuckled remembering how theatrical Molly could be sometimes. "And how's school goin'?"

"Good, sc…school's good," she stuttered. "Heading into senior year." She then proceeded to tell me a little about her classes and some job she had at a law office. I watched her closely as she rambled on about school and work, but no matter how hard I tried I couldn't make myself feel any anger toward her. It was weird, but I just didn't care.

She was speaking so quickly, like she was nervous, and it began to dawn on me that maybe it was because of me – that *I* was making her nervous. And I have to admit, there was a little piece of me – okay, maybe a big piece of me – that kind of enjoyed it. As she rambled on, I just nodded and inserted comments in all the right places, but I wasn't really listening. I was paying more attention to the way she touched my arm every couple of minutes, or the way she leaned in as if she was sharing a secret with me. She was flirting. That's when I began to wonder - how much did she know about what was going on with me? With the band? A simple Google search would've told her the whole story. Was that why she was acting that way?

I continued to watch and to listen, not to her words, but to her tone. That's when I saw it - clear as day - her eyes were filled with regret. But was it regret over what she'd done? Maybe, but I couldn't help but think it probably had more to do with my success and the fact that she wasn't a part of it.

Suddenly her eyes darted to the left of me but before I could turn to see what'd grabbed her attention, I felt an arm slip around my waist. I didn't have to look twice to know that it was Jayne who'd just sidled up next to me.

If I thought Leah was talking fast before, it was nothing compared to how fast she was talking now. It was actually comical to watch her stumble over her words after Jayne greeted her with a simple, classy, *Hi Leah*, as she leaned her head against my shoulder.

I had to bite the inside of my cheek to stop myself from laughing as Leah nervously returned Jayne's greeting and then made some lame excuse about having to get back to Molly before hightailing it outta there.

As soon as she'd disappeared into the crowd I turned to Jayne, her arm already slipping from my waist.

"Hey, sorry," she said. "I probably shouldn't have done that, but..."

Before she'd had a chance to finish her sentence, I leaned down and kissed her. I don't know what I was thinking – *clearly, I wasn't*. In that moment, though, it just seemed like such a natural thing to do. I quickly realized my mistake, though, and pulled away.

"Shit, sorry," I said as I hastily stepped back. "I...I don't know why I, uh...hey, you're not gonna go all kung fu on me again, are you?"

"Oh relax." She rolled her eyes. "You were trying to make it look real; I get it."

"Uh, yeah, right; exactly, of course that's what I was doing." I paused. "So we're good?"

"Yeah, we're good." She glanced over her shoulder in the direction Leah had headed. "Is that the first time you've seen her since...?" She trailed off.

"Yeah," I said as I glanced past her, hoping Leah was well out of sight. "Fuckin' weird."

Jayne looked over her shoulder again. "Hey," she began as she turned back. "I know I should've let you handle that yourself because it's really none of my business, but after the shit she pulled I just couldn't help myself."

"Forget about it," I said and I meant it. I was glad Jayne did what she did because, honestly, I had no idea what else to say to Leah. As it was, the encounter had already been pretty awkward and if Jayne hadn't swooped in when she did I'm sure it would've only gotten worse. Plus, at this point so much time had passed – nearly two years – that I could pretty much say I'd moved on and didn't really give a shit anymore. Sure, there were times I'd fantasized about what I'd say if I ever ran into her, but those days were long gone. I was in a good place now. I slid my eyes to Jayne who had stooped down and was picking through Brody's cooler. A *really* good place.

▲   ▲   ▲

I felt off the next day, or maybe distracted was a better way to describe it, and I knew why. As much as I tried to convince myself that what Jayne said was true - that I'd kissed her only to make things look convincing to Leah – I wasn't so sure. Truth was, I really didn't know why I did it, but I doubted it had anything to do with "making it look real." At this stage of the game I didn't give a shit what Leah did or didn't think. Now, much as I tried, I couldn't seem to get that kiss out of my head.

That odd feeling lasted a few days, surfacing usually after I saw or spoke to Jayne. Then Dirty Bushwick got even busier, and Matt started putting even more pressure on us to write new songs, and I eventually forgot about the kiss and the feelings it evoked. It was stupid anyway. Jayne and I were just friends – good friends – but nothing more.

▲   ▲   ▲

A few weeks later, Jayne and I were sitting on the floor of my apartment surrounded by empty Chinese food cartons and beer bottles. I'd only been in the apartment a short time, yet it felt more like home than Jersey had in ages. Not to mention dealing with that long-ass commute – it was a wonder I even made it to practice, let alone putting the extra time we had to in order to keep Dirty Bushwick's momentum going. Like tonight, after finishing up at the garage, Jayne and I decided to keep at it because the apartment was only a few blocks away. If I'd been in Jersey we would have hemmed and hawed and maybe even called it quits. Then again, the two of us were on such a high over the news we'd just heard that commute or no commute, it would have been hard to unwind.

A few hours earlier, just before we started jamming, Matt had gotten a call from Reynolds – apparently a few of the suits from Sony wanted to get together and iron out some last-minute details. They'd be in the city Thursday and wanted to know if we'd be available that night. So, fingers crossed, that meant in just a few days we'd find out the official release date of the album. It was all Jayne and I could talk about, starting from the short walk to my apartment to the last bites of dumplings, lo mein and General Tso's chicken.

"I should get going," Jayne finally said as she stood. "It's getting late."

I glanced at the clock on the kitchen wall. "Shit, it's nearly one," I said as I got up from the floor.

I began gathering the empty food cartons and bottles as Jayne fished around in her bag for her ringing phone. When she pulled it out and looked at it I saw her brow furrow.

"That's weird," she mumbled, "It's a Florida number."

I shrugged, not thinking much of it as I threw the empties into the trash, but then I heard her quietly ask, *Is he alright?* I stopped what I was doing and looked over.

"Okay," she said politely to the person on the other end. "Thank you for calling. I'll try to get there by morning."

She ended the call but continued staring down at her phone, a fearful expression on her face.

"What's up?" I asked, eyeing her warily.

She was still staring down at her phone when she said, "It's, uh, my dad. There's been an accident. That was the hospital on the phone." She looked over at me. "They're taking him into the O.R. now."

"Shit, how bad is it?"

"They...they don't know; won't know until they get him into surgery."

In an instant I was brought back to that rainy night when I was seven years old and we got the call from the hospital saying my mother had been in the accident. I remember having this horrible feeling in the pit of my stomach as my father sped down the highway towards the hospital with the three of us kids in the back seat. It was probably the same thing Jayne was feeling now.

I moved across the room to her, but she shook her head as if any comforting act on my part would make her lose it.

"I...I gotta get down to Tampa," she said, her voice cracking. Then she grabbed her bag and quickly threw it over her shoulder. "Can, uh...can you let Matt know?"

"Jayne, wait, you shouldn't be alone. I'll go with you."

She shook her head again. "I'll be fine Jackson, really."

"Well, let me at least drive you to the airport."

"Airport? Shit, I gotta figure out flights, which airport..."

"Let me do it," I quickly offered. "You go home, pack a bag and I'll check on the flights. Once we figure it out I'll pick you up and get you to the airport."

"Yeah...okay; that'll be a big help." She reached out and touched my arm. "Thanks, Jackson."

"Jayne...it'll be okay."

But she was already headed out the door.

⋏   ⋏   ⋏

As soon as Jayne left I got on my laptop and started checking flights from New York to Tampa, finally finding a six a.m. out of JFK that would get her into Tampa a little before nine. I was just about to book her a ticket when I shook my head and said *fuck it* and booked one for myself too. She'd probably be pissed but I didn't care. Better to have her pissed at me for going than for her to be alone if the news wasn't good.

I texted her with the flight information and told her I'd pick her up at four, then started scrounging around the bottom of my closet for my backpack. I quickly tossed in some clothes, my toothbrush, razor and phone charger before zipping it up.

At a little past four I got to her apartment and pulled out my phone again. A few minutes after my text she appeared in the doorway, and even in the dark I could tell by the set of her shoulders how upset she was, and how could she not be? I knew how tough it was to hear news like that; I couldn't imagine how shitty it was to hear it from so far away.

As she approached the car I reached over and unlocked the passenger side door. She got in and tossed her bag into the back.

"Thanks for doing this, Jackson," she said as she reached behind her for the seatbelt, then buckled it.

We drove most of the way in silence except for when I commented here and there about the lack of cars on the road. We ended up getting to the airport in no time.

"What're you doing?" she asked when I pulled into the long-term parking lot. "You could've just dropped me off; I don't need you to walk me in."

I didn't say anything but when she saw me reach into the back seat and grab my backpack her eyes got wide.

"Jackson, I told you I didn't need you coming with me." She sounded annoyed but I didn't care.

"Yeah, I knew you'd be pissed, but I still say you shouldn't go alone."

"Jackson, we can't *both* miss the meeting with Sony. How does that look?"

"Relax, it's not a big deal. I got myself a roundtrip ticket; I'll be back in plenty time for the meeting."

"Fine, whatever," she said in a tone that conveyed she wasn't up for arguing.

Once we were settled at our gate, I went to grab us a couple of coffees. On the way back, I stopped at one of the kiosks and bought Jayne a bunch of magazines and some snacks, anything to distract her from thinking about her dad. I'd been in her shoes more than once and doubted it would help, but it was worth a shot anyway.

It felt like an eternity before we finally boarded, but at least once we did we took off almost immediately. It was a smooth flight and we even touched down in Tampa a few minutes early. As soon as we were allowed off the plane we grabbed our bags from the overhead bin then quickly maneuvered our way through the crowded airport. Once outside we jumped into the first cab we saw and headed for Tampa General, where her dad would hopefully be out of surgery.

When we got to the hospital I waited back in the lobby while Jayne spoke to the nurse at the front desk. I couldn't hear what they were saying but I saw a lot of nodding and sympathetic looks from the nurse. The nurse handed her a pass and pointed to the elevator across the hall. She craned her neck around and when she spotted me, motioned with her head to come over.

"What's up?" I asked.

"He's on the fifth floor, intensive care." She pushed the elevator button. "It was a hit and run." Her voice sounded shaky.

"Shit," I said as I shook my head.

"The doctors'll fill me in on the details when they get in."

"Can you at least see him?" I asked as the elevator doors opened.

"Don't know," she shrugged as we stepped inside.

I pushed the button for the fifth floor as the elevator doors began to close.

▲   ▲   ▲

I shifted slightly in the waiting room chair, trying to ease the aching in my left butt cheek, and wondered what sick son of a bitch designed such an uncomfortable thing to sit on, and what even sicker son of a bitch had decided to place it outside the ICU. Weren't the people sitting there suffering enough? After what felt like hours, I grabbed the TV remote and flipped through the stations before returning to the local news I'd had on earlier. Fuckers, I muttered, noting they were still covering the same bullshit story. Some scandalized local politician – the usual crap. I'd just shut if off again when a bleary-eyed looking Jayne appeared and took the seat next to me.

"Were you able to get in to see him?" I asked.

"Yeah, but he's still unconscious." She looked utterly exhausted. "Why don't you split. This could be a while..."

"You sure?" I asked, because although I wasn't crazy about leaving her there, I knew at some point we'd need somewhere to stay.

"Yeah, I'll be fine. I want to be here when he wakes up."

"Alright," I said as I stood and flung my backpack over my shoulder, "I'll see what motels are around." Then as an afterthought added, "Unless you'd rather stay at your dad's?"

She shook her head. "Not an option – he lives about forty-five minutes from here. There're some motels down the street, I figured we'd stay in one of those..." She began digging in her bag. "Let me give you my card."

I put my hand on her arm. "Really, Jayne? Don't worry about it."

She nodded. "Alright, just text me the name."

"Okay, and you text me if you need anything or if you get any news, okay?"

She nodded.

⚔ ⚔ ⚔

The nurse at the front desk told me the best spot to hail a cab. I thanked her although it sounded more like a grateful grunt because at this point I was too exhausted to muster up anything more. I walked out the front doors of the hospital, hopped in the first cab I could find and slid into the back seat. After about five minutes I saw the string of slightly dilapidated motels serving travelers passing through and presumably other people visiting hospital patients. I randomly directed the driver to a Holiday Inn Express and with a sigh heaved myself out of the car. When I got to the room, I didn't even spend any time looking around for amenities – I just dropped my bag, kicked off my shoes and fell onto the bed. When I woke a few hours later I checked my phone but there was no word from Jayne. After I showered I decided I'd pick up some food and bring it to her in the hospital. I stopped at a deli I'd noticed earlier and picked up two turkey sandwiches, a couple bags of chips, some Snapples and a little pack of cookies for Jayne.

When I got back to the hospital I went up to the fifth floor and asked one of the nurses if Jayne's dad had been moved to a regular room yet. She must have thought I was a relative, because she told me he was still in ICU, then pointed down the hall where those rooms were. I slowly walked down the hallway, peering into each room until I spotted Jayne standing at her dad's bedside. Her back was to me and I was about to go in but stopped myself. I saw she was holding onto her father's limp hand as she reached up with her other hand to wipe away a tear. When I heard her choke back a small sob I took a step back, not wanting to intrude on what clearly was a very private moment.

I returned down the hallway and bypassed the nurse's station until I came to the waiting room where'd I'd been earlier. I put the bag of food on the small coffee table in front of me and waited. Jayne finally appeared about a half-hour later and slumped into the empty chair next to me. I wouldn't have thought it possible, but she looked even more exhausted than when I'd seen her earlier.

"The doctors said he's stable and it's just a matter of waiting until he regains consciousness to see how much damage there is...if any," she added hopefully.

"Maybe we should go back to the motel, eat something." I motioned to the bag of food. "You should try and get some sleep. You could come back first thing tomorrow."

Jayne shook her head. "No, I don't want to leave him. What if he wakes up and no one's here?"

"If he wakes up they'll call you and you'll be here in ten minutes, tops. The motel is practically around the corner."

She finally agreed, so after she checked in on her dad one last time the two of us headed to the Holiday Inn Express.

When we got there, I set the food out on the small round table in the corner of the room, but aside from two small bites of her sandwich and a few chips, all she ate was the little pack of cookies.

"I think I'm just gonna take a shower and turn in," she said as she yawned. "I want to be back at the hospital first thing in case he wakes up."

As soon as she was done I hopped in the shower for the second time that day. The water pressure wasn't great, but I didn't care. It felt amazing. The warm water relaxed my muscles while once again washing the grimy Florida humidity and slight smell of sick from the hospital off me. When I came out Jayne was already in bed. She appeared to be asleep, and not wanting to wake her, I slipped quietly between the cool sheets of the other bed and closed my eyes. I didn't bother turning the TV on. Who was I kidding? I was still so tired I would have been out before the first commercial.

"Jackson..." I heard Jayne quietly say a few minutes later. "...thanks for coming."

I turned my head and eyed her in the dark. "I thought you were asleep."

"I can't sleep." I heard the rustling of sheets as she turned over. "I keep thinking..." she trailed off.

"He'll be fine, Jayne," I said with a confidence I didn't necessarily feel.

I heard more rustling of sheets and a few seconds later her warm body slid in next to me.

"I'm scared, Jackson." Her voice sounded small. "Is it alright if I lay here with you for a while?"

"Uh, sure," I said swallowing hard as I moved over to give her room while mentally cursing the fact that I hadn't bothered putting on a t-shirt.

She curled up next to me as I awkwardly put my arm around her.

We laid there for a while, not saying anything; then, just when I thought she'd fallen asleep, she moved her hand so that it was resting on my chest. I didn't think much of it, aside from the fact that I liked the feel of her warm hand on my bare skin. A couple minutes later I felt her leg twist around mine. I didn't move as I tried to block out how good it felt to have her body pressed up against me like that. I kept my breathing steady. The last thing I wanted was for her to realize the effect she was beginning to have on me. Slowly she slid her hand down to my stomach where she let it rest. She pressed herself closer so that half her body lay on top of mine then rested her head in the crook of my neck. I tried to ignore my now racing heart as I felt the warmth of her breath against my skin. When she tilted her head slightly and kissed the side of my neck my eyes shot open in surprise. *What the fuck was she doing?* It wasn't until her fingertips slipped beneath the waistband of my shorts, though, that I knew I'd have to stop her because she was about to do something I was sure she'd regret in the morning.

I quickly grabbed her wrist before it got any lower. "Jayne, wha...what are you doing?"

She twisted her wrist out of my grasp then, placing her hand lightly over my mouth, she moved real close to my ear and whispered, "Don't ask me to stop."

She was putting me in a nearly impossible situation. If I stood firm and said no, I was rejecting her; if I went ahead, I was taking advantage.

"Jayne...wait..." I stalled.

Before I could get out the rest of my sentence, she'd straddled me. Other than the light from the moon coming through the break in the curtains, the room was dark. I could still see her staring down at me, though, with a hand resting on each of her thighs, her breathing now matching my own.

"Listen," I began, "You're upset; you're not thinking clearly."

She hung her head low and brought her hands up to cover her face then choked back a small sob. "My dad...he's all I've got, Jackson. If he doesn't make it, I...I've got no one."

I'd never seen her like this - could've never *imagined* seeing her like this. I grabbed hold of both her hands. "Hey, that's not true...you got me."

She collapsed in tears onto my chest, her arms wrapping around my neck like a vise. I didn't know what to say so I didn't say anything, instead I just held her. Then in what seemed like a moment of clarity she lifted her head and took my face in her hands and said simply, "...I'm sorry," before leaning in to kiss me.

$$\blacktriangle \quad \blacktriangle \quad \blacktriangle$$

The next morning, I waited until I heard the motel room door shut before turning over. Definitely not my proudest moment, but after last night I didn't know what to expect from Jayne and decided to buy myself some time by pretending I was still asleep.

When I reached for my phone on the floor beside the bed, I found she'd left me a short note. It was scrawled on a little motel notepad she must've found in one of the drawers and said only that she'd left for the hospital and would see me later. I stared at the note for a moment as if there might be some kind of hidden meaning in it, but quickly realized how ridiculous that was and tossed it aside.

I leaned back against the pillows and began to replay fragments of the night before in my mind. Jayne kissing me...the moment I gave in and started kissing her back. When that happened all sense of reason flew right out the window. Clothes were quickly tossed aside and the next thing I knew I had her on her back, my hands roaming over every inch of her. Her skin...I'd never felt skin that smooth before. And her hair...she usually had it tied up either in a ponytail or knotted some crazy way, but last night it was loose and still damp from the shower and looked hot as fucking hell. It wasn't until afterward, though, that it hit me – I mean *really* hit me. I'd had sex with Jayne - *Jayne*. I reached over, grabbed the pillow next to me and covered my face with it as if that would solve everything.

What happens now, I wondered. Maybe nothing...Maybe it was just one of those things that just kind of *happens*. Who was I kidding? It hadn't been that way for me; in fact, it wasn't until now that I realized I'd been fighting my feelings for Jayne for a long time. The countless hours spent together, long after practice with the band had ended or the latest song had been written; the touch that lasted a little longer than necessary when we pretended to be together for the sake of some clingy fan – through it all those feelings had been there, just beneath the surface. I thought back over the last couple years, over the many times we'd hung out, and immediately Beth and Brody's wedding popped into my head. I vividly recalled how I'd felt like punching out that dirtbag who was eye-fucking her during the cocktail hour. And *Tim*...when he cut in during the reception. I remembered having a weird feeling as I watched the two of them slow dancing...Jealousy? Possessiveness? I wasn't sure, which is probably why I had dismissed it at the time.

I also thought about the *Die Tryin'* premiere...holding onto her as we walked the red carpet together; how good it felt having her so close. And the tour out in California...that night we hung out together in my hotel room...her *sleeping in my hotel room.*

But as crazy as it sounded, all that was nothing compared to the way I'd felt when she sidled up next to me at the concert and, in front of Leah, quietly slipped her arm around me. If I had to pick one moment when I should have known I cared for Jayne, that was it. *That's* why I had kissed her that day. It wasn't because of Leah, it was because I'd wanted to do it for so long and in that moment, *it just felt so right.*

▲   ▲   ▲

I had never taken so long to leave a motel in my life. A fifteen-minute shower, followed by two checks of the room and three checks of my backpack under the guise of making sure I hadn't left anything behind. All to postpone the inevitable face-to-face with Jayne. It was ridiculous, I knew. Whatever drama last night stirred up paled in comparison to everything she was going through with her dad. Even so, that didn't stop the knot from forming in my stomach the minute I closed the motel room door behind me. It also didn't help that the generic *how're things going* text I'd sent earlier had gone unanswered.

I was still stalling as I approached the entrance to the hospital, I even took the stairs to the fifth floor. By the time I got to the waiting room and texted her to let her know I was there, I had to admit I was a full-fledged chicken shit.

It wasn't long before she appeared at the end of the hallway with one of the doctors. As they spoke, I was relieved to see the hint of a smile on her face - something I hadn't seen since we'd arrived in Tampa. As soon as she caught my eye, she motioned for me to come over. I nervously got up and began to make my way down the hall towards them.

"Good news," she said as she grasped my hand. "My dad's awake."

"That's great news," I said feeling relieved and a little awkward at the same time.

"Oh, uh, Dr. Ramos, this is my friend Jackson. He flew down with me from New York."

He stuck out his hand to shake mine. "Nice to meet you," he said politely before turning back to Jayne.

I stood by and listened as they finished their conversation, all the while hyperaware that she hadn't let go of my hand.

"Okay, so we'll touch base again after the MRI this afternoon," Dr. Ramos was saying.

"Sounds good," Jayne replied with a quick nod before turning back to me, her smile still in place. "Great news, right?"

"The best," I replied.

She shook her head. "I swear, I feel like I just woke up from a nightmare."

"I can imagine..." I trailed off, feeling slightly guilty that I was still replaying last night in my head and wondering if some small part of her was doing the same. "When you, uh, think'll get out?"

"Not sure," she said as she let go of my hand to grab her phone from her back pocket. She scanned it quickly before returning it. "He's not out of the woods yet. They have a few more tests they want to run before they'll consider letting him out."

"So...you'll be hanging around for a while?"

"At least until he's discharged, maybe longer. Depends on how much help he'll need."

"Yeah, he'll probably need you for a while," I agreed.

She glanced down, just then noticing the backpack in my hand. "What time's your flight?"

"Uh, one," I said awkwardly. "I'm gonna head to the airport soon."

"Yeah, you definitely should. You don't want to miss your flight and by the time you check in and get your boarding pass . . ." She reached out and grabbed my hand. "C'mon, I'll walk you down, it's nearly noon now.

We made small talk on the walk down to the lobby, mostly about her dad and what she thought his recovery would be like. When we got to the revolving doors, she stopped and turned to me.

"So, you'll fill Matt in on everything."

I nodded. "Sure."

"Tell him I'll call him at the end of the week. And that I'm sorry I'm missing the meeting with Sony."

"Don't worry about it; he'll understand."

She turned to me. "...and Jackson..."

"Yeah?"

"Thanks...for being here...you know, for everything. I couldn't have gotten through this without you."

Thanks for being here? I looked at her, trying to see what she meant, but her face was unreadable.

Before I had a chance to respond, she added, "You're the best," then she leaned up and kissed me.

That's when any doubts I'd had about where we stood disappeared.

I thought of nothing else the whole plane ride back to New York – nothing else but Jayne and the unexpected shift between us. I wondered what would happen when she got home, but I pretty much knew the answer. Knowing Jayne as well as I did, she definitely wasn't going to want to advertise this and, honestly, neither did I. The last thing we needed was Matt finding out and thinking we'd be distracted from everything we'd all worked so hard for.

I don't know about the rest of them, but I had never worked harder on anything; well, anything except maybe getting over Leah. I'd never thought it possible, but over the past year she had become little more than a distant memory and now I knew why. Jayne. Without her, I never would have gotten through what Leah did to me, let alone losing my grandfather right afterwards. And she did it without taking any of my shit. Hell, now I couldn't even imagine being with Leah – how I was *ever* with Leah.

Suddenly, a wave of exhaustion hit me; the past few days were finally taking their toll. I leaned my head back against the headrest as my lids began to slowly droop. Lately, it seemed as if every time I turned around something else was going my way. The album...the apartment...and now this.

The Sony meeting was awesome, at least it was once I got over the sticker shock at the bar Matt chose, some swanky place on the Lower East Side called Copper & Oak. I figured he thought the fact that it was a whiskey bar made us look sophisticated, and it might have, if we knew anything about whiskey. I mean, they had to have two hundred kinds. Good thing I double-checked the menu because some of them cost a couple hundred bucks a drink. The guys from Sony certainly seemed in their element and once we ordered they immediately got down to business, filling us in on the album release. Turns out it would hit the shelves in less than four weeks! They also said they were ironing out the details of the tour and that they had their eye on a mid-January start date. I was relieved when I heard that because Jayne would surely have everything squared away with her dad by then.

I called her as soon as the meeting ended because I figured she'd be on pins and needles, but though she sounded sort of excited, I couldn't help but notice she seemed kind of off. Or maybe distracted was a better word to describe it. At first I thought maybe her dad had had a setback, but that wasn't it. In fact, he was doing much better and might even go home sooner than expected. I chalked her mood up to the sheer exhaustion caused by the stress of everything she'd been through. Once she got back to New York and everything returned to normal, she'd be back to her old ball-busting self; I was sure of it. We ended the conversation with her saying she'd call the next day. When one day turned into three I called her and was genuinely surprised to hear that she had already returned.

"You're back?" I questioned, trying unsuccessfully to keep the surprise out of my voice.

"Yeah, I got back last night," she answered, like it was no big deal.

When I asked why she didn't tell me so I could pick her up at the airport, she mumbled a kind of non-answer.

When I questioned her again, she skirted around the issue, saying just that I'd done so much for her already and that she didn't want to bother me with anything else.

Bother me? Was she serious?

As crazy as her reasoning sounded, I decided to let it slide, not wanting to make waves after everything she'd been through.

It wasn't until I half-jokingly asked if she Uber'd home that I got my first inkling that something was up.

"Uh, no, um, Eddie picked me up," she answered in a tone that tried but failed miserably to convey nonchalance.

Eddie? WTF? Was she serious?

At that moment there was no pretending or playing it cool; in fact, I was too stunned to respond at all. Why would Jayne ask that douche to get her, especially when she knew how I felt about him, and especially after the night we'd spent together in Florida? Honestly, if it were anyone other than Jayne I'd say they'd done it purposely just to piss me off, but Jayne wasn't like that – she didn't play games. If Jayne was anything, she was a straight-shooter, always had been. At least that's what I'd always thought.

I decided it was best to hold my tongue and end the call before I said something I'd regret. Jayne had had a rough couple of weeks and probably wanted nothing more than to just relax at her apartment and unwind. As pissed as I was, I didn't want to add to her stress.

The next day I called her and asked if she wanted to stop by before we got together with Matt and Skid. I could fill her in on the details of the meeting with Sony since I'd just given her the basics over the phone while she was still in Tampa.

"Oh yeah, um, I already spoke to Matt about everything so I think I'm pretty much up to speed."

Was it my imagination or was she...*avoiding* me?

"Oh, okay..." I mumbled, "I'll just catch you later at the garage then..."

I ended the call feeling like I should have said something else, but what, I had no idea.

Later on at practice everything appeared to be fine. Everyone was psyched that the meeting with Sony went so well and things seemed to be on the fast track with the album release and tour. Jayne seemed to be back to her old self and I began to think it must've just been my imagination.

After we quit for the night we all headed to Token's for a celebratory beer. To be honest, I didn't feel much like drinking; I was just hoping to get Jayne alone, if only to ask how her dad was doing and if she needed anything. But she seemed to be glued to Matt's side, even trailing after him when he went to talk to one of the bar's owners. Again, I let it go, figuring she was just preoccupied with all the shit she had going on. It wasn't until I came back from the bathroom to find her gone that I again began to think something was up.

I was definitely pissed that she'd jetted so quickly without saying goodbye, but even more so that ever since she got back into town she'd been blowing me off every chance she got.

When I got home that night I thought about getting her on the phone and calling her on her shit. No, I thought, this is best done in person and when I didn't have three beers in my system. We were practicing again the following night, so I decided to wait until then.

I approached her as soon as Matt called it quits. Jayne, I noticed, hadn't even waited until the words were out of his mouth before she started packing up her stuff. No doubt planning for another quick getaway.

"Hey, uh, Jayne..." I began.

"Yeah?" she replied without looking up from what she was doing.

"Can I, uh, talk to you a minute?"

She hesitated. "Yeah, uh, sure," she said before turning around. "Gotta make it quick, though; I got like a million things to do at home."

"What's...what's going on Jayne? I've been trying to talk to you since you got back but I can't seem to get you alone."

She stared at me a moment, then said, "Well, now you got me, so talk."

Just then I heard Matt say he'd catch us later as the door closed behind him. Skid followed a few seconds later, leaving just the two of us.

"What the heck, Jayne? What's with the attitude?"

"No attitude; it's like I told you, I've got a lot to do at home, that's all."

I looked at her a minute, then decided to soften my approach. "Listen, I'm sorry, it's just that..." I shrugged. "I don't know, I'm worried about you. You haven't said anything about your dad and-"

"He's fine, Jackson," she said, quickly cutting me off. "The doctors say he'll make a complete recovery and he's home now taking it easy." She hesitated a beat. "Anything else?"

"What about you? How're you doing?"

"Me? I'm fine."

"Do you wanna, I don't know, maybe go down to Token's and get a beer, hang out...talk?"

"Like I said, Jackson, I've got a lot to do at home and I'm really beat... raincheck?"

I shrugged again, trying to hide my disappointment. "Yeah, sure, raincheck."

▲   ▲   ▲

Getting that "raincheck" proved to be nearly impossible. Every time I suggested we get together Jayne had another lame excuse at the ready. It was as if she had compiled a list. Finally, I'd had enough.

"We need to talk," I said one night after we finished up and Matt and Skid were just about to leave.

"Jackson, I can't, I'm -"

"Busy?" I hissed, cutting her off. "Yeah, I'm aware of your sudden *busy-ness.*"

"What's that supposed to mean?" she snapped and folded her arms across her chest.

I waited a beat until I knew the others were gone. "I'll cut to the chase, Jayne...are we gonna talk about what happened in Tampa or are we gonna continue to pretend like nothing did?"

"Fine, you want to talk about it," she said with a sweeping gesture, "Go ahead, talk."

After nearly two weeks of rehearsing what I wanted to say, I suddenly found myself tongue-tied.

"I'm waiting..."

I drew back at her tone, the anger I was feeling replaced by confusion. Why was she acting this way?

"I don't know, Jayne, I guess I thought we had something...some kind of connection..."

"Had something? Some kind of 'connection'," she repeated using air quotes. "Is that what you wanna call it? Gimme a break, Jackson...yeah, something happened, but let's not make it out to be anything more than what it was - a quick fuck in a cheap motel and nothing more."

She might as well have punched me in the gut. "You're kidding, right?" I didn't wait for her to answer. "A *quick fuck?* That's what you wanna call it?"

"Yeah, that's what I wanna call it because that's what it was."

"Seriously?" I said as I stared her down with narrowed eyes. "C'mon, Jayne; you're gonna stand there, look me in the eye and tell me it meant nothing? Really?"

She stared me down just as hard before saying, "It meant *nothing.*"

"You're full of shit and you know it."

"Don't kid yourself, Jackson," she huffed. "What? You think every time you hop in the sack with someone it has to 'mean something'? Believe me when I tell you, it didn't."

I looked at her, unable to hide the genuine hurt I felt. "You *used* me."

"I *used* you?" She laughed humorlessly. "Well, I sure as hell don't remember hearing you complain."

I was beyond pissed. I couldn't *believe* what I was hearing. Did she really feel that way?

"Do you have anything else to say?" she asked very matter-of-factly. "Because I really need to get going."

I started to step back and let her pass when I stopped myself. *Fuck it.* I wasn't letting her off that easy.

"Ya know what, Jayne? I'm *done* with this fucking attitude of yours."

She started to speak, but I put my hand out to stop her.

"You wanna blow off what happened in Tampa? Hell, I can't stop you, but either way I sure as shit don't deserve to be treated the way you've been treating me. I've dealt with a lot of shit the past couple years; fuck, I think I can pretty much say I've been through hell and back. But ya know what? I'm past it. Yeah, it's taken a while, but for the first time in maybe *ever* I'm in a good place in my life, a really good place. I've worked hard to get where I am and can honestly say I've fucking earned it. Especially with how far I've - *we've* - come with the band."

Again she looked like she wanted to interrupt but thought better of it.

"I don't know what *the fuck* happened with you, but what I do know is that life's too fucking short to waste trying to wade through other people's bullshit." I took a few steps back and gave her a long, hard stare. "You got anything else to say? Cuz otherwise, I'm done." She just stared back at me. "Yeah, didn't think so."

I turned and took a few steps toward the door then I stopped and turned back to her. She had yet to utter a word in response, not like her at all. "Oh, and hey, just a side note...no need to worry about any awkwardness on the home-front. I'll have *no* problem keeping things professional between us."

I paused for a beat, then reached for the door handle. Clearly she had nothing to say. "See ya around, then."

▲　▲　▲

I was so worked up over my run-in with Jayne that I couldn't sleep for shit that night. Her sudden about-face just didn't make sense. She'd made one thing clear, though, and that was that she obviously deemed what happened in Tampa a mistake. She clearly wanted nothing more than to go back to the way things were before, although judging from the way she'd been acting, I wasn't sure she even wanted that.

If Jayne wanted to erase what happened between us then fuck it, that was her choice, but there was one thing I knew for damn sure and that was I wasn't letting her shit affect my music. I remembered all too well what happened last time I let my personal life get in the way of the band and I had no intention of letting it happen again.

It was obvious early on that Jayne felt the same, because two days later when the four of us got together for practice, things appeared completely cool between us – on the surface anyway.

I actually convinced myself that things had worked out for the best. I'd always thought Jayne was different but as it turned out, she was just another psycho-bitch who didn't know what the fuck she wanted. In the meantime, I'd try like hell to put it outta my head and stay focused on what was really important - the *band*, the *album*, the *tour*.

▲   ▲   ▲

"Awesome session, guys," Matt said as he set his guitar down, "I hate to jinx us, but I think we're ready."

I tried to ignore the clenching feeling in my gut. Awesome, yes. Ready? I couldn't speak for the others, but I felt anything but ready. In fact, I felt nervous as shit.

I couldn't believe that in just three days we'd be on a tour bus to Baltimore, about to dive head-first into an experience most musicians only dream of. Unless of course we crashed and burned, making it every musician's nightmare. I kept reminding myself what Artie had said – that we had nothing to worry about because most of the shows were sold out and the album was still climbing the charts. If what he said was true, this would make last summer's West Coast tour of the college circuit look like fucking band camp.

I still couldn't believe all that had happened over the past few years. I'd like to think making it was inevitable, that we were just that fucking good, but who was I kidding? If Decker hadn't heard us at that Labor Day festival and tapped us for the *Die Tryin'* soundtrack, we'd still be working our way through the worst dive bars in the Tri-State area. I also knew that it wouldn't take much – maybe one or two crappy shows – for us to wind up right back at the bottom. Sometimes that seemed worse than never having the opportunity at all.

I was packing up my stuff when I heard Jayne say, "Hey, can I, uh, talk to you a minute?"

For a minute, I thought she must be talking to Matt or Skid. Other than band business, Jayne and I hadn't spoken since our confrontation the week before. She didn't even hang around after practice anymore, just exited full throttle as soon as the last note was played.

I didn't say a word, just closed my guitar case and turned toward her with an expectant stare.

She cleared her throat before she spoke, almost as if she were stalling.

"Listen," she began, "I, uh, wanted to talk you, explain things." She slipped her hands into her front pockets. "I feel like I owe you that."

"I get it, Jayne," I said as I grabbed the handle of my guitar case. "You're just not that into me." I chuckled humorlessly at the lame joke but Jayne looked even more uncomfortable. In fact, she actually looked *nervous*.

"It's not that, Jackson."

"Well, what is it then? I mean, you made yourself pretty clear the other night, but if I'm missin' something..." I placed my guitar case at my feet and gestured with my hand. "Go ahead, I'm all ears."

She didn't answer, and for a minute I actually felt a little bad for her. Then I thought to myself, *fuck it.* Why should I give a shit if she obviously didn't?

"It's just that I've been down that road." She hesitated. "With Damian. It didn't end well and I...I don't want to make the same mistake again. You know, getting involved with someone I work with. You're important to me - too important to take that risk."

Wow. Jayne expressing vulnerability? Definitely hadn't expected *that*. Still, I wasn't going to just let her off the hook; I had been through my own shit too.

Finally, I said, "I get it, Jayne, really, I do, but to me, some things are worth the risk." I shrugged. "But I guess for you I wasn't one of them."

"That's not what I meant, Jackson, and you know it."

"Well, from where I stand it's as clear as day - you're saying you and I were a 'mistake' the same as you and Damian, right?" I didn't wait for her to answer before adding, "And, hey, just for the record, I don't appreciate being lumped into the same category as your douchebag ex."

We stared at each other for a moment then I took a step back.

"I was never some 'guy in the band' looking to score, Jayne. If you can't see that then maybe you're right. Maybe what happened in Tampa *was* a mistake." I shrugged. "Either way, I'm not holding a grudge. Hey, you know what they say - *What happens in Tampa...*"

This time my chuckle was met with a scowl. *Shit, I can't seem to lay off the clichés tonight.*

I grabbed my guitar case from the floor next to me. "I gotta get going; haven't even started packing yet." I moved past her toward the door, then turned and added, "See you in a couple days."

She nodded but didn't say anything more.

▲　▲　▲

I turned up the collar of my jacket against the chilly night air as I slowly walked the four or so blocks to my apartment. *A mistake.* Not for one minute did I think what happened between me and Jayne was a mistake. Apparently she did, though, which is why I needed to just suck it up and move on. It just seemed so crazy - Jayne came home from Tampa a totally different person from the one I left there. How does someone do a complete one-eighty like that? *You mean like Leah? When you gonna stop asking yourself the same stupid questions? Better yet, when you gonna stop playing the schmuck for these girls?* I thought it was ironic that Jayne mentioned her douchebag ex when she was acting a hell of a lot like mine.

Fuck it, I thought, and picked up the pace as if to put more distance between myself and the drama. There were more important things to think about, like the ton of packing I had to do before we left at the end of the week. Not tonight, though. Tonight I just wanted to chill on my couch with an ice-cold beer and some mindless bullshit on TV.

I reached into my jacket pocket for my keys as I walked into the building. The three flights of stairs to my apartment seemed steeper than usual, or maybe just my body felt heavy. Between dealing with Jayne's bullshit and all the preparation for the tour, I hadn't realized how exhausted I really was. Yeah, I'd chill for a few hours in front of the TV then turn in early.

I'd just grabbed a beer and kicked off my black Chucks when I heard the muffled sound of my ringing cell. A quick scan of my tiny living room turned up empty so I followed the sound back to the second-hand sofa I'd picked up on Craigslist just after I'd moved in.

By the time I'd reached between the cushions and felt around for it, the ringing had stopped. *Missed call from Brody.* It seemed odd that he'd be calling me this late, but before I had a chance to think too much of it a text came through, *On way to hosp. Brody Jr on the way!* My eyes widened in surprise, which was silly, really. It's not as if I didn't know my sister was about to have a baby.

"Holy shit," I said to the empty room, "I'm gonna be a fuckin' uncle!"

▲   ▲   ▲

By the time I got to the hospital, Joannalise Elizabeth Foxx-Cooper had already arrived. It was just a couple weeks shy of her due date, which was a good thing, because I'd be leaving in a few days and would've hated not to be there for them. I wasted no time in getting a quick peek at my niece who everyone, including Beth and Brody, was sure would be a boy – hence the "Brody Junior" reference in the text. Not me, though. I said from the get-go that they'd have a girl and that they'd better have a girl's name picked out just in case. They must've, too, because they could've never come up with that name on the fly. Joannalise, after my grandmother, Joanna, and my mom, Annalise; her middle name, Elizabeth, was for Brody's mom who'd passed away from cancer when he was in high school. I told Beth that although I thought it was a mouthful for such a tiny thing, the name couldn't have been more perfect.

"You want to hold her, Jacks?" Beth said, then looked to Brody who was staring adoringly at the little pink bundle in his arms. "Brody, let Jackson hold her."

"Hmm," Brody murmured as he continued staring down at the baby.

"Brody," Beth repeated with a smile, "Give her to Jacks."

Brody stood with the sleeping baby cautiously cradled close to his chest before carefully placing her in my arms. She was so tiny and weighed practically nothing. I stared down at her and without thinking much of it whispered, "Hi, Joey." Apparently, I didn't say it quiet enough though because I immediately got a look of reproach from my sister.

"*Joannalise*, Jackson," she said sternly, "not *Joey*."

Brody laughed, but I knew Beth meant business since she rarely took that tone with me, or with anyone for that matter.

"Yes, ma'am," I joked as I carefully eased myself down onto the chair near the foot of the bed. "She's beautiful, Beth," I said as I smiled down at the baby. Beth beamed proudly. "Kind of takes after her Uncle Jacks," I added with a chuckle.

I hung out with them for a while, then stood reluctantly. All the excitement had given me a second wind, and I needed to get home and get my shit packed.

"I should probably get going."

Neither of them argued; in fact, they were probably relieved to see me go. They both looked utterly exhausted, especially Beth. I carefully handed the tiny baby back to Brody and looked down at her nervously when she let out a little cry.

"Is she okay?"

"Yes, Jacks," Beth said, as if she already knew everything about the baby. "She probably has gas."

"Yeah," Brody deadpanned, "Full of hot air, just like her uncle."

"Whatever." I rolled my eyes at him, then walked over to Beth and kissed her on the forehead. "I'll see you..." I was about to say "soon" when I realized I probably wouldn't be seeing them again for at least six months. There was a piece of me that actually felt a little bad about it. How could I be fun Uncle Jacks when I wasn't even going to be around? I'd have to make it up to her when I got back – maybe bring her back a pony. I laughed to myself as I imagined Beth and Brody's expression when I arrived at their doorstep with a freakin' miniature horse in tow. They'd wanna wring my neck for damn sure.

After a round of hugs and plenty of well wishes about the tour, I was on my way. I was just about to walk out the door when for some reason I stopped and turned back. Just as I did, I saw Brody place the tightly swaddled baby back into Beth's arms. Beth scooted over to make room for him as he sat down next to her on the bed. He slipped his arm around her as they both continued to stare down at the baby with contented smiles on their faces. I stood there and watched the scene before me for a moment and wondered...was it like that when we were born? I shook my head. It was hard to imagine a time my dad could've *ever* been that affectionate with us *or* with Mom, no matter what he claimed.

As I turned to leave again, I began to think about how much it sucked that Mom wasn't here for Beth and to meet her first grandchild. I shook my head in disgust. *Fuckin' Dad.*

CHAPTER 56 - JACKSON
Six Months Later ...

I felt the tour bus pull to the right, then glide down the exit ramp. Outside the window, I could see the bumper-to-bumper traffic, and beyond it, the buildings of downtown Miami. *I can't believe it's almost over*, I thought. Had we really been gone six months? Best six months of my life. The tour had taken us all the way down the Eastern seaboard – Philly, Atlanta, D.C, and a whole mess of cities in between before heading down the east coast of Florida. There were just two more shows here, then we headed home. I had never been so exhausted, and I had never been so fucking happy.

Before this tour began, I was so sure I knew what to expect. Shit, it was all I had dreamed about for as far back as I could remember. How many times had I watched Bon Jovi's "Dead or Alive" video and imagined myself on that bus, one city blurring into another as we threw back beers and travelled from show to show? And when we played those gigs on the West Coast, I thought I had died and gone to heaven. But this was on an entirely different level. Venues packed with fans who *knew* us; who had heard our songs on the radio and were buying our album. Their energy was like a drug, and we couldn't get enough of it. We'd leave the stage each night, sweaty and spent, to find dozens of them – mostly girls, of course - waiting to meet us after each show. I'd never turned down so much tail in my life – of course if I'm being totally honest, I didn't turn down *all* of it.

And we weren't only kicking ass on stage either. Album sales were steady and Decker said that if it did as well as predicted Sony would be on us by summer – maybe even sooner – about coming out with a follow-up.

It was like hearing the four of us had hit the mega-millions jackpot. *Even better!*

With all the excitement there had been little time to reflect on the whole Jayne situation. Jayne and I were good, actually more than good; sometimes it even seemed as if things were back to normal. She had even gone with me one day while I shopped for some gifts to bring back for little Joey. Beth had kept me in the loop with pictures and Facetime, and I had never seen my sister look happier. I don't know how happy she was gonna be with the clothes Jayne and I picked out for the baby – concert tees and a tie-dyed onesie – but I figured it was appropriate given my status as a fledging rock star and cool uncle. Anyway, Jayne and I'd had fun that day, but I didn't read anything into it. What had happened in Tampa - and her reaction afterward - was always simmering just beneath the surface. Though sometimes we'd be hanging at some bar after a show and I'd catch myself nonchalantly scanning the crowd to see if she was with anyone, then I'd want to kick myself for even giving a shit.

It could've been my imagination or maybe wishful thinking, but a few times I thought I saw her glancing my way, as if to see what I was up to, which made me think maybe she had some regrets about the way things had gone down. Then I'd look again and she'd be talking to some guy or even on the dancefloor, and I'd think I had to be imagining things. That wasn't the only thing I was imagining, either. Early in the tour, I saw this guy I swear could've been my father's twin. The first time I saw him, standing in the crowd, a few rows from the front, I almost fucked up the song. I knew I was being ridiculous - this guy was thinner than Dad, had a beard, and wore a faded Mets cap pulled down low. I had never even seen my father wear a hat and even if he did, he wouldn't be caught dead in a Mets cap. He had always been an avid Yankees fan, which was probably why I had always rooted for the white, blue and orange. But then I saw the guy at two other shows – a split-second glance at his profile followed by his back as he slipped through the crowd – and I couldn't deny the resemblance. I told myself it didn't make sense; as far as we knew he was living in Arizona, and we hadn't heard a peep from him since he moved.

In fact, other than occasionally wondering if he'd heard about the baby, I rarely gave the man a thought.

▲   ▲   ▲

We spent our last day in Miami at the hotel, throwing back a few beers before our final show. It was nearly time to head down to the bus when Matt got a phone call. He signaled for us to go ahead without him and mouthed that he'd meet us in the lobby. Ten minutes later he joined us near the front desk.

"What's up?" Skid asked.

"That was Brett...from Token's...he had kind of an interesting request."

We all looked at him impatiently. Matt had a way of always dragging out these revelations that was both exciting and annoying.

"Let's have it, Matt," Jayne said in that sharp tone she had when she wasn't in the mood for any bullshit.

Matt smiled. "He wanted to know if we'd consider closing out the tour there. Said we'd be doing them a big favor."

"No shit!" I said. It'd be so cool to wrap up at the place where we'd gotten our start. Then I glanced over at Jayne and saw she was shaking her head. Skid didn't look all that excited either. I shot them a "what gives?" look.

"I know what you guys are thinking," Matt said, "That the space is too small, considering ..." He paused for effect, "how much our fanbase has grown since the last time we played there. But since I couldn't say no to him either, I said we'd do it as long as they don't advertise. It'd be a real blast and will put Token's on the map."

"But if they don't advertise how will anyone know about it?" Skid asked. "It'll be pretty tough to get on the map if no one shows up."

"Well, what if we put something out on social media...something cryptic. Something that only our most loyal fans would pick up on." He looked from me, to Skid, then to Jayne to gauge our reactions. "This way, Token's gets a decent crowd, but nothing crazy and it's great future advertising for them." He turned back to Jayne. "You're our social media guru, Jayne; think you could come up with something?"

I glanced over at Jayne and could almost see the wheels turning in her head. "I'm on it," she said. She was in her element with this kind of thing.

"Good," Matt said, a grin splitting his face. "I was getting down thinking tonight was our last show."

That night was our best performance of the tour. It almost felt like a swan song too, and I wondered whether it was a sign that the Token's gig would fall flat.

We didn't have to wait long to see what Jayne came up with. The next morning I reached for my phone and there was her tweet: *Paying token visit to our hometown this Saturday night...stay tuned. #DirtyBushwick #WhereBrooklynAt.* It already had a couple hundred retweets.

I thought it was too cryptic, but Jayne was convinced our die-hard original fans would definitely get the message. Matt and Skid didn't look so sure, but since no one was able to come up with anything better, we went with it.

▲   ▲   ▲

We'd been back in New York for three days and I was still dragging ass. It was as if I had been on a six-month workout and now all the adrenalin had drained from my body. I didn't say anything to the others, but I knew they felt the same. Shit, even Matt looked like hell when he showed up at the jam session he insisted we have before the Token's gig on Friday night.

"Dude," Skid had groaned when he suggested it, "We've been killing it for months – the songs are perfect."

Jayne and I nodded in agreement. "Seriously, Matt," Jayne said, "I was planning on sleeping until Friday."

"You can sleep all you want after Token's," Matt said, smiling. "And *perfect*, Skid? Really?"

We knew he was right. This was not the time to be lazy. Token's might even be the most important show of the whole tour. Whatever reviews it got would be the ones everyone remembered, at least around here. I just prayed Jayne was right and that her vague-ass tweet drew a respectable crowd. I tried to tell myself I didn't really care if Token's was crowded or not, that it would just be fun to play there again, but that was only half true. I remembered all the times we played to crowds in the single digits and knew that a triumphant return to our home turf would be the ultimate validation.

On Friday night we got to Token's early and slipped through the back door. We'd set up our equipment earlier that afternoon so we could chill and have a few beers before we went on. When I took a quick peek at the bar area, I was surprised by how many familiar faces I saw. Jayne had been right - her tweet had been picked up on by a lot of our loyal fans and by the looks of it, Token's was nearly filled to capacity.

"Ready guys?" Brett said as he poked his head into the back office. Before anyone could answer he added, "And, hey, I just want to thank you guys again for doing this."

"No problem," Matt said, "We're glad to do it."

"Hey," I chimed in, "Just think of us as *Southside Johnny* and Token's is our *Stone Pony*."

Brett looked at me blankly, and for a minute I thought maybe he didn't get my reference. Known as "The Godfather of the Jersey Sound," Southside Johnny and his band The Asbury Jukes was a legend to any self-respecting New Jerseyan. Shit, Jon Bon Jovi called them his "reason for singing." And, like a lot of Jersey bands, they had gotten their start down the Shore, at a bar called the Stone Pony.

I was about to explain myself when Brett laughed.

"Can take the boy out of Jersey, huh Jackson?" he said, then gave me the thumbs up before closing the door behind him. A second later, he popped back in. "Oh, hey, I almost forgot," he said as he reached into his back pocket. "There's a guy sitting at the bar; been here since we opened. Said he's been following you guys your whole career."

The four of us looked at each other and laughed.

"Our *whole* career, huh?" Matt said, raising an eyebrow. "We haven't been around that long."

432

Brett shrugged. "Looks like you guys have your first super-fan. Anyway, he wanted me to give you this." He handed Matt a twice-folded piece of notebook paper, then shrugged again. "Didn't say much else; seemed like a nice enough guy, though."

Brett hurried off, closing the door behind him as Matt unfolded the note. I watched his forehead crinkle in confusion as he read it. "It's a request," he said, running a hand across the scruff on his face, "An *odd* request."

"What's it say?" Jayne asked as she took the paper from Matt, her brows pulling together as she stared down at the handwritten note. "What the -? New York...? *New York Groove?*" she said, a small but audible laugh escaping.

As soon as I heard her say *New York Groove* I felt the hairs on the back of my neck stand up. "Gimme that," I said as I grabbed it from her.

As soon as I saw the shaky cursive, I knew exactly who'd written it. It said simply: *Been following you guys for a long time. I know it's not part of your routine to take requests, but it'd mean an awful lot to me if you could play New York Groove in honor of my late wife. It was the first song I ever played for her back in my garage in Jersey on my second-hand acoustic. She was the best. Thanks.*

Suddenly I was a little kid again, maybe six or seven, asking my mom to tell me the story of how she'd met my dad. I made her tell me that damn story so many times I used to mouth the words right along with her. I never got tired of hearing it, not until the day she died.

"'Annalise, my name's Annalise – Anna for short,'" I told him. 'Nice to meet you, Keith.'

He introduced the rest of the guys and then they began to play a song that they claimed was New York Groove. I couldn't really tell what it was, all I knew is that they sounded awful, but I didn't care. I was with Ace and that's all that mattered.

Our eyes didn't stray from one another's for even a second during the whole time I was there. And it wasn't just me. I knew he felt something too. . . "

It *was* him I'd seen in the audience all those times on the tour! And it was him last summer too on the West Coast. I remember telling Jayne I could swear I'd seen him in the audience...like he was haunting me.

"Jackson," I heard Jayne say. "Are...are you okay?" She sounded like she was a million miles away. She touched my arm, pulling me back to the present.

"Huh? Uh, yeah, I'm...I'm okay."

She looked at me as if she wasn't so sure.

"Could, uh... I mean, would you mind if I did it...?" I blurted out to no one in particular.

"Did what?" Matt asked, sounding genuinely confused.

"The, uh, the song...*New York Groove*. Would you mind if I sang it?"

Matt looked at me as if I had three heads; the reason, glaringly obvious: he'd never heard me sing so much as a single note.

"*You?* You wanna sing?"

"Yeah," I shrugged, "I'd kinda like to do it."

"You're kidding, right?" he asked incredulously. "This is like totally outta left field. Since when do you have any interest in vocals?"

"Um, since about five minutes ago," I mumbled, but I was dead serious. "Would you mind?"

"I've heard him sing, Matt," Jayne interjected, referring, I knew, to my solo at Beth and Brody's wedding. "He's actually not bad."

Not bad? Really? Though the compliment was lukewarm at best, I looked to Jayne, silently thanking her for backing me up; then I turned back to Matt.

He looked as though he were mulling it over and for a moment I was sure he'd shoot down my request. But then he just shrugged and said, "Hell, why not? It'll shake things up a bit."

"Yeah," Skid laughed, "It'll take us back to our 'Free Bird' days. Sometimes I miss doing covers."

I let out the breath I was holding, then thanked Matt for giving me the shot.

We decided to do New York Groove midway through our set since we only planned on playing for a short time. Brett didn't want us playing too long. He was nervous if word got out, there'd be a stampede through the front doors that his bouncers might not be able to stop.

When we took to the stage, I nonchalantly scanned the crowd but didn't see him. It wasn't until we were about fifteen minutes in that I noticed him. He was alone and sitting on a stool at the end of the bar nursing a bottle of Bud. I stole glances his way but avoided eye contact. It was going to take more than a note to make up for all the shit he'd pulled.

For years all I had thought about was showing him up. Succeed where he had failed, then rub his face in it. But a couple songs into the set, I remembered that letter he'd left for me and how he'd flat-out acknowledged he thought I had talent and that I'd go far with it. So, really, what did I have left to prove? *Nothing.* Suddenly, it felt like a weight had been lifted from my shoulders, and when I glanced at my father again I actually found myself feeling sorry for him. Sitting at the bar he looked like a shell of the man he once was, aged well beyond his years. Forgiveness had never been an option but maybe it was time to let go. Beth, Tim and I had lost our mother and nothing could ever make up for that, but he'd lost *everything* – his wife, his kids, and now a grandkid as well. It was by no fault but his own, but the fact that he owned it – that he knew he'd fucked up and there was no coming back from it – well, maybe that was punishment enough.

The band took a short break, and when we came back out Matt started talking to the crowd, getting them pumped like he usually did.

"Folks, this next number's an old one but I think it's a perfect way to say how happy we are to be back on our home turf." He glanced at me and smiled. "Take it away, Jackson."

I felt a little nervous at first but as soon as I strummed the first few cords the crowd jumped to their feet, immediately recognizing it. By the time the first words were out of my mouth the crowd was in such a frenzy that I could barely be heard above the noise. I sang my fucking heart out and by the time I finished I could actually feel the floor vibrating beneath my feet from all the cheering.

We brought the song to a close amid thunderous applause that was almost deafening. Token's wasn't very big and was filled to capacity with our most die-hard fans but as I scanned the crowd, I noticed only one - the guy in the faded Mets cap standing near the bar. He raised his bottle to me but I just stared at him, still debating whether or not I wanted to acknowledge him. It was then that I realized, I didn't feel angry as I usually did when I thought of him, but something akin to pity or mercy, or was it compassion? I couldn't be sure, so I raised my chin to him in greeting before turning away. That's when Jayne grabbed me by the shoulder and said, "Holy shit, this is fucking *awesome*! Do you hear them? That was the perfect song to come home to."

She was so thrilled to be back in New York, we all were, and that her tweet had worked out so well. I looked down at her for a moment - her pale blue eyes dancing with excitement beneath the bright lights above us – and I knew that no matter how many times I told myself I was over her, I was kidding myself. I was still fucking crazy about her and probably always would be. *Fuck it*, I thought, then leaned down and kissed her, not giving a shit that we were standing on a stage in front of a few hundred people and that she'd probably knock me on my ass for doing it.

I pulled away and rolled my eyes at her. "Sorry, yeah, I know, I shouldn'tve done that, but…"

She looked me square in the eye, her face unreadable, as she grabbed the collar of my sweaty black tee and pulled me toward her. I braced myself for the *wrath of Jayne*, but to my surprise, I saw the corners of her mouth turn up slightly.

"…Yeah, you should have," she said, and then she leaned up and placed her lips on mine.

EPILOGUE

The buzzer rang just as I finished putting on my lipstick. I glanced at my phone. *Right on time, as usual.*

I hurried the short distance from the bathroom to the hallway and pressed the button that opened the front door to my small Hoboken apartment, then scurried back to the mirror for one last inspection of my makeup. Not perfect, but pretty good.

I heard Ryan's confident footsteps coming down the hallway and forced myself to take a few deep breaths. We had been dating for about a year, ever since we met at a coffee shop halfway between our offices in Midtown. The barista mixed up my non-fat latte with his Americano and when we went to sort it out he struck up a conversation. He was tall, fit and handsome, too handsome to be so friendly, but it all made sense when he revealed that he had just recently transferred to New York from Wisconsin. I left that day with a date for Saturday night, and since then he had proven himself to be nothing but kind, decent and honest. Perfect, really. Lately I had even begun to feel that he may be "the one," but I tried not to let my mind go there too often. I'd thought that before about other guys, only to end up losing interest for one reason or another. Then again, Ryan was willing to travel to Hoboken to pick me up for a date, so he just may be a keeper.

The thought made smile as I pulled open the door to find him standing there, looking gorgeous as usual in black slacks and a grey cashmere sweater. In one hand he held a lovely bouquet of colorful spring flowers.

"Happy Birthday, babe," Ryan said as he handed me the flowers.

"Oh, Ryan, they're beautiful!" I gave him a peck on the cheek, then stood back so he could enter the apartment. "Come in, let me put these in water."

Ryan made himself comfortable on the couch while I searched through the kitchen cabinets for a vase big enough to hold the bouquet. Easier said than done – though I had been living in the apartment for nearly a year, some of my stuff was still in boxes. I always meant to unpack them, but by the time I got home from work I usually only had enough energy to wash my face, undress and pass out.

Working for a real estate law firm wasn't exactly my dream job, but what could I expect? Being an attorney wasn't exactly my dream career either. Law school had been a struggle, mainly due to my lack of interest. After a lifetime of watching gripping legal thrillers on TV, wading through statutes and mind-numbing caselaw was an unpleasant reality, but I had muddled my way through. It's not like there was something else I wanted to do with my life. Besides, the firm paid me enough to outweigh any disillusionment – at least most of the time – and afford this place on my own. The last thing I wanted after a twelve-hour-day was to deal with a roommate.

Sometimes it was a bit lonely, though. Most of my friends were either engaged or newly married, which left me with an increasingly smaller pool of people to go bar hopping with. *Barhopping*, ugh, even that was getting old. Or maybe it was just me getting old. Sometimes it felt as though life were passing me by. Jeez, even Molly was around less and less ever since she and her boyfriend Derrick had gotten serious. It was just like college, only this guy was as obsessed with her as she was with him. Kinda sickening, actually, or maybe I was just jealous. Jealous and bored with life in general. I just couldn't seem to shake the feeling that something was missing.

"Ahh, here we go," I said as I freed an old vase of my mother's from a dusty box. I rinsed it out, filled it with water and placed the flowers inside. They really were beautiful. What was I complaining about? I had a great boyfriend, a great job, and tonight I was going to have a great birthday. Ryan was taking me to The Chart House in Weehawken, which was a favorite of mine because it had *the* best coconut shrimp and was right on the water with a gorgeous view of Manhattan.

I went into the living room, where Ryan was rapidly typing on his phone. Most likely a work email.

"So what time are the reservations?"

"Not 'til eight..." Ryan turned to me, his face stretching into a grin.

"What?"

"I have something else for you." He reached into his jacket pocket and pulled out a card. "Happy birthday again, Leah."

"Dinner, flowers and a card?" I chuckled as I took the envelope from him. "You're spoiling me."

"I hope you're into it..."

"Into it...?" I looked at him, my curiosity piqued.

When I opened the card, there were two tickets inside. My heart dropped when I realized what they were – two tickets to see *Dirty Bushwick* at Madison Square Garden.

Immediately, a flood of memories came crashing back. That first time I saw Jackson, how hot I thought he was; the first time we kissed, feeling like I would die of happiness... That awful night when I walked into my dorm room after leaving Chase's and finding Jackson sitting on my bed with that devasted look on his face. And finally, the last time I saw him at Ramapo, when he looked at me like I was a complete stranger. That might have been the worst of all.

"They're for this Saturday night," Ryan said, interrupting my dark thoughts. "You wouldn't believe how hard these were to get," he added. "I had to ask a client for a favor." He paused, waiting for a reaction.

"You *are* into them, right?" He chuckled. "I mean, what girl isn't?"

I just nodded slightly as I continued to stare down at the tickets, now feeling a subtle, undefinable dislike for Ryan, which I knew was ridiculous. He had no idea about my past involving *Jackson Foxx, lead guitarist for Dirty Bushwick, currently the hottest band in the fucking country.* Dirty Bushwick was *all* over the radio these days, so much so that I'd taken to listening to music on my phone to avoid having to hear about them. The *last* thing I needed these days was a constant reminder of how I'd screwed up. My one consolation was that at least he hadn't ended up with *Jayne*. Yeah, there'd been rumors floated about them being together, but there'd also been rumors about her and Matt...and her and Skid. The tramp had probably been with all of them at one point or another.

I sighed inwardly, my birthday night all but ruined.

"You know," Ryan was saying, "they're not really from Bushwick; in fact, I think the chick and one of the guys – maybe the guitarist – are from Jersey."

"Yeah," I said absently, "He grew up not far from me."

"No shit," he said, then lightly elbowed me in the ribs. "Do you know him?"

I stared blankly at the TV with the card and the tickets now resting on my lap. *Do I know him?* I wanted to say, *No, but at one time I did. In fact, there was a time I knew him very well, maybe better than anyone else. Believe it or not, there was a time when I was the love of his life, a time when he would've done absolutely anything for me. When he said I was the inspiration for the music he wrote. He was a good person. A kind person. A beautiful person. And he loved me.*

I looked over at Ryan, who for all his good looks and sweet smile, suddenly didn't seem so perfect.

"No," I said, forcing a laugh, "I don't know him."

And he doesn't know me.

EPILOGUE
Jackson – Five years later

"**B**eth's gonna be pissed, you know that, right?" Jayne said as she slid into the first-class seat next to mine.

"Probably, but it's better than the alternative." I shot her pointed look. "Am I right?"

"I guess," she agreed as she shook off her jacket. "Do me a favor, though, fill her in when I'm not around."

"Oh, no," I laughed as I grabbed her hand. "You're not gettin' out of this one...*Mrs. Foxx*."

"Whatever," she said as she closed her eyes and reclined the seat, but I could see the hint of a smile.

A few minutes later the plane began taxiing down the runway of McCarran International Airport. Jayne and I had gotten hitched the night before at one of those cheesy little wedding chapels the Vegas Strip is famous for. It wasn't exactly what we had planned – standing under multicolored strobe lights as a gyrating Elvis pronounced us husband and wife – but somehow it had been perfect. Now we just had to get back to Jersey and break the news to my sister before any photos popped up online. Not that Beth had a problem with Jayne and I getting married, in fact she'd asked me about it countless times over the years. She was just going to be upset that she wasn't there. She'd envisioned a big blow-out with the church, the white dress – the whole nine yards. What she couldn't seem to understand was that was *so* not our scene, or that it would've ended up becoming a media circus. Gone were the days of obscurity, of playing in clubs and on college campuses. Dirty Bushwick had just wrapped a nine-month tour, headlining in huge arenas in major cities around the country. And now, with our first European tour in the works? We never would have been able to keep a wedding between two of its members under wraps.

Looking back, I don't know how we kept our relationship a secret as long as we did. Of course, we told our families – who were thrilled – and Matt and Skid, who didn't care so long as it didn't hurt the music. If anything, it had made it better! Still, Artie insisted that we hide it from the public, said it worked better for our image if we were all unattached. Not exactly convenient, but we couldn't argue with Artie, who since becoming our manager had been spot-on about everything having to do with our success. Of course, there were always rumors circulating – about me and Jayne, Jayne and Matt, and even about me and Matt, which was hilarious – but we always managed to keep the paparazzi guessing. Now, though, we were finally done sneaking around.

To be honest, I still couldn't believe we'd ever *had* to sneak around; it still blew my mind how big Dirty Bushwick had gotten over the past couple of years. What made our success even sweeter, though, was the fact that we'd stayed true to ourselves. For us, it was always about the music, not the fame. *Anna's Leash*, the song with the lyrics my mom wrote, was still a staple on the radio and our biggest hit to date. We also always made it a point to play *New York Groove* whenever we were in town, and it still brought down the house every time, the same as it did when we played it for the first time at Token's. I'd be lying if I said we never made any compromises where our music was concerned, because everyone sells out a little – it just goes with the territory. What I *can* say is that we sold out a hell of a lot less than most.

I glanced over at Jayne, a little envious to see she had dozed off. As exhausted and burnt out as I was after the tour, I was too keyed-up to sleep. At least my mind was racing with good things, mostly all the things I wanted to do during the couple months of downtime we had before getting ready for Europe. I didn't know about Jayne, but I was dying to see the progress they had made on the construction of my – *our* – new home since they'd broken ground about a month earlier.

The house we were building was in Jersey, of course, and on a beautiful piece of land in upper Ringwood, my hometown. I'd originally purchased the land for Beth and Brody – hey, what's the good of having money if you're not going to spend it on the people you love, right? I was genuinely surprised when she turned it down. At first I thought she just didn't want to accept such an expensive gift, but it wasn't that at all. She said she couldn't bear to part with all the memories of Mom that our childhood home held for her. I told her I understood, but I didn't, not really, not when that house held so much pain for me. But then I saw how she and Brody, along with my grandmother, who sadly passed away last year, had made it such a warm, happy home for their three – yes, three! – little girls. It was almost as if they had healed all the hurt that had gone on there when we were kids. *Almost.* Still, I preferred to hang out at the cottage I'd bought them down the Jersey Shore. It was awesome when we all got together down there, especially when Tim, who was still stationed in Texas, was on leave and could join us for a few days.

My thoughts ran to my nieces, who, other than brief FaceTime sessions I hadn't seen in nearly nine months. Joannalise was nearly five now and about to start kindergarten, Jacklyn was three and the baby, Jennifer-Jayne, was almost two. Beth had her hands full for sure because Joey, Jacks and Jay-Jay – as I liked to call them – were three rough and tumble little girls, especially when *fun Uncle Jacks* was around.

As for my father, nothing much had changed, not for me, anyway, and not for Tim. I knew from Beth that he came to a lot of our concerts but with the size of the venues we played it would've been nearly impossible to single him out. Not that it mattered. I wasn't all that angry anymore, and I certainly wished him no ill will; I just had no interest in having any kind of relationship with him. Probably never would. Of the three of us, only Beth kept in touch with him, mostly through email, Skype and the occasional phone calls. She'd reached out to him at some point after Joey was born, saying he had a right to know his granddaughter. I didn't agree, but it was her choice and I wasn't about to judge her for it. I guess mine wouldn't be the first shitty father to try and redeem himself through his grandchildren.

Somewhere over Colorado I plugged my headphones into the seat and began flipping through radio stations. I should have been used it by now, but my heart still raced a little when I heard one of our songs playing on one of them. This is fuckin' surreal, I thought, then glanced at Jayne, and nearly laughed out loud. *Jayne is my wife. Talk about fuckin' surreal.* I thought back over when I first met her, how bitchy and weird she had seemed, then our childish dance around each other as we pretended there was nothing but music between us. Actually, she probably wasn't pretending, and who could blame her? I was a fuckin' wreck back then – always drunk and pissed off over what Leah had done to me.... That's when it hit me - I had Leah to thank for me and Jayne getting together. If she hadn't kicked me to the curb I would never have been with Jayne . . . shit, I might have even given up music if Leah asked me to. I was *that* hung up on her. Wonder what had happened to her anyway? I hadn't seen her since that day at the outdoor concert at Ramapo College. It was an idle thought that evaporated as soon as I saw Jayne stirring in the seat beside me. I reach over and slipped my hand into hers. Yeah, losing Leah was definitely the best thing that could've ever happened to me.

The End

ACKNOWLEDGEMENTS:

Special thanks to my husband, John along with our two children, Tom and Jen for their constant love and support and for their continued encouragement day in and day out.

I'd also like to thank my two biggest critics - my sister Jean and my friend Lisa - for their endless help in critiquing each and every page of 'Finding Jackson'. They're support and encouragement along the way turned this third journey into the best one yet!

My sincerest gratitude goes out once again to my editor Dana for providing me with her expert input and guidance every step of the way. I couldn't have done it without you!

I sincerely hope you enjoyed reading 'Finding Jackson' and as always would love to hear from you!

Anne Holster
Anneholster.author@yahoo.com

Made in the USA
Middletown, DE
03 November 2019